COACHING RAYNA

BOOK 1

PEBBLES LACASSE

Model: Chris LaPointe

Photographer: Sharon Seguin

Edited by: Off the Shelf Editing

https://www.offtheshelfediting.com

This book is intended for adults only. Characters, organizations, and events
portrayed are fictional. Resemblances are purely coincidental.

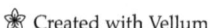 Created with Vellum

Sharon Seguin, the photoshoots were so much fun, and I can't thank you enough for all the work you put into getting the perfect shot for this cover. Sometimes we meet people and feel like we've known them our whole lives. We'll have to get together soon to have that drink.

Chris LaPointe, what can I say? Thank you for posing for the cover of this book and several more to come! I'm so grateful for all the advice you gave to help with my social media ignorance and not poking fun at me for it. We had some interesting chats, didn't we? I wish you only the best life has to offer.

CHAPTER 1

 ayna

Doing the laundry isn't what I planned to do on my first Saturday off work in three weeks. Having lunch with my friends or taking the kids on an adventure would be so much more fun. But the chores have to get done. The kids are running out of clean clothes and all of my work scrubs are too dirty to wear again.

Shutting the door to the laundry room and pretending the piles of dirty clothes don't exist would be so much easier, but I can no longer avoid this mundane chore.

Would it kill the kids to throw in a load once in a while? I've taught them both how to do it, so I know their laziness isn't due to their lack of know-how. I'm a firm believer in teaching children how to do real-life tasks.

Instead of having a fun day with me, they're shut away in their rooms. To be honest, I'd rather that than have them follow me from room to room complaining that they're bored. Not like that's possible; their rooms are full of interesting distractions that should keep their imaginations alive and blooming.

I'm shaken from my thoughts. Is that a lawnmower I hear?

I immediately stop sorting colours from whites and pull the button to halt the gushing water filling the washing machine. I can't tell whether it's the dreamboat next door mowing his lawn or the neighbour directly behind my house...

My legs can't carry me up the stairs quick enough, even though I'm stepping two at a time. I nearly smack my head off the patio doors trying to look for *him*.

Yes! Damn, he's so fucking hot! I've been looking forward to this show all week.

I quickly pour a glass of wine three-quarters full of the nice pinot I opened last night. I must act aloof, as though I'm not outside to watch his sweaty, tanned skin as it stretches over his bloated muscles. My pussy tightens as I slide open the glass door and take a deep breath. Without glancing his way, I step out and close it behind me.

After setting my glass on the table, I squat my ass on the cushiony deckchair and rest my feet on the chair opposite. Being the smart cookie that I am, I always keep a book at the backdoor to make him think I'm reading and not ogling him while dreaming up a naughty fantasy.

Damn, it's hot today! I don't mind; the glistening sweat accentuates the ripples of muscle.

I always sit facing his yard. This way, I can drink him in without being too obvious. I open the book and pretend to read with my head tipped downward.

Nearly every Saturday for the past three years, I've lost myself in my imagination while staring at my hunky neighbour. His muscles flex as he pushes the mower around his enormous yard while wearing nothing but shoes and a pair of shorts that fit snug on his thick, muscular thighs.

His name is Simon Brenton, but everyone calls him Coach because he owns a gym and coaches people on how to reach their peak level of physical fitness. He's as strong as an ox; I can't stress that enough. The man's arms, chest, and thighs are massive, his waist tight and ripped. I imagine he can fuck like a machine. The power behind those thunderous thighs would have any woman screaming through multiple orgasms until she lost consciousness.

My fantasies have me in his arms, his thin lips on mine, pelvis rhythmically grinding against my needy vagina as he sinks himself deep into me.

Sigh...

I'm divorced, thankfully. I've had no intimate encounters in the four years since I gave the asshole the boot. My life is too busy working and raising my kids. I'm sure that's why I love to picture myself getting sexually mauled by my hot neighbour more often than what's probably healthy for anyone.

The best thing that happened out of the shitty marriage is two children. Kim is eleven, and Ken is thirteen. There's never enough time in a day for us to connect other than dinner time when we sit at the table together and discuss what's on their minds. There are days when I almost have to poke them with a stick to get them to talk.

My son is getting to the age where he thinks mom isn't cool enough to hang out with anymore. He used to be my little shadow, clung to me wherever I'd go, but things have changed. I miss that. My daughter still enjoys my company, but I'm sure she'll think I'm stupid soon enough, especially if she takes after me. I was rude to my mother too often during my teen years. Hopefully, she'll be wiser than I was.

Between my job, the kids, and the household, I'm exhausted when I flop into bed at night. Doing everything myself, without a partner or an accountable ex, is sometimes overwhelming.

Sex comprises me occasionally masturbating while using my helpful aides: my fat dildo and a vibrator. I'm usually so tired at the end of the day that I only want to sleep. Sometimes, when I've been unusually excited—like after watching Coach mow his lawn, for instance—I'll zip through masturbation just to ease my sexual tension enough that I can sleep.

I've gone weeks without having an orgasm. It's depressing, I know. I used to be extremely sexually expressive. What happened to me?

Coach probably knows exactly why I'm out here, but he's kind enough not to call me out. If he looks up and sees me, he'll wave. I'll lift my head and wave back, and he'll continue to mow while I quietly observe his sculpted body. I'm sure he gets an ego boost from women checking him out, and I imagine it happens a lot. I'm an out of shape older woman and not his type.

Sometimes we chat over the fence, but it's rare. We've had conversations over the years, ranging from politics to religion and even about our childhoods.

He's intelligent and well-spoken, which I find to be an alluring trait in a man. The sexiest thing about him is his ability to hold eye contact and not flinch, which intimidates the hell out of me. He's definitely an assertive man, and that excites me. He's far more alluring than my arrogant, cheating coward of an ex-husband who has no spine to speak of.

Coach occasionally has his friends from the gym over to his place. I love those days! They're all fit and muscular like he is. They sit outside shirtless under the heat of the sun, and I can't stop watching their brawny chests and backs as they carry on, boasting about their wild adventures with naughty women, or telling tales of their high school football highlights.

I wonder what it would feel like to have one of their thick bodies above me, using those powerful thighs and strong backs to fuck me hard. My pussy twinges at the thought. I couldn't pick their faces out in a line-up even if I had to, because I never stop staring at their bodies. I wish I could see what they have in their shorts that might please me.

The day after Coach moved in, three years ago, I went over to introduce myself and welcome him to the neighbourhood. I was captivated by his physical size, but his confidence attracted me most. I could barely speak. Everything I muttered sounded stupid, especially when I asked to meet his wife and kids.

There was a woman and a few children helping with the

move, so I assumed they were his family. That's when he told me that he's never married and never plans to. The woman was his sister, and they were her children. Strangely, it pleased me to know that he was available but sad that my excuse to visit with him for arranged playdates with our kids was now void.

Coach has had many women come and go, but his present girlfriend doesn't talk to me even if we're both outside. Occasionally she'll wave, but we've never carried on a conversation. She doesn't seem shy. Judging by the occasional leers directed at me, she dislikes me. I don't recall saying or doing anything to her she could have taken offensively.

I'd rather not get to know her well, anyway. It would be too hard to fantasize about her bulked-up man tearing off my clothes and ravishing me if she complains about all his nasty habits. That might turn me off, and then I'd be right back to having nothing tantalizing to stare at on these scorching summer days. This is all I have to make me feel like a sexual woman, and I need it. I don't want to see him as an actual person with flaws. He's the perfect sex machine—at least, in my vivid imagination.

My tummy flutters just before he bends to pick up the metal table to move it out of his way, allowing him easier access to mow the grass beneath. When he lifts, his muscles flex and his skin strains to maintain them, but he moves the heavy table with barely a struggle.

That task would take the effort of my ex-husband plus his clone if he had one. Thankfully, there aren't two of that asshole. Just one of him is too many.

I've sucked back the entire glass of wine way too quickly and it's already going to my head. Maybe I should have eaten something today before I bled this glass dry.

Coach finishes and puts the table back and the mower in the shed before starting to pick weeds out of his vegetable garden. I've never seen his girlfriend lift a finger to maintain the yard, even if a weed stands tall right beside her foot. I see the way he looks at her, and I don't think she'll be around much longer.

He's down on his widely spread knees and bent over to reach for a well-rooted weed. He pulls, flexing his back muscles ever so slightly. The lumps on his arm shift and grow as he moves, stirring something primal inside of me. His flesh glistens under the vibrant sun.

I want to taste him. I imagine what it must feel like to lie beneath such a powerful man, my legs wrapped around him while he looks down at me, readying himself to penetrate my body with his swollen manhood.

My eyes close and I take in a deep breath, suddenly realizing that my book rests on my lap, covering my hand slid down between my thighs. I've been pressing on my excited clit.

I jolt back to reality, yanking my hand from my groin. My eyes shift here and there, looking to see if anyone has been watching me masturbate through my shorts while I stare at the sexy guy next door like the neighbourhood pervert. I'm relieved no one else is outside until my eyes meet Coach's accusing glare.

He's still on his knees, but the table has turned, so to speak. He's been watching me. I want to run away and hide, but it's too late. There's no denying he saw what I was doing. I'm so embarrassed and the heat flushing through my cheeks proves it.

A smile slowly grows on his face. I try to return the gesture, but my bottom lip quivers, distorting my mouth. He probably can't see that detail from this distance. I feel the embarrassment continuing to fill my cheeks, proving my desire for him.

He lifts his thick arm to wave at me. I tip my head down while I wave, wishing I could go back in time to redo the last ten minutes. This time, I wouldn't have lost myself in the fantasy.

Coach tosses the weed he pulled before standing and brushing the dirt off his hands and knees. He looks up at me, still grinning like a man who has naughty intentions.

Oh shit! He's walking toward the fence separating our yards.

Should I go to the fence or tell him that I can't chat and then hide in the house? Damn it! I'm horribly embarrassed, but it would be rude to run away at this point. I grip the railing, fearing my trembling knees might give out, thus tumbling down the stairs in a most humiliating fashion. The way my luck is, it wouldn't surprise me.

As I approach the fence, his deep voice greets me. "Hi. Are you enjoying the day?"

The grin on his face boasts his sinful thoughts. His lips are thin, but the well-groomed beard and mustache frame them perfectly, as if they're a target for my lips to aim toward.

Snap out of it, damn it!

"Um, hi, Coach. It is a beautiful day." I swallow hard. "I see you mowed your lawn."

I sound like such an idiot. I'd have to be blind and deaf to not know he mowed it. Couldn't I have thought of something less ridiculous to say? Why can't I say anything brilliant to this man? I bite my lip again; I do that when I'm nervous or intimidated. At the moment, I'm both.

"So it would seem. You watched me mow my lawn." He accentuates the word "watched."

I can imagine what he wanted to say: "...while you were flicking your bean."

I'm so relieved that he's respectful enough not to comment on my masturbation, further humiliating me. I'm not even sure that's possible at this point.

I shrug, crossing my arms over my chest and trying to be aloof by looking anywhere other than at his seductive eyes. Even still, I feel their gaze burning into me. They stare right through me and into my soul, setting it on fire.

Fuck! Timidly, yet trying to seem nonchalant, I say, "Yeah, sorry. There's nothing else to look at that's remotely as exciting as you mowing your lawn."

Shit! I said he was exciting. Damn it!

"Watching me excites you?" He beams, resting his large, tattooed arms on the top of the slatted wood fence.

Each time we've talked in the past, he's been an absolute gentleman. He's insinuated nothing sexual could happen between us. Is it his intention to aim this conversation in that direction, or am I reading too much into his words?

"I don't know how to answer that. I mean, yes, you *are* nice to look at, obviously, and nobody else is outside, so there really is nothing..."

My words fall away. I swallow hard, suddenly realizing that my mouth is parched. I just might cough up the wad of cotton manifesting in my throat.

He must think I'm a sex-deprived, slightly older woman with ridiculous fantasies of being with a very fit younger man who has absolutely no reason to think of her as anything but a mother. He must laugh inside his head at my idiocy, but I'm relieved that he isn't blatantly obvious about it.

I'm not a perfectly thin or physically fit woman, but I'm not overweight. My stomach is still flat after having had two cesarean sections. I'm very proud of that. My legs are thick and strong, and my waist is small, but my butt is jigglier than I'd like and my arms are getting flabby. The best part of me is my breasts; they're large and still somewhat rest at the same altitude they originally grew at. Gravity hasn't had its demonic way with them yet, but I have noticed that they are not as solid as they were ten years ago.

I look up at him only to see his eyes staring at my breasts, which are barely hidden beneath my light pink halter top. I look down and discover my nipples have betrayed me. They're pointing straight out, directly at Coach, as if trying to torpedo me toward him.

He sighs and whispers, "You have beautiful breasts. I'd like to see them without the shirt."

Wait! What?

Shivers ripple up my spine, prickling my skin and forming tiny bumps from head to toe. Every strand of hair on my head feels like it's lifting. My bottom jaw once again quivers uncontrollably, so I bite my lip between my teeth but cannot hold it steady. I stare at his eyes a little too long and it feels very uncomfortable between us.

Say something!

"Thank you," I whisper with barely an audible voice. Damn it, that was a dumb thing to say! I could have said something more flirtatious than that, such as, "I would like that, too."

My eyes follow his Adam's apple as it slowly bobs in his throat when he swallows. I would love to wrap my lips around it while he fucks me deeply. I shake my head, hoping to clear the arousing thought, but it lingers.

"In fact, I'd like to see your entire nude body. You're a sexy woman. You know that, right?"

"Um..." I stutter, "I-I am?" Oh please, compliment me again.

He chuckles, replying, "Sweet thing, I know you watch me, but what you don't know is that I watch you, too. I can see straight into your kitchen from my office window."

He turns to point to the window facing my house. My eyes look back at his in time to see his tongue lick his top lip.

He confesses, "I positioned my desk so I can catch glances of you while I work. When you're in the kitchen at night, in that light blue nightgown, the really thin one," he pauses, "Well, it's my favourite. With the light behind you, I can see the silhouette of your amazing body. I fantasize about touching you over that nightgown."

My eyes are wide, face flushed a feverish red, and my mouth hangs open in surprise.

"Do you have any idea how often I jerk off while watching you make your kids' lunches at night?" he pauses again. "Almost every night."

Oh my God! Did I just hear that? He finds me sexy and masturbates while watching me perform a mundane task. Holy shit! No, he must be taunting me simply to see my reaction and then he'll let me down hard. A guy like him doesn't fantasize about a mother of two who's ten years older than him. He can have almost any young, fit woman he desires.

"You do?" I ask doubtfully. My mouth is painfully dry, and that glass of wine I guzzled is making me feel more uninhibited than my usual self. "I like watching you. I touch myself sometimes."

His sexy crooked smile is enough to make me swoon, but when his eyebrows bounce only once, my knees weaken. He radiates testosterone like an invisible aphrodisiac, making my thoughts cloudy. My pussy is so wet that I can feel its slickness. I wonder if other women experience his allure as intensely as I do. How could they not? He sure knows how to turn up the heat.

"Do you want to come over for another glass of wine?" he suggests with a deeper than usual voice.

He's sporting a very serious expression with salacious eyes that seem to pierce right through me. I can't prevent them from reading my deepest, darkest thoughts.

A bead of sweat trickles down the tanned skin on his well-formed bicep, and I nearly lean in to lick it simply to quench my ravenous thirst. My curiosity and desires are no longer my kept secret. I've opened a can of worms here, but I'm not sure I want to put the lid back on it yet. I've fantasized about this moment so many times.

In those dreams, he's always lived up to my expectations. What if he doesn't compare in reality? The fantasy will forever be tainted.

But what if he does?

"Yes, but I shouldn't," I reply, hating myself for turning down his offer. Whether or not his performance measures up to my high expectations, I'm sure we could have had an entire afternoon of steamy sex, had I accepted the offer, but I have priorities. "The kids are home and they'd eventually notice my absence."

He suggests, "Tell them you're going for a walk. I won't keep you more than an hour...unless you'd like me to. I'll gladly entertain you for the rest of the day."

I swallow hard while forcing myself to look anywhere but at his beckoning brown eyes. My body trembles and my skin craves his touch. His gigantic hands would feel so rough against my womanly flesh. Having two of his fingers inside of me, pleasuring me while he kisses and suckles my nipples, would drive me to cum within seconds.

My legs wobble, weak from the thought. I quickly grab the fence to steady myself. Surely, he knows the effect he's having on me.

His hand hovers over mine, middle finger delicately caressing my middle digit. The contact feels electric. A whimper escapes me. My eyes meet his once again. A smirk has grown on his thin lips and his eyes seem darker, so much more dangerous and enticing than I've ever witnessed. I'd be a fool to deny myself this opportunity. It'll likely never happen again.

"Okay, but I need a little time."

I have done no maintenance on myself for a very long time. Sex is absent from my life, so I don't bother. My stomach tightens like a vice when he wraps his massive hand around my wrist, slowly and assertively pulling me closer to the fence. We are face to face, looking at one another, our breath brushing over each other's faces. My entire body shakes, and I can't control it.

"Don't take too long, okay?" he whispers. His sweet breath is hotter than the summer breeze that caused his skin to glisten so perfectly. "When you're ready, walk in the front door and come down the stairs. I'll be waiting for you."

He releases my wrist but watches me as I slowly ascend the stairs, painfully aware that my weak legs could fail me at some point. I can feel the heat from his stare as it burns into my body.

The instant I'm inside the house and sure he can't see me, I slide down the wall, planting my ass on the cool hardwood floor. I rub my wrist, making sure he isn't still attached to me. My skin is super-heated from just one touch.

How will his touch to my more delicate regions affect me?

My endorphins are easing; panic sets in. Oh god, what have I done? I can't go to his place! If I walk into that house and he touches me, I know I won't be able to maintain control over my primal needs.

Do I want to hold back though? That's a good question. It's

11

been too long since anyone has touched me. I hope I don't make a fool of myself.

Shit!

Even though I'm still unsure if I'm going to go see him, I hop in the shower and shave away all my stubble. I wash my hair and my skin with the prettiest scented products I own.

Yes, I think I'm going over there.

No, no, I can't!

But I really, *really* want to. I deserve this, don't I?

After quickly drying my hair and dusting some powder on my face to reduce the shine, I flip through my closet, looking for something to wear that might be appropriate, but everything I own is so damn boring. I've been a single, overworked mom for so long that my sexy attire has been stowed in boxes or given away. I figured someone should get use out of them.

Frustrated, I settle for a light summer dress and a pair of white silky panties.

I'm still shaking when I enter my daughter's doorway. She's sitting on her bed reading a book assigned to her for a school project. Knowing her as I do, I'm sure it's due soon. She puts everything off to the last minute. She's always looking for an excuse to avoid anything that doesn't completely captivate her attention.

"Hi, baby. I'm going for a walk."

"Can I come?" she asks while bookmarking her page and edging herself off the bed.

"No, you have to get that book read. When is the project due?"

"In two days," she confesses, pouting.

I sigh heavily and give her the GET IT DONE look. "Okay then, you'd better get busy reading. I'll be back in about an hour."

"That's a long walk. Where are you going?" she asks with her face crinkled up as she re-situates herself on her bed.

"Just walking. I need some exercise and the fresh air will help me clear my thoughts." I try to sound convincing. "Don't worry, you won't even miss me."

I blow her a kiss only to witness the infamous eye roll. She acts like she's too mature for silly love gestures.

I enter my son's doorway, even more nervous now. I take a deep breath to calm myself before poking my head in. "Hey, I'm going for a walk. You don't want to come with, do you?"

He turns his contorted face to ensure I see the over-exaggerated expression of his disinterest.

"Okay then, keep an eye on your sister and don't go anywhere."

Without a word, he turns back to his computer to continue with his online game. Maybe they won't miss me.

I make my way out of my house, locking the door behind me.

CHAPTER 2

I<small>T'S AS IF MY FEET HAVE A MIND OF THEIR OWN; NO MATTER HOW</small> hard I try to slow my pace, they move quicker than I'd like them to.

Before I know it, I'm inside his house and halfway down the seven steps, unsure of what I'm going to find once I get to the bottom. Will he still be wearing his shorts? What will I do if he's naked? I stop with two steps to go and take a calming deep breath, hoping to erase the terrified expression from my face.

He's wearing a clean pair of shorts and I smell the soft scent of cologne. He leans against the back of a black leather sofa, which sits in the middle of the room, and offers me a glass of wine. It wasn't all that long ago that I sat on it while we chatted. The girlfriend he had back then sneered at me the whole time, making me feel very unwelcomed.

I'm standing here braless, knowing that he will probably touch me in ways the woman he's dating now would definitely disapprove of. I'd love to record this moment and shove it in her bitchy face. What does he see in her?

He extends his arm further, expecting me to take it, but I can't get my planted feet to move. Strange how a moment ago I couldn't get them to halt. Betrayers, that's what they are!

Coach slowly stands and walks toward me, handing me the glass. I take it and take a gulp while his eyes burn into mine with volcanic heat. Although it's cold in his house, I'm boiling hot, and my womanhood is about to burst into flames.

I sip from the glass once more and then cast my gaze to his well-formed pectoral muscles. His tiny nipples jut out from the base of them. His chest cavity expands and contracts slowly as he breathes the air between us. I feel like I'm gasping, as if he's consuming all the oxygen in the room, leaving me breathless. I suck back another gulp of wine before he takes the glass from me, leaning toward me to set it on the table behind me. His steaming chest touches my arm, and I shiver.

Instead of him pulling away, his face hovers next to my neck. His lips almost touch my skin. His caressing breath raises tiny bumps that seem to spread throughout every cell in my body. I shake violently, eagerly waiting for a solid touch to confirm that this isn't just another daydream and I'm soon to awaken.

He whispers, "I want to taste your skin, kiss your sexy mouth and fuck you hard, the way you deserve to be fucked."

The instant his mouth presses under my ear, my legs waver. He wraps his powerful arms around my waist, taking my entire weight as if I were light as a feather. I nearly faint when his hand cups my ass cheek, pulling my groin against his concealed, erect penis.

Oh God, it's huge! I always imagined it would be, but figured reality would prove otherwise.

Coach lifts me and presses his lips hard to mine. His tongue digs deep into my mouth, exploring every inch. My mind whirls as our first kiss burns into my memory. I never want to forget how sweet his mouth tastes or how passionately he's kissing me.

I wrap my legs around his waist and my arms around his neck. My fingers weave into his thick black hair. I want to be as close to him as I can.

If this is a dream, don't let me wake from it.

He carries me to the sofa, his lips locked on mine. I remain wrapped tightly around him as he lowers us, pressing me into the cushions with some of his weight. He's so solid and heavy that I'm pinned and could not get out from beneath him if I wanted to; which I absolutely do not!

I'm enjoying that he has me under his control. I can pretend that I have no way of escaping his desires, thus not being responsible for my actions, but why deny the truth? I absolutely want him.

He takes both of my wrists in one of his massive hands and holds them together above my head, further restricting my movement and taking away whatever control I thought I still had.

A wave of panic tears through me. Will he let me go if someone walks in? Would he stop if I change my mind?

As if he can read my thoughts, his face pulls back and seems to soften. "If you want this to stop, say 'red' and it stops. Do you understand?"

I nod, not knowing why I can't simply tell him to stop.

He demands, "Tell me you understand."

"I understand, but why…" My whisper evaporates. I breathe heavily, knowing I'm about to give in to his sexual prowess.

He explains, "Red stops everything. If you tell me to stop, I won't. Do you understand?"

I nod, still not understanding why "stop" won't make him stop.

Our eyes remain holding one another's gaze while his hand glides up my thigh, lifting my dress up as it travels. When his hand is between my upper thighs, nearly touching my panties, he urges my legs further apart. Only my damp panties separate the most sensitive part of my body from his rough exterior.

The instant his thigh presses firmly against my damp panties, I gasp. He pulls at my other thigh until my legs spread wide, but he doesn't lean down against me. His body hovers just above mine.

Coach's deep growl seems to vibrate my chest as he kisses down my neck, his free hand squeezing my breast through the thin fabric of my dress. He pinches my nipple until I wince. I yank my wrist free and grab his bicep.

What the hell? That hurt.

In one swift movement, he's up on his knees, each of my wrists in his hands, and he sits me up. He tucks my arms behind my lower back and then pushes me back down, pinning them between me and the sofa. What is he doing? I try to pull them free because it feels awkward and confining. He stops moving and holds my shoulders still. His eyes burn into mine.

"Stay," he commands abruptly.

His voice is deep and threatening. My breath catches in my throat, fear ripples through me, but only for an instant. I decide to play along and remain in this position to see where he's going to take it. He removes his hands from my shoulders, giving me the choice to stay put or pull them free.

I don't move, not yet. I'm curious.

Coach's mouth covers the gusset of my damp, silky panties, instantly soothing away any concerns. His moans match mine as his teeth nip at my pussy lips through the thin fabric while biting and tugging on my panties with purpose. His fingers slip beneath the thin material, brushing against my excited clitoris and it twitches appreciatively. He tugs quickly, tearing the crotch of my panties in two, freeing my womanhood for his mouth to ravish.

I glance down to see why he's not kissing my pussy, only to see him staring at me.

"Do you want me to eat your cunt?" I simply nod excitedly. "Tell me."

"I want you to lick me," I reply in barely a whisper, my cheeks flushing at my uncharacteristic boldness. I've never been a verbal lover.

"Tell me you want me to eat your cunt," he insists and then blows cool air on my clit.

I can't say that word, it's absolutely too vulgar. His eyes remain focused on mine, but he isn't touching me. His mouth is an inch away, his breath now heating me to near volcanic temperatures.

I'm going to scream soon. I can't remember a time I have ever wanted anything this desperately.

He leans back on his knees, looking down at me, disappointed. "Tell me what you want, Rayna."

Nervously, I say, "I can't say that word." I feel awkward, like I'm being put on the spot.

"Cunt?" he asks with a grimace. I nod, biting my lips between my teeth. "Say it, Rayna. Say the fucking word. It's only four letters. I promise the world will not cave in around you."

"Please, I don't want to," I whisper, suddenly feeling insignificant.

He breathes in deeply. I watch as his eyebrows furrow and his eyes seem to soften. "If you can't say something as simple as 'cunt,' I don't think we are a suitable fit. I'm sure, as you've discovered, I'm not a gentle lover, and I want what I want."

He leans forward, uncharacteristically brushing a lock of hair from my cheek. Does he have a softer side?

"I'm sexually dominant; brutal at times. When I play, I play hard. I don't mess around with my pleasure. If you want to expand your mind, I'll be happy to take you into my world, but you have to want to do the things I tell you to, without questioning my motives. I'll expect you to do things that might be uncomfortable. All I'm asking right now is that you say the word 'cunt.' Do it now, or I'm going to ask you to leave and not come back until you are ready to do as I ask."

My mind is whirling, unable to decide. If I stay, he could do things to me that scare me. If I leave, I'll always wonder what he means by taking me into his world.

"Take a chance, Rayna. What do you have to lose?"

"You really are bossy," I sharply reply, not enjoying that I'm being given an ultimatum. "So, either I say that disgusting word or I go home, and you're done with me?"

"Yes." He hasn't moved, still kneeling and staring at me as if reading my chaotic thoughts. He's patiently waiting for me to decide. "It's only a word and nobody is within earshot to hear you say it other than me."

The best I can manage is to whisper. "Cunt." I feel my face flushing red; my shame becoming all too obvious.

"I'm sorry, I couldn't hear you. Try again, louder this time."

Even though he is calm and absolute, I watch the corners of his lips lift, alerting me to the pleasure he's getting from my mortification.

I nearly yell, "Cunt! Are you happy now?"

I swallow hard, trying to keep my emotions held back. I do not want to cry. I hate confrontation. My anxiety spikes and tears typically spill.

"You tell me," he replies as he grabs his erect cock through the fabric of his cotton shorts, proving the excitement my humiliation brings him.

His seductive smile makes my tummy flutter. I want him even more now, which confuses me. Why wouldn't I get up and leave, stomping my feet? Instead, my body proves its need for his touch. I think I'm more aroused than I have ever been. Could it be from saying that awful word, or because I did something I never do?

He lowers his face to my smouldering pussy, sucking my clit between his teeth and flicking it gingerly with the tip of his tongue.

Holy hell!

The world falls apart around me. I moan so loudly that it echoes throughout the room. His barely audible, devilish chuckle gently whispers into my ears. I'm spellbound. Take me, devil man!

He started off worshipping my swelling clitoris. But now,

Coach teases me with his scarce flicking. He's enjoying how my body bucks in frustration.

"Your cunt tastes so sweet. Your juices are thick and slick, perfectly preparing you for my meaty cock. I want to drink you in." His lips press a full kiss onto my pussy. My hips lift in appreciation. With a deep, assertive voice, he demands, "Beg me to make you cum."

He wants me to talk nasty again. No, I can't do this. It's not in my nature. Besides, I'm not ready to cum yet.

Feeling ignored, he covers my clit with his open mouth, sucking hard while stroking his tongue up and down over my aching button. He pushes two of his fat fingers deep inside me with one quick thrust.

I cry out as his digits push completely in, his knuckles pressing firmly against my labia. Coach stays focused on one particularly sensitive spot inside of me. Each time his fingertips thrust, the sensations his tongue generously provides intensifies. He's not fucking at a steady pace but keeping it torturously sporadic and I never know when he's going to lick my clit or leave me craving it. He's making me come apart.

He lifts his mouth long enough to repeat his demand. "Ask me, Rayna."

I look down at his sexy, dangerous face as he mashes it against me. The world fades around me, my focus aimed at my pleasure button. I'm almost there. He lifts his face and I know he's going to ask again. I'll do just about anything to keep this going.

I scream, "Please, let me cum!"

"Cum, Rayna." His calm, deep voice sounds so far away.

He doesn't let up as my pussy clenches around his fingers. A violent orgasm erupts from deep inside of my soul. It is finally free to ripple throughout my body, setting fire to every cell of my being. I scream as my mind slowly falls into blackness, but his mouth and fingers don't let up for a second. My body bounces and jerks under the command of his tongue.

Coach kneels up quickly, unbuttoning his shorts and yanking

them down his thighs and tucking them between his knees and the sofa cushion. His impressive, rock-hard prick juts straight out from his body.

It's glorious! He's so big! His is probably the most perfect erection I have ever seen. A tiny gleam of pre-cum glistens at the tip, catching my eye.

His teeth tear at a condom package, revealing the hidden sheath inside. He rolls it over his weapon with the skill of a man who's done it a million times. He leans forward, touching the fat tip against my slit.

He stops.

"Tell me you want me to fuck you," he demands, his excitement revealed in his voice. When I pause, he tilts his head and glares at me.

"Yes, please fuck me," I reply with aloud, quivering voice.

In one smooth movement, he's buried deep inside of my body. The shock of it ripples through me. I gasp, nearly coming from the sudden invasion. He's spreading my walls wider than any man ever has.

I open my eyes when he doesn't move. He's looking down at me. A dark, trance-like expression has enveloped his face. He looks like a testosterone-filled, emotionless machine, ready to fuck me harder than I've ever been before. And I want him.

He doesn't disappoint me when his hips lift, slamming back down onto me, shoving himself even deeper inside. The initial fullness shocks me and my hands spring free from behind my back, immediately slapping his ribs. He doesn't even flinch at my weak attempt to make him ease up. He continues to pound into me again and again.

The pain quickly becomes something entirely wonderful. Each time the tip of his prick pounds my cervix, my body weakens a little more. I want him even deeper if it's at all possible.

My fingernails dig into his arms, which brace his weight on either side of my chest. I slide up the cushion each time he crashes into me. His massive hands clutch my hips, lifting my lower half off the cushion and pulling me with him as he kneels back.

He flashes me a crooked grin that would signify a fistfight to another man with a quick temper. I'm quickly learning that he loves his dominance and the fear it creates in others.

He pushes his prick deep into me and holds me still. Only the rapid swelling and shrinking of his chest prevents him from looking like he's made of stone, a perfectly sculpted statue for my eyes to soak up and burn into my memory.

"Tell me to fuck you hard and fast. Tell me your hungry cunt wants to cum on my throbbing cock."

Coach isn't fucking around.

I now know that when he insists I say something, I'd better say it. Otherwise, the pleasure stops. I wonder if he's this persistent with his gym clients and if they appreciate it or hate him for it. I want to sample more of what he's offering, and I'll do almost anything to make that happen.

I yell, ensuring he'll hear every word, "Fuck me hard and fast until my starving cunt cums on your fucking cock!"

Wow! I sound like a loose-tongued whore.

An evilness burns from behind his eyes that fills me with a sudden unease. His expression softens as he studies my fearful eyes.

"When you cum, I want you to thank me. Do you understand? If you don't, I will stop." His gently spoken words ensure that he is not a vicious beast intending to hurt me, but a man with an intensive need to pleasure me. My anxious fear has me undeniably lusting for him.

"I understand," I say breathlessly, hoping he'll quit talking and get back to fucking me.

He nearly sings, "You're a good little slut and you deserve to cum."

The violent fucking ensues and doesn't let up. I don't even care that he called me a slut. This pounding is totally worth the humiliation of the insult. I know I'm not a slut, so it doesn't faze me.

He rams me like a wild man, pounding into me with impossible speed and force. The thudding against my body forces the air from my lungs in rapid succession. I can barely think.

My body is his toy to take as he will, my mind no longer able to make intelligent, responsible decisions. An orgasm locks every muscle in a seizure of painful pleasure I hope never to recover from. Screams pour out of me as wave after wave of heightened climax shreds through me, rendering me stiff and useless.

I open my eyes to make sure a man is fucking me and not the devil, but I can't be sure. Coach still fucks me hard while watching me with black pools surrounded by skin so red it's nearly purple. His eyebrows furrow. Soulless growls escape from deep in his massive chest as if the devil himself is tearing into me. Perhaps he is.

His eyes widen and glare, and that's when I remember his instruction. "Thank you!"

Coach stands quickly, grabbing me by my arms and yanking me to my feet. My weak knees give out and I nearly fall, but he scoops me up like I weigh nothing more than a bag of potatoes. He doesn't even grunt like I do when I pick up a grocery bag off the floor. He sprints to the back of the sofa, and then sets me down onto my feet, spinning me until I'm facing away from him.

His huge hand grabs the back of my neck firmly, bending me forward until I'm at a ninety-degree angle over the back of the sofa. He gently but assertively kicks my feet wide apart. His thick, powerful spread thighs press against my much smaller ones, pinning me to the back of the sofa and that throbbing prick buries deep into me again.

Oh, fuck! I didn't think it was possible, but he's reaching so much deeper inside of me in this position. I can't even cry out to beg him to go easier, but do I really want to if I could?

It hurt at first when he entered me on the couch, but my body quickly adjusted, and I will this time, too.

I've never been this full and overwhelmed by anyone in my entire life. I'm surprised to realize that I really like not having any say in what he does to me. I trust him in that he said he'll stop if I say "red" and that brings me comfort.

With one hand on my hip and the other on the back of my neck, he fucks me like it's the last time he will ever fuck a woman. The power behind his muscular body has me flopping around like a rag doll. If he wasn't holding my neck, I might get whiplash. The skin on my body feels like loose clothing as it ripples with each hard thud. Even the skin on my cheeks and lips bounce and I don't have a shred of decency left in me at this point to care what I look like.

I cum, hard. My wetness trickles down my parted inner thighs.

He releases my neck only to grab a wad of my hair, pulling me back until his mouth is next to my ear. My scalp hurts but I'm still coming so I don't give a shit what he's doing to me as long as he doesn't stop.

My pussy spasms around his thickness. He holds deep inside me. I relish the pause and gather my senses. His rapid, heated breath bounces off my ear. The only other sound is from my vigorously pounding heart rushing blood through my veins.

"Say 'thank you, sir,'" he whispers next to my ear as shivers continue to ripple through me.

"What?" My mind is still foggy from the violent fucking.

"Say 'thank you.' Since you forgot again, you will start calling me sir to acknowledge my sexual dominance over you."

"I don't like that." My voice sounds fragile and timid through panted breaths.

"Then you should have remembered to thank me," he whispers in a growl. "Now thank me properly, or we're done."

To get him to shut up and bring me back to that level of euphoria, I comply with his demands. "Thank you for the incredible orgasm, Sir! May I have another?"

Yes, I'm being a smartass, but what's he going to do about it?

He won't throw me out. He hasn't cum yet and I'm sure he'll want to accomplish that before he tosses me aside.

His hand comes down on my ass with a thunderous clap. My ears ring and my eyes fly open. I wail! I pant as the heat from his hand singes my flesh, no doubt imprinting a giant hand-shaped welt on my flesh.

Before I can complain, he fucks me even quicker and harder than he had been, which is a tremendous feat. I didn't think he could be more intense, but I thought wrong.

Within seconds, I'm coming so hard that my body desperately wants to fuck back against him, but he's too powerful for me to compete with. He has all the control, and I am simply along for the ride. And what a ride it is!

Before I can finish thanking him, I'm coming again, and again.

A loud, beastly growl wrenches from Coach's throat, lasting longer than any breath I could manage right now. His prick swells, stretching my inner walls and forcing me into one final vicious orgasm. His muscles jerk, jolting his massive body.

A complete stillness overcomes him, and my hair slips from his grasp. A long, quiet exhale seeps from his very core as if he has satiated his devil.

I remain flopped over the back of the sofa, gasping for a full breath with his pelvis still pressed against me. I am limp, like an overcooked spaghetti noodle. He groans softly, leaning forward to kiss my back a dozen times before resting his forehead on it. His withering prick still lives inside of me.

He suddenly pulls away, his prick sliding out of my well-used vagina. I attempt to lift my chest, but I'm too tired. With more gentleness than I thought he had in him, he grips my shoulders, raising me up and turning me to face him. He pulls me against his sweaty chest and wraps his massive arms around my shoulders. Tenderly, he kisses the top of my head. It's a loving gesture that seems out of character from the man I knew a moment ago.

"You did well." His whisper compliments me while his body rocks me safely back and forth.

"What?" I ask, not sure why he thinks I did well when I did nothing to contribute, not even follow his simple verbal requests.

"You learned to appease my requests, even though you had an attitude. Also, you didn't beg for mercy." He seems proud of me.

I thoroughly enjoyed that, so why would I beg for mercy?

"I didn't know that was an option."

Coach scolds, "The option was always there. You accepted whatever I was doing to you. Do you remember when we first started, I told you to say 'red' if you wanted it to stop?" I nod against his solid chest. "You didn't use the word. You surprised me, is all."

"I should go. My kids will wonder where I walked off. The last thing I need is for them to report me as a missing person."

He chuckles as he releases me from his hold. He walks around the couch to get a tissue to wrap the condom in. His glistening muscles hypnotize me as he performs the simplest task of pulling his shorts back on. That man is a glorious mountain.

Now that I've seen him totally naked, I think he's even bigger than I had thought he was, or maybe that's the perception I have of him because of how he just overpowered me.

He fucks like an angry man with something to prove. I wonder what his reasoning is for needing to have that much control. Is he like this with everyone he's ever fucked or just the meek people such as myself?

"Can I ask you something?" I utter as he hands me a small towel. I watch him pat his forehead and chest with another towel while focusing his attention on me.

"You can ask me anything."

I clear my throat before beginning my interrogation. "Why were you so rough with me?"

Coach seems concerned. "Did I hurt you?"

"No," I reply quickly, easing the tension from his expression.

"I enjoy a good, hard fuck. As you can tell, I like control and dominance. The thought of making love bores me. And, before you ask, there is no deep-rooted reason behind this compulsion of mine. I simply prefer sex this way."

I cross my arms after handing him the towel. "Do you ever make love?"

Coach tilts his head, furrowing his eyebrows, and tells me an affirmative, "No." He tosses the towels through an open door.

"Why not?"

He sharply responds, "Why would I?"

I shrug, not really knowing how to answer that question. "I don't know. You love Alissa, right? So, do you two ever get romantic with each other? I mean, how do you show her that you love her?"

"She knows exactly how I feel about her."

I nod, waiting for him to elaborate, but he doesn't. "You do love her, right? If my calculations are correct, you've been dating her for nearly a year."

"I care about her wellbeing, sure. Making love is for people in love, and I am not in love with her."

He picks up the glasses of wine and hands one to me.

"You're not in love with her? That would explain why there's no ring on her finger," I say with a smile, hoping I'm not overstepping.

He stares at me, his expression beginning to look intense once again. He no longer has the calmness in his voice, taking me off guard.

"I will not marry her."

He's so sure of his statement. I can't say I've ever been that sure of anything in my entire life. When I married my ex-husband, I convinced myself that he was the best I could ever hope to have in a life partner, but I wasn't sure I loved him with all of my being. He turned out to be a son-of-a-bitch who spent his time chasing loose women and not caring for his wife and children like he should have been. The man only cared about one thing: his dick.

To this day, I sneer when I see him with his arm around his

chosen tart of the month. When our kids had court-ordered sleepover visitations, which he rarely followed through on, I didn't know who would stay with them while he was out doing God-knows-what with God-knows-who. I think most of the girls enjoy playing housewife for a while, but when shit gets too real, they always leave him.

"If you've been with her for this long already, and you're sure you will not marry her, why not let her get on with her life so she can find someone who wants to marry her? I mean, if that's what she's looking for."

"Rayna, she knows I'm not the marrying kind. She is free to find another if she chooses to. I am not holding onto her. The two of us enjoy one another's company; we are plus-ones to special occasions, and we have a well-matched sexual rhythm between us. But that's it."

"Yeah, but..." I want to continue questioning him about this, but the look he gives me tells me to leave it for another time, if ever. "I should go."

"Thank you for coming over. We should do this again soon if you're still curious."

I clear my throat, ready to ask him what there is to still be curious about, but I decide not to. I gulp from the wineglass and set it on the table and then turn to walk toward the stairs. I don't even get to the first step before he grabs my arm, spinning me around to face him.

The warm palm of his hand cradles my cheek with shocking tenderness. His eyes look down into mine and for the first time, I notice the flecks of green in his eyes that break up the intensity of the brown. They don't seem so dark and intimidating at the moment.

How can these pretty eyes of his reveal that much petulance and yet still seem to have an overflow of kindness hidden within them?

Coach delicately touches his lips to mine, stirring the heat within me. Before the fire burns out of control, he sets me free and leads me by the hand up the stairs to the front door. He twists the handle and pulls it open, slapping me lightly on the ass as I take my first step outside.

I spin around and smile, blushing hotly as I recall the pain from the other slap he gave me while he fucked me, and how my body surprised me by reacting in an orgasmic explosion because of it.

The moment I walk through my front door, I immediately head to the bathroom to check my appearance. I can almost guarantee that I look like I've been repeatedly bounced off a fleshy brick wall. After burying my torn panties deep in the trash bin, I burst into a laughter that echoes off the bathroom walls. I immediately cover my mouth to muffle the sound. I don't need the kids asking me why I'm so happy.

Oh, what an interesting afternoon this has been!

CHAPTER 3

 *oach*

THE HOT WATER SPLASHES AGAINST MY BACK AS I SOAP MY CHEST AND think about what just occurred with the woman I've been fantasizing about for three years. I always imagined that she'd be sexually uptight, and I wasn't wrong. However, she lets loose when her pleasure is at stake.

It might be possible to convince her to be submissive to me. I'll have to take my time breaking her in and teach her what that role entails. I can't rush anything with this woman. She'll likely run for the hills if I do.

I wasn't sure if I pushed her too hard today, but she didn't quit on me, which surprises me. I'm so thankful that she stuck it out. If she had left when I asked her to say "cunt," I would have been very disappointed at myself for being such a twisted fucking asshole.

I know I'm a dick when it comes to sex; I get that, but rough sex gets me off, always has. Rayna didn't seem to mind. Whether or not she returns to me will prove or disprove that theory.

If she'll let me, I'd like to bind her with rope, limiting her movements. Rope binding has always been something that I find to be very sensual. With her helpless and at my mercy, I'd caress and kiss every inch of her milky skin, occasionally nipping her with my teeth just to keep her on edge. I want to spank her ass until it's red hot and then fuck her so hard she screams and cums, drowning my cock in her wet pleasure while her pussy clamps down so hard I can no longer move inside of her.

All this thinking about Rayna being at my mercy has my prick standing at attention. I don't have a lot of time to jerk off, but it won't go away on its own, especially since Rayna is still vivid in my mind and probably will be all day.

I squirt a blob of body wash in my palm and turn my back to the running water. I grip my prick and stroke it quickly, squeezing its firmness while imagining Rayna's tight pussy wrapped around me, sucking me in deeper just before she cums and then bearing down on my hard-on as she reaches her climax. It isn't long before I blow my load, relieving my tension and the stiffness of my cock.

I've been secretly watching Rayna for three years. When I first moved into the house next to hers, she came knocking at my door to introduce herself. The moment I opened the door and saw those gorgeous green eyes, I immediately imagined how intoxicating it would be to look into them while I slid myself inside her body. The thought of it had me trying to hide the hard-on I was growing in my sweatpants.

Her voice was soft and sexy, which didn't give ease to my throbbing dick. Something about her held my attention, captivated me in an instant, unlike anyone ever had.

I watched her cheeks flush after she stammered through informing me that she was divorced. She must have thought what she said was inappropriate because she seemed to ramble nervously as she tried to shift the conversation away from her ex as quickly as possible. It was strangely titillating.

She said she had two kids. I wondered if she was lonely. She didn't seem the type of woman to sleep around randomly just to get the physical relief she likely needed.

Right then, I made a vow to myself that she was off-limits. Back then, I needed a woman hanging on my arm while dragging a shit-load of baggage with her like I needed a hole in the head. I had enough baggage of my own. No, I was sure I'd keep my distance, but I thought it would be interesting to tease the fuck out of her every chance I got.

When our eyes met at our first encounter, I held her gaze and didn't look away. She averted her eyes quickly and then ran her fingers through her hair, nervously tucking a loose strand behind her perfectly adorable ear. She liked me. It was obvious from the way her eyes kept dropping to my chest. I stirred something inside of her that had been dormant, but she didn't act upon her desires and I needed to leave her be.

Perhaps my intuition knew there would be a better time for us to be physical. Maybe I subconsciously feared she would run for her life, thinking that I'm a sadistic fucker. She wouldn't have been wrong. Or maybe I'm different now; not so angry and dangerous as I was then.

She never so much as said a single thing that led me to believe she physically wanted to be with me other than the way she ogled my body when she thought I wouldn't notice.

Over the years, I've gotten to know her two exceptional kids. I occasionally play with them, usually with water guns or cannons. I chase them outside our houses and it's a riot. They're sneaky when they want to be, especially the little girl, Kim. She is small and can hide just about anywhere, rendering her almost invisible, thus allowing her to sabotage my plans of attack. Ken is older, and he's not nearly as sly as his little sister, but he runs as quick as lightning when he wants to get away from me. I'm too big to run quick enough to catch him.

Every night, Rayna makes her kids' lunches wearing only a nightgown, which is usually thin enough to see her shape when the light shines perfectly behind her. Little did she know, her silhouette was being admired by my eyes from my office window.

I didn't lie to her when I told her that I usually jerk off while watching her. I can't help it, she's so fucking sexy and she doesn't even know it. Maybe that's what I find to be most attractive about her.

Little did I know back when I first met, but her life looks pretty good from where I stand now. Perhaps I've matured. Her kids are awesome, too. The only issue is her deadbeat ex-husband, but he rarely enters the picture enough to be a problem. I wanted to play with her back then, to sample her, but I knew I'd only hurt her, and she deserved better. She's a respectable woman and too good for the likes of me.

I have a fun girlfriend, of sorts. Alissa is more of a submissive than what I would define as being a girlfriend. Before we started playing, she and I agreed that love will never enter the picture and if one of us felt like we were getting too close, we'd end it. She's a toy that I play with when I need entertainment, and she gets off on doing anything I tell her to; submitting. As I said, she's a fun girl.

Alissa and I have been together for about a year now and I think it's about time to send her on her way. Even though we agreed that this relationship was only for convenience and sex, I think she allowed herself to develop deeper feelings for me. She tries to kiss me romantically and cuddle when we're finished having sex, and that isn't something she would ever consider doing in the beginning. I should really think about letting her go as soon as possible, as Rayna suggested.

I'm meeting my long-time friend, Brett, for a late lunch and if I don't get a move on, I won't be on time. I despise people who are always late. Sometimes, like today, for instance, things come up that need taking care of before other pre-scheduled plans. If Brett was given the opportunity to fuck his infatuation, I doubt I'd be upset that he was late or missed our appointment altogether, but he's a little different from me. He takes things too personally sometimes.

Brett is someone I tag-team women with. Most women have fantasies involving two men, and we are more than happy to help them live out that fantasy. It's a lot of fun, especially when we're both fucking her at the same time. First off, it feels amazing on my cock. Second, I get to rock a girl's world with my good buddy. The women we do this with are nothing more than a plaything that we send on her way because we have no heartfelt feelings for them.

I'd never share Rayna with him, not that she'd allow it, anyway. It's not that I have deep feelings for her, but she differs from all of those other women. She's better than them, more deserving of respect. No matter the reason, I'd never let Brett put his hands on her.

He's much rougher with women than I am, and that's not a simple task. He has no problem leaving ghastly bruises on them or choking a woman out until blood vessels around her eyes burst and she's nearly unconscious. He likes to fuck anally, but his dick is too huge for most women to handle in their ass. If I think she's too tight, he won't fuck her ass, at least not while I'm around. After she's schooled in how sadistic he is, if she's daring enough to go to him alone, it's on her.

When I pull up in front of Charley's bar, I see Brett sitting at one of the outside tables, drinking a beer. Damn, that beer looks cold and soothing. I think I'll order one, too.

"Hey! Sorry, man," I apologize as I approach Brett and grasp his hand, bumping our firm chests together while we pat each other on the back only once. It's a manly way to show our level of friendship without seeming too affectionate.

"No worries. There must have been a damn good reason since you're never late. What's your excuse? It had better be a detailed story about nailing a hot chick," he jests.

"Brett, do you remember me telling you about my neighbour?" I ask as I take a seat across from him.

He tilts his head and asks, "The one with the blonde hair and hot little body? You pointed her out last year when a bunch of us were over for a barbeque. Fuck, it was hot that day."

"Yeah," I nod, remembering how steamy it was. "Well, I finally got to play with her."

His eyebrows rise high on his forehead. "Fuck off! No way! Yeah? Damn, you're a lucky man," he exclaims and then sips his beer while smirking. "She's hot for an older woman. I can't wait to fuck that broad." He laughs sadistically.

I shake my head. "Not with this one, buddy. She's special. I don't know why, but she is. She's a classy woman, not just some fucking slut who'll do anything to ride a cock." I point directly at him and sternly say, "Hands off. I'm not fucking around. Sorry, man."

"Since when do we keep the hottest chicks to ourselves? We always share. Well, almost always. I wouldn't subject you to a boring starfish," Brett says, referring to lazy women who only lie on their backs and spread wide, waiting for us to do all the work. If we give her the opportunity to move about at her will and she refuses, she's a starfish. We always take the lead, but I don't like bitches who expect that.

He looks pissed off, so I assure him, "The next chick I fuck, I'll make sure she's one of those fiery bitches you like so much. She'll be a chick who wants her two-man rape fantasy played out by two vicious, well-built men. We can take her hard while she play-fights. Those chicks are a riot, am I right?" He looks at me, lost in thought. "Brett, is it a deal?"

"But I like your neighbour. She makes my dick hard," he pouts.

"Sorry, Brett, not this one. I mean it, stay away!" I demand, hoping he'll let her go. I chuckle. "You know what? Alissa is available now. On the way over, I called her and told her not to come around anymore. We're done."

"No, you didn't! Really?" He's shocked. He sips his beer, pondering taking her on as solely his. We've played with her together many times, so he knows how insanely wild she can be. He shakes his head. "Nah, I don't want to play with her without you. She was your chick and I don't want her to think she'll be dating me. There's something not right about that woman and I can't put my finger on it. She's fun to play with, but not to keep. It was about time you dropped her."

"I think she has the fucking warm and fuzzies for me, and that's why I sent her packing."

"Why the sudden change?" he asks, then swigs his beer.

I grumble, "Rayna suggested I let her go if I'll never commit to her. She's right."

"So, this Rayna chick is telling you what to do already, and you only fucked her once? She must be an impressive piece of ass," he teases, sucking back the last gulp of beer from his bottle. He hisses, "Now I really want her."

"Kindly keep the python in your pants. There are other people around," I remind him. I take a big gulp from my bottle but wave him off when he asks if I want another. "No thanks, I'm driving."

"Suit yourself," he says while tilting his bottle toward the watchful waiter.

"So, why don't you give Alissa a call? Like I said, she's available and you know she's a freak for vicious sex. She loves your cock in any hole. I'm sure she'll agree to play with you. That girl is perpetually horny, and as you know, she'll do anything you ask and love it."

"I know. Alissa is a fine piece of ass. I didn't think you'd ever let her go. That girl is a screamer, especially when we DP her." His attitude shifts and he leans in closer. "That always feels so fucking good, doesn't it? I'm not saying I'm gay or anything, but I can feel your cock fucking her ass when I'm deep in her pussy. It's like you're stroking my cock, good buddy."

"When you say it like that, it sounds a little gay." I look around to make sure nobody is listening in. "Can we change the subject before you get it in your ugly fucking head that you're going to rub your cock on mine before your next beer arrives?"

"Since you want to keep her to yourself for a while, you can at least tell me what she's like? Start with her body. Give me something to jerk off to. Does she have any weird moles, fish scales, four tits? Leave no detail untold," he begs.

I grimace and shake my head. "She's magnificent. That's all I'm saying."

He scratches his perfectly shaved chin. "She's a single mom, right?" He frowns as if that's a huge turnoff for him.

"Yeah, so?" I wonder what his issue is with fucking single mothers.

"Dude, if you date her, you'll have her fucking brats hanging around all the time. They'll start calling you Daddy. How will you get to use her body whenever you want if she has brats running around? Fuck that shit!"

I smile and reply, "Wow! Take a step back. We aren't dating. We only fucked once. It's not like we're in a committed relationship, for fuck's sake. If it turns into something bigger, I'll accept her kids, too. They come as a package and I think I'd be okay with that. Those kids are pretty cool!"

"Who the fuck are you and how do I get my crazy friend back?"

I laugh. "We all have to grow up sometime. You will, too, when it's time."

"So, you'd consider having a relationship with her? I thought your motto was to use them up and spit them out."

"Yeah, well..."

I stop talking to watch the couple sit at the table next to us. A tinge of panic sinks in my chest when I imagine them as being Rayna and me. I've held my heart behind a barrier for a long time. I wonder if I ever could truly love anyone.

"So, let's say you do date he and things are great at first, but soon she convinces you to buy a minivan—"

"No fucking minivan! I like my truck, thanks."

"We'll see," he teases, sips his beer and continues. "What happens if it doesn't end well? First off, now you're stuck with a minivan." I roll my eyes. "You two live next door to each other. That could get awkward. And the kids; what about them? They'd be knocking at your door, calling you Daddy and shit; crying because you hurt their mommy and now she's sad all the time. Did you think about that before you fucked her?"

"No, Brett, I didn't. My cock was hard, and she was there. As I said, we only fucked once. I probably scared her away with my sinister ways." I sip the water the waiter brings me. "So, just calm the fuck down and drink your beer. You know me; I live for today and don't fear tomorrow. I'll deal with shit if I need to."

He shakes his head and snickers. "I almost forgot! I met this chick today. She's a natural blonde; tall, thin, dangerous dark brown eyes, and pouty lips that could make a man beg for mercy. What do you say? I can set us up for tonight." He takes out his phone and taps the screen, searching for her number.

"No, I think I'll pass this time. You have fun with her and tell me about it tomorrow." I tease, "Are you asking because you know you can't completely satisfy her without my expert sexual talents?"

When he frowns and flings his coaster at me like it's a Frisbee, I burst out laughing.

"I'll do just fine, thank you. I know what I'm doing. I'm just saying that it's not as much fun without you. I mean, she'll fucking get off a lot more with two guys. I know how much you love to watch a slut lose her mind."

He looks at me with dreamy eyes while licking his lips.

"Stop looking at me like that. You're making me wonder if it's me you want to fuck. Cut it out!" I hiss, and he laughs.

There's something to be said about how great it feels when we both fuck a chick. Each man can feel the friction from the other man's cock through the thin skin separating the two canals. It's not a homosexual thing, I don't think. But, to have my dick stroked while I'm ass fucking a chick is mind-numbing. It's like having a tongue lick the underside of my cock, but while I'm fucking.

Brett is always the first to cum. He can never hold back. I often tease him about it, of course. That's what friends do.

"Are you heading to the gym today?" I ask, hoping to get away from this subject.

He shrugs, muttering, "I don't know. You?"

"Yeah, right after this. I have a new yoga instructor starting today. Carol will observe her, but I'd like to see how she does." My words seem to fall on deaf ears. "Hey, are you still with me or are you too busy concentrating on peeling your beer label?"

"What?" he asks, quickly shifting his eyes up to meet mine. "Yeah, yeah, I'm still here. Carol—new yoga chick—I heard you. Continue."

"What's going on?" I ask, but he simply shakes his head, not replying. Much louder than I should, I ask, "Is it the gnarly butt rash flaring up again?"

"Oh, come on!" He snickers while looking at the disgusted couple nearest us. "I got it from him." They look at me, then go back to eating.

"What's up?"

"Nothing. It's dumb," he says while shaking his head.

"Don't be a dick. Tell me."

"Am I losing you to a chick you barely know?" he asks. As if something gross dawns on him suddenly, he shivers. "Holy fuck! I sounded like a chick just there, didn't I?"

"I'm not going to lie; you kind of did."

"Damn!" He cups his pecs as if checking to see if they grew. "They have been sensitive lately."

"Are you getting your period?"

He debates. "If you're just finishing yours, then yes. Our mensies are almost synced."

"Brett, you aren't losing me. We're friends first, chick-swappers second. I will always think of you as one of my closest friends. And I didn't *just* meet her!" I exclaim, tossing the coaster back at him, hitting him on the nose, and then throwing my arms up as if I just scored.

Brett glares at me as he touches the bridge of his nose. He smiles and replies, "I don't want it to end and I hate that you won't share her. I know that we'll always be friends, no matter what either of us does or won't let the other do. You're my brother from another, and I love you."

We grip hands like men do, but when the couple looks at us, he leans in and licks my hand. They roll their eyes.

"What? Are you against man-on-man love?" he asks them, to which they shake their heads. He's a scary-looking guy when he means to be.

"We're just messing with you," I tell them after seeing the fear in their eyes.

As if he didn't just terrify the people next to us, he casually looks back at me and asks, "Are you sure you don't want another beer?"

Sometimes the man worries me. He hasn't always struck me as a totally mentally sound person. But he means well, even though his ways of thinking aren't always what I would consider being of societal norms. Who am I to judge? I have my own fucked up issues.

"Yeah, all right. You talked me into it. I'll have one more, but I'm cutting myself off after that. I have to drive to the gym to do some paperwork and can't be sloshed while doing either task," I explain as he waves his hand at the waiter, pointing to his bottle and holding up two fingers.

CHAPTER 4

 *ayna*

I SLEPT PEACEFULLY LAST NIGHT. I CAN'T REMEMBER THE LAST TIME I felt that relaxed. Perhaps I should have sex more often, and with an actual human, not with a hard plastic vibrator. Adult bedroom toys are great, but the satisfaction that comes from being physically touched by someone's hot skin, listening to their moans and feeling their weight pressing down on my body? Well, an inanimate object can't match it.

What am I going to do today?

Last night, I finished the chores I had planned on doing today. After I'd gotten home from Coach's, I had newfound energy which had me dancing around the house and cleaning every room lacking a good dusting and polishing. All the dirty clothes were laundered and put away. I even went to the grocery store before it closed so I could restock the kitchen for the coming week. My mind swayed between dreamland and reality, so I overlooked some items on my list.

I definitely should engage in this type of extreme sexual activity more often. I get more accomplished afterward.

With my second cup of coffee down, I make my way to the bathroom to take a shower. Right after I pull my nightgown off, the doorbell rings, of course.

After quickly pulling my nightie back over my head, I rush to the door, hoping to open it before the person pushes the bell again, possibly waking the children. It's Sunday and I have no plans for them today, so they can stay in bed all day if they choose.

When I get to the top of the stairs, I see my sister waving at me through the window in the door. I knew I should have bought curtains for it.

She holds up two large coffees, smiling and bobbing up and down like an idiot. I shake my head and then lift my wrist to look at an imaginary watch as if we're playing a game of charades. She stops bouncing long enough to roll her eyes like she always did when she was a kid. It used to make me instantly angry, but since she never outgrew it, I learned to let it go.

I pull open the heavy door to invite her in, taking the coffee from her hand before I let her pass the threshold. I'll think of it as a fee for the early intrusion. She kisses my cheek before flashing me another silly smile that's way too toothy to be legitimate.

"Please, come in," I say, sarcastically.

"Thanks, sis! I think I will. So, what are you up to?" She's way too happy and energetic. It's not even nine in the morning. I'm still groggy and I've been up for an hour.

"Why are you here this early? You never come over before noon. And on Sundays, it's never until around three in the afternoon." I follow her up the stairs and into the kitchen. "Did you shit the bed again? I keep telling you to pick up a bag of adult diapers. They rave about them on the television."

"Hardy-har-har! You're hilarious! And I didn't shit the bed. Gross!" She contorts her face for a quick moment before joking adding, "I haven't done that in a very long time." She pauses while her face lights up. "Funny story…"

Here we go! Every time she tells me something that starts with a "funny story," it usually means she was out drinking and had a life-altering sexual experience with some guy or girl.

She sets her coffee on the counter before reaching into the small paper bag she sat on the counter and pulls out a bagel. She peels the wrapper back and I see that it's smothered in cream cheese, exactly how I like it. I smile, so she hands one to me before lifting another from the bag. She picks up her coffee and makes her way toward the glass patio doors.

"Do you want to sit outside? The weather is perfect this morning, isn't it?" she asks, and I shrug since I have no idea. "So, I was out last night, met a girl at that old tiny diner down the street from where I work." She points north with her bagel. "She was hot, I mean *so* hot! We talked for about half an hour, and by that time, I'd already decided I would ask her to come home with me."

We sit at the table; me facing Coach's house and her facing me.

She continues with her arms flailing to embellish the story. "That's when she got a phone call. I tried not to listen in, but she made that impossible. She was talking, more like yelling, to the caller about some curtains that she wants back, and threatening that she's going to send her cousin to take them. So, I decided I wanted no part of the crazy bitch."

"Probably wise," I say.

"Right? So, I stood up, took my coffee and walked out the door, leaving her at the table, still yelling at her phone. I don't even think she knew I left until she hung up."

"That's quite a story," I say with exaggerated sarcasm because this story doesn't surprise me. Renee has this magnetism that attracts societal losers. "Are there any napkins in that bag?"

She looks in and replies, "No, lick your fingers. Germs are our friends." She licks her fingers as if showing me how. "So, back to my story. I went home, watched TV, and fell asleep on the sofa. That was around seven. I woke up at eight this morning!"

The sun reflects off her bright white teeth. I don't think she could smile bigger if I offered her money to do so.

"Are you telling me you slept for thirteen hours?" I stare at her in disbelief.

"Yup! Are you jealous?" She giggles while still smiling like a fool.

"Did rigour mortis set in?"

"You are so funny, but I can tell you're jealous. I'm more well-rested today than you are," she teases.

I snicker, no doubt blushing like a young schoolgirl recalling a kiss from a boy. Her statement has me picturing Coach fucking me from behind. I'm unable to wipe the smile off my face.

"No, I'm not jealous. I slept better than I have in a very long time."

Renee chews while looking at me with questions behind her gaze. I giggle, shrug, and then take a big bite, knowing she's trying to read my thoughts. She swallows after a sip of coffee.

"What's going on? You're being weird."

I cover my mouth so I won't spit on her. "What makes you think something's going on? Can't someone have a great night's sleep without there being a hidden cause?"

"Sure, they can, but you're blushing." She sips her coffee again.

We hear patio doors slide next door. We both turn our heads toward the sound. The amazingly well-built man, who fucked me so extensively yesterday, walks outside with a basket of wet clothes. He waves when he notices us. I lift my arm and wave back, trying to hide my growing grin.

"Coffee and breakfast? Did you bring me any?" Coach shouts.

Under her breath, Renee whispers, "Oh, yeah, beast-man! I got something for you right here in my panties."

I shake my head and fight back laughter. "Sorry, my sister only brought enough for two, but I'll share some of my bagel if you're hungry."

He grins, waving his eyebrows. "Sweetheart, I would gladly

eat whatever you'd like to share with me. All you need to do is ask."

My face is fiery hot. I quickly glance at my sister, who's staring at Coach with her lips slightly parted. She doesn't blink. Knowing my sister as well as I do, I can tell she's fantasizing about him.

"Maybe I'll bring something over later, after you finish your chores," I tease, surprising myself how flirtatious that sounded. I've never been good at flirting.

He licks his bottom lip while smiling, tilts his head to the side, and says nothing. We share an intimate look between us, a hot and steamy moment that makes my pussy twitch and my body temperature suddenly spike. I gasp and bite my lip. My sister slowly turns her head and looks at me with wide eyes.

She whispers, "Tell him you have something better for him to eat than a bagel. Go ahead, tell him. I dare you!"

I look from her to him. "I have something better than a lousy bagel for you to eat. It's hot and fresh, but no cream cheese."

Renee groans. "Why point out the cream cheese? Christ, woman!"

He shakes his head and crinkles his forehead. "You're really not all that good at the art of flirting, are you?"

I shake my head, cheeks flushing. "Apparently not. Sorry for having painted that image."

My sister whispers, "Way to be cool, Rayna!"

Coach snickers, and then turns to go down the stairs with his basket. Renee and I watch every movement he makes, both mesmerized by how his incredible muscles move as he performs such a mundane task. How does he make hanging laundry on a clothesline look so damn sexy?

"How the fuck do you live next door to that gorgeous creature and yet have never made it to his bed?" She moans. "What the hell are you waiting for? I would be all over that."

"He's with someone." I struggle to act like I don't have a dirty little secret.

Renee turns her face to me, and I know she thinks something's up.

She demands, "Spill it! Now, woman!"

I burst into belly laughter that I can't reign in while shrugging to suggest that I don't know what she's talking about, despite my hysterics and unconvincing, overdramatically, innocent expression.

Her eyes light up with surprise. Coach walks up his stairs with his attention on us. I don't doubt he's curious about what she's saying to me. I laugh even louder. He stops at the glass doors and watches us with a curious expression. Renee turns her head to look at him. He smiles at her and nods as a pleasant gesture since he's still unsure of where our conversation has taken us. I'm sure he assumes that I've said something about last night.

When she looks back at me, he slides his hand in his pants, smiling suggestively and pointing at himself, then me, and then giving me the come-hither, one-finger wave. My face lights up, eyes wide and mouth opening with a gasp.

What if the neighbours see him do that?

Renee quickly spins to look at him, but he's already in the house. She didn't see his rather lewd suggestion.

The look she gives me is priceless. Damn, I wish I had my camera handy. She's in total disbelief that her *innocent* older sister could ever be with a sexy beast like Coach. You'd think I'd just told her that I won an impressive award. Then again, I suppose in some ways, I did. She shrugs her shoulders, urging me to spill the beans.

"Okay, yes." I pause. "Him."

"Holy shit! Seriously? When?"

"Yesterday, actually."

I smile like an idiot, mocking her typical silliness. She frowns in disapproval of the teasing. Renee leans into me with her elbows on the table.

"You've got to tell me; is he good?"

"Good, how? His body? Obviously, he has an impressive body; you can see that for yourself."

She's seen him many times before today, so she's familiar with his physique. I'm playing dumb purposely to drag this out and make her slightly crazy with anticipation. For once, I hold the crown as the woman with the best sex story. She rolls her eyes. *Annoying!*

"No, you ass! How is he in bed? Wait! No, don't tell me. Okay, it's okay, tell me. Damn it, no!"

Renee's torn, unsure if she wants to know. If he's a lousy lay, it'll ruin her infatuation with him. I snicker and wait for her to decide. She covers her eyes for a second and squeals before looking at me.

"Give it to me."

"He's very," I pause, "dominant. Coach needs to be in control. If you like that sort of thing, then yes, he's very good."

"And, did you like that sort of thing?" she asks with her eyes half shut as though she were in a trance-like state.

I giggle. "I really did. Several times, actually."

"Oh, nice! It's about fucking time you got laid." She sips her coffee. "How long has it been, anyway?"

"A long damn time. Too long," I confess.

She takes another sip of her coffee. "Are you getting together again soon? Oh, shit! What about his girlfriend? I mean, you said he's still with her. He's kind of an ass because he obviously doesn't give a shit about her. But on a better note, good for you, Rayna! Tame that wild beast. And fuck her. She's a bitch, anyway."

"He might have told her, I don't know. They have a strange relationship. He told me that she knows he will never marry her and that she's fine with it. He's obviously afraid of commitment."

"Uh-huh! But are you going to be hopping on that horse again soon? You need to be sampling more of that regularly." Her voice shifts to sound more jealous. "I can't believe that Adonis banged you yesterday. Are you full of bruises today?"

I sip my coffee, then nod. "The front of my thighs are a little bruised."

"Really?" She considers the unorthodox ways that could have happened. "What position were you in?"

"That's a smidge too personal, don't you think?" I exclaim.

"Don't be a bitch!" she hisses. "Tell me!"

"Probably when he had me over the back of his couch."

She moans. "Please give me more details. Let me have all the glorious details, you lucky slut. Leave nothing unsaid."

She leans back in her chair, holding her coffee with both hands, and resting it on her lower belly. She's quiet while I explain.

"He went down on me, and it was so good. He insisted I say 'thank you' after every orgasm he gave me, which I thought was weird. He swatted my ass when I copped an attitude after he reminded me that I had forgotten to thank him. It shocked me to realize that I quite enjoyed that swat." I look down at the table, embarrassed. "He pulled my hair, gripped my body, and then fucked me so damn hard; harder than I have ever been fucked."

She moans, again. "Damn!"

"When he looked at me, I'd swear he could read my thoughts. He's very intimidating."

She asks, "Will you do him again?"

"If he'll have me, I'll gladly visit him again. I could really use more of what he's offering."

Renee looks over my shoulder, most likely picturing him fucking her hard while pulling her hair. Having told her makes it so much more real. The entire thing seems like something I read in an adult magazine and not a genuine story I personally experienced.

"Sis, you'd better get your ass over there today and take off your clothes. Going by the picture you're painting, I'd say he could be exactly what you need to break you out of your abstinence. You're so busy being a mom that you forgot how to be a woman. You have needs; physical needs that vibrators can't fulfill." Her arms flail. "Go get him, babe! Just be sure to tell me every detail. Oh, if you can get pictures of his nakedness, that'd give me a better reference when you're telling me about him."

I'm about to tell her to fuck off when the backdoor slides open. My son's head appears. "Hi, Aunt Renee. What are you doing here so early?" He aggressively wipes the sleep from his eye.

"People, I get out of bed before noon, you know," she huffs. "Hi, big guy. How did you sleep?"

"Fine. Mom, where's the cereal?"

"Good morning to you, too," I tease, wishing he would have greeted us more politely.

He sighs. "Good morning, Mom. Where's the cereal?"

"I put it in the pantry. There wasn't enough room in the cupboard."

He shuts the door without saying thank you. I should be more like Coach and give his ass a little swat for being impolite.

A giggle quietly escapes me.

CHAPTER 5

$\mathcal{C}$ *oach*

I'VE BEEN STANDING BY THE KITCHEN WINDOW, WATCHING RAYNA AND her sister, Renee, ever since I walked back into my house. Both sisters are beautiful with their matching blonde hair and bodies that have every heterosexual man wishing they could have them.

Even though I find Renee incredibly sexually desirable, I've held an interest in Rayna for far longer and on a deeper level than what I'm used to. She's special; different in that she could easily steal my heart. What's worse is that I might actually want her to. It's unlike me to feel this way about any woman.

I don't know why I'm even considering it. She'll never let it happen. She's out of my league and I'd be wise to remember that.

Judging by how brightly Rayna's blushing, I believe she's telling her sister that I fucked her. I can't see her sister's face, but once in a while, Rayna bites her bottom lip and then smiles, tipping her head down shyly.

The main difference between Rayna and Renee is that Rayna is a lot more reserved than her sister. Renee seems to have no issue with expressing herself, no matter who's listening. She doesn't apologize if she offends anyone. Renee and I would get along great if we were to become strictly friends, which is not likely to happen, especially now that I'm fucking her sister. When Renee finds out I'm not into commitments, she'll hate me for leading her sister on.

Why am I even thinking Rayna would consider me as a romantic interest in the first place? Rayna is an incredible woman, but why would she be interested in an asshole like me as being anything more than a fuck-mate? She wouldn't.

She's a bit older than me and much more sophisticated and grounded. Maybe her being divorced and raising the kids, basically alone, has granted her a level of maturity that I know I can't match. I'm an asshole, and I know it.

I admire Rayna for her courage and strength. If it were me in her shoes, I would have shot the ex-husband; not because he was a cheater, but because he's a shitty father. The man has no idea how fantastic those kids are.

Ken is smart, no doubt smarter than I am, and he's only thirteen. He's going to grow up and be noticed for his intelligence.

Kim is younger; eleven, I think. She's smart, too, but has a shitty attitude, much like her Aunt Renee: carefree and happy to be herself and not strive for anything more. She might not become a household name for winning a Pulitzer, but she'll have a fun and interesting life to talk about in her old age. Who knows? Maybe she's smart as hell, but good at hiding it.

Rayna has done an amazing job raising those kids by herself. She's sacrificed her own happiness time and time again with no sign of appreciation from anyone. I'd have gone postal by now if I were in her situation.

I need to see her again.

My cock swells in my shorts. I ache to smell her hair, feel her soft, creamy skin, watch her sexy eyes as the lids slowly close when she's at the apex of her orgasm. That's when she forgets to breathe. I need to be inside of her, feel her heat around my cock, and the pressure when she's squeezing me so tightly as her juices begin to spill.

I slide my hand down my shorts and start to pump my fist around my erection. I focus on her innocently blushing cheeks. She's biting that same bottom lip I had pressed mine against not twenty-four hours ago.

My ass muscles flex as I push my pelvis forward, making my cock more accessible for the simulated fucking of Rayna's mouth. I can't be bothered to stop my shorts from falling to my ankles. I close my eyes to help me recall how shy and embarrassed she looked when I challenged her to say the word "cunt." That was a test to see if she would do whatever I demanded. If she had refused, we would have been over before we even got started. I needed to know she would be willing to try new things, no matter how ridiculous she thought the command was.

She should know that she can say and do unconventional things without the whole world falling apart around her. Her simply verbalizing that offensive word helped confirm my belief that she is brave and courageous.

I want her naked and under my control once again, and doing everything I demand of her. I want to awaken her to the possibilities of intense sexual fun and freedom. I know she's never allowed herself to be sexually liberated.

Rayna is standing when I open my eyes. I hadn't noticed that she's wearing my favourite nightgown. She walks to the glass doors, sliding it open. I watch for a full minute as she talks to someone inside the house. Her strong legs are bare and kissed by the bright morning sun.

With my knees slightly bent, my thighs flex until they hurt, which helps me cum. I jerk my cock so fast that my arm aches. My teeth clench and I tighten my abs, straining them as well. Sweat forms on my forehead and upper lip as I beat my meat at the sight of such a tasty woman.

I reach down with my free hand, cupping my balls and pulling them away from my body. Fuck! Rapid slapping sounds echo through my kitchen. I'm going to cum. I'm so close. Rayna steps into her house and out of my view.

No! Damn it!

Her sister is still sitting outside. I suppose I could picture my hand twisted in her hair, forcing her to suck my cock until she fucking gags on it. No, this hard-on is from Rayna and I'll keep it that way. I close my eyes again. I want to fuck Rayna's mouth until just before I cum, and then pull out and let go on her pretty face, temporarily marking her as mine.

Oh, fuck, yes!

My grunts are loud, but my windows are closed so I know Renee can't easily hear me despite the stillness of the early morning neighbourhood.

My eyelids open slowly. I'm elated to see Rayna coming out of the house in her nearly see-through nightie that does nothing to hide the fact that she isn't wearing a bra.

She plops down on her chair while looking directly at the window I'm watching her from. I'd swear she's watching me, and it thrills me. That woman's eyes seem to burn into mine, even if she can't see me through the tinted window. The instant she looks away, I close my eyes, remembering how hard I fucked her dripping wet cunt.

My climax shreds through me. I fuck my hand with every bit of reserved strength I have. A loud growl erupts from deep within my chest. My legs shake violently, urging my cock to let it go. Cum spits in short spurts onto the floor. My hand glides slowly, forcing wads of cum to collect on my fist as the few last wads dribble from the end of my dick. I squeeze the last remaining glob from my shrivelling shaft and raise my eyes to look at the woman who I know will somehow change me forever, and it scares me.

I flip on the water and begin washing the sticky cum from my hand and then wipe the floor with a damp paper towel. I get a pen and a small piece of paper from the drawer beside the fridge, jotting down my phone number, and slip it into my pocket.

Just as I'm about to step outside, it dawns on me that I should wipe the sweat from my face and make sure I'm not noticeably flushed. Rayna and her sister knowing that I recently jacked off is a hot thought, but I'd rather them not think I'm some kind of peeping Tom, pervertedly watching them while I choke my cock, even though I confessed to doing just that. Because her sister is there, I'd rather her not know. Rayna is probably freaked out enough after how rough I was with her yesterday.

I hate that I'm sadistic with a need to dominate, to watch women physically or morally suffer in order for sex to seem worthwhile to me.

The psychologist I saw years ago didn't really give me a straight answer as to why, so I stopped seeing her. Besides, she was really hot and I wanted to fuck her, but she let me know that was off the table. If I'd thought there was a chance I could bang her, I might have kept attending the sessions to see how far she was willing to go to understand me.

I pull open the door and step out, closing it behind me. After carefully walking down the stairs, because of my weakened leg muscles, I notice that she's gone in the house. Renee is still sitting at the table, drinking from a water bottle.

Instead of going back to the house, I walk to the fence to wait for her. Renee looks over as she's sucking back a rather large gulp of water that bloats out her cheeks. She nearly spits and has to take several swallows to get it all down.

After emptying her mouth, she shouts with sarcasm in her tone. "So, ah, what did *you* do yesterday?"

Rayna told her.

My lip twitches and my jaw clenches when I see her expression. The conniving little smirk she wears makes me want to grab her by her hair and slap her sassy fucking mouth before kissing her hard enough to hurt. I imagine myself fucking her mouth to shut her up if the slap doesn't do it.

I don't trust that broad to not make a move on me, even though she knows I fucked her sister. She might even do it simply because her sister sampled me. I can usually tell when a chick is a backstabber and I'm very sure Renee is exactly that. She wants to overshadow her sister; it's just her personality. Call it jealousy or low self-esteem. Either way, it's wrong.

"I mowed the lawn, did some cleaning and then I had a very heated workout with a new friend," I reply without a glimmer of emotion. My face is locked in a statuesque way, my eyes staring at her with intense intimidation. She will not control this conversation.

Renee laughs as she stands and hops down the stairs, quickly making her way to the fence. She reaches up and begins tracing a muscle on my forearm. She's making me want to throw her over my knee like she's a bad little bitch who needs to be taught boundaries.

If I ever had sex with her, which I won't, I'd love to punish this little cunt, but for my pleasure, not hers. I would get off on watching her plead with me to let her cum, and I'd consider denying her. It's not that I particularly want to fuck Renee. I'm simply annoyed at how she's so quick to flirt with me right after her sister told her that she and I were together. Bitches like this make my inner demon twitchy.

"From what I hear, you gave her one hell of a workout. You know, I've been known to enjoy a good workout now and then, but I've never sampled a musclebound fox like you. Maybe I should drop by after I leave here so you could fuck me the way—"

In a deep, fatherly tone, I hiss, "Stop talking right now. Just shut the fuck up and stop being a backstabbing cunt. She's your sister. Have some respect for her, if not for yourself."

She gripes, "You're a fucking asshole!"

My inner demon breathes fire at this point. I growl, "Bitch, you have no idea how much of a fucking asshole I am."

"Is that so?" she says while trying to sound cute and innocent.

I absolutely can't stand that immature, sassy female tone. My demon clenches his fists and trembles with a need to punish her. I'm going to fucking slap this twit if she doesn't fuck off. I know she's doing it to piss me off; I turned her down flat and insulted her pride in the process. But I haven't finished knocking her off her fucking pedestal quite yet.

My eyes burn into hers. After a few seconds of glaring, her cocky attitude is shaken, and I see her discomfort growing in her eyes, but she's stubborn.

In the deepest voice I can manage, I say, "Renee, get your fingers off me this instant. I know you feel insulted because I'm not caving into your immature act of betrayal toward the one person in your life that you should respect more than anyone. I will not fuck you, ever. Let's get that straight right now."

She snips, "Yeah, we'll see."

I look at her hand and she removes it from my arm.

"If you're stupid enough to ask me again, I'll be sure to tell Rayna about this little conversation. I still might, I haven't decided. You know what you're doing would hurt her, and I don't think you want that. So, why don't you get your sneaky self up those fucking stairs and get your hot sister back outside so I can talk to her."

She takes a step back from the fence. When she's far enough away that I can't reach her unless I jump over this fence, she tries to create a cover story.

"Well, good! You passed the test. I was checking to see if you'd agree to have me over with the promise of sex." She's back-peddling like a fucking coward. Her tone shifts. "I'm going to say outright that your eyes are fucking intense, dude! What the fuck is with that *I'm going to own your soul* stare? Fucking wild! No wonder my sister couldn't resist you. I knew there had to be something special about you to make her break her long-running marathon of celibacy."

I speak slow and deep. "I don't know if you're telling me the truth or if you're trying to cover your tracks. If it's the latter, I'd bet my house that you fucked her husband at least once. If that's the case, you'd better pray she never finds out. Now be a good girl, and go get your sister."

She laughs nervously as she walks away, swinging her tiny ass with every step. I'm usually great at reading people, but this broad has me second-guessing my intuition. What is it about these sisters that has me so off my game? I want to pleasure one while punishing the other.

Before Renee makes it all the way up the stairs, Rayna walks out the door. She looks at her sister and then glances past her and sees me. I shake my head, letting her know that I have no interest in the mouthy woman. She seems to sigh heavily, as if she had been holding her breath.

Renee says something that makes Rayna scowl at her. Her face slowly softens before she meets eyes with me. I pinch the small piece of paper between my forefinger and middle before holding it up. Renee sits down and watches as Rayna approaches me. The little bitch looks like something I said to her touched a nerve because her eyes look more sombre than usual.

Rayna walks down the steps and approaches the fence. She takes the piece of paper and sees that it's a phone number. "Yours, I take it?"

"Text me when your mouthy little sister fucks off. What's her problem, anyway?"

"Her problem?" she asks, unsure of what I'm referring to.

I tilt my head. "She was hitting on me. She said it was a test to see if I was a creep. But I didn't get that vibe. It just felt wrong. I'm all into sisters if that's your game. I doubt it is, and that woman doesn't interest me."

"She told me she tested you and you passed. Who knows with her? I think she's lonely. Hey, do you know someone who might be interested in entertaining my crazy little sister? Perhaps someone who looks like you and likes their women rather sexually wild?" She tilts her head and taps her lip with her finger. "Come to think of it, you'd be perfect for her."

"Like I said, she's not on my agenda." I try to frown even though I secretly wish I could humiliate that slut, enough to make her cry and call me an asshole again.

The thought makes me snicker.

I say, "I do know a guy that fits that description, but I don't want to set them up if she's only going to use him and spit him out. My friends are important to me. Tim is a really nice guy who wears his heart on his sleeve even though he has a bit of a wild streak. He's the bad boy with a good heart."

"So, just like you," she accuses.

"Nothing like me. I'm an asshole, through and through." If she only knew me better, she'd already know that to be true.

She rolls her eyes, not believing me. "I do understand the meaning of friendship and I can't promise she'll be on her best behaviour with him. You could ask him if he'd be interested in being with someone who loves a lot of sex? Tell him she's really cute; that'll help."

"Yeah, I could set her up with Tim. He's a good man who's good to women and does love a challenge. He's always been wild but has mentioned wanting to find someone special to settle down with. They might be perfect for each other. He's Black, is that a problem for her?"

She furrows her brow. "Why would it be? Love is love and it doesn't matter who you're giving it to or getting it from, as long as you're good for one another." She crosses her arms over her chest. "She won't care either way. If he's kind to her, that's all that matters. If he's not, I'll kick his ass, and I don't care how big he is."

I nod and snicker. "I have no doubt that you would. You're protective over family, and I admire that quality in a person. Let me think about it, and maybe I'll ask him tomorrow if I see him."

"Thanks," she says, looking back down at the folded paper.

"So, let's go back to the subject of you and me getting naked. I need your body and I think you want more of what I'm offering."

I purposely make my voice deep and speak slowly. Many people have told me that when I do that, I'm scary as fuck but its effects are like an aphrodisiac to most women. It seems to work well on Rayna, judging by how hard she just swallowed.

She refolds the paper and palms it as she steps closer to me and looks deep into my eyes and doesn't blink or look away, trying to get me to back down. She has no idea how doing exactly that makes my cock swell. Rayna easily intimidates me like no other woman ever could, other than my mother, of course.

My thoughts flash back to yesterday when I had her on her back and I was on top of her, fucking her. Her face flushed a cherry red when she was at the peak of her orgasm. She's so angelically beautiful when she cums.

"More of what you're offering," she repeats with an undertone of suspicion.

Her arms fold over her chest as she steps back, subconsciously letting me know that she's putting up her guard. Maybe I should have been a bit less obvious about my sexual intentions for this afternoon. Asking her to come over for a drink or something less devious might have been more appropriate, but I don't do romance.

I want Rayna to be my fuck toy; a hot body that I can entertain, pleasure and explore without worrying she'll become my love interest. It'll be hard to keep her out of my heart, but it's for the best if I do. This woman could seriously hurt me if I let my guard down. Besides, I'm no good for her.

I didn't fear falling in love with Alissa. But Rayna draws me in more than any woman I've ever met. Having secretly fantasized about her for several years, my need for her has almost overwhelmed me. I'll do almost anything to have her again. Just when I think I have her under my control, I want her to look at me exactly the way she is right now—with defiance.

"After yesterday, aren't you curious to see how far I can take you?" I ask with the same intimidating voice.

"Take me?" Now she's being obviously cynical. "And where is it you think you can take me?"

Good, I have her asking questions and not running away. Even though she seems doubtful of my ability, I know she's curious to find out how crazy things can get. I smile at her and then lick my bottom lip as my eyes intentionally scan down my favourite nightie.

"Rayna, I want to take you into my world, teach you how your body can receive pleasure in ways you haven't even thought of. Have you ever been bound and fucked?" She looks shocked but not scared. Good! "I want to do that with you today. If you're interested, text me. It's your choice completely, sweetheart."

That being said, I turn around and walk away from the fence without another word. As I make my way to the patio doors, I glance back at the fence where she remains. She's watching me with squinted eyes, as if trying to assess me. Maybe she's unsure of whether I really would tie her up. The paper I handed her is unfolded and pinched between her fingers, not crumpled up against her palm. That's a good sign.

With my hand on the door handle, I speak loud enough that she and her sister can hear. "Be more daring, Rayna. Satisfy your curiosity. You're allowed to do something for yourself once in a while."

With a crooked grin, I wink and then open the door and step inside, closing it behind me.

She'll text me. I know she will. Won't she?

CHAPTER 6

 ayna

MY HEART POUNDS AS I WATCH HIM WALK INTO HIS HOUSE AND CLOSE the glass door behind him. He wants to tie me up. Why?

It's becoming more and more obvious that he's into some kinky shit. If tying me up to fuck me is the next step in this adventure, over time, how far will he take it? Will he want to beat me or hurt me for his own pleasure? I've heard of it, but I don't understand why anyone would want someone to hurt them. What pleasure can be derived from that? Then again, he spanked me once and I came very hard. Coincidence?

Do I even want to venture into the unknown? Better yet, do I have it in me to allow him to take my body however he wants? Is it even possible for someone as stubborn as me to give up control to that extreme; to become obedient?

I sit back at the table with Renee while silently reading his phone number repeatedly. She stares at me without saying a word. Am I trying to memorize his number in case I lose the paper? I don't know, but when I look up at my sister, she's grinning like an idiot. She contorts her face into the most overly dramatic expression I think she can manage without using her fingers to support it.

"What?" I ask rather harshly.

"What do you mean, *what*? Spill it, girl!" She leans toward me, putting her elbows on the table while hugging her water bottle close to her chest.

"It's his phone number. He wants to see me again," I say without trying to sound either too scared or too excited about the possibilities that lie in that statement. "So, what are your plans for the day?" I ask, needing to change the subject.

"Hmm, you're holding back. I think he said more than that. But if you would rather keep it to yourself, I totally understand. Just know that I'm pissed you feel the need to keep secrets from your one and only sister. Why won't you let me live vicariously through you?" she begs, wearing an exaggerated pouty face.

"Why? I've been living vicariously through you for years and it's not a fun place to be. Live your own life, Renee. Yours is much more interesting than mine, anyway."

"Not anymore," she huffs. "I haven't had an interesting person in my life in months. Sure, I've picked people up but as soon as I get to know them, they show their true colours and trust me, it isn't always pretty."

She leans back in her chair, looking more emotionally distraught than usual. She's always hidden her loneliness well. That must be a family trait because I can exude happiness even when I'm feeling emotionally desolate.

"Okay, what's really going on with you?" I ask.

She hesitates, then shakes her head. "Nothing you need to worry about. I'm fine. All is good. Let's talk more about your sex life."

"Bullshit, you're fine!" I accuse. "There's something going on and you need to tell me. I'm your big sister. You can tell me anything and it'll stay between us. You know that, right?"

She nods while looking down at her fidgeting hands. "I want

to meet someone who is normal, or at least not fucking psychotic. Lately, I've been wanting someone to fall asleep with every night and wake up beside in the morning. I want something permanent, someone who won't fuck me over after I give them my heart. I wish I could find someone to grow old with."

"You're lonely," I tell her as if she doesn't already know.

"Yeah, I am, but I'll get over it. So, are you going to text hot-stuff next door?" she asks, suggestively waving her eyebrows at me while directing the subject away from herself, which is also a family trait.

I look down at the folded paper in my hand, trying to decide whether to continue this...this, what? Is it a relationship? Are we dating? I've never had a casual sex partner before. I've always committed to everyone I've been intimate with.

We are obviously not dating. This is just sex, right? Sex is exactly what I need, but can I separate my emotions from the physical? I've never had to. If I text him, I'll have to learn how to do exactly that. He wouldn't want to commit to me, anyway; I'm too old for him and my life is far too boring for a wild man like him.

"Probably, yes," I reply as my face flushes.

She's pleased with my response. "You need an untamed man to break you out of this lonely funk you've gotten comfortable being in ever since you kicked the asshole out."

"Tell me something and be honest," I suggest, waiting for her to agree. She nods, so I continue. "Were you really checking to see if he'd take you up on the offer to fuck you, or were you hoping to sample him for yourself?"

She looks down at her hands and confesses. "Honestly, if he would have said yes to me, I can't be sure. He's physically incredible, you have to admit that. His body is to die for and that sexy, deep voice of his vibrates my chest when he talks. I could melt under that man."

What a bitch!

"Thank you for being honest, but if I'm to be honest with you,

I'm a little ticked off that you would do that to me. You're my sister. I would never do that to you."

She drops her head and swallows before nodding.

"I could ask him if he has any muscular friends who would be interested in being in a casual sexual relationship, or are you leaning more toward an emotionally committed relationship?"

I already asked him, but she need not know that.

"Um, sure you could ask him, but I'd like to have more than just a sexual thing. I don't want him to think I'm desperate for a man, so don't ask him outright. But if it comes up in conversation..." She cuts her sentence short and then shrugs.

I wonder if I should ask her about something that's been chewing at me for a long time. I'm a coward because I fear I already know the answer. Should I leave it in the past? People say that sometimes not knowing something is better than learning the painful truth, but I'm tired of carrying this question on my shoulders. Fuck it!

"Renee, can I ask you something else?"

"You just did," she replies with a chuckle. Her face falls serious when she sees that I'm not responsive.

"Did you proposition my husband?" I blurt out.

Her eyes tell me everything I need to know. For a moment, I wish I hadn't asked, but before I can stop her, she's quick to reply.

"Yes, sort of," she blurts out while tipping her face down. She slowly raises her eyes to better gauge my reaction.

I crinkle my forehead. "Sort of? What does that mean?"

I need to know everything. A painful fire burns inside my stomach and I'm not sure I can stifle it. Am I ready to hear the details? Judging by her reaction to the question, I'd better prepare myself for the worst.

"You will hate me."

I feel the heaviness of regret in her tone. I take a deep breath and let it out slowly. If she says what I think she's going to say, will I hate her for saying it? I suppose it depends on what she tells me.

With a coldness in my voice, I reply. "I could never hate you, you're my little sister. There's a chance I'll be furious, but you need to say it. I'm sure whatever you're about to tell me has been eating at your conscience for quite some time."

She swallows to prepare herself. "Shortly after you two got married, you had that party for New Year's Eve. Do you remember?" I nod, remembering it as best I can. I was very drunk that night. "Well, after everyone left and you passed out in bed, I was trying to help him clean up. I was drunk from all the tequila shots and beer chasers I had through the night."

I wear a pained expression from remembering the hangover that ensued. "We did drink a lot. It's hard to believe you were still standing when I was falling all over the place."

I smile when recalling that ridiculous moment we shared after I stumbled and slid down the wall onto my ass. I was sitting on the floor and she was helping me stand while we laughed so hard that I peed. I remember little after that. I have never been so drunk before that night, and never since. I don't care to experience that again.

"He grabbed me around my waist when I drunkenly stumbled into the kitchen and nearly fell. We were face to face. I tried to walk away, but he held me in place. I was so drunk. That's not an excuse for what happened next."

Renee shifts in her chair and looks at the patio doors to make sure the kids aren't listening. "Everything was whirling around me and I felt like I was in a dream. I thought he was trying to help me until he kissed me. I don't know why, but I kissed him back. To this day, I can't understand why I did that. We didn't stop there."

Angrily, I ask, "Did he fuck you?" I swallow hard, fearing her response.

Renee nods while tears stream down her cheeks. My mind swirls with so many images of the two of them fucking, and it turns my stomach. I can't believe she didn't tell me the very next morning after we had sobered up. I understand how things happen when you're drunk that you might regret in the morning. But she kept this a secret for far too long.

I feel so deeply betrayed by her, my sister. Betrayal by him became commonplace in our relationship. After a while, it no longer shocked me. But, not by my sister, whom I've never kept a single secret from.

"I'm so sorry," she sobs.

"I can see that you are. I am furious that you didn't tell me." I look down to see my hands shaking. "I always wondered if something happened that night because the two of you were different around each other. I suppose I should have asked. Knowing the truth at the time probably would have ruined me. But that doesn't excuse this. One more question; did you two get together again after that night, sober or not?"

She shakes her head rapidly. "No, absolutely not. I avoided him as best I could. He kept calling my phone and trying to flirt. I had to threaten him that I'd tell you everything if he didn't stop. He doubted I'd confess because of how much it would hurt you if I did. I wanted to tell you, but I didn't want you to hate me."

Sarcastically, I say, "Now your conscience is clear." I growl through gritted teeth, "He is such an asshole. I wish I had known that before I married him. Although, if we had never married, I wouldn't have my beautiful babies. If you had told me the next morning, they wouldn't be here because I would have left him."

"I'm so sorry. I know that doesn't solve anything. I should have told you, but you were so in love. I was selfish because I didn't want you to hate me. It was a stupid mistake. It only lasted a few seconds. I was so drunk that it almost seemed like a dream until he started calling me."

"I will eventually forgive you, but keep nothing this important from me again. If you even bat your eyelashes at any man I'm with, from this moment on, I will probably punch you square in the eye, hard!"

She sniffs and wipes the snot from below her nose with her napkin.

My hands aren't shaking as much, and I'm calming down. "It'll take some time for me to work through it, but you're still my sister and I love you. But you've got to give me some time."

I lean over and hug her while she bursts into a chest-heaving, blubbering mess. It should be me needing the consoling, but I expected this confession would come one day. I've already dealt with the anger, even though I wasn't positive. The worst part is, I will not cry because of what he did; I've cried from his betrayals too many times already. He isn't worth even one more spilled tear. The tears I spill will have Renee's betrayal written all over them.

I whisper, "He can be very convincing when he wants something. I swear, that man could talk an Inuit into buying a snow-cone maker."

After talking with Renee for a few hours, I think we've rebuilt our relationship, perhaps even stronger than it was before she confessed. I'm still hurt and will always harbour resentment, but maybe now we can be more like best friends than sisters. We love each other, there's no doubt about it, but now we're no longer holding anything back.

Renee left at around one o'clock with the kids. She said she would take them to the mall to catch some sales, maybe get them some new shoes. She has always loved buying them footwear. Her primary intention was to free me from my responsibility. She wants me to visit, and I quote her as saying, "the dominant fucking machine next door."

If I do, maybe he'll fuck the anger out of me, at least for a little while.

It's only quarter after one and she doesn't plan to bring them home until after dinner. I have plenty of time to visit with Coach. If I don't chicken out first, that is.

My heart thumps a little harder each time I picture his eyes staring into mine. I try to breathe slowly to ease the reminder that I'm a weak coward. After opening the folded paper, I can't help but think about how incredible his tongue felt on my pussy. It's been so long since anyone has touched me, let alone licked me.

His tongue was so hot and wet, soft yet strong, gentle while still quite aggressive.

Yes, I desperately want that again.

I input his name and number into my phone, but instead of writing Coach as his name, I call him Sexy Muscleman. I type out a text with wildly shaking fingers.

Me: The kids are with my sister for a few hours. I am free. Do you still want me to visit?

He replies immediately.

Coach: Yes, I want you. Come now.

Me: I need to shower first. I'll be there in 15 minutes.

Coach: Sooner or I'll come over, drag you out of the shower and carry you over my shoulder to my house while you're still naked and dripping wet.

Me: Then you'd better stop texting me and let me get ready so the whole neighbourhood doesn't see my naked ass.

I wait, but no more messages come. I hope he isn't on his way over. The doors are locked, so his threat isn't a heavy concern. After a quick shower, I dry my hair while putting on a little make-up. I dress in a simple, light blue sundress and leave the undergarments in the drawer. I'll waste no time while waiting for him to take off my panties. Besides, I'd rather him not destroy another pair.

I slip my feet into my flip-flops and quickly make my way over to his house. For a moment, I debate whether to push his doorbell but decide to check first to see if he left it unlocked. He did. I push it open and walk in.

"Hello?" I call out.

"Up here," Coach yells.

I look toward where the voice came from. As I walk through his immaculately clean home, I notice he doesn't have any family pictures on the walls, only artistic paintings and drawings. I'm no expert, but they are impressive.

"Are you coming?" he asks loud enough for me to hear him from in the living room.

I follow a strange sound but can't figure out what it is, even as I get closer to the room. When I step through the doorway, I realize this must be his bedroom. I suddenly feel awkward.

The noises I was hearing were metal on metal. The buckles twang on the metal as he secures the leather-wrapped hand and ankle cuffs to the steel posts on each corner of his king-sized bed. The wall behind the headboard is jet-black but the other three are a soft creamy off-white. The bed dons a silky black fitted sheet but nothing else. A pile of bedding in the corner suggests he removed the other blankets and comforter, along with all the pillows.

His dressers look solid and heavy. The grain on the wood is not like anything I'm familiar with.

"What type of wood are your dressers made from?"

He looks at me oddly, as if wondering why I'm not questioning him about the situation he's about to put me in. He then glances at the dresser behind him before casting his eyes back to me. "It's Teak."

"Oh, I like it," I tell him as I stroke the top of the shorter dresser beside me.

I'm so nervous that it feels like I'm about to be de-virgin'd. I can't stop biting my bottom lip or cracking my knuckles. I don't know where to look or stand, and I don't know where to put my hands. My nerves are getting the better of me and I'm shaking, doubting I should be here at all. I have to remember to breathe.

Coach is wearing a pair of loose black shorts without a shirt. He's barefoot but has nicely manicured toenails, unlike most men. They typically have horrible, unmaintained feet and that turns me off.

"Do you need a drink, or can I get you to take your clothes off straight away? I want to watch you."

"I don't need a drink," I say, immediately doubting the legitimacy of my answer. A drink would help to calm me, but by the time it kicks in, we will have already started, and I likely will be too occupied to be nervous anymore.

"Would you like some help or do you know how to get naked all on your own?" he asks in his deep, seductive voice.

He leans his ass on the footboard of the bed, arms crossed over his chest, ankles crossed over one another, waiting impatiently for me to remove my dress so he can observe me—whatever that means.

"Why are you staring at me? It makes me uncomfortable," I whisper innocently, hoping he'll look away or something, but he doesn't.

"Are you ashamed of your body, Rayna? I sure hope not. You are beautiful, sexy, and I get hard from watching you." He licks his lips. "So please entertain me."

"I'm not twenty-one anymore," I say before giving in to his request and reluctantly pull my dress up and over my head, revealing my complete nudity.

His focus is on my eyes, not my body.

"I don't want twenty-one. Besides, you'd put most twenty-one-year-old little twats to shame. You are absolutely beautiful."

His eyes glide over my body, admiring every inch of my skin. My heart pounds quickly in my chest and I wonder if he can hear it as loudly as I can. I stand perfectly still, pretending I'm not being ogled by a man in his physical prime, while I'm aged, imperfect, and vulnerable.

"Turn around and bend over. Grab your ankles."

"What?" I ask, crossing my arms over my breasts as though I'm suddenly desperate to hide my nudity. I have never bent over and grabbed my ankles for anyone. Does he plan to just stand there and watch me?

"Put your arms down," he whispers assertively.

I keep them clenched. His eyes appear to soften, revealing a kinder side of him that rarely reveals. They remain focussed on mine and ease my anxiety.

"Come on, you can do it. Remember that you are beautiful to me. Now, drop your arms, turn around, and show me your ass. Entertain me, Rayna."

I slowly drop my arms down to my sides. I continue to look at him as he watches my face. He's patiently waiting to see what I will decide to do. It's my choice to play along or simply refuse. I can decide to be more sexually daring than I have ever been in my life by doing as he has requested.

Life is short, as the saying goes. I turn around, bending as far forward as I can before the back of my legs strain.

He speaks slowly and sensually. "You are so sexy."

I'd swear I can feel his gaze burning into my vagina. There's a sexual side to me that he seems to awaken so easily, like I'm under his spell.

"Stand up and turn around. Look at me with those gorgeous eyes of yours."

I do as he says, happy to feel less exposed.

Coach comes to his feet, rushing toward me with eyes that seem to read into my soul. He wraps one arm around the small of my back, hocking me against him. His other hand cradles the back of my head, holding me still while his brown eyes scan my face as if he's burning each feature to memory.

His mouth suddenly comes down on mine with so much passion he takes my breath away. My legs weaken, so I wrap my arms around his thick chest and hang on. I like how his calming words gave me positive strength, but I need the roughness of his body inside of me to pleasure me beyond my imagination.

He slowly drops to one knee, kissing and painfully nipping at my nipples before continuing further down until his fat tongue slips between my folds, finding my hidden gem, and then my eager wetness. I open my legs slightly, enough for him to get his face in a better position to lick my stiffening clit.

When I cast my eyes downward, I'm surprised to see that he's looking back. Our eyes meet and hold one another's gaze as his mouth tastes me. I moan when he sucks my clit between his teeth, holding it in place so he can flick his tongue over the most tender part of it.

My hands grab his head to keep it in place, as well as to help with my balance. My eyes close, and the world slowly spins around us.

If he continues, I will cum soon. My breath is heavy and erratic; my pussy twitches involuntarily. He must know I'm getting close. He is relentless, licking and sucking so perfectly that I'm nearly there in only a few moments.

"Oh, yeah! Don't stop!" I insist.

He continues working his magic, not altering the sensational rhythm of his licking and sucking. His mouth is ever so perfectly loving my pussy. The tension in my belly builds quickly.

I'm coming already.

Oh, fuck! My tummy muscles tighten, pulling my upper body forward. I'm still gripping his head, forcing it against my pulsing, fiery pussy. I jerk, gasp, and cry out. His tongue is still slurping until the hypersensitivity forces me to push his head away from my shuddering body.

Coach rises quickly, sucking my right nipple into his mouth, biting hard enough to make me yelp. He presses his mouth to mine, and I can taste myself on his lips and tongue. He explores my mouth, and all I can think is this beautiful tongue is my favourite muscle on his body.

His hands scoop my ass, lifting me off my feet. I wrap my legs around his firm waist and hang on tightly. My hands hold his head once again. My heart continues to pound wildly in my chest, having not yet escaped its confines despite its efforts.

Coach grips my waist, tearing me away from him and dropping me onto my back on the bed. He grabs my left ankle before I have even stopped bouncing. As he walks around the bed with my ankle in his grip, I laugh at how easily he can manipulate my body.

He rolls me onto my belly and pulls me so he can secure that ankle in a cuff. He doesn't waste any time fastening me down, spread wide like a starfish, face down, arms and legs tied to each corner post on the bedframe.

Fear of the unknown has me questioning my choices.

I'm so much more vulnerable than I was when I was simply bent over, grabbing my ankles. If he wants to hurt me, he could, easily. It's not like I can fight back in this position.

When I turn my head to see what he's doing, his shorts are sliding down his legs and dropping to the ground, revealing a very hard, fat prick.

I'm fearful of the unknown, but I desperately want him to fuck me like he did yesterday.

 *oach*

FUCK, SHE'S SO PERFECT. THE SIGHT OF HER SPECTACULAR ASS TAKES my breath away. I want to fuck it today, that's why I want her in this position. For her, it'll be the most comfortable when I slide my dick inside her tight little rosebud. If she'll let me, that is.

My cock twitches at the thought of entering her backside. I really hope that isn't off-limits. If it is, I'll respect her wishes, but it will disappoint me.

She looks like she's getting more nervous than I'd like her to be, but watching her squirm against her bindings turns me on. Time to occupy her thoughts before she insists I set her free.

I step onto the mattress beside her and look down at the glorious creature with skin smooth as butter. She turns her head toward me, but the draping of hair conceals her expressive eyes.

I gently drop with my knees above her head and gather her hair in my palm. She's breathing heavily, nervously awaiting the unknown. She pulls her extremities to test their confinement in case she should want to escape. Using her gathered hair, I deliberately lift her head until she can see my face.

In a voice as composed as my excitement will allow, I tell her, "Red is the safe word. Use it if it gets too intense for you. If you can't speak, wave your hands and feet, and I will stop immediately. Do you understand?"

She nods. Her wide, inquisitive eyes have me wanting to kiss her to ease her worry. I don't want her to be afraid.

"It'll be okay. You'll like this, I promise." I smile to reassure her. "Verbally tell me that you understand using Red sets you free."

"I understand," she tells me, her voice quivering. She's nervous now, but won't be once I get started.

"Very good." I brush my hand down her cheek and cup her chin. "You will suck my cock now."

"Okay," she quickly replies, giving me permission.

I hadn't expected her to agree so easily. It's almost disappointing. I was hoping she'd put up a bit of an argument like she did when I asked her to say cunt and thank you. I wonder if she knows that I wasn't asking her to suck my cock; I was telling her what I was about to do. She has the option to say no, but I'm thrilled that she's copacetic about sucking my cock. I would never force Rayna to do anything she didn't want me to do. Talk her into it, yes, but I'd never force her.

"Open that pretty mouth as wide as you can. Let me see down your throat," I say, and then watch her do as I command.

She's eager to suck my cock. I rest only the tip between her lips. She tries to take more, but with her limited movement, she's forced to have patience. Is this a tease for her? Does she enjoy taking men in her mouth?

I want to jam my cock all the way down her throat, purposely, to watch her gag on it. To me, watching a beautiful woman choke on my cock while tears roll down her cheeks is fucking amazing, especially if she gets horny doing it. I've been dreaming of doing this exact thing for what seems like a lifetime; three years is a long time to hold a fantasy.

Now it's happening, and I have to maintain control. I take a deep breath to compose myself. She isn't used to hard sex, not that I know of, anyway. I doubt she's done anything nearly as rough as I am used to.

It's a struggle to stay in control; to harness my barbarous self. Terrifying Rayna isn't my goal. If I'm not careful, I could easily scare her away. However, not ramming her face against my belly while burying my prick into her throat until her body wretches, for me, is a hard lesson in self-control.

She looks up at me with the head of my prick between her straight, white teeth. She threatens to bite my cock, but her smile proves she never would. I pull my prick back and stroke it several times while I watch her study my hand movements.

With conviction, she asks, "Are you going to jerk off on my face or fuck my throat?"

What the fuck?

Is Rayna secretly a wild woman? Or is she acting the part to impress me? We will get along great!

"Oh, I'm going to fuck your throat."

I push my prick into her mouth so far that it's near the back of her throat. I hold still while watching her to see if she's going to protest. She's looking at my abdominal muscles, in particular, the V pointing toward my prick.

She hasn't gagged. Damn! Should I push further in, perhaps test the depth?

I pull out completely and wait for her eyes to meet mine again. When they do, I smile at her with wicked intention, letting her know that I'm pleased, but to prepare for more. She returns my grin and then opens her mouth wide, inviting me in while waving her eyebrows.

I slide in; all the way in. She holds true. I hold still and wait for her to gag. I'll stay like this until I think she needs air or she gags, whichever comes first. Nothing happens after five full seconds. I pull back a bit while she takes a few breaths from around the head of my cock, and then I push back in. This time, I don't hold still. I fuck her face, slow and steady, allowing her to breathe between penetrations.

What an incredible sight; my cock fucking deep into Rayna's throat. I've dreamed of this moment too many times. Am I dreaming now?

Holy shit, she is so fucking hot! If I keep fucking her mouth, I'm going to cum. All the times I've jerked off to the thought of doing this to Rayna are flooding back.

Instead of risking coming too soon, I pull out and lift my cock, pushing my balls against her lips. She sucks one into her mouth, gently pulling at it.

I can't hold back the loud moan that rewards her efforts. Fuck, this feels so good!

She releases that testicle, taking the other. Another moan escapes me. I have to stop. She's too good at this.

I want to own Rayna's body.

"Have you ever had a spanking that made your ass red hot?" She shakes her head after spitting out my testicle. "You're getting one today."

When I release my grip on her hair, she turns her head to the side, her cheek coming to rest on the silky sheet. Her eyes are wide and anxious, and she bites her bottom lip.

I step off the bed and pick up the firmest pillow from the pile of bedding in the corner. After sliding my left arm under her pelvis, I lift, allowing enough room to slip the pillow beneath. Her heart-shaped ass rests higher than her chest, giving me one hell of a view. I can't wait to fuck her, but I must stay in control of my needs.

My palm slaps on her right ass cheek with a crack, not hard, but she jolts, and an odd-sounding squeal fills the room. She holds her breath, waiting for the next hand-to-ass contact. I tease her by waiting until she exhales before slapping her left buttock. That cute yip doesn't fill the room this time and I find myself rather disappointed.

Between slaps, I delicately caress her reddening cheeks,

occasionally pressing my lips to her heated flesh. There's a fine line between pushing her limits and crossing them. I want her to realize that pain can be sexually stimulating.

She's panting and crying out with each slap. *Enough!* I pull her cheeks apart and dive in to tongue her asshole. I lap at it feverishly.

An exasperated groan escapes her, as if deflating every morsel of tension she's held onto for far too many years. I repeatedly let my mouth ride down her slippery slit, from asshole to clit and back, paying special attention to her swollen, stiff button.

I soak my finger with saliva and cautiously insert the tip on my middle finger into her ass, holding steady while I lap at her clit. Her body tenses, but she doesn't ask me to stop. I continue to slurp at her labia, hoping to distract her attention from the invasion. She quickly relaxes. I push deeper, inch by inch. I gingerly pull and twist to stretch her tiny hole until she can tolerate another spit-soaked finger. The gentle assault continues until my digits glide easily.

I'm not used to being this tender with a submissive, but Rayna is different. She isn't a submissive, she's more than merely a plaything I keep around to occupy my time and entertain my body. I want to please her so much more than I need to be pleasured by her.

My hands roam over her back, gliding down to feel the curve of her waist and the arch at the small of her back. She's a fucking goddess.

I kneel between her spread thighs and roll a condom over my cock before shoving it deep into her slippery pussy. She cries out and pushes back against me, eager to take me deeper.

My fingers find her asshole and glide in easily. She moans and bucks despite her restraints.

My pelvis presses forward, forcing my fingers deeper into her ass. She groans sharply. I don't hesitate for even a second. I pound into her, while my digits fuck her ass with the same rapid tempo. I pause only to pour some lube over my fingers. She doesn't even notice the third digit I slip into her ass.

"Yes, fuck me!" she yells as her arms pull forcefully at the restraints. Her legs battle just as ferociously.

I pull my fingers free, quickly punch my fists onto the bed on either side of her chest and lean forward to balance my weight. I fuck her sloppy wet pussy, slamming my hips against her rippling ass with so much force that her hips sink into the pillow. She springs up when I pull back, but I'm already coming back down on her.

The second time she cums, I quickly pull out of her. I can't get too carried away and cum too. Not yet! It takes me several breaths to regain enough control of my senses to speak.

"Has anyone fucked your ass before?" I ask her as I dribble lubricant on her pre-stretched hole.

She lifts her head, her voice soft and meek. "I've done it to myself but never with anyone." She pants, "I'm nervous."

Normally, those words wouldn't concern me, but with her, they do. I lean forward, pressing my body over her like a giant blanket, trying not to put too much weight on her. I must weigh twice what she does. I lovingly kiss her shoulder twice and wonder what the fuck I'm doing. I never show my gentler side.

"Would you rather I not?" I whisper behind her ear, knowing the heat of my breath will raise tiny bumps on her skin.

"Um," she hesitates. I feel her relax when I brush her hair off her neck and kiss the tender skin, ever so softly. "I want to try, but please be gentle."

"If it's too much, use the safe word. I'll go slowly at first, I promise. You will feel very full, like you have to take a shit. Sorry, there's not a more pleasant way to describe it. Try to relax and let your body accept me. If you want me to hold still, say 'still.' I won't move until you're ready."

"Okay, let's do this," she whispers.

My lips press to her neck once more.

I remain leaning over her, hoping she'll feel more at ease.

Using great caution, I push the head of my prick in. I'm doing my best to relax my cock so that it isn't as thick as it usually is when I'm extremely aroused; like when I remember I'm with Rayna.

She tightens up and holds her breath, but says nothing. She's too tense to continue and likely too stubborn to tell me to stop, so I hold still.

"Breathe slowly," I whisper behind her ear. "Remember your safeword."

To occupy her thoughts, I continue tasting her neck with tender kisses. It isn't more than a few seconds before she relaxes. She nods, so I push forward, pausing when her muscles flex. Soon, every inch of my cock is buried into her backside.

With one arm slid under her upper chest, and the other hand weaved into her hair, I lift her head so I can kiss her parted lips.

She is so fucking luscious!

Our mouths mesh while the rest of our bodies wave against one another. I'm impressed she hasn't asked me to stop, or at the very least slow down. Instead, she's rocking her hips to meet my steady movements.

When I let her head rest back on the bed, I lift myself until I am up on my knees, looking down at my cock gliding in and out of Rayna's ass. The site is enough to make me want to let loose and ram her hard. I have to close my eyes for a moment to distance myself and regain my composure.

"Fuck, you're so beautiful!" I mumble as I caress my hands down her glistening, tanned skin as it catches the light just right, revealing the muscles on her arms and back.

Soft moans slip from her depths, ringing sweetly through my ears. She's enjoying this; I'm so pleased. My hips bump against her butt in a steady rhythm; it's hypnotic.

She's fucking back on me, welcoming me into the taboo.

God damn, she feels fucking amazing!

Get it together, otherwise, you'll cum before her and ruin it!

Beautiful Rayna...

I want her to cum a hundred times tonight.

"Coach, please rub my clit," she begs.

Using my free hand, I reach under her right thigh and slide my middle finger over her incredibly swollen, stiff clit. I dip my finger into her pussy to make it slick before caressing small circles over the bundle of highly sensitive nerves.

I slide my other arm up her chest, beneath her, resting my weight on my elbow, and then wrap my hand around her neck. My grip is firm, but I'm not applying enough pressure to restrict her breathing or blood flow.

She moans each time my cock glides in, breathing in as I pull back. My lips press behind her ear with the most tender pecks. I let my panting breath heat her skin.

"Oh, God... Yes!" she cries out.

Rayna's high-pitched whimpers grow louder with every exhale. Suddenly, she shrieks and falls silent, her arms and legs pull forcefully against her bindings as her body fights to fold in on itself.

Her hot cum drains from her spastic pussy, coating my fingers as they continue to roll circles over her very swollen, twitching clit. My cock is being strangled by the muscles inside her body.

That's it; I'm done!

My pace increases, as if my body has its own agenda. Five more thrusts and I'm holding steadfast. It's my body's turn to stiffen; frozen in the euphoria of a perfect orgasm.

My abs clench as I dump my seed into the condom.

Gradually, as if deflating, my weight presses down onto her. My lungs ache and burn, begging for me to breathe. A deep bellow rips from deep in my chest, followed by quick breaths in rapid succession. I'm dizzy. I can't recall the last time I'd cum that hard.

What the fuck is this chick doing to me?

"You're killing me, woman," I whisper as my prick slithers out of her ass. I gather my strength to lift my heavy chest off of her back.

Her cheek is flushed bright red, but it's her relaxed smile that captivates me. Her eyes are closed, so I carefully pick the scattered tresses of hair from her cheek and wait for her to open them.

She whispers under her breath, "Wow."

I remove the condom and toss it into the trash before freeing her wrists and ankles from the cuffs. I kiss and quickly massage each one. She doesn't move, remaining in the same position as if she's too exhausted to lift herself. I slide onto the bed on my back and pull her over until her head is resting on my bicep, her arm lying over my chest.

My gaze falls on her glistening face and I'm lost in the thought of what life would be like to wake next to this woman every morning. Could I love her enough to want to commit to her; to belong only to her? Could I ever be respectable enough for this remarkable woman?

I shake the thought clear, telling myself that it's simply an infatuation with my new human toy that's putting those thoughts in my head. I'm sure I'll tire of her soon and send her on her way, as she will do with me. She'll quickly realize how sick my inner demon can be when I finally set him free. Besides, she has a lot on her plate and I'm not sure I'm man enough to deal. The kids are pretty cool, but her ex-husband is a fucking dick.

Rayna pulls away from me. She gets off the bed and makes her way to the en suite bathroom, closing the door behind her without a word. I immediately hear water run and then the shower door close. I weave my fingers together behind my head and take a deep breath, releasing it slowly. I'll give her a few minutes before joining her.

CHAPTER 8

ayna

A SMILE GROWS ON MY FACE AS THE SUPER-HEATED WATER RUSHES over my head. I just had a man's cock in my ass for the first time and I loved it!

My entire adult life and I've been too afraid to let someone touch my asshole, let alone stick their fingers and cock into it. I can't remember a time when I ever came that hard. I am utterly exhausted but feel amazing, kind of like I could run a marathon, even on my cooked spaghetti noodle legs.

Coach's hands slide around my waist, startling me. I didn't even hear him come into the bathroom. He guides me back against his chest, kissing my neck only. He exhales loudly before setting me free. I turn and look up at his handsome face. He looks down his nose at me. Even after what he just did, as gentle as he was, he still intimidates the hell out of me.

"Hi," I say, and then burst into a silly schoolgirl giggle, only stopping when I bite my lip.

"Hi," he replies. A sultry smile creeps on his face as he

watches me acting oddly. "So, you enjoyed having anal sex with a real cock?"

Realizing that he will not be coy about what just happened, I decide not to play shy with him either. I nod a lot; too much.

"Yeah, so it would seem. If I had known that a long time ago, I would have done it a lot over the years."

"Can I ask you something?"

"Yes, of course," I reply.

He pulls several strands of hair off my face, tucking them behind my ear. "When was the last time you had sex, any sex, before me?"

"Honestly, I don't know. Aside from occasional masturbation, my best guess would be about six months before I kicked the asshole out of the house for the last time."

"So, the sex would have been with your husband, I assume?"

"Yes." I grimace.

My fingers glide along the muscles lining the center of his abs. His hands continue to pull wet hairs from my cheek.

"What was he like sexually?"

"Sexually?" I consider how to answer. "He wasn't anything like you, that's for sure. I mean, he was okay, but I rarely reached orgasm. I faked it a lot so he wouldn't pout. If he had gone down on me for over five minutes, I may have cum more often than I did. He was always in a rush to fuck me."

He smiles and shrugs. "I can't say I blame him. Fucking you is a pleasure. But you taste damn good. I'd be happy to lick you stem to stern for an hour if that's what it took to make you scream your way through an earth-shattering orgasm."

He waves his eyebrows. Coach's hand cups the back of my head, and his lips press to mine. Our tongues dance the tango as the water pours over our faces, rinsing away our sweat.

After we're clean, he steps out, gathering two towels from the closet. He tosses one on the floor just outside of the shower and then takes my hand, helping me step out. I try to grab the towel from him, but he refuses to hand it to me. Instead, he dries my body from top to bottom. When my toes are dry, he gets to his feet, flips the towel over my head and lets it flop around my neck to catch the water dripping from my wet hair.

I'd be wise to keep my heart and romantic ideals to myself. I should think of our visits as learning experiences only. We are not in a committed relationship!

He's not the type of man a single mother should give her heart to. He'll grow bored of me in no time, realizing that he craves the indecency of a sexually uninhibited woman. I am not her. I'm reserved, sexually uneducated, and painfully inexperienced. He'll quickly tire of my innocence.

He goes back to the closet to retrieve another towel to dry himself. I stay where I stand, eyeing every inch of his body as the towel skims along his muscles. He looks so strong. His thighs are thick and powerful. Perhaps one day, he'll let me measure them.

Coach hangs his towel on the back of the door and then turns toward me, placing his hands on his hips. He quietly stands in front of me, looking at me with a lost-in-thought, flat expression.

"Are you okay?" I ask, unsure of what's happening.

He smiles, "Yeah, I'm great! I'm contemplating what I should dare to do to you now."

I smile and shake my head in disbelief. "Are you kidding? I'm exhausted. How can you possibly still be horny?"

"Sweetheart, I'm perpetually horny. Even when my dick is soft, it'll only take a few seconds to be hard; if I think about sex, that is." He snickers and crosses his arms over his chest, making himself look even bigger. "I love sex. I thoroughly enjoy everything about it. The thought of exploring a woman's body is an incredible stimulant for me. And girl, your body has a lot of hidden secrets I want to uncover."

"So, what do you have in mind?" My face flushes, wondering what crazy position he'd like to put me in and if he plans to fuck my asshole again. Not that I'd mind.

His smile reveals his filthy thoughts. "My intentions? If you must know, my intention is to try something new with you every day until I know your body like the back of my hand. I'll learn all of your triggers so that I can fire you off with only a few touches. That's my goal, if it pleases you, Madam."

"Madam?" I crinkle my nose. "That makes me sound old, and I don't need reminding of that when I'm with you."

"Okay, I won't call you Madam."

"Why do you want to do this with me?" I ask, suddenly feeling self-conscious. "I need to know what you see in me. I'm so much older than you, and I'm not perfect. I have scars that only motherhood provides. So, what is it?"

Coach steps toward me, his eyes locked on mine. Strong in his conviction, he tells me, "I like you."

"Yeah, I can tell," I say, gesturing toward his stiffening prick.

He shrugs innocently as if his cock has a mind of its own.

My arms wave as I speak. "But why me? I mean, Carrie across the street is hot, and Lana two doors down is a long-distance runner so her body is strong. I just... I don't understand why you're with me and not them? Am I a joke or a pity fuck? Is that what it's called? I don't even know. See! I'm not up to date with the new terminology."

"No, never!"

Coach scoops me up by my ass. I squeal and wrap my arms around his head. He leans back so my chest presses to his. My feet lock together behind his back. He doesn't look away from my eyes for even a second as he carries me back to the bedroom. He lifts one leg to kneel on the bed and then lays me down, our bodies never separating.

As his lips press to mine, they open slightly to take my tongue into his mouth. His warm hand cradles my cheek and the other slips between my thighs. With his softest touch yet, his finger slips between my folds, tenderly stroking my clit up and down in a slow, rhythmic motion.

How does this man have so much knowledge about how a woman's body works? I wonder who taught him where to touch; how hard, how soft, when to do what, and when not to. He must have been an exemplary student because he has it down to a science.

I feel my clit stiffen under his expertise. His fingers slide effortlessly inside of me and a soft moan rides my exhale. I tighten my legs, pulling him into me. His fingers push deeper and fuck me faster while his palm presses down on my aching clit.

His heated breath caresses my neck, sending a powerful shudder throughout me, raising tiny bumps all over my flesh. He lifts himself onto his elbow so he can better study my face.

My only thoughts are of how much my body wants him; right now, and every single minute to follow. I've never had a lover this focused on granting me so much attention. He truly enjoys giving me pleasure, and that's something I've never known. Nobody has ever made sex all about me and my satisfaction.

My inner self screams at me to guard my heart.

To prevent my heart from wanting to feel for him, I close my eyes. If I can't see him, I can concentrate on how this delicious man is owning my body with incredible ease and not on how much I've missed the emotional closeness intimacy creates. What will sex be like when he knows my body's secrets, as he claims to be his goal? I'll be putty in his hands. Then again, I already am.

Leaving his fingers inside me, Coach slowly slides down my body, kissing and nipping at my tender flesh. In my thoughts, I beg him to lick my pussy. He takes extra time kissing above my clitoris, forcing me to lift my pelvis to trick him into slipping his fiery tongue over the most sensitive part on my body. That desperate bundle of nerves rules my every thought at this very moment. I yearn for his talented tongue.

The second his open mouth surrounds my clitoris, his delicious tongue presses flat. My arms spread wide across the bed, hands clutching the sheet to hold on as if I'm about to float off this mattress. I'm light as a feather, ready to blow away if he exhales too forcefully. The last thing I want is for the bond between his mouth and my eager body to sever, so I hold, unrelentingly.

Coach laps against my clit from the base and up over the tip, with quick repetition.

Oh, fuck!

I'm so close to losing control and completely giving myself, body and soul, to him to manipulate however he desires. I'll even risk him crushing my heart into a million pieces. I am his puppet. I am putty in his hands, permitting him to use me in ways I've never even dreamed of.

My head whips side to side in an ill-fated attempt to keep my mind clear, but I fail, and the delirium of orgasmic fog sweeps over me like the calm before the storm. I'm stuck at the peak of my climax.

An erotic scream fills the room. I'm sure it came from me, but it sounds so distant that I can't be sure. Blackness, like the darkest of night, envelops me. I hear nothing but the sound of my heart's vicious pounding until suddenly, nothing.

Ecstasy. Euphoria. Perfection.

Air rushes to my lungs as my consciousness revives, awakening a flood of racing thoughts. My lungs burn and my throat is as parched from voicing my approval.

He's going to make me love him.

My hands grasp his hair, holding his face to my twitching clit as the second wave of exhilaration tears through me, igniting every nerve in my body. Every muscle locks in a tight flex, and it's unrelenting.

My climax all too quickly rides to a close. His mouth lifts off my painfully sensitive clit, but his fingers continue exploring my pussy. He hasn't yet finished toying with me. He inserts another finger, waving and spinning his hand.

Oh, yes! Do what you will.

I am putty in his hands to mould however he desires me to be. He fills me more and more. My back arches, lifting my hips to take all he's offering, and quickly dropping to the sweat-soaked bed sheet.

I cannot get enough.

The stretch is exquisite. I want more; need more. My body opens itself up to devour him. I've lost all inhibition.

The pressure is immense, so much so that I fear he might split me in two. But I want him to do exactly that and worse; to shatter me into a million pieces, body and mind. I need my heart to feel again, to feel something, if even for a moment.

I'm jolted back to complete clarity. It feels like his entire body just popped into me. I screech, then instantly freeze. Pain and pleasure; both are overwhelming. Not a single muscle moves other than my pounding heart, which is desperate to burst from my chest. Tears seep from the outer corners of my eyes.

What the *fuck* just happened?

"Slow your breathing, Rayna," he whispers, with his face near to mine.

"It hurts, but..." My words fail me but my tears no longer flow.

My fingernails have dug into his shoulders, and he doesn't seem to care. He's so calm. Fuck, he's handsome! I'm baffled why this man desires me.

"Is the pain easing?" The deepness of his voice and the sedate manner in which he speaks has me eager to hear more. "The female body is designed for childbirth. You will accommodate my fist if you can relax and slow your breathing," he explains with surety.

Fist? *What?*

With monumental effort not to freak out, I take several slow breaths to help ease my anxious muscles from their tensed state. I begin by pulling my nails from his flesh and dropping my hands back to the sheet beneath me. I take another calming deep breath, blowing it out as slowly as I can all while my eyes remain focused on his caring, brown eyes. My heart steadily pounds like a drum.

"Your whole fist is inside me?" I ask in disbelief.

He nods, wearing a tranquil smile. "Everything about you is beautiful, Rayna."

His free hand slides under my head, lifting enough that he can easily kiss my lips. The tenderness in his kiss is out of character for the badass lover I know him to be.

His buried hand spins gradually. I whimper against his lips. A strange sensation of coolness radiates from his fist outward. My thoughts fall away from our kiss. I break our connection as my head flops to the right.

I reach up, gripping a muscle on his back. My other hand strokes the powerful arm with the gingerly moving fist. This is becoming overwhelmingly magnificent.

This fullness is unconscionable. It fucking hurts, but brilliantly.

Coach cautiously moves his hand. From the deepest depths of my being, a phenomenal orgasm builds. If the world erupted into a molten lava hell around me, I wouldn't care as long as he continues doing exactly what he's doing.

I am calmly bursting at the seams, mute while screaming inside my mind without a hint of an audible sound. The fire within me rages while my very being remains motionless, wishing I could buck against the one thing that fills it so immensely.

My pussy spasms once, twice, three times.

A meek whisper has the effort of a thunderous scream. "Oh my God!"

My entire essence is floating. I've lost myself in a place that is blank, absent of everything except euphoria. I can't think or speak, nor move under my own power. My pelvis remains tilted upward, allowing his hand to invade me.

The room spins, darkening evermore. I think I'm dying and I'm grateful for the release.

He slides his hand out of me, and it's followed by a flood. I want to stay right here in this intoxicating moment. Nothing matters. Here. Now. Him. Me. Us.

My cheek stings, snapping the world into focus. I gasp.

"You hit me!"

He snickers. "Rayna, you were blacking out, and I didn't hit you hard. Your senses are heightened."

I've never felt this relaxed in my entire life. My body feels like it weighs a ton. I can't even lift my arms off the bed. My legs have fallen open in a very unladylike manner, but I don't have the strength to regain some of my lost dignity. Judging by the sopping wet sheets beneath me, I think it's too late for that, anyway.

"How was that?" he teases with a smug grin.

"I never thought I could stretch." I take a breath. "How did you do that? I've never..." Inhale. "I mean, the kids were cesarean sections, so I've never been that open." Breathe. "Oh my God! How?"

Matter-of-fact, he says, "Constant pressure and patience."

"You must do this a lot. I mean, you're very good at," I listlessly wave my hand over my vagina, "at, you know...*that*."

With calm assurance, he replies, "I don't do it with everyone, but it's one of my favourite ways to bring a woman to a state of pure ecstasy. I love watching their faces when they slip away from reality and drown in their physical selves. Bringing a woman there is like a tremendous stroke to my ego, I suppose."

"Well, bravo." I clap with very little enthusiasm. "I'm so damn tired," I confess while shifting to snuggle up against him and burying my face on his warm neck.

He wraps his thick arm around my back, pulling me tighter against him. I feel safe, warm and much more comfortable with myself than I have been in a very long time. My emotions well up in my throat and despite my effort to hold back the tears, I fail and they spill.

Coach's arm holds me tighter still, without judgement, comforting me in my moment of weakness as though he were expecting this to happen. I sob for several minutes until I finally regain my composure.

"I'm sorry. I don't know why..." My words don't come.

"It's the adrenaline. No need to apologize. Just let it out."

His voice is deep but whispered with compassion. Even the vibration in his chest seems to comfort me.

The tears quickly ebb, followed by a deep yawn. I'm so sleepy.

Coach releases some tension from his hug so he can better look at my face. With a delicate touch that doesn't suit his dangerous exterior, he caresses away my tears. His eyes look into mine, failing to suppress a heartfelt emotion that a playboy like him should rarely allow. He's revealing a frailty that I hadn't expected from him.

As if he suddenly snaps out of a fog, he clears his throat while quickly sitting up. He picks up my towel from the floor to wipe the sweat from his forehead and chest. He then lays it over me, patting my covered tummy before making his way to the bathroom and closing the door without another word to me.

COACH

There she is, asleep on my bed in the same position she was in when I left to shower and regain control over my emotions. Christ, she's even more beautiful when she's asleep.

This incredible creature has me feeling things I'd convinced myself no longer existed. Over the years, I've fought so hard to suppress heartfelt emotions toward women. But here she is, unbeknownst to her, waking my heart from its cold, dark grave. I want her with me every day and all the time. I need to touch her, kiss her, hear her soft but stern voice, and drown in her orgasmic screams.

I bite down, close my eyes, and clench my fists. My inner demon is screaming at me.

Shake it off, Simon Brenton! Smarten the fuck up! She's just a broad, like any other. Rayna will not want you in her life forever. Get it together, dammit!

"Rayna," I bark.

She jolts awake, sitting up immediately, looking surprised and then embarrassed.

Goddamn, she's so fucking pretty. She winces when she shifts herself to the edge of the bed. Strangely, I feel sorry because it was my selfish doing that caused her to have this much discomfort.

She smiles apologetically, putting her hand out to accept the glass of water I hand her. She gulps some before giving it back to me. Her eyes never meet mine.

"Thank you," she says. Her sweet voice caresses my ears as well as my resistant heart. "I didn't mean to fall asleep. I should get going."

She stands, grimacing once again, and covering her breasts behind crossed arms. Her unnecessary self-consciousness reveals itself yet again.

I watch her sensuous body glide over to the small heap of clothing on the floor. She squats and shakes her dress as she picks it up, turning it this way and that until she finds the opening at the bottom. She pulls it over her head. Her small hands smooth it over her body while she looks down.

I'm overwhelmed with a flash of sadness, desperately wanting to grab her and rip that dress from her flesh. Now she's hidden from me, and no longer mine. Once again, she's my neighbour, Rayna, fully and completely.

Her eyes glance up. I nod, understanding that she doesn't belong to me. I must keep her at a distance. This woman is too much for me to handle. I'd probably beat her ex-husband to death if he came to pick up the kids, saying something vicious enough to stab at her confidence for the mere enjoyment of hurting her. He's like that.

I don't want her to leave without making her feel at ease and that we are still friends who can chat outside of sex.

"That guy I was telling you about said he'd be interested in meeting your sister. Text me her number when you get home and I'll forward it to him."

"That was quick," she says.

Another painful silence falls between us and lingers for a bit too long, making the situation seem unbearable once again.

"I have to get to the gym. I have a client coming soon."

Okay, that sounded like a bullshit line to get her out of here. I am; I don't have anyone scheduled until seven o'clock tonight, but I need to get away from her before she weakens me further. I can't shake the dreaded fear that if my heart opens for her, something bad will happen, possibly destroying both of us.

"Um, yeah, okay," she murmurs, nervously tucking her hair behind her ear. Her eyes have yet to meet mine.

As she tries to pass me, I put my arm up, preventing her from walking out of my life. I lean down and steal a kiss before dropping my arm, allowing her to continue on her way.

I stand, frozen in place, listening to her footsteps fade as she makes the distance between us seem vast.

Why do I suddenly feel so alone?

Christ, Coach, get your shit together!

ayna

I'VE BEEN SOAKING IN A HOT BATH SINCE I CAME HOME. WHY WAS Coach so distant with me before I left? He did his best to make small talk, but it felt awkward. We went from being so connected to what felt like strangers in only a few minutes. Was he upset that I fell asleep in his bed? I can't see any other reason for his sudden frigidness.

Renee returns with Ken and Kim. The house goes from being so silent I could hear the distant sounds of laughter as people walk past my house to being as loud as a schoolyard playground seconds after the recess bell sounds. You'd swear I had five kids, not just two.

"Mom," Kim yells so loud that it echoes throughout the house. "Hey! Mom, are you home? Where are you? Aunt Renee bought me some new shoes. They're green and I love them."

Her voice grows louder as she runs up the stairs, down the hall, and into my bedroom. I think the new shoes have cement soles. As if I didn't already know that she's standing outside my door, she bangs on it loudly, making my ears ring. So much for having a quiet bath.

"I heard you, baby. I'm in the tub. I'll be out in a few minutes. Is Aunt Renee still here?" I ask, getting ready to unplug the drain and let my relaxation time disappear along with the lavender essence oil-infused water. Well, it was the perfect way to unwind from my exciting afternoon, even if it was fleeting.

"She's coming," Kim yells, louder than necessary to penetrate the flimsy door separating us. I hear them mumbling and then Kim's shoes stomp as she makes her way out of my bedroom.

The door pops open quickly, startling me. I cover my chest and crotch with my hands, sitting up so fast that the water splashes over the rim of the tub, forming a puddle on the ceramic-tiled floor.

She rolls her eyes in her carefree manner. "Calm down, it's not like I've never seen you naked before. Shit, we used to bathe together, remember?"

Renee plops her ass up on the counter, folding her legs like a child parked on the floor in front of the television to watch her favourite Saturday morning cartoon.

"Um, a little privacy, please," I spit.

"Get over yourself!" Renee smirks and looks as if she's about to learn the secret of youth. "So, tell me all about it."

"Before I forget to tell you, a guy from Coach's gym might or might not be calling you for a date. I asked Coach to set you up. So, expect a gentleman caller. It's not a sure thing; I'm letting you know that it could happen."

"You're setting me up on a date with one of Coach's friends?" she asks with irritation in her voice. She beams, "You're the best sister ever! Is he built like Coach? I hope so. Yay!"

"Don't thank me. I didn't set you up with anyone, Coach did. I'm not involved. After you meet the guy, you can either thank him or blame him, depending on how the date goes."

I look at her, then the door, and finally back at her as if asking her to leave.

She shakes her head. "We haven't finished this conversation yet."

I groan. "I would imagine he'll be fit, but I have no idea to what extent. I suppose you must meet him to find out."

"Now that *that's* out of the way, tell me all about your hot rendezvous with the smolderingly sexy stud next door," she pleads with a breathy voice. "Was he as aggressive as the last time?"

I nod and quickly explain, "I went over. And he was amazing. That's it. End of story. Now get the hell out of my bathroom!"

She laughs sarcastically. "Yeah, fat chance of that happening, bitch. Details, now!" I stare at her with wide eyes. She hisses, "That look only works on your kids and you didn't birth me, so spill it and don't leave out the tiniest detail." She throws her arms out to her sides. "I'm not leaving here until you tell me everything. Get out of the tub before you prune."

I mimic with a scrappy attitude. She will not leave. I stand quickly, not bothering to cover any part of my body. The bubble bath suds slowly glide their way down my skin in puffy patches, tickling my tiny hairs along the way.

Her eyes don't veer away from mine to look at my nudity. I don't care who you are; if you're naked in front of me, I'm going to look, even if I don't want to. It's an automatic reaction for most people, but not for my sister, strangely enough.

"If you're planning to sit there, could you not stare at me, please? If you look away, I'll start talking."

A fair ultimatum for my privacy. She rolls her eyes, smiles idiotically, and then covers her head with the hand towel she pulls off the towel rack beside her.

"Okay, I can't see your beautiful and no doubt well-used body. Spill your guts, you dirty little slut!"

I begin, "He used me very well."

While drying my body, I give her most of the glorious details, leaving out how I burst into tears when it was all said and done. She need not know that her sister is a big crybaby. I'm sure she'd tease me, never letting me live it down. Even though she looks ridiculous with her head under that towel, I appreciate her giving me privacy. With my housecoat on, I pull the towel off her head. Her long hair scatters about her face as if she's just come in from a windstorm.

As she's finger-combing it back in order, she grins. She whispers, "You're a fucking slutty little MILF, aren't you?"

"Hey!" I groan.

"It's not an insult. I'm just saying that it's about damn time. Girl, you were so sexually repressed. I'm extremely happy you're getting your pussy pounded, finally! They say that after five years of abstinence, your virginity can grow back."

"That is so not true!"

"Yeah, I suppose it's not. If it were, you wouldn't have taken his fist." She taps her chin. "If I recall correctly, his hands are massive. How the hell did he get one inside of you? I mean, I have taken a fist now and then, but they were women's hands and much smaller. I'm impressed."

"He was gentle. It's obvious he's experienced," I reply as I run a brush through my hair.

"So, what do you think he'll do to you tomorrow?"

"Tomorrow? No, I have to go to work."

"So, blow it off!" she instructs while waving her hand in the air to add emphasis.

"You're a terrible influence," I exclaim as I hit a snag in my hair, gently tugging at it with the brush. "I'm a fool to trust you with my kids."

In her happy-go-lucky, cartoon-ish mannerism, she hops off the counter, laughing wildly while dancing herself out of the bathroom, leaving the door wide open behind her. I can still hear her laughing until she gets to the kitchen. I can't make out what she's saying to the kids, but laughter fills the air. She'd better not be telling them anything about Coach and me.

I dress quickly in a pair of shorts and halter top before making my way into the kitchen to see the new shoes Renee bought for them.

Renee looks at me and I mouth, "Thank you." She knows it's for more than just the shoes.

Coach

My appointment won't be here for another hour, so I decide to get in a quick workout before then. The hour speeds along as my thoughts of Rayna scramble around in my mind, making me lose count of my reps.

I stop to look at my watch and try to recall exactly what I've been doing for the past forty minutes. It all seems like a hazy dream. I'm sweaty and my arms ache.

Loreen is standing behind me with her hands clasped behind her back, quietly watching. She's donning a gentle smile. Her long hair is tied back in a tight ponytail that falls down in soft waves to her mid-back. The spandex she wears shows off the hard work and dedication she's put forth over the past six months. She's now thirty-two pounds lighter, only needing another twelve to meet her set goal-weight.

I'm very proud of her. Never has she given up, much less whined about the workouts I've assigned her. Even I complain sometimes, and I live for this shit.

"Sorry, have you been standing there long?"

She shakes her head. "Not too long. I called your name, but you were lost in thought and didn't hear me." She crosses her arms over her chest. "What's on our mind, Coach?"

"Nothing that you need to worry about, angel," I tell her while setting the weights down as gently as I can. "You should have slapped me."

"Uh, no! You're a powerful man, in deep thought. If I had slapped you, what do you think your instinctual reaction would have been?" She flexes her thin arms. "Besides, with these weapons, if I had, you would have never recovered."

"Hmm, you were probably wise not to hit me then. Okay, are you ready to crank it out?" I ask, clapping my hands together while smiling with cruel intentions.

"You bet! Make me beautiful, Coach!" she says, throwing her arms up in the air, gleefully.

I hold my hands out from my sides. "You are beautiful. You're gorgeous! Look in the mirror behind you." She does as I suggest. "Do you see that tight ass? You did that, not me. That's on you, babe!"

She admires her ass while rubbing her hands over her curves. A smile lifts the corners of her lips, but she quickly fights it off, pulling her lips tightly together.

"Enough of this shit. I don't want to get an ego. Besides, it's time to kick my ass."

I get her working hard. Sweat glistens, making her skin reflect the light, revealing more definition to her arms, which I find very sexy. As I watch her, my mind drifts to this afternoon spent with Rayna.

It wasn't so much the sex as the way she made me feel. That has me so distracted. I felt things I haven't allowed myself to in a long time. How is she so easily breaking through the iron-clad walls that surround my heart?

Loreen deserves my full attention, so I blink several times to bring my mind back into focus before she notices that I'm not watching her.

I'm introducing Loreen to a different machine when she rudely interrupts. "Enough about me. What has you so distracted tonight? Don't say 'nothing,' either. You owe me an explanation of why I'm not your one and only girl tonight." Her hands are on her hips and she's very intimidating for such a short woman. "Who is she, or is it he?"

"Oh, sweetie, I would court you if you were available and you know it," I tease with a sexy smile.

She laughs and waves the idea away. Loreen is happily married with six kids that drive her crazy most of the time. She once told me she would not wish it any other way.

"Oh, so it is another woman then, huh?" she teases. I shake my head, but she doesn't fall for my bullshit attempt at denying it. "Who is she? Don't play shy with me, kid."

I'd better tell her something, otherwise, she'll never let it go. "I've known her for some time now and we just started...something."

I don't say what exactly. I don't have to. She knows to what I'm referring: sex.

"You really like her and it's terrifying you. Am I right?" She doesn't give me time to reply. "Coach, you may have it in your head that you will never settle down with anyone, never marry, and never have children. But your heart seldom does what your brain tells it. It will do as it pleases. You can try, but you'll soon learn that you can't prevent it from wanting what it wants. You like her, I can tell. You like her a lot. So, what's the problem?"

"For starters, I was sort of with someone," I lie.

"Honey, if you're telling me that you're sort of with someone, you aren't really with them, and you need to let them go. Your heart is with someone or it isn't. If it's not, don't you think you should let her go on her way?" She talks to me like a mom to a son. "Maybe this woman, who has you all knotted up inside, is who you should be with. Obviously, she has a powerful effect on you. Maybe you should ask yourself why that is."

She makes sense, I suppose. I should listen to this woman. She's been married forever and seems wise about relationships. Deep down, I want Rayna, but taking on her issues? I don't know about that.

"Does she have a complicated history?" she asks. When I nod, Loreen looks at me with sad eyes. "You know, we all have some issues that follow us throughout life. If she didn't carry her history on her back, she wouldn't be the amazing woman that plagues your thoughts. It's our struggles that make us who we are. Try to keep that in mind."

I nod because she's right. I am who I am because of my life experiences. I lost my father at a young age. He battled cancer for a few years but eventually lost his fight. I watched him wither away while my mom did everything she could to keep everyone's spirits up and hopes high, even though she was screaming inside. We could all see it in her sullen eyes, but she let no one see her cry. She is the toughest lady I know.

My father's struggle taught me that one day I'll need to find an exceptional woman like my mother, and to care for her, knowing she will care for me, should the need arise. Also, not to take my health lightly, which is probably why I exercise so much. I try to live my life to the fullest, and I don't care what other people think about my choices. This is my life, and I'll live it how I want. If you don't like it, fuck off!

"All right, enough of this lazing around. Get back to work," I scoff.

She leers at me while taking another gulp of water. When I smile as if thanking her for her advice, she smiles. This lovely woman has nothing but honest friendship to offer me, and for that, I'm grateful. Loreen is a first-rate lady and I cherish the day she walked into my gym.

After she leaves, I shower quickly before swinging by the grocery store to pick up a few things.

CHAPTER 10

 *ayna*

I<small>T'S</small> <small>EIGHT</small> <small>O'CLOCK</small> <small>AT</small> <small>NIGHT</small> <small>AND</small> <small>THE</small> <small>GROCERY</small> <small>STORE</small> <small>IS</small> <small>NEARLY</small> empty when the kids and I arrive. They want a different cereal than what I bought yesterday. I send them on their way to each choose a box that costs less than five dollars.

None of the fruit looks all that fresh, and the lettuce is limper than it was a day ago. I pick through the bananas for a bunch that don't already show the blackened scars from the abuse they endured before arriving on this shelf.

As I'm looking at the tomatoes, trying to find two that aren't as squishy as the majority, a hand presses against my lower back and I jolt, then freeze. Whoever it is, is standing very close. I can feel the body heat they're putting off. I turn my head and I'm met with smouldering eyes.

"Hello, sexy. Fancy meeting you here," he whispers, leaning in to place a fervent kiss on my neck.

I swiftly step away from him. "My kids are with me," I

promptly announce as my eyes scan up and down the produce aisle.

He nods, seeming to understand why I don't want him to touch me. "How are you feeling?"

My face flushes. I look around to see if anyone is privy to my embarrassment, thus questioning why this super fit, younger man is kissing the neck of a less than perfect woman over the age of thirty.

"I feel great. If I could have soaked in my bathtub without my sister bursting in on me, I'm sure I would be less jumpy." My voice lowers more. "You have an efficient way of relaxing me, Mr. Brenton."

"You're so cute when you blush, Ms. Baxter." He scans the immediate area around us before adding, "I want to fuck your ass again." He licks his lips and I swallow hard, remembering how talented they are. "What are you doing later? I want to fuck your beautiful pussy, but I will taste you first. I get so fucking hot when you writhe on my tongue."

This man is a machine! I wonder how many times in a day he can ejaculate. Maybe one day, I'll ask him if he ever tried to set a personal best.

He's mesmerized by my body as his eyes drink me in. Most likely, he's running some wild fantasy through his mysterious mind. My pussy twitches at the possibilities. I shudder when an icy shiver runs up my spine.

"My eyes are up here, Coach," I tease.

His gaze meets mine. He takes a slight step forward, closing the distance between us. His deep, sexy voice whispers, "My beautiful little slut, I'll look anywhere I damn well want. If it were up to me, I'd spin you around and force you to bend over those tomatoes you seem so fond of groping." He takes another step toward me.

"I'd yank those shorts down and then bury my face in your ass, licking and tongue-fucking you. Then I'd stand up, free my stiff cock from its denim prison, grab your hair in my fist, and ram deep into your little snatch. I'd fuck you relentlessly. Everyone in the store would hear you screaming through your pleasure and they'll come to watch. What do you say; do you want to play a little game with me?"

I'm lost in the dangerous, erotic fantasy while noting that it's more thrilling than anything I could ever see myself doing. I shake my head as soon as I picture the very plausible scenario that would follow: either my kids would see Coach ramming me or the cops would put handcuffs on us. The thought of either horrifies me.

"It's okay if you don't want to play the public sex game. It's not for everyone. Come over to my house later. I'll be gentler this time since you're most likely still tender."

Coach tilts his head, looking even more enticing than usual, as if that were even possible. How the hell am I supposed to resist him? Damn those eyes!

"What about your girlfriend, Alissa? I mean, what will happen if she drops in when we're... You know; while we're doing something deviant?"

"Deviant?" he chuckles. "She can join in if everyone agrees."

"All joking aside, I'm serious."

Does this man trivialize everything that doesn't pertain to sex?

He replies, "She's not permitted to drop in on me unannounced. When we first started playing, we discussed boundaries. She knows better than to show up unannounced." Coach slowly licks his bottom lip while looking me up and down. "Come to my bed tonight."

Note to self: never show up unannounced.

I run my fingers through some errant locks of hair, tucking them behind my ear. "I don't know. If I decide to drop in, I'll text first. But don't hold your breath waiting."

His captivatingly white smile makes him even more desirable. How can I resist him?

My face doesn't flush, but the rest of my body heats quickly. When my clit gives me another shot of tingles, I cast my eyes back onto the tomatoes I've squeezed a little too hard. Its juice drips from where my thumb perforated its skin.

He looks at my hand and snickers. "You want me," he confidently teases.

"Hi, Coach," Ken says as he and Kim walk up, tossing their cereal boxes into the plastic shopping cart.

I was so taken by Coach's charms that I didn't even notice them approaching. My demeanour immediately switches from desirous sexpot to mama bear who needs to protect the children from the knowledge of my illicit affair with their friend and neighbour.

"Hey, little man! How are you?" Coach says while they do some weird handshake, fist-bumping routine. I wonder when they created that and why I didn't notice at the time? Whenever the kids were outside, I was never too far away. When Coach was playing with them, I was usually on the porch watching his sexy body, not so much the kids.

"Hi, Coach!" Kim says while admiring his giant arm as it waves around while greeting Ken. "Why are you here?"

He leans down and whispers, "Us big guys have to eat plenty of healthy food to keep us moving. We're like enormous trucks and use up a lot of gas to keep ourselves running. My tank runs out quickly. Why are you here and not at home doing your homework, little lady?"

She giggles while she high-fives him. "I already did my homework."

"Well, it's late. You should be in bed."

"It's not that late," she insists.

"Oh, I suppose you're right. It's almost past my bedtime." Coach feigns a yawn.

"We needed cereal for the morning and Mom bought yucky stuff. But she made us come with her even though Ken is old enough to babysit me. It's legal; my teacher said so. I don't know why Mom makes us come with her everywhere." She rolls her eyes just like her Aunt Renee and I shudder.

"I know why! Because she loves you and wants to keep you safe. In about ten years, you'll be wanting to spend lots of time with your mom, trust me. Moms are amazing and yours is the best mother of all time." He straightens and pats her shoulder while looking at me. He says, "I'd be honoured to spend lots of time with your mom."

His eyes don't leave mine until my son curiously asks, "Why? Do you have a crush on her?"

Coach raises his eyebrows and taunts Ken. "And what if I do?"

Ken looks up at him as if he's trying to decide if Coach is teasing him or if he really likes me. In my mind, I beg everyone to change the subject.

"You want to date my mom? Ew! Why?"

Nope, he will not let this conversation simply slip by. My eyes beg Coach not to answer him.

Luckily, Kim interrupts. "You can date my mom. You'd be good to have around for when we have to move the heavy furniture. I'd bet you could lift a car."

Ken turns his attention to his sister. He teases her in that annoying way kids have of harassing their siblings. "He can't lift a car, idiot!"

I hiss, "Hey! No name-calling."

"He could lift more than you can because you're a weakling," she hisses back at him.

Yes, the conversation has shifted, thankfully. Now's my chance to get away from him.

"Hey, Mom, can I go home with Coach in his car?" Ken asks.

Coach recently bought a sports car that's incredibly fast right out of the factory. Ken has been drooling over it ever since Coach drove it into his driveway.

The sizable man looks at me and puts his hands together as if he's praying. His eyes beckon me, much like a hungry man would beg for food. He hops from leg to leg like an energetic child, and in the same tone, begs. "Please, Ken's Mom, can he? Please, can he? Pretty please! With a big, red cherry on top."

I shake my head and whisper, "Never do that again."

He looks unfittingly uncool but also immeasurably adorable because of how well he's relating to Ken and Kim. They admire him and think he walks on water. He's the fun guy who gives them popsicles in the summer and runs around the house with a water-gun, sneaking up and soaking them on sweltering days. Ken never seems to manage a successful surprise attack, but Kim hides well, jumping out when he least expects her.

"As long as you're not a bother to Coach and you mind your manners," I tell Ken.

I look at the big goofy guy who's now holding his hand high in the air to taunt my son into giving him a very high five of which the boy can't possibly match, no matter how hard he tries to pull down Coach's arm.

"Are you sure? You don't have to."

"Nah, it'll be fun. Right, tough guy?" he replies, still holding his arm over his head. Ken finally gives up trying to reach.

Kim asks, "Can I go, too?"

Coach looks at Ken's smile drop from his face and sees the disappointment. He pats her on the head and sadly tells her, "Not this time, butterfly. This drive is for Ken. I'll take you to buy some ice cream on the weekend, but only if your mom says it's okay. If I take Ken now, you can use it as leverage to get her to agree to ice cream. I like ice cream. Rocky Road is my favourite. Do you have a favourite?"

"Yeah, strawberry. Okay, I'll wait to go for ice cream," she tells him, smiling oddly at him. Her cheeks flush. Holy crap, she's smitten!

I respond, "We'll see about ice cream."

"Kim's Mom," he begs, "come on, please?" Coach tilts his head and sticks out his bottom lip like a pouting three-year-old. I know he's doing it for their benefit. He adds, "We love ice cream so much!"

Standing before me is a troublemaking kid stuck in a seductive, full-sized man's body. I grimace and shake my head.

"You're an intolerable child."

"I'll never grow up! I'm like Peter Pan, Momma Bear. My green tights are at home, though." He winks at me.

I picture him in tights with his steely cock straining against the stretchy green material, my lips covering its thick girth as I try to kiss it through the tights. I bite my bottom lip, unsure of why picturing a muscleman in tights has me all flustered.

"I'd like to see those," I sass, shifting my weight to one hip with my arms defiantly crossed over my chest and a flirty expression on my face. Would he appease me as I do him?

He grins, winks and then heads off to finish his shopping without coming back at me with one of his witty wisecracks. My son is in the custody of someone who, not over three hours ago, took his mother's asshole virginity, if there were such a thing.

This is definitely weird.

"Come on, Kim, let's go get the toilet paper that's on sale and then hit up the ice cream aisle."

COACH

As Ken and I leave the store, I notice Rayna and Kim just getting into the long check-out line. The woman in front of her has a full cart so they'll be waiting there for a while.

Kim is gesturing purposely with her hands to help better relay the story she's telling her mom. Rayna bites her bottom lip, lost in thoughts that have nothing to do with what Kim is going on about. Every once in a while, she nods, making Kim believe she's listening to her.

Ken asks, "Can I drive?"

"I tell you what, when you're of age and have a license, you can drive it in a parking lot, an *empty* parking lot. Preferably one that doesn't have any poles, curbs or people. That's provided I still have this wicked girl."

"This car is badass," he says after he slides onto the leather seat and shuts the door.

I slide in behind the wheel after putting the groceries in the trunk. "Thanks, little man. Put your belt on?"

"Of course!" he replies, sounding very much like a thirteen-year-old kid who is coming up to the age when he thinks he knows everything and adults are stupid. "Fire this bad boy up!"

"No, no!" I take my hands away from the start button to teach the kid the lesson that every kid should learn from his father. But Ken's father is a dick, so I assume they haven't had this discussion. "This car, and every car, should be referred to as female. She's a wicked girl, with a bad boy behind the wheel. Get it?"

Here comes the question every kid asks: "Why are cars girls?"

"Let me teach you the similarities between cars and women. Never repeat what I'm telling you to a female because they freak the fu..." I rethink my wording. "Well, let's just say they won't like it. Okay, so the similarities between cars and women: both have a cool exterior, they're sleek and curvy, and they feel really nice when you're in them. You'll understand that when you're older."

"I understand it now," he says. I look at him strangely and he adds, "Phys. Ed."

I nod before continuing. "Some are loud and obnoxious, while some purr like a kitten. Some will run you right over if you aren't paying attention because some are fast, real fast—stay away from those, kid. Trust me. And that, young man, is why men refer to cars as being female. Oh, I almost forgot. Some are temperamental, so you need to give them a little extra care. And never, ever call them temperamental to their face unless you want to feel their wrath. Learn to duck; women like to slap."

"Oh. Okay," Ken says while nodding, absorbing the information.

I fire up the bitch and slow-roll out of the spot, eventually weaving my way around all the parking lot medians and onto the street. Instead of heading straight home, I stay on the main road for another five minutes before turning off. Ken looks out the window, noticing that I've passed by our turn off.

"Are you taking me to a secret location so you can kill me and hide my body?"

I look at him with an expression that screams 'you're-a-sicko.' "Nah, little man, too many people saw me leave with you."

I turn onto an empty road, barren of any other vehicles, and stop the car. She rumbles under our asses, anxiously waiting for the imaginary green light. I look at Ken, meeting his wide eyes. I smile and then look through the windshield. My foot slams down on the pedal and she launches, exactly as I knew she would. The tires grab the pavement and she's flying.

Ken laughs and squeals in the passenger's seat. He's a big kid so I figure he'll be safe from the airbag's velocity, but hopefully, my assumption won't be tested for factuality.

In seconds, we're zipping so fast that I'm nervous, not for my safety but his. If Rayna finds out that I took her only son on a dangerous ride, she'll likely flip out. I want to touch that woman again, soon. I let off the gas and coast, letting her gear down on her own.

"Hey, dude, don't tell your mom that we went this fast, all right? She'll kick my ass if she finds out."

He's still laughing when the car slows to an acceptable speed.

"I won't tell her we went this fast." He laughs. "Are you kidding? She'd kick my ass for not making you slow down. There's no way my mom could kick your ass, though."

"Should you be swearing?" I ask, not expecting an answer because I'm sure Rayna wouldn't allow it. "Another lesson about women: never doubt a woman's strength when she's protecting her young. Women will go psycho when their offspring are in danger. Enough talk about cars and your mom. Tell me what you really want to talk to me about."

Ken casts his gaze down at his fidgeting fingers, a trait he no doubt learned from his mother. He asks, "I tried to talk to my dad, and he said to ask Mom, but there's no way I'm talking to her about this."

"It's okay, little man, you can ask me anything. No judgements," I assure him.

He pauses momentarily before spilling his worries. "There's this girl, she's nice and I really like her. We've been hanging out together for about a month. Please don't tell my Mom about this." He pauses until I look over at him and nod. "Well, we've been kissing for a few weeks, but I want to, you know, touch her. How can you tell when a girl wants you to?"

Shit! It couldn't be something simple about jacking off, for instance.

"Well, I'm sure it's a little different with my women than yours because of the age difference. But when she's kissing you really nice, with tongue and passion behind those lips, she'll do this little exhale that has a subtle whimper in it. Usually, if you hear that, you can give it a shot. But, little man, be patient with her, okay? She'll let you know where she's going to draw the line. If you ever cross that line, you and I will have a problem. Do you understand me?"

I'm not sure he's falling for the bullshit tip about a whimper being a cue. But, if he does, and she doesn't do that whimper while he's waiting to hear it, he won't try to progress and therefore, there's no worry of accidental pregnancy. When he's a more mature age, he'll figure everything out for himself. For now, he's too young to fuck girls.

I remember being thirteen and terrified of the female gender. My dick would get hard whenever I looked at a hot little high school girl's ass or perky tits. I must have jerked myself raw a dozen times a day. Even back then I was a horny bastard. Not much has changed.

"Yeah, I would never make a girl do anything she didn't want to. I'm afraid to touch her so how can I cross any lines? I don't even know where the lines are."

Even though he's smirking, I know he's confused and needs more advice.

Why the fuck is the sperm donor that made him such a selfish asshole? His son needs his father's advice. I suppose I'll have to be a substitute for the loser. It's probably better this way, anyway. I'm sure the advice he'd give the kid would be to dip his wick whenever and with whoever would spread their legs for him.

I'm nobody to be teaching a young, impressionable guy what to do and not to do to a woman. I know very well that I'm not exactly the pillar representative of lovemaking. I'm rough; I know that. Sometimes I push harder than I should, but I'm never out to hurt a woman and I'd never make her do something she doesn't want to.

Hearing women scream excites me, but only if she's screaming because she's coming and not because I'm causing her serious physical or mental injury while doing something that she forbids. I won't cross any lines a woman has drawn. Never have, never will.

"Don't be afraid of sex. It can be a lot of fun, just be sure you're both mentally ready for it. If you're not prepared to take care of a screaming brat with a shit-filled diaper, keep your dick in your pants. There are a lot of things to consider before it gets to that point. All right?"

He nods, so I mess his hair.

"Do it for the right reasons, especially if it's your first time, or hers. Make it special for both of you, okay? It's something that the two of you will look back on for the rest of your lives. The question about how your first time went will come up in conversation more often through your life than you think it will. Make the true story a remarkable story."

"Thanks," he says, less uncomfortable with our conversation about sex.

"No problem, little man. Hey, if you ever want to talk—you know, guy to guy—and your dad isn't available, I live right next door. Come see me."

 *ayna*

KIM AND I HAVE BEEN HOME FROM THE GROCERY STORE FOR ALMOST fifteen minutes, but Ken and Coach are still missing. They should have been back long before we were. We would have taken the same route home since we're neighbours, so had he broken down or had an accident, I would have seen them.

I'm sure they're perfectly fine. Maybe they're doing guy things. It's not as if his father would ever take the time to play the dad role. How I married a man who turned out to be such a shitty husband and father will forever baffle me.

My phone rings so I quickly dig it out of my purse, thinking it'll be Coach calling to inform me that they stopped somewhere else.

Can my ex-husband read my hateful thoughts? His name is lit up on my phone. I roll my eyes and wonder if I should answer or let it go to voicemail. I just know he's calling to say he can't pick the kids up from school tomorrow. I wonder what ridiculous excuse he'll give this time.

I click the green square. "Hello, Rick."

"Hey," he replies sharply. "So, I'll pick the kids up at school tomorrow and bring them back to your place. I can't stay long so you have to go straight home from work, otherwise, I'll have to leave them there alone."

"What's so important that you can't spend a few hours with your children?" I ask, not too upset because at least he's putting forth an effort.

"Nothing you need to worry about," he spits. "So, will you be going right home or not?"

"I had plans, but I'll try to change them. Just don't leave them alone, okay? I'll go straight home, but you might have to stay for an hour until I can get there."

"Fuck," he whispers under his breath. "Fine, don't be any later!"

Rick hangs up without giving me a chance to say anything else, not that I care to acknowledge his little tantrum with a response. There isn't anything important that I had planned after work, but I didn't want him to know that. I'll take my time getting home tomorrow so he's forced to spend his slotted time with his kids.

It's nice when someone picks the kids up from school, that way I don't have to rush to get to the school on time. I close my eyes and take a deep breath, letting my resentment toward my ex-husband escape my thoughts.

The groceries are put away, and the fresh foods are washed and set in their appropriate spots. But still, no men walk through my door. Shit. Maybe they tried to call, but I didn't hear my phone ring. I left it in the living room.

I'm disappointed to see that they haven't tried to call. I look out the front window to see if his car is in his driveway. No sooner do I look out when I see Coach following behind Ken as they cut across my slightly overgrown front lawn. I make a mental note to mow that tomorrow.

Ken opens the door and walks in with Coach in tow. Both of

them are laughing, easing my concerns. Seeing Ken having fun and relating to a man who's older than him makes my heart flutter. Coach does not understand how much this means to Ken, and to me.

"Hey, Mom, Coach let me drive the car!" he says with a lot of excitement.

My heart instantly feels like it dropped into my stomach. I literally push my hand against my tummy to get my heart back in my chest where it belongs.

"What the f...?" I ask, not finishing the swear word. My eyes immediately widen and scan Coach's face to determine whether I should scream at him or laugh at their joke. He's stoic and impossible to read.

"Was I not supposed to let the guy drive? He asked nicely, and he said please."

His lips aren't smiling but his eyes seem different, sort of wider than normal. He's going along with the joke, if it is a joke. It had better be a joke!

"If he drove your car and christened her with some scratches and dents, it's not on me. If you hurt my son, I will have to kill you," I say, not as much threatening as I am promising.

Coach leans in toward Ken and whispers, but I can hear him. "See, little man, your mom knows my car's a she, and did you see how she changed into a momma bear in the blink of an eye?"

Ken nods in agreement as he studies my face.

He tells me, "Coach said that cars are always female. I had no idea. I lied, Mom. I didn't drive his car, but he said I can when I'm sixteen and have my license."

Coach assures me, "Only in an empty parking lot. Ken, buddy, you can't leave that out. It's important to remember the detailed rules of said future endeavour and to ease your mom's concern."

"I look forward to driving her in a few years. Keep her polished for me, okay?" Ken teases.

"Anytime you want to come over to wash her, you let me

know and I'll get you set up. Shit, I'll even help you start a fund for gas money."

Ken walks down the hall to his bedroom with an extra bounce in his step and shuts the door.

Coach and I are alone in the kitchen, and we make eye contact.

Instantly, the heat between us sparks, burning hotter than it should. The kids are only a few steps away. I clear my throat and shake my head to clear my naughty thoughts. I scoot over to the sink and begin washing the bowls from our ice cream.

Two huge hands slide around my waist, coming to rest on my belly. A set of sensuous lips press to the right side of my neck. I take in a sudden gasping breath as the tiny hairs all over my body stand on end. It's as though he's electrocuted me with his lips. His hard body presses against my back, and he pulls me into him. The bulge in his pants has my pussy clenching.

I stand with my wrists on the edge of the sink, a sudsy sponge in one hand, a half-washed bowl in the other. The water still flows. His touch has completely captivated me, recklessly taking over my sensibility. My eyelids sag shut when he lets out a heavy breath as if he'd been holding it for a long time.

I open my eyes when I feel his hand leave my body and reach for the tap's handle. He flips it down, shutting off the water before whirling me around and taking my mouth hostage with his.

Coach's hand is in my hair, cradling my head. His powerful tongue invades my mouth as I suck it gently. Our tongues dance a seductive tango. Coach's other hand is up my shirt and under my bra, squeezing my breast while pinching my stiffening nipple. Shockwaves ripple from the stiff little nub, shooting straight to my clitoris, plumping it as an insatiable hunger grows within me.

He has me pressed against the counter and under his control. I reach behind me and place the bowl and sponge in the sink.

His sexual aggression fires me up like no man ever has. If I want it to stop, I know he would. All I have to say is the safe word, and it's over just like that. I welcome his touch.

I try my best to keep my ears honed for the sound of the kids' bedroom doors opening.

Coach suddenly grabs me under my ass, lifting me, and setting me down on the edge of the sink. His hands have my shirt and bra lifted while his mouth sucks my left nipple with brutal harshness. I nearly cry out, instead imprisoning both of my lips between my teeth and bite down hard.

I really should put a stop to this. But, fuck if this isn't the hottest spontaneous sexual thing I've ever done!

He sucks, nibbles and squeezes my breasts, setting my vagina into a frenzied state of need. Coach lifts me off the sink by wrapping his arm around my waist, taking my weight like I weigh nearly nothing. His lips press to mine, exploring my mouth with a newfound yearning.

My legs wrap around his waist, and my arms fling around his neck, holding onto him. He couldn't shake me off if he wanted to. He takes me to where the two counters join and presses my ass against the corner, leaving me teetering on the edge of the counter.

I moan under my breath when he grinds his pelvis against mine, rocking like he's fucking me in an easy rhythm. Each time he presses his swollen bulge against my wanton pussy, I want to scream for him to get my shorts off and fuck me hard. For obvious reasons, I can't do that. As if he's reading my secret desires, I feel him pull at my waistband and the button on my shorts popping open.

"Red," I whisper when a moment of clarity breaks through. My legs release their ironclad grip. I shift so that I'm sitting more balanced on the counter's edge.

Coach stiffens. He groans softly, as if struggling to suppress his need to have me. His hands grip the counter so tightly that his fingers lose colour. He takes a step back, breaking all physical contact with me.

"Kids?" he asks, swallowing hard.

"Yeah, kids." I'm winded. "Sorry, I can't do this right now.

Fuck, I want to!" If not for my flushed face, my quivering voice proves my need for his touch.

He lifts me off the counter and sets me onto my feet with one swift movement. He continues to look at me even though he's stepped away. He takes a few deep breaths and adjusts the bulge in his pants while I run my fingers through my hair. Hopefully, I don't look too dishevelled.

"Come over to my place," he instructs with a voice so seductive I nearly leap into his arms.

I hesitate momentarily, desperately wanting to take his hand and run to his house this very instant. I want him to fuck me like we're wild beasts in heat, but I have responsibilities.

"Kids. I can't." I cross my arms over my chest to keep from reaching for him. "The battle over showering should begin soon. It's getting late and if I have any hope of getting them to bed on time tonight, I'd better get things rolling. If they're tired, they're impossible to wake in the morning. It is a school night, and I have to work tomorrow, so I'll have to sleep, too." I'm rambling, so I bite my lip to stop myself.

"The shower battles? I don't follow," he questions, curiously.

I keep forgetting that he doesn't have kids. He wouldn't understand the struggle parents have to endure over their children's hygiene or lack thereof.

"I have to fight with Kim to get her in the shower, but I can't get Ken out until the water runs cold. They are opposites with personal hygiene."

Coach nods as if he understands. "He's jerking his meat." I stare at him, not sure I heard him correctly. "That's why he's in there for so long."

Oh, the horror! Not my baby boy!

"No way, he's just a kid," I hiss, doubting the truth to his statement.

"Come on, Rayna. Don't be naïve. When I was his age, I used to crack out two knee-shaking orgasms before the water ran cold.

If you think I'm a horny fucker now, you should have known me back then."

"Um, no thank you! You were a child, and I was a grown woman. They would have sent me to jail, and I'd be deserving of the lengthy sentence."

"I would have wanted you back then, too. You're smoking hot." He stands with his hands on his hips, smirking at me. "I'd put money on it that Ken's friends have fantasized about seeing you naked."

I shake my head and roll my eyes. "Oh, come on! You're being ridiculous. No way! To them, I'm an old lady."

"Older than them, yes. Hot as fuck, definitely." He looks up at the clock on the wall above the kitchen table. "Well, I should let you get at it then."

I trail behind him as he makes his way down the stairs to the landing. Coach opens the door but turns and leans toward me, pressing his cheek to mine. He whispers in my ear. "Text me after the kids fall asleep."

I want to tell him not to wait up for a text in case they don't fall asleep until late, but he's sprinting across the lawn before I can. I'm not leaving the kids alone while they sleep just so I can get fucked the way every woman should be at least once in her lifetime.

"Kim, get your little butt in the shower," I yell while locking the door and shutting off the outside light. "Kim, *now*!"

~

COACH

It's ten o'clock and I'm sitting on my bed playing solitaire. I know this is a massive waste of my time. There are more productive things I could do, but I'm waiting for Rayna to text me.

I need to see her tonight, to touch her soft skin and taste her exquisite lips. I can't see any lights on at her place, so maybe she called it a night. I'll give her ten more minutes, and then I'll call it a night, too.

Fifteen minutes later, I'm lying naked in bed, about to doze off when my phone lights up and vibrates on the nightstand, jolting me from the weightlessness of consciousness escaping me.

Rayna: The kids are asleep.

Me: Come over right now.

Rayna: I can't. I'm not leaving the kids in the house alone at night while I'm busy getting some action from the guy next door. I can imagine the horrible headlines that would come from that.

Me: You think too much.

Rayna: I'm a mom. It comes with the job title.

Me: Meet me in your backyard.

Rayna: Why?

I don't respond to her last text. I'm too busy digging through my dresser for a pair of black fleece pajama pants and shifting my erection once they're on. After picking up a condom and my keys so I can lock the door, I make my way from my front door, through her gate, and into her backyard.

She's standing on her patio, looking toward my yard.

"There stands a sexy woman," I say in a low, deep voice, cutting through the silence of the night.

"Okay, you have me outside. I have to stay right here, so if you plan to coax me to go home with you, you might as well save your breath."

The cotton nightie she's wearing hangs halfway down her thighs. With great thanks to the light that's shining from the opposite neighbour's house, I can see clean through it. Her silhouette might be turning me on as much as seeing her naked does. Maybe it's the mystery of what's underneath that has me so aroused.

"I could throw you over my shoulder and take you home with me," I threaten.

She shakes her head. "If you do that, I'll scream, alerting the whole neighbourhood."

"And if they come, I'd lie you on the ground and fuck you hard while they watch."

"You wouldn't!" she suggests, proving that she doesn't know me very well. I simply raise my eyebrows as if to challenge her.

Not wasting another minute, I give her an order. "Get your sexy ass down here. I want you."

"What? Outside?" She whispers under her breath, "Oh my God!"

"Yes, outside."

"What if someone sees us?" She looks mortified as she glances around with her arms crossed over her chest.

"I could just fuck you on that lit up patio. The whole neighbourhood can watch. Although that sounds like a fun fantasy to play out one day, not tonight."

I know she would never allow me to fuck her where the neighbours could see us because she has kids that could suffer some backlash from our deviant behaviour.

"No, I'm not coming down there. I won't be able to resist you if I do," Rayna confesses through a quirky grin.

"Do you want to resist me?" I ask, knowing the answer. The kitchen make-out session had us both burning hot.

She hesitantly descends the stairs, looking at me with her seductive eyes. I could completely drown in them. She stands in front of me, nearly touching me but not quite. Her eyes have yet to leave mine as if she's daring me to make the next move.

She smells of sweet lavender. Fuck, I want this broad sucking my cock under my control. I'd really enjoy humping deep into her throat, again.

"Get on your knees," I demand.

"What if someone sees us?"

Her eyes jerk away to examine every backyard connected to hers. She takes a step away from me, showing me that she isn't as daring as she was trying to be a moment ago.

"Nobody's looking. People's lives are too busy to sit and stare out their windows at the empty yards. It's not entertaining." She's still looking around. "Now get on your fucking knees."

"I don't think so," she replies, making my blood boil.

If she were anyone else, I'd grab her by the hair and force her onto her knees, and then bury my prick in her mouth, stopping only if she spoke the safe word. I clench my fists, hoping to fight off my demon's urge to make her regret sassing me. I stand before her, my cock more rigid than ever. Rayna looks down, noticing that my fleece pants are no match for my obvious lust.

"Do you like it when I tell you that you can't have what you want?" she whispers in her alluring voice, making my cock twitch. "I think you do."

My nostrils flair and my jaw clenches.

Fuck, she drives me crazy!

"Take my cock out of my pants," I growl while glaring into her eyes as if threatening her.

Rayna doesn't look at all intimidated, and that turns my inner demon on even more. He loves a challenge.

She steps toward me while reaching for the waistband of my pants. Her eyes don't veer from mine. She slips both hands beneath the fleece material. She strokes the sensitive skin on either side of my prick but doesn't touch my erection. Her fingernails lightly scratch, tickling and teasing me. My upper lip twitches in defiance. She delicately caresses me, never touching my eager dick, and I let her do it.

She's driving me insane!

CHAPTER 12

ayna

COACH IS UNDER THE ILLUSION THAT HE HOLDS ALL THE CONTROL, but he's sadly mistaken. He's my subject and I'm feeling feisty. I know he won't stand here much longer and allow me to tease him. Soon, he will take back the control.

Giving myself to him is exciting. For once in my life, I don't have to be the responsible one who makes the world spin. It's a relief to give it all a rest and let someone else hold the reins for a while.

Sensing that he's about to lose his cool, I grab his cock with both hands and squeeze. His breath catches, releasing with a deep grunt. He approves.

"Pump my cock," he instructs. He lowers his pants until the waistband rests on his thighs, just below his balls. I don't immediately comply. At this moment, I determine what happens, not him.

Instead of jerking him, I squeeze the base until a small glob of pre-cum seeps from the slit at the end of his tense cock. Using my thumb, I rub circles on the tip, using the lubrication his prick was kind enough to spit out.

Coach stands tall, his entire body stiffer than usual. He looks so fucking vicious in the shadows of the night. I should shake in my boots, so to speak. But I don't fear him anymore.

"Why are you defying me?" he murmurs through clenched teeth.

I smile at him while biting my bottom lip, not answering his pointless question. My thumb is still rubbing the tip, but my other hand is slowly caressing up and down his shaft. Not pumping it, as he suggested.

Coach's jaw relaxes, just enough to suck in a deep breath. He's so massive. He towers over me, and he's probably twice my weight. Yet, here I am driving him wild. This is hot! So fucking intoxicating! I can see why Coach gets off on being in control.

"Because I want to. Why don't you get on your fucking knees and pleasure me?" I suggest with the same insisting undertones he so effortlessly uses with me. Any second now, he will have had enough of my entertainment, and the shift in position will change.

"Do you want me on my knees?"

"Maybe I do," I reply with a stern attitude.

"Tell me what you want, Rayna," he whispers.

His face tilts toward me while he licks his lips. He scans my body, taking in my curves. My knees weaken. Who is actually in control of the situation? I don't think it's me.

He's going to pretend to be my submissive, take orders and follow them through? What a role reversal this is turning out to be. I think I like it. In fact, I'm sure I do, even if it's only happening because he's allowing it.

Coach slowly sinks to his knees while looking into my eyes. His steamy hands caress down my body along my loose-fitting nightie. His fingers lightly tickle down my thighs by barely touching me. I fight off the urge to giggle by biting my bottom lip.

His fingers catch the hem of my nightie and lift, revealing my bare pussy to the whole neighbourhood. If they're looking. I know it's dark on this portion of the patio, but still, it's entrancingly dangerous. I could get used to being a naughty girl.

My eyes scan the yards, ensuring nobody is outside to witness my body being ravished by this brawny man. This is sexy as hell, like one of those stories people write in the erotic romance books I like to read.

Just the premise of getting caught is a thrill. Add in that a hulky, younger man is about to lick my pussy under the night's sky, is almost enough to make me cum before he even touches me. I can't wait for his tongue.

The air is chilly, so Coach's super-heated breath on my pussy sends shivers from head to toe.

I demand, "Eat my pussy."

He looks at me and grins devilishly. "Cunt."

I know what he wants. I had better say it even though I hate that word.

He's looking up at me, breathing hot on my anxious clit but refusing to taste me until I satiate his need to corrupt my moral values. I am definitely not the one in control.

"Coach, I'm demanding that you eat my cunt," I whisper to him with strong certainty in my voice. Embarrassment flushes my face. That was so vulgar!

"Good girl."

He smiles before grabbing my ass and pulling my womanhood against his mouth, allowing him to bury his tongue between my folds.

Oh, hell yes!

I am putty in his hands, willingly allowing my thoughts to slip away.

Anyone who's silently listening out their windows could hear my soft moans. My right leg shakes wildly. I open my eyes to the night and scan my neighbours' homes, making this much more spectacular.

Coach suddenly spins me around, positioning me so that my

butt cheeks are directly in front of his face. His breath is fiery on my derriere.

"Bend over and put your hands on the railing," he insists.

Without question, I do as he says, no longer caring whether our neighbours are enjoying the show. His tongue is my best friend, and I want it on me again. After several hard ass-slaps that echo off the surrounding houses, my clit twitches wildly. I consider looking around to see if there's movement but prefer not to know if anyone has stepped outside.

Coach buries his mouth on my asshole, licking it softly and pushing at its puckered opening. My entire body shivers in delight. Before Coach, I had no idea a tongue on my asshole would feel so fucking wonderful.

My clit won't stop twitching.

"Bend over more and spread your legs wide," he demands.

I do as he says, bending and spreading until my feet are a little wider than my shoulders and my back is flat, putting me at a ninety-degree angle. The cool wind bites at my pussy.

His tongue licks from clit to asshole. I'm suppressing my moans, but still wonder if I'm too loud.

Oh my God! This is so fucking wrong!

Two fingers push into my pussy and flutter, twirling and fucking me so brutally that my entire body is bouncing off his hand, despite bracing myself with the railing. I hang on with all the strength in my hands.

He slows his punches, and then gently slides a finger into my asshole, burying it completely. Coach sucks my clit between his teeth, flicking wildly with his tongue. His hand pulls back, sliding all three fingers at the same time.

This is sensational!

He increases his tempo until he's fucking both holes in a quick and steady rhythm.

His tongue whips at my sensitive clit with impressive speed, nipping now and then.

He moans, and not quietly either. I shush him, but either he

PEBBLES LACASSE

doesn't hear me or he's simply ignoring my plea. He opens his mouth wide, engulfing my swollen clit, swirling his powerful tongue as he sucks forcefully. The vibration from his moan has me hanging on the edge of orgasm. I fight to remain quiet, but he's louder than I am.

Mix his sexual talents with the fear of being caught, and I'm about to lose all control.

"Yes, oh, yes! I'm coming! I'm coming! I'm co..."

My voice fails. My breath burns in my chest. My heart ferociously pounds as my body stiffens. Anything else known to women, even chocolate, can not match this momentary sublime euphoria.

~

COACH

I'm moaning, licking, sucking, and finger-fucking her two holes simultaneously. My arm tires, but I will not stop unless she's satisfied or my arm falls off. I'll do whatever it takes to get her to lose herself. She tightens around my fingers for the second time tonight. Another orgasm will soon sweep through her.

"Yes, Rayna, cum on my face."

Her pussy forces against my fingers while her asshole tries to pull my digit deeper. She clenches and my cock twitches. Her clitoris swells at the command of my tongue. Her orgasmic whimpers grow louder. At this rate, soon the sounds of her pleasure will echo off the surrounding houses.

It's fascinating how Rayna's sounds have me unable to think rationally. This woman has me wanting to give all of myself to her; my body, my heart and my soul. I know the neighbours can hear her and the thrill has my cock harder than ever. She deserves so much more from me than a quick fuck, but I won't last long tonight.

She cries out; lost in orgasmic ecstasy. I continue until I know she's completely finished. Before I stand, I slap her ass cheeks twice with both of my hands. She yelps while pulling her ass away from me.

As I'm getting to my feet, I wipe her cum off my chin and then lick my fingers to taste her once more. She tries to stand upright, but I grab the back of her neck and urge her back into position. She whimpers but plays along with my silent insistence.

I reach in the tiny pocket of my pajamas and find the condom. I rip it open with my teeth and then pull it out of the package with my one free hand and roll it over my aching prick with an incredible skill that only years of practice provide.

I aim my cock at her glistening slit and push all the way forward in one quick motion until I'm entombed deep inside of Rayna's remarkable body. She gasps and I grunt, neither of us caring in the slightest about the neighbours. Like me, she doesn't seem to give a shit what anyone thinks. We're lost in each other, and I will never have regret or apologize for it.

With both of my hands, I grab hold of her pelvis and pull her toward me as I buck forward. The lustful sounds of our panting mixed with the clapping of our bodies crashing together echoes off the houses with a sensuous beat that's music to my ears.

The moonlight casts a glow on her back, emphasizing the two shadowed dimples on either side of her tailbone. They wave to me after each thrust. I can't resist pushing her nightgown up to her neck, so I can watch her muscles move in the moon's light as she battles to maintain position.

My legs shake. I'll cum just before my legs ache so brutally that my mind will be too distracted to cum.

Rayna has orgasmed three times already, and she's building up for a fourth. She's so loud that I'm sure she's going to draw someone's attention. I see lights flicker on at the Jennings' household. I'd better shut her up or the cops will show up soon.

I reach forward, grabbing her hair and pulling her up so I can cover her mouth with my hand. I pin the back of her head against my chest so she can't pull away. She grabs my arm, trying to free her mouth, but I'm too strong. She squirms in my hold, trying to turn her face away.

That's right, sweetheart, make me work for it.

I muffle her cries under my grip, and the sounds stir my inner demon into a frenzy. It's hard to get enough oxygen when the mouth is covered, adding an element of fear.

I whisper, "If you need me to stop, tap my arm three times, but only if you absolutely have to."

She grips my forearm but doesn't tap. She doesn't know it yet, but when she cums, her mind will fog from lack of oxygen, heightening the euphoric intensity of her orgasm.

I place my other hand on her lower belly to keep her in place while I continue to fuck her with brutal force. My legs are really shaking now. I'm not only holding my weight but hers as well. I'm barely able to keep us upright.

My teeth clench, lips parting only when I suck in a quick breath. If I open my mouth to exhale, I'll grunt like a barbarian, and this is not the place for that.

She's still grabbing at my arm, trying to pry it from on her mouth, but she isn't tapping. I lift my palm long enough for her to take two deep breaths before replacing it. She wiggles in protest but realizes that there's no point in struggling. She cannot overpower me.

It's up to me to keep Rayna quiet. She has lost awareness of her surroundings. I very much like her this way.

A wave of newfound energy floods my body. I pound my cock into her, lifting her with each thrust. My legs have gone numb from the abuse. My body can't take much more. It won't be long now. I'm so close to giving in to my body's need to let it go.

No sooner do I consider letting my cum fly does her body stiffen, her pussy squeezing and forces so hard that I absolutely can't pull back, otherwise she'll push my cock out of her. Hot liquid seeps from around my prick and drips down my thigh. I need not move at all; the spasms her pussy inflicts on my shaft are enough to throw me over the edge. But I fight to resist.

My cock begs for release. I'm hanging on the edge, waiting for her to finish her orgasm before I allow myself the reward of a soul-trembling orgasm. Her muscles soften, and I know it's my turn to free my inner demon, but Mr. Jennings opens his backdoor and steps outside.

Bad fucking timing, dude!

He looks around, trying to see what woke him.

I don't fucking care anymore!

I slam her so hard that her arms and legs flop like a rag-doll. The sound of our bodies clapping together echo, revealing our not-so-secret fuck-fest.

There's no denying Mr. Jennings knows people are fucking somewhere nearby. I know he can't see me; the shadow I'm standing in casts a black hue over my body, blocking my presence from the full moon's bright rays. I believe Rayna remains hidden from his view by the large flower pot. He continues to search the shadows for the source of the sexual sounds.

I've spent all my energy pounding into her as if I were Satan himself. My inner demon is pleased. It's time to let myself go.

I clench my teeth, trying to contain the wails from my barbaric, growling demon. She holds as still as she can while I dump my super-heated cum into the condom. Her pussy twitches around my throbbing shaft, adding to the perfection of the moment. My muscles can barely keep us standing.

With an exasperated exhale, I have reached my goal of making her cum many times and then finally relieving myself.

Between breaths, I whisper in her ear, "Mr. Jennings has been outside for a few minutes. He's been listening to us while looking for the source." Rayna holds her breath. "Don't worry, he's been looking at my backyard. He's wise to think I'd be the sexual deviant performing such a daring act. What he doesn't know is that you are a bad little slut who likes to get drilled outdoors. Aren't you?"

I lift my hand from her mouth now that I'm sure she'll remain quiet.

She whispers as quietly as she can manage. "Can he see us?"

"No, we're hidden in a shadow. Just stay quiet for a minute. He'll give up and go back inside."

Rayna pushes my hands away and then spins to face me. "That was so exciting!" She looks exhausted and utterly dishevelled, but happy. Her hair is a mess, and her skin bears a thin layer of sweat. "Was I too loud?"

"Baby, you can never be too loud for me. You can scream if it makes you cum harder," I assure her with an exhaustive smile.

"Do you think he knows you're with me?"

She's beginning to let panic seep in, ruining this copacetic moment.

I pull her into a hug and kiss her head. "No, Rayna, he thinks it's me, not you. He does not know you're involved." I lean forward in time to see the man return to his house. "He's going back inside."

She pulls back from the hug and looks up at me, still wearing a freshly fucked and completely satisfied expression. "I'm going inside. You can't come with me. Go home. Oh," she takes a breath, "and thank you."

I pinch her cheeks between my thumb and forefinger, watching as her lips pucker to look like a fish. People rarely enjoy this. Judging by her frowning brows, she's irritated by it.

I kiss her fish-lips lovingly and then turn to leave without another word. She watches me open the gate and disappear through it, the gate latching behind me after it gradually swung shut.

This chick is really getting to me, and it's scaring me.

She's sexually inexperienced. She's not like any woman I've ever had the pleasure of seducing, but she's willing to learn.

Normally, I wouldn't give a woman like her a second glance. I would never take the time to train a woman from scratch before introducing her to my kinks like I'm doing with Rayna. She isn't ready for my level of kink.

Coaching her on how her body can be manipulated in ways

that will take her to an incredible orgasmic state of being will be fun. I can't deny that. But I prefer a woman who has done all of this before and knows her role as a submissive.

What will she do when my inner demon sneaks out in full force, wanting to punish her with electric shocks or genital piercing for the simple pleasure of hearing her scream? Suppressing his need for torture will not be an effortless task.

Rayna may never be willing to go as far as I am accustomed.

This captivating woman differs from all the other women in my past. I don't know why I feel this way about her, I just do.

I want to take her into my world and teach her everything I know. But if I attempt to do that, she'll most definitely run away screaming. For that reason alone, thinking I can keep her as mine is off the table.

I can't let myself feel anything more than friendship and sexual desire.

It's better this way. Right?

 *ayna*

THIS DAY HAS BEEN GRUELLING. I CLEANED THE TEETH OF EIGHT adults and two children.

One person came in with an abscess that stunk horribly. The youngest of the two children, while attempting to x-ray, bit me. Lucky for me, I was quick to pull my hand out of her mouth before she could chomp down hard enough to break the skin. She only made an impression but hadn't yet cut into me.

Her mother laughed through her embarrassment at how horribly behaved her child was while I sat there wanting to punch her in the face; the mother, not the child.

There's no way in hell I would have allowed my kids to behave so poorly. I wish I could yell at the idiotic woman about setting boundaries by demanding the kid show respect to people. That little girl will soon become a teenage nightmare who thinks the world owes her something and demands they pay up while she sits on her ass complaining about how awful society is.

I did the best I could with her teeth and suggested to our

receptionist that she urge this family toward a pediatric dentist for the next time she needs a cleaning. Let her be someone else's problem.

By the time I pull in my driveway, I'm truly exhausted. Maybe that's because of the exhaustive pounding I received from Coach last night. I smile coyly at the thought of Mr. Jennings hearing me pant and moan through my heated orgasms.

Going into my house to face my ex-husband will be the absolute worst part of my day.

It's Friday, his day to pick up the kids from school. The courts assigned him only two days a month to do this, and he usually has an excuse for why he needs to cancel. A loving father would take this time to enjoy them and to go anywhere other than straight home. He's simply too self-absorbed to realize how great his kids really are.

As I stand in my entryway, I can see into each room he's allowed to be in. He knows he has to stay in the kitchen, living room, or TV room, but he's in none of those places. I'll bet that fucking asshole is in my bedroom again.

In the past, he's gone through my private things. I've never been able to catch him in the act. Today, I will. I bought this house for the kids and me with my money after Rick and I divorced. He has never lived here and never will.

As quietly as possible, I set my bag on the steps and slip off my shoes. I sneak down the hall without a sound. The kid's bedroom doors are closed, but I can hear their televisions. I would bet this house that Rick told them to go to their rooms and close their doors. He wouldn't have to deal with them then. At least I'm comforted in knowing they're home safely.

I come to my bedroom door and it's closed, instantly infuriating me. Rage flushes through my veins as my adrenaline spikes. I never leave my door closed when I'm not home. How blind was I when I walked down that church aisle and said *I do* to this dickhead?

I open my phone and start recording video before slowly

opening the door. I can show it to the courts one day if it comes to that.

Careful not to make a sound, I push open the door. He's digging around in my t-shirt drawer. I don't know what he thinks he's going to find since there's nothing but shirts in there. I wait while he closes that drawer and opens the one directly below it.

"Rick, what the fuck are you doing in my room?" I yell.

He jolts and spins, suddenly looking like a dog who got caught taking food off the table. "Nothing! I'm just looking at your t-shirts." He looks at the drawer, then me, and back at the drawer before continuing. "I was hoping to buy you a shirt as a gift from the kids one day and needed to know the correct size."

"You're so full of shit, Rick." I look at my phone's screen to ensure I have him in the frame. "Get the hell out of my house. You will never step foot in my house again. Do you understand me?"

Fury rages through every cell in my body. I want to beat the bullshit right out of this fucking asshole!

The kids are standing in their doorways, their faces hanging in disappointment from their father's actions. Unfortunately, this isn't the first time they've witnessed their dad doing something sneaky. Nobody deserves to have their privacy invaded by anyone, especially by a person they've divorced.

Ken steps around me and begins a rant. "Why, Dad? What's wrong with you? Why do you always have to screw things up? Can't you just be a normal father for once? You need to leave. We'll be just fine if you leave and never come back. We don't need you. So, go! Get out! Leave us alone!"

By the time he's done his speech, he's screaming as loud as his cracking, teenage voice will allow. My heart breaks when his tears burst forth, pouring down his cheeks. I wonder how long Ken has been holding that anger inside, afraid to confront his father.

He's a soft-hearted kid who never wants to hurt anyone's feelings, other than Kim's, of course. She's his sister so she's fair game in the unwritten sibling rules of conduct.

I pull him into a hug to comfort him. He's gasping with sobs.

Suddenly, he pulls away from me to pick up the small ceramic bowl off my dresser. He whips it at his father before I can stop him.

Rick tries to block it but fails. It hits him on the head and falls to the floor, shattering in tiny pieces. He looks at Ken and finally realizes that his son hates him, or at the very least despises him enough to want to hurt him.

Kim is crying loudly as well. She's still standing in her doorway, her little body frozen with fear. None of us have ever seen Ken this angry and it is heart-wrenching.

My poor little boy is hurting and has been for a long time. I failed him because I didn't see the anguish he's been carrying. I grab him and wrap my arm around his chest, pulling him against me. He's trembling.

Rick rushes past us, angry and embarrassed. Maybe he'll finally realize what a horrible father he's been to his kids. It's a slim chance, and I seriously doubt it. He's a hopelessly selfish human being. Somehow, he'll turn this around so that he's the victim and our son is the horrible attacker out to hurt him at my command. He blames me for everything that goes wrong in his life to this day, even though we divorced four years ago.

In the softest, calmest voice I can manage, I whisper to Ken. "Take Kim in your room and close the door. I'll be in to see you soon." My fingers brush through his hair. "Stay in there, okay?"

I hurry to follow Rick. He's standing in my foyer, furious, his face tense and flushed.

He points at me and I notice his hand shaking. "You turned those kids against me and I'll see you in court. Those are my kids, too. You made them hate me."

How dare he? My hands shake from the fireball raging in my gut. I pull open the door and point toward the road, urging him to leave. I don't dare speak because I'm too pissed off. I might cry which shows weakness, and he'll berate me for it. Besides, I know I'll say something I'll regret.

He stands before me with his arms folded across his chest,

wearing a smug expression and looking down his nose at me. "I'm not fucking leaving until I talk to my son."

Probably louder than I should, I yell, "Were you not listening? He doesn't want to talk to you. Don't you get it? Did you even hear a word he said? Just go or I'll call the police."

He yells, "Call the fucking cops! I don't fucking care! This is my day with those kids and I'm not leaving until I talk to my son."

"I said get out! Ken doesn't want to talk to you and I will not force him. Just go! Get out of my house!"

I'm seeing red while dialling 9-1-1.

"Rayna, is everything okay here?"

Coach is standing a foot outside the door on the porch with his hands on his hips, filling the doorway. He must have been outside when he heard the yelling. I'm relieved to see him and yet worried that he won't be calm enough to deal with Rick's hot-temper.

"It's okay," I tell him while holding my hand up, urging him to keep his distance and not to get involved.

"Oh, and who the fuck is this asshole? Is he your knight in shining armour that's going to rescue you from the evil ex?" He looks Coach up and down. "Are you fucking this piece of shit?" Rick accuses while pointing at Coach.

"What?" I question. It takes exceptional restraint not to punch this asshole straight in his foul mouth. In a hushed tone, I spit back. "Are you kidding me? Who I sleep with is none of your damn business. You have no right—"

The operator picks up and I ask him to send the police because my ex-husband won't leave my house, he's scaring my children, and is becoming threatening to me and my neighbour. I give him my address before hanging up, even though the operator tells me not to. I want to record this interaction on my phone as proof of his defiance. Coach steps in the door, walking past me so he can stand between the two of us.

"The lady asked you to leave. You need to go now," he says in a very calm and deep voice.

If I were Rick, I'd be running out the door in fear of getting clobbered. But I know him, and he's too stubborn to reveal his cowardice. He'll try to pick a fight so that Coach will hit him, so he'll look like the victim when the police show up.

Coach looks huge standing beside my ex. Rick is not a big guy, by any means. He's tall but extremely thin. Ken takes after him with those traits.

"Are you going to make me leave? Try it! Put your hands on me. I'll fucking sue your ass!" Rick says while stepping toward Coach to taunt him. "This doesn't involve your stupid ass, so go pound more weight. You're looking a little flabby."

"Don't be an asshole in front of your kids. Leave."

How is Coach staying so calm?

"Or what? What are you going to do about it, huh? Do you want to punch me? Is that why you're here? Do you think it'll make you look like a tough guy in front of my wife?"

I cut in. "Ex-wife!"

Coach speaks slowly and clearly. "If you're challenging me to a fight, you must hit me first. But heed my warning; you will not come out of it well."

He has his fists clenched, and his jaw is tight. Rage is building inside of him. He's ready to pounce should Rick decide to initiate a physical fight. If Rick is dumb enough to swing, Coach will pummel him. I'm not sure I want that to happen; he is the father of my kids. Even though he's useless in almost every way, he's still their father and I don't want them to hear or see him getting a beat-down.

Rick slowly lifts his arm, putting one finger on Coach's chest to coax him into swinging first. Coach simply smiles at him. Holy fuck, he's scary!

I'd piss my pants if that look was aimed in my direction. Although, sometimes he glares at me with an expression much like this one, but it's not as intense. The difference is that he wants to fuck me hard, not fuck me up. I know how strong he is, and although I shouldn't care, I fear for Rick.

"Leave, Dad!" Kim stands at the top of the stairs, yelling at her father with a tear-soaked face. Her little body jerks from broken-hearted sobs. "Why are you trying to fight with Coach? He's a nice guy and wouldn't hurt anyone. And he's my friend, and you're not because you're mean!" She hiccups. "I wish you weren't my dad!"

Rick looks at Coach and then at me. An 'aha' expression erupts on his face. "You *are* fucking him! This muscle-head? This gets you off these days?"

He should never talk like that in front of the kids. I'm seeing red, on the verge of punching Rick myself.

Coach is ready to boil over but speaks in a soft voice to the tiny, weeping child. "Kim, please go to your room and shut the door. Wait there for your mother. I don't think your father wants to pick a fight with me. I won't hit him, Kim, I promise. He's leaving right now." Coach looks at Rick. "Isn't that right?"

Kim rushes off to her room, still crying and obviously angry, judging by how hard she stomps her heels. These kids will need a lot of hugs and time to talk it out. I want to make it all go away, give them a normal life, but their father defies me at every turn.

Rick glares at me. "You're a fucking whore and a shitty mother. Are you fucking this asshole while my kids are in the house? I'll see you in court, bitch!"

Coach growls through clenched teeth. "You'd better shut the fuck up right now. I will not tell you again. Not another word. I do not want to break my promise to Kim. Unlike you, I will always keep my promises to those kids."

"Don't you dare tell me what to do. You're nobody but a fuck toy for this whore. You don't have a say in what happens here, so fucking go home and shoot some steroids or drink some eggs."

Rick will not shut up. At no other time have I ever seen him reach this level of stupid while bearing no common sense.

For the benefit of the video recording, I announce, "Coach, I give you permission to remove this asshole from my house. I've asked him to leave countless times and he refuses. He has no right to be in my house. He's trespassing on private property."

Coach looks at me. "Are you sure?"

With my eyes wide and my head nodding, I reply, "Oh, I'm sure!"

Rick looks at the camera. "Make sure that thing's recording so I can sue him for assault."

Coach reaches out, grabbing the front of Rick's shirt. He spins him around with ease and then quickly shifts his hand to the back of the shirt's collar. He grasps the back of his belt with his other hand while Rick swings his arms, never hitting Coach hard enough to cause him any discomfort. He lifts Rick by the belt. He falls forward and hangs as if being held by a harness, like a dog, suspended by his shirt and belt with his feet and hands barely touching the floor.

Coach takes a few steps toward the door, but when he tries to get through, Rick grabs the frame and holds on. I swing the phone so it doesn't capture what I'm sure will happen next. Coach lifts his knee quickly, nailing Rick's fingers against the solid wooden doorframe. He screams and grabs his fingers with his other hand. I'm sure I heard bones break in at least one of his fingers. Judging by his pained expression, I'd bet money on it.

"You a fucking asshole! I'm going to sue your dumb ass! I'm going to take your fucking house! Let me go, cocksucker!"

I don't know when they showed up, but the police are walking up my driveway, watching what's happening with their hands on their pistols.

The female officer calls out. "Take your hands off that man and step away. Do it now."

Coach lets go, dropping Rick to the grass with a thud. He raises his hands to signify that he isn't a threat to the police. Rick jumps up and lands a punch to Coach's jaw. It barely moves him.

Coach doesn't even drop his hands, but he's focussed squarely on Rick and I'd swear his eyes turn black.

Oh, shit!

The officer yells, "Get on the ground, now!"

While still glaring at Rick with evil eyes and flared nostrils, Coach obeys the officer's commands and slowly gets on his knees. He lays down, his eyes never leaving his assaulter. The asshole stands there, staring at Coach with hatred in his eyes and clenched fists. He wears a smirk that tells me he thinks he's won this battle.

"Get down now or I will Tase you," she yells as she steps closer to him with Taser in hand, pointing it directly at Rick. "Do it now, sir."

He looks at the cop and then nods, finally realizing that she's talking to him. He complies with her demands by dropping to his belly with his arms over his head. Damn, I was hoping she would blast him. He deserves it for everything he's put me and the kids through over the years.

I slowly walk toward Coach. "This guy is my neighbour and he was helping me. This is my asshole ex-husband who brought our kids home and then went through my belongings in my bedroom. I caught him on video, so he can't deny it. Coach came over when he heard Rick yelling at me. He only came to keep me safe." I pour it on, hoping they'll arrest him.

"He scared me. He wouldn't leave even after my kids and I begged him to go. He was very belligerent, so I asked Coach to get him out of the house for the sake of my children."

The officer nods at Coach. "You can get up now. Do you need medical attention?"

"No, thank you. I've been hit harder by frail women."

This has been quite an event, making this really shitty day even shittier.

Coach stands and joins me, wrapping his arm around my shoulder. He lets go of me almost right away so that nobody thinks we are a couple, especially the kids who are standing on the front porch, watching their father being handcuffed. They must have heard their father screaming or seen the flashing lights from the police car through Ken's bedroom window and were curious.

I race over to them and pull them both into a hug. "It's okay, don't be afraid. Dad simply got angry, that's all. I'm sure he'll feel terrible after he calms down, and then he'll apologize for being so mean to us today."

Kim whispers through her sobs. "Is he going to jail because he punched Coach?"

Damn, I was hoping they hadn't seen that.

"They will arrest him for assaulting Coach, but I'm sure they'll let him go later tonight." I look from one set of tear-soaked eyes to another. "Fighting is never okay. There are other ways to resolve issues. Can you two sit in the kitchen so I can talk to the nice policewoman? Will you do that for me?"

They both nod and then turn to walk into the house after taking one more look at their father, who is now being escorted to the police car. These wonderful, loving kids shouldn't be going through this.

Most of the neighbours are outside, watching as the worst moment of my life unfolds publicly; displayed for all to see. I'm a private person, so this is one of my greatest fears. People need not know my business. I approach Coach, who's talking to the policeman.

He asks, "Are they okay? They shouldn't have seen that. I'm sorry. Maybe I should go talk to them." He runs his hand through his hair, obviously upset. "If I wouldn't have come over, the situation may not have escalated."

"No, don't say that! I needed help, and you were there to give that to me. I can't thank you enough."

A lump is welling up in my throat. I smile and lean in to hug him, but the female officer calls to me before I can.

"I have to get your version of the events," she explains. "I'm sorry you had to go through this. How are the kids?"

"Shaken up. They're strong. They'll be okay."

"Can you tell me what happened here?" she asks.

I tell her the entire story, showing her the videos I took as evidence of what led up to him getting arrested. She asks me to send the videos to them. She tells me not to show them to anyone until the courts say it's all right to do so. It's not like I'm going to splash my business all over the internet, inviting strangers into my humiliating personal trauma. I hate it when people do that.

"Do you think he would have caused you physical injury had your neighbour not shown up when he did?"

"I don't know. Maybe. He is a very selfish, angry man."

She asks, "Has he caused you physical injury in the past?"

I look down at the grass and cross my arms. "Only one time. He slapped my face, and then pushed me backward. I fell onto the coffee table. My lip split and I was bruised, but that was years ago. Do I think he would have hurt me today?" I scrunch my face and tilt my head.

"Yeah, maybe. He was furious because our son yelled at him. I wouldn't put it past him to take his anger out on me. It enraged him when his daughter told him to leave. He thinks I turned them against him, but he's a shitty father and the kids have had enough."

"You don't have to allow it, but is it okay if I talk to the kids to get their side of the story? You can be present, of course." She's a soft-spoken woman.

If the kids can tell their side, they might feel as though they hold some power in a situation that is so far out of their control. They probably feel helpless at the moment. Kids don't understand the mindset of adults, it's beyond their capability, thankfully.

"Um, yeah. I think they'd like to tell their side. You'll be kind and understanding, right?" I suggest.

"Definitely. Kids process things differently than adults do. I have three of my own." She shakes her head and shrugs. "So, I'll be considerate. I'll talk to them like I would my own kids, only nicer," she promises with a snicker.

"Come with me," I tell her, leading the way to my kitchen so she can talk to them.

She allows them the freedom to tell what they saw and felt, thus giving them back their strength. After she's finished, she gives them each a sucker. The officer heads back outside to join her partner and bring Rick to the jail for processing.

 *oach*

THE COPS JUST LEFT WITH RAYNA'S ASSHOLE EX-HUSBAND handcuffed in the backseat of their car. I kind of hope they crash and he's pinned in the car while it goes up in flames. I'm sure Rayna wouldn't miss seeing his dumbass around.

I should keep in mind there was a time they were married, and she loved him. He's still the semen donor that created Rayna's two exceptional kids. They deserve so much better than him.

Rayna is in the kitchen talking to the kids to make sure they're not too freaked out while I wait just inside the front door. They seem calmer after talking to the officer. At least they aren't crying anymore. Seeing Ken and Kim upset like that broke my heart. Once again, father of the year!

I hear Ken say that he wants to get back to his video game. Rayna suggests that Kim take a nap. She promises to wake her for dinner. After the kids head to their rooms, she comes down the steps towards me. She looks at me with the most vacant expression and I can't read her.

I ask, "Are they okay?"

She takes a deep breath, releasing it slowly, and I see the anguish in her face. It's obvious she's emotionally drained. Instead of answering me, she wraps her arms around my chest, grabbing my shirt in her fists. I hold her as closely as I can and then I place a long kiss on the top of her golden hair. I gently rock her back and forth, soothing her the only way I know how; like my mother used to soothe me.

I keep my voice as calm as possible. She needs to hear that she did all right tonight. "You're an exceptional mother. Those kids love you so much. Don't listen to what that asshole said. He was trying to hurt you. Babe, the kids; are they all right?"

She nods against my chest. "I think so. They seem to be better than I am."

"I can stay the night if you're worried he'll come back."

I hope she'll accept. Leaving them alone scares me. If he comes back, he won't be pleasant. What if that fucking asshole wants revenge?

I overheard her tell the cop that he hit her once before. She didn't know I was listening, and I won't ask her about it. But, after hearing that, it took every ounce of strength I had not to rip that car door off, drag him out by his neck, and beat him to a bloody pulp. I would have gladly served a jail sentence for it; it would have been worth it.

My parents raised me not to hurt women. Yes, it's ironic, and believe me when I say that it's a personal struggle within me not to hate myself for my kinky, sadistic ways.

I want to plead with Rayna to let me stay with her, in her bed so I can hold her all night. But I know I can't. The kids have enough to deal with.

As if she can read my mind, she says, "Sleeping the night with me, in my bed? I don't think so. The kids—"

"First off, I didn't say I'd sleep in your bed with you, although the thought crossed my mind. I'm suggesting I'd sleep on the couch. I think the kids would be perfectly fine with that."

"I don't know. I wouldn't want to put you out. You don't have to do that. You've done so much already. I'm sure we'll be fine with the doors locked."

I yell, jolting Rayna from this quiet moment between us. "Hey, kids!"

Rayna jumps away from me, ensuring they won't see us sharing physical contact. Their doors fly open, and they come rushing to find out why I yelled.

"Would you guys feel safer if I spent the night on the couch?"

They look at each other with concerned expressions before turning their gazes to their mother.

Ken asks, "Do you think Dad is coming back tonight? Would he hurt us?"

Rayna replies, "No, I don't think he's coming back tonight, and he would never hurt you. He loves you, even though he doesn't know how to show you that."

I add, "Look, little man, if he comes back tonight, it'll be to yell more, not to fight. If he sees me here, he might not try to cause any trouble, and if he does, it'll be directed at me, not you. Besides, wouldn't you sleep better knowing I'm here to keep you safe?"

I raise my arms and flex. Rayna's breath catches in her throat. She looks away, needing to collect herself before the kids notice her swooning. They both smile and nod.

Kim says, "Wow! You're the biggest man ever! I want you to sleep over."

Ken asks, "Mom, can he?"

"If Coach wants to stay, it's okay with me," Rayna replies, crossing her arms over her chest and clearing her throat after her voice cracks.

"Cool!" My arms drop to my sides while I smile at the kids as if I just won a grand prize. "Okay, I'll go get what I need and come right back." The kids smile as if they've won that same imaginary prize.

I slip out of the house, closing the door behind me. After grabbing my gym bag out of my truck and bringing it in the house, I quickly toss my pajama pants, a t-shirt, and a toothbrush in a small bag. Just as I'm about to head out, an idea pops into my head.

A few minutes later, I'm back at Rayna's. I take the baking ingredients out of the plastic bag, setting them out on the counter, away from where she's preparing dinner. She looks at me as if to ask why I've brought them.

I gloat. "I make the best oatmeal raisin cookies. Some have said they're better than what their grandma used to make."

"You don't have to go through the trouble. Really, this is too much."

I take her hand and kiss it. "Sweetheart, it was my choice to stay. I love baking cookies but rarely do because I'll eat them all. Here, I can make my *cake* and eat it, too, so to speak." I shake my head. "You know what I mean. It's a win/win situation."

"Thank you. Truly, thank you for everything," she whispers, looking at me with a loving kindness that turns me to mush. For a fleeting moment, I'd swear we can see into one another's souls. I like what I saw but fear that she'll discover the demon that lives inside of mine. I blink to hide him from her view.

"Think nothing of it." I'm quick to change the subject, averting my eyes, preventing her from seeing my evil side. "What are you cooking?"

"Chicken, mashed potatoes, corn, and steamed carrots."

"Damn, woman, that sounds delicious." I open the oven door enough to take a long sniff. "Mm-mmm! What can I do to help?"

She laughs and points to the table. "You can sit down and let me cook. You're too big for me to keep moving around you. Now get out of my way and park your rear."

Dinner goes well, as if nothing traumatizing happened a few hours ago. I had the kids laughing so hard at one point that Kim snorted. Even Rayna laughed to the point of wiping away tears. The kids think I'm hilarious.

Fear floods my thoughts when I realize my heart is waking up for Rayna and her kids. Fuck, don't do it! I'll only hurt them.

I stand quickly, take the plates, and set them in the sink. It's dangerous to sit around the table like a happy little family. It'll serve me well to remember that we're not.

Rayna will soon realize I'm a demonic fuck-monster, not a potential life partner. She'll be right to believe I'm not worthy of her and her kids, because I'm not. She doesn't understand the level of asshole I can be. She doesn't know I get my thrills from watching women scream.

While keeping my heart on ice, the kids and I hang out in the kitchen baking cookies and laughing while Rayna takes a soothing bath. I have to keep reminding Kim not to lick her fingers each time she balls up a wad of dough and then drops it onto the cookie sheet. It makes me laugh, but I secretly hope she isn't catching a cold or some weird childhood disease that she'll surely spread to the rest of us. But then, I wonder if the baking process is hot enough to kill off anything she might be carrying.

It isn't long before we've stuffed ourselves with cookies, having saved her only two. We're sprawled out on the U-shaped sofa, watching an animated movie. I jolt and see Rayna standing at the bottom of the stairs, looking at me. I must have dozed off. How long has she been standing there?

She tucks her hair behind her ear and then walks around the sofa, taking a seat next to her daughter. Kim crawls over to her, placing her head on her mom's thigh. Rayna brushes her fingers through Kim's hair, pulling some stray locks from her face and neck.

She looks up at me with a gentle smile so full of love that it reminds me of my mother's kindness. I can almost see how much love Rayna has for her daughter, and it makes my icy heart feel warm and full.

Ken stares at the television, lost in the excitement on the screen. I look back at Rayna, hoping to watch her with her daughter, but she's still looking at me. We don't smile; we simply hold each other's gaze.

What's she thinking?

My eyes slowly lower, noticing the nightie poking out from under her robe. I gently shake my head while biting my bottom lip. She's wearing that same light-blue nightie that makes my dick hard every time I watch her from my office window. My mood instantly changes from admiring her love to wanting to ravish her body.

I've told her how excited I get when I see her wearing that, so I'm sure she put it on to torture me. She knows I can't touch her tonight, not with the kids around. The wicked grin she's wearing while eyeballing my reaction proves her deviance.

Touché, Rayna! You win this time.

I shift, trying to hide my swelling prick, and she snickers.

At ten o'clock, Rayna finally tears the kids away from the television and gets them into bed. It's been a very long, trying day and I can see how it's taking its toll on all three of them. When Rayna returns, she's carrying two glasses of white wine, handing one of them to me. I sip it while watching her walk away from me and sit on the opposite side of the sofa. She folds her legs under her, letting her housecoat fall open, revealing more of the provocative nightie. She's not wearing a bra.

"Why are you teasing me?" I calmly ask with a deep voice. She drives me wild. She shrugs, smiling innocently, but says nothing. "How do you expect me to be on my best behaviour when you're this close to me, dressed in the nightie I fantasized about fucking you in?"

"Behave. Think of it as an incentive for when you can have me again," she teases in a sweet and sultry voice. She sips from her glass, keeping her sexy eyes set on me.

"You don't fight fair," I whisper, knowing I'm defeated.

"Are we fighting? Are we at war? If that's the case, is my strategy working? Am I winning?" She's being a brat; she's aggravating me, and I fucking love it.

"You're winning the prize of a spanking until your ass is red-hot," I say, sounding as if I'm joking when I'm really not.

Defiantly, she repeats, "Red-hot, huh? I'm not so sure that's a prize I want."

I snicker. "Oh, you'll like it. I'll reward you afterward."

Rayna teases. "It's too bad you can't take some of your frustrations out on me right now. I'd bet you could use my body as a stress reliever."

She knows me well.

I wish she'd open her legs and touch herself to further torment me, but I doubt she would. If she does, she'll be under me in a second, with my hard cock ramming into her, as I take what I want like the selfish man that I am.

"So, tell me about your sister. Why is she so…" I take a breath. "What's the word?" I ask, hoping to shift my thoughts. Talking about her sister will help simmer her sexual drive as well.

She quickly offers an appropriate word. "I think the word you're looking for is slutty."

"Okay, we'll go with that even though I appreciate sluts. Why are you saying it like it's a bad thing?"

Unless it's in the bedroom during sex, I don't think women's sexual proclivities should deem her a slut. That suggests a double standard between the sexes. If a man plays around, he's excused because it's considered sowing his oats or playing the field. If a woman does it, she's crucified and ostracized.

I like sluts. I am one; or at least, I was.

"I don't know why she hasn't settled down. She has always been a free spirit and tries to enjoy life to its fullest, which I admire. I think she's only had a few actual boyfriends, but they were fleeting. She had a girlfriend for a while that she really cared about. I'm not sure what happened, but it ended badly." She sips her wine. "She might be ready to settle down."

"Maybe Tim will call her soon," I inform her. "Now tell me, how is that delicious pussy of yours?"

She snickers. "My pussy?"

"I love hearing that word come out of your mouth. Would you like to ride my mouth?" I ask, hoping she'll say yes.

Her face flushes and I'm once again reminded of how naïve she is.

I can imagine the dilemma in her mind battling between her motherly instincts and her womanly desires. She shakes her head to turn me down. I know we can't start playing. But I want to make this woman cum hard on my face and then ride my cock, but we can't risk the kids hearing.

"Damn, you look delicious and smell like coconut. Strangely, I happen to be craving coconut."

"I'm sitting way over here. How do you know I smell like coconut?" she asks, doubting my nasal keenness.

I flash her my very best come-hither expression. She gulps down the last of the wine before standing to get some pillows from the chest. She then reaches behind the cushion on the sofa, grasping something and giving it a quick tug. The cushion flips over, immediately changing the sofa into a bed. The sheets are already on it. She tosses the blanket from the back of the sofa and a pillow onto the bed before turning to look at me.

"There you go; a nice, soft bed to lay your weary head."

"Lie with me," I whisper, not asking but telling her what I want.

"You know I can't," she whispers, filling us both with disappointment.

I want her to lie in my arms so I can hear her breathing and smell her coconut-scented skin. It's not about sex, although that would be the highest point of my day. I chug back the last of my wine and set the glass on the coffee table.

I wave her over. "Come here." She shakes her head so I place my hand on my heart. "I'll behave. I won't touch your body, I promise."

She hesitates before deciding to come to me. My eyes stay on hers. It's almost impossible not to look down at her nightie as it brushes against her thighs with each step. I lean forward and take her hand when she's close enough. I pull gently, leading her down until she's straddling my thighs, facing me.

"You are an exceptional mother. You're strong and kind. It's obvious that they are your universe. They're lucky to have you."

"Thank you, but I'm lucky to have them."

She leans in, pressing her lips to mine. I let her set the pace, gentle and patient, not rough and eager as it usually is when I kiss her. Her hands hold my face as our lips mesh, and our tongues calmly explore.

I'm not touching her, as I promised. My hands grip the edge of the cushion with tight fists. Keeping my hands to myself is like a punishment. I'm sure she can feel my appreciation of her attention swelling beneath her. I'm careful not to tilt my hips. I know it will push me beyond my ability to maintain myself.

Our lips separate, her sweet breath caresses my face. We're both eager to rip our clothes off and mould our bodies into one sweaty, erotic heap. She rests her forehead against mine. It's abundantly clear she's fighting the overwhelming urge to let me take her right here, right now.

She sighs heavily before sliding off my legs and taking a few steps back. I have yet to release the cushions from my vice-like grip.

My prick is uncomfortably entombed in my sweatpants. I am in such a heightened state of arousal that if I move even the slightest, I might grab hold of her, going against my vow not to touch her body. I want to give her what pleases me most: intense, orgasmic pleasure.

I see her swallow hard before whispering. "Sleep well. I'll see you in the morning."

I slowly nod, not saying anything. Instead, I watch her run up the stairs, waiting until she's out of view before flopping my head against the back of the sofa and taking a few deep breaths. My hands finally release the cushion. I open and close them several times to get the blood flowing through my white knuckles.

Remaining quietly seated for several minutes, I listen through the silence in the house for any cue that she may have changed her mind and is making her way back down to me. I don't know why I think she'll return, but I'm disappointed when she doesn't. I debate whether to jerk off before going to sleep. I'm deterred when I look around and remember the kids were sitting in here only an hour ago. That thought is enough to stifle my desire and soften my cock. I go to the bathroom and brush my teeth and then slide onto the sofa bed.

It's been an hour since Rayna went upstairs and I still can't fall asleep. I'm sexually frustrated. Knowing that she's upstairs lying alone in her room is enough to keep me awake. I keep fantasizing about sneaking upstairs, climbing into her bed and ravishing her body while looking into her seductive eyes.

I lift my head to listen to the hushed sounds coming from upstairs. Someone is tiptoeing down the steps. Even though it's dark, I can tell it's Rayna approaching the bed. She says nothing, which I find odd. She startles when I raise my hand toward her.

Perhaps she thought I was asleep, and she was hesitant to wake me. I wait for her to decide whether to take my hand and get in with me.

I'm relieved when her delicate fingertips glide along my palm. I lift the covers and roll onto my back. She slips off her panties and tosses them to the floor while I slide my sweatpants down to my mid-thighs.

She straddles my pelvis. Her lips quickly find mine. She will set the pace tonight.

I place one hand on her lower back while the other cradles her cheek. Rayna can use me tonight, taking what she needs. I'm ready to let her take her pleasure, but I hope I'm capable of having an emotional connection, should she desire it.

Our lips never part. In one swift motion, I am buried deep inside her. Our breathing is quiet but increasingly more impassioned, even though she hasn't moved.

This is fucking amazing; she is fucking amazing.

Rayna's curvaceous hips lazily rock, pulling me in and out of her as she glides her pussy against my belly, never once lifting her weight off my pelvis.

My heart is warming and becoming a part of her. It's abundantly clear that tonight means something more to both of us than did our previous raging sexual experiences. We are connecting on a deeper level, despite my efforts to keep my heart out of this.

Tonight, she's mine and I'm hers, completely. We are one. Tomorrow, things can go back the way they were. Right?

She makes love to me, letting her orgasm slowly build and easily take her over. I'm careful not to force my pelvis upward by remaining still so she can take me how she chooses.

This is easy for a control freak like me. My inner demon throws himself against the imaginary cage in which he's confined. I would much rather flip her over and take her hard and fast, but I sense that's not what she needs tonight. If I'm rough with her, it won't please her as much as being gentle.

Her orgasm rolls through her. She quietly rides the high, not moaning any louder than a whisper. Instead, her body trembles against mine. Her eyes meet mine, and that's when I see her tears welling up. Her emotions are so strong that she can't contain them.

For me, sexual intimacy has always been for sexual gratification or to gain a feeling of dominance, but for no other purpose. This is the most unbelievably loving moment I've ever experienced.

I couldn't possibly be more intoxicated by this woman.

My fingertips tenderly wipe the tears from her soft cheeks. We slowly roll, ending with me above her. I raise myself onto my elbows while kissing her forehead as her tears spill. I don't hump her; I stay inside her while kissing her cheeks and brushing away her tears with my thumbs. Never had I imagined wanting to be this gentle and loving while having sex. This is how I want to be for Rayna because she needs me to be.

"Please, don't stop," she whispers.

Following her request and make love to her, the same way she did to me. I kiss her lips, neck and cheeks, loving her with a newfound compassion that had been dormant. Her body slips into a silent orgasm.

I watch her in the silent calmness of the night. Her mouth opens as a quivering breath escapes her. Her eyelids remain tightly shut and her brows furrowed, lifting in the center just slightly.

I'm drowning in this moment. It's taking away any doubt I may have had that I care deeply for Rayna. At this very moment, I realize that I'm not afraid to love her, and willing to let her love me. I can't fear something I have no control over and I can't stop it.

My own euphoric, full-body and mind climax overtakes me. My body stiffens and then jerks above hers. A muffled grunt slips from my throat. As my lungs release a halted breath, my body suddenly becomes weightier on my elbows.

She looks at me and peacefulness graces her eyes. I stroke her cheek with my fingertips and hold her gaze for several minutes until my softening manhood slips from her, ruining the best moment of my life.

She lifts her face and kisses me lovingly once more. As quickly as she got into my bed, she wiggles out from beneath me and tiptoes back up the stairs, disappearing into the lonely darkness.

I feel warm and complete, something I have never felt.

It's only for tonight. Come the light of day, Rayna will remember that I am nothing worth loving and everything will go back to the way it was. She won't want to build a life with a man like me.

A fullness builds in my throat, but I harden my emotions, preventing my regret from spilling from my eyes. Instead, I close my lids, subconsciously waving goodbye to this incredible night. I felt the vastness of her love, if only for a fleeting moment.

I fear I will never recover.

~

RAYNA

I make my way back to my bedroom, stopping only to peek into each child's room to ensure that they're in their beds asleep. When I shut my door, I lean against it, suddenly feeling alone in the darkness of this stillness of the night. Although the air is cool, I can still feel the warmth from his kiss on my lips.

What happened between us? I can feel his love in my soul while his cologne graces my skin. I wrap my arms around myself, inhaling his scent and remembering how endearing his eyes were when he held my gaze. His patience stole my heart.

I will never be the same. *We* can never be the same.

My silky sheets caress my body with a delicate touch. They don't compare to how tender Coach's fingertips were as they brushed away my pain. He broke something in me.

I've been hiding behind the facade of a happy, single mother with few regrets. He let my heart reveal all of its wounds through the silence of my tears. Then he kissed them away without judgement or expectation of anything in return. He fixed what he broke.

Tonight, in Coach's arms, my wounds scarred over and I feel whole again. I will always treasure those moments in the darkness and how he loved me, even if it won't last.

How could I allow myself to love him? He told me that he will never marry. I cannot change him, nor should I fool myself into thinking I can. He's a playboy, and I'm too complicated.

The beautiful man, whose bed I crawled out of, will never be happy with me alone. I should stop fooling myself into believing that we could live happily ever after with the fairy tale ending people would envy long after we've passed. Actual life isn't like that. I, of all people, know this and should keep it in mind.

There was a time when I loved Rick and thought he was everything I could ever need a man to be. How wrong I was! Maybe I'm a terrible judge of character who will inevitably fall for the wrong man over and over…

Am I blinded by Coach's incredible ability to take my mind

away from life's ugly realities, using only his sexual talents? My ex-husband's bullshit promises of having a happy ever after fooled me, so why should I think that Coach is any different?

I will not ask him to be with me and only me because he'll shoot it down.

Why do writers always taunt us with a forever after happiness when it doesn't exist? Books and movies should better reflect actual life, not spin tales of untruths that give us all false hope.

My eyes close. I recall how he looked in the darkness. His loving eyes stared at me as if begging me not to hurt him. His fragrant flesh was hot against mine; hot enough to thaw my frozen heart. He was everything I needed him to be, just then, and I will forever be grateful to him for that. My mind drifts off, holding his image.

I dream of his tender, loving touch. I welcome this sleep because I get to enjoy him more. We are one while the moon hangs overhead, but when the sun awakens, I will once again be boring Rayna and he will be Coach; eternally single and unavailable.

CHAPTER 15

 *oach*

SOMETHING PULLS ME AWAY FROM THE SENSUOUS DREAM I WAS having about Rayna, instantly annoying me. I dreamed that the beautiful goddess was sitting on a stool, her arms tied behind her back with rope in an elaborate design effective in both immobilizing her arms and creating a sensual image. I had her at my mercy. She was mine, body and soul.

Why do I hear kids talking in my house?

My eyes open. I'm blinded by the bright light beaming into the room. Damn, my eyes feel scratchy and ache painfully from the glare that's bleeding through my lids. I blink several times and rub them harshly. Where am I?

Oh, right! I'm in Rayna's basement. Her scent flashes through my mind, along with the sound of her hushed moans, the softness of her skin, and how lonesome her eyes looked when they were full of tears. She nearly broke me. Maybe she did, and I simply haven't realized it yet.

Something smells very appetizing. I'm starving. I would really enjoy a steaming cup of coffee to help chase the drowsiness away. I suppose I should get out of this bed and start the day.

With significant effort, I pull my legs to the edge of the foam bed. I step down onto a pair of silky white panties; Rayna's, I presume. I remember her taking them off last night. She must have forgotten to bring them with her. I scoop them up with one finger and hold them to my nose, breathing in her sweet scent. My cock instantly springs awake. Is it a pee-hard-on, or do I need a release? Perhaps it's both.

I slip my t-shirt on and stand, re-adjusting my sweatpants and the rock-hard sausage that's begging to take a piss. After flipping the bed back into the sofa, I stuff the pillow into the same chest I watched Rayna take it from. I visit the bathroom to relieve myself and jerk off as quickly as I can just to make my hard-on go away. Thankfully, it only takes a few minutes. I wash my hands, brush my teeth, and then head upstairs to see what all the giggling is about.

The kids and Rayna are busy in the kitchen and don't notice me make my way up the stairs. The sun beams through the patio doors, making it possible to see her silhouette through her nightie. I'm so thankful that I jerked my cock before I came up here, otherwise I'd be hard as steel from seeing how fucking sexy she looks right now. This woman does not understand how she affects me.

I fling myself from around the wall and yell, "Good morning!"

All three of them jolt and screech. I burst into hard laughter. Their faces are priceless!

"What the f... Fart?" Rayna yells, holding her chest, her eyes wide. "Dammit, Coach, that's not funny!"

"*Au contraire, mon ami.* From where I'm standing, it's hilarious."

"Coach, don't do that," Kim complains with a sour expression.

I pat her head on the way to the coffeemaker. "Sorry, little woman. I only meant to scare your mom."

"Nice," Rayna retorts, slapping me on the shoulder. I laugh even harder.

"Are you hungry?" Ken asks. "There's a lot to eat."

He isn't upset that I startled them. He thought it was as funny as I did. Scaring people to make them shriek must be a guy thing.

I stand next to Rayna as she holds a spatula, getting ready to flip a pancake. I want to wrap my arms around her, press my lips to her neck, and breathe in her scent. She carries her natural beautiful well, even though her eyes are still puffy from the lack of sleep, and her hair is unkempt. A light purple haze hangs under her eyes, reminding me of how late it was when she left my bed last night. If she would have stayed with me, maybe we could consider ourselves to a couple.

Nah, Rayna would never settle for a schmuck like me.

"Pancakes? Eggs?" She asks, stepping a little closer to me as she turns her back to the kids and adds teasingly, "Me?"

My voice isn't quiet. "The latter sounds tantalizing enough. I'll have some of that, please."

"Eggs it is." She smirks at me. "How many?"

"Hmm, how many do you have?"

"I only have three left. How do you want them?" she asks as she flips a pancake that's been swelling in the hot pan.

"Any way you want to give it to me," I suggest and she blushes.

I take a mug from the cupboard. I fill it with coffee and then sit at the table with the youngsters. "How did you two sleep?"

"I slept great," Kim replies.

"Okay, I guess," Ken tells me. "How about you?"

"Well, I fell asleep feeling very tranquil. I can't say I've ever experienced anything like that before. It was the best *sleep* I've ever had," I reply while looking at Rayna and trying to assess her thoughts.

She's looking at me, expressionless. I wish I could read her mind. Her face isn't giving me any clues whether she's happy with how things went last night or if she's regretting letting me glance at her heart.

Rayna looks away, scooping the pancake up and flopping it on a plate. She slips it in front of Kim and pours syrup on it, casting her eyes up to glance at me. She blinks several times, and walks back to the pan, still wearing no discernable expression.

Did I read too much into last night?

She breaks the eggs into the heated pan, sprinkles something over them and then covers it with a glass lid. I'm waiting for her to look at me, but she doesn't. She stares at the eggs, watching them cook while lost in her thoughts. What's she thinking? If the kids weren't here, I'd ask her what's taking her so far away.

After we finish eating, the kids head to the basement to watch cartoons. I hear the television blasting out strange noises, and the characters talking in annoying screeching voices similar to nails on a chalkboard. It's way too early in the morning for that. How does Rayna do this every morning and not go insane?

Rayna is putting the milk in the fridge when I slide up behind her and wrap my arms around her waist. She instantly stiffens and holds her breath. She doesn't have to hit me with a brick; it's obvious she doesn't want me to touch her. I immediately step back, putting some distance between us. She slowly closes the refrigerator as she exhales.

Without turning to look at me, she apologizes. "I'm sorry. It's just that I," She takes a breath, "I don't think we should read too much into last night. I was vulnerable. Not that you took advantage, obviously! It was my fault completely. I should never have been so..."

I interrupt her. "Rayna, it's okay."

She turns to look at me. Her face is flushed, and her eyes are glossy. "I shouldn't have put you in that position. It was cruel of me and I'm sorry. Please don't read more into it other than a pathetic moment of weakness on my part."

I look down at the floor, remembering how perfect she felt in my arms last night. "If that's what you want."

"I think it's best, don't you?" she asks.

"For who?" I ask, my heart suddenly thumping wildly in my chest.

"Please don't do this now. The kids are downstairs."

"Yes, they're downstairs and the TV is blaring. They can't possibly hear our conversation, Rayna. Do you really want to pretend last night meant nothing?"

It's as though she's trying to convince herself more than me. She clears her throat before explaining. "You know this can't happen. We are so different. You're young, single, and a bit of a playboy. No offence. I'm divorced, older, a mom, and definitely not as sexually experienced as someone should be in order to properly entertain you for the rest of your life. We both know I wouldn't be able to keep up with your needs. You'll tire of me and my boring, vanilla life, and then leave me and my kids broken, which is exactly as their father did. I can't put them through that again. So, yes, it is better for all of us if we don't read too much into last night."

Rayna is using her head, not her heart, and her face reveals that. She's being a protective mom. I can't blame her for that. It's one reason I respect her so much.

Maybe everything she says is right. I don't know. I can't see the future. All I know is that I'm drawn to her. From the moment we met, and after having been intimate with her only a few times, she's weaved her way into my heart. I want her and those kids in my life.

She crosses her arms over her chest. "Where has Alissa been these past few days? I haven't seen her car in your driveway."

"Alissa and I are over. I broke it off after you came to visit me on Saturday. It was time to let her go. You were right when you told me to send her on her way." I take a step toward her and stop. "At this moment, sweetheart, you couldn't be more wrong about us. I want you. I want those kids. Are you listening to me? Look at me!" I demand, but she refuses.

Rayna stares at the dishes in the sink with tear-filled eyes.

She says, "I'll bet you broke her heart. Understand, I don't want to be in her position in a year from now. I can't be a notch on your headboard, a conquest that you use for your own purpose and then toss away when some newer shinier toy comes along. I think we should stop before this gets out of hand."

"No, Rayna, I don't think we should stop. I want you because somehow you do something to me that nobody has ever done. You see me for me, for who I am. You always have. All those times we shot the shit about everything and nothing, I wanted more of you than you will allow." I step toward her again. "I can't see myself being apart from you, not anymore. The thought scares me. I don't know why, but it does. Rayna, I want to live with you, marry you, maybe give you more children, if that's what you want. You're such an incredible mother."

I inhale deeply, watching her examine my face to see if I'm weaving a web of lies or telling her the truth. That's when it happens. My heart speaks for itself.

"I love you, Rayna."

She struggles to take in a breath, as though all the air has been sucked out of the room. She puts her hand on her forehead, the other on her stomach. She whispers a heart-wrenching plea, "Simon, please don't hurt me."

I rush to close the distance between us, pulling her into my arms and kissing her passionately. It's something I've wanted to do since I woke up without her beside me. She kisses me back.

"You won't hurt me. Will you?" she whispers as she clings to me, her golden head pressing against my chest.

"I will try every day to do the exact opposite of that. I never want to hurt you. Date me. Date me like we're a proper couple. What do you have to lose, Rayna?" I ask while holding her to my chest with one arm draped around her shoulder. My fingers comb through her soft hair, brushing it away from her pale face.

"A lot if it doesn't work out," she utters, her hands gripping my back a little tighter.

"Mom? Coach?" Ken startles us and we leap apart, nervously.

My heart is suddenly pounding in my chest, desperately trying to break free. "Are you two boyfriend and girlfriend?"

"Um, well," Rayna scratches her head, stalling. "It's complicated."

"Ken, I asked your mom to go on a date with me."

"Are you going to go?" he asks her, not frowning or smiling to give me a clue whether he approves. He's his mother's son, for sure.

"Um, I don't know," she replies while fiddling nervously with her fingers.

"Do you think she should say yes?" I ask him, thinking it'll give me bonus points with him. "Since you're the man of the house, I should ask your permission to take your mom on a date. So, what do you say about that idea, little man?"

"I think Mom should say yes," he quickly tells me.

We both look at Rayna. She looks scared as her eyes peer from him to me and back to him.

"You think I should go on a date with Coach?" she asks him, not sure she heard him correctly.

"Yeah, I do. He's a nice guy, Mom."

I yell, startling Rayna and Ken. "Hey, Kim! Come here, darling."

She runs up the stairs and into the kitchen. "What?"

"Tell me something. Do you think I should take your mom on a date?"

She looks at me for a few seconds before meeting eyes with her mom. "Yes, I do. I like you. You're nice to us and you're hilarious."

"Okay, fine! I'll go on a date with you," she blurts while rolling her eyes dramatically to make the kids laugh.

"Hey, kids, can I kiss your mom?"

Ken nods. Kim giggles, covering her mouth as shy girls do. My eyes meet Rayna's.

I spread my arms wide and announce, "I have their permission to kiss you."

As I'm slowly stepping closer to her, she puts her hand up to stop me, but she's smiling and laughing, confirming that she doesn't hate the idea.

"No! Stop walking! You don't want to kiss me," she says for the benefit of keeping things innocent in front of the kids. She's laughing as her face flushes bright pink.

The kids are watching and laughing. Ken cheers me on. "Kiss her, Coach!"

"What do you say?" I ask with a ridiculous toothy smile while she looks at me with wide eyes.

She playfully pushes me to make me stop advancing, but finally drops her hand when I'm standing only a foot away from her. She looks at me with delicate eyes. "Fine, kiss me then."

My lips touch hers and hold perfectly still. I tenderly slide my hand onto the back of her head. Our faces separate but hold near as our eyes meet. I press another tender kiss to her velvety lips while breathing her in. We don't open our mouths because the kids are watching us. It's hard to pretend they aren't; the laughter is a constant reminder that they're in the room.

When my face pulls back from hers, she playfully pushes me away, curling her lips into her mouth so she can taste me. Her face flushes brighter than I've ever witnessed, and I notice her hands are shaking when she tucks a tress of hair behind her ear.

"Okay, now that you've had your kiss, go home so I can get the kids ready for school. I have to go to work. Don't you have to go to work, too?"

I pout. "Yeah, I do. All right, I'll see you all later. Thanks for breakfast and saying yes to a date and a kiss."

"I can still change my mind on the date. You know that, right?" she teases.

"Nope, I have witnesses that will back me up. Right, guys?"

"I'll back you up, Coach," Ken assures me.

Kim corrects Rayna, throwing her words back at her in that spiteful way children love to do to their parents when the roles reverse. "You said you'd go, Mom. You always tell us not to make promises we have no intention of keeping."

I snicker and pat the kids on their heads as I pass by them. "See you kids later." I make my way across the lawn to my house but cringe when I look up to see a familiar car in my driveway. "Shit!"

I walk in the front door to find Alissa sitting on the sofa, staring at me with a furious expression. Her lousy attitude is not something I care to be privy to right after having the best night and morning of my life. The last thing I want to do is ruin this incredible high I'm on.

"We are no longer together. What are you doing in my house?" I ask as I walk past her.

She's not threatened by me. She's a true submissive so I'm taken back by her courage to confront me with so much attitude, but I won't let her know that it's pissing me off. I won't give her the satisfaction.

She crosses her arms while continuing to glare at me. "Just like that?"

I reply matter-of-factly. "Pretty much, yeah. What were you expecting; a sympathy card, a parting gift, what? Alissa, you knew we were only friends with benefits, nothing more. We did not have a deep spiritual connection. The arrangement was that we would spend time together, have sex, and go about our own business. And now it's done."

She scoffs at me while shaking her head. "Wow! I can't believe it's so easy for you to cast me aside. So, do you want to tell me who the new tart is?"

"New tart?" I repeat, snickering at her word choice. "What makes you think there's someone new?"

"This," she says, holding up a condom wrapper and a used condom that I had put in the trash bin. She must have sifted through my garbage and unwrapped wads of tissue to find it, which is absolutely disgusting. "And you didn't come home last night."

"Get the fuck out of my house and give me my damn key back. Better yet, keep it as a parting gift. I'll be changing the locks, anyway. If you ever come back here again, I'll have you arrested for trespassing. You need help. Digging through my trash is beneath you."

"Oh, I need help? No, mother fucker, *you* do! You should seek professional help. You beat the fuck out of women for sexual gratification. That is fucked up!"

"Is it? I don't recall you disagreeing when you were bound and coming while I was slapping your ass. But now, when I suddenly don't want you anymore, I'm a mother fucking abuser? Go fuck yourself! Get out of my house."

She stands and throws the used condom at me, pissing me off even more. If she'd have hit me with it, I can't say I wouldn't have thrown her over my shoulder and carried the bitch out of my house. My fists clench and my nostrils flare. If a man had done that, I'd beat him to a bloody pulp. But she's female and I will never put my hands on a woman when I'm angry.

Alissa stands right in my face, staring at me, but I refuse to look at her. I look to the right of her head, which I know irks her in ways that give me a slight satisfaction.

"Look at me!" she demands, but I don't. "Is she the bitch next door with the kids? You always had a thing for her. Didn't you? She seems to be way too vanilla for someone as messed up as you. But maybe she's a dirty hoe like the rest of the whores you fucked behind my back."

"I never hid anything from you."

I glare at her with obvious rage, and she flinches. She can't deny that I'm wickedly pissed off. My upper lip twitches and I know I'd better walk away before I do something I will absolutely regret. I take two steps back before turning around and rushing out the front door. I'm not giving her enough time to jump on me.

This psychotic bitch standing in my house is nothing like the woman I thought I knew. Now that I look back on our time together, I can see the tiny clues that should have tipped me off that she's a crazy, possessive bitch.

"Get out of my house or I'm calling the cops," I tell her as I make my way outside.

I stop when I reach the lawn, plenty far enough away from the door for her to walk through it without touching me. I don't need her telling the cops that I physically assaulted her. Because of how aggressive I look, and what happened last night with Rayna's ex, they'll likely believe her over me.

"I'm not leaving until I get my shit."

"Just go, I'll send your shit via courier."

"No, fuck you!" She turns and runs back up the stairs, disappearing down the hall toward the bedrooms.

Instead of dealing with her bullshit, I dial 9-1-1 and ask the cops to come so they can take an intruder out of my house. I let them know that I'm a big guy and I'm worried she'll try to say I hit her. I'd much rather they come and take her out of my house. It doesn't take more than a minute for them to arrive. They must have been close by.

Once again, the neighbours trickle out of their houses, curious why I'm being confronted by the police for the second time in less than twenty-four hours.

I have my hands up when they approach. These cops differ from the two last night and I'm grateful. If I'm involved in two incidents in such a close timeframe, I think they might develop some concerns.

"Sir, are you the one who called?" the first officer asks as he's stepping out of the car.

I nod. "Yes, I called. There's a woman in my house who will not leave even though I asked her several times to get out. She's my ex who never lived here, so she has no right to be inside. She says she isn't leaving until she gets her shit. Will you please get her out of my house?"

"Does she have any weapons on her or does she have access to anything inside that could harm us?"

"Does her evil glance and bitchy attitude count as a weapon?" I reply with a smirk, but they don't appreciate the humour.

"Does she have anything in the house that belongs to her? If so, what?" the second officer asks.

"She has two t-shirts, three panties, one pair of yoga pants, a pair of jeans, one or two pairs of socks, and a bra. Black, I think. I can give you a full description of each item if need be. Oh, don't forget her pink toothbrush and her hairbrush in the top drawer in the guest bathroom. She can take her shit and get the fuck out, but I want to make sure she isn't taking anything that belongs to me. She knows where I keep my money and my valuables. I do not put it past her to take everything she can get her fingers on. She wants to hurt me."

"You're very specific in the list of her belongings," he says, looking at me as if I've suddenly grown a second head.

"Well, I know the contents of my house. Will you check her to make sure she's taken only her belongings?"

The officer nods. "I'll call a female officer to pat her down and go through her purse."

Thankfully, they aren't simply going to let her walk off with anything she feels like. The officer puts out a call on his radio and then tells me to stay put while they go inside my house.

I wait for the cops to come back out while I yell at the nosy neighbours. "Mind their own fucking business! There's nothing happening here that concerns any of you."

Most of them go back in their houses, fearing my wrath, but a few nosy mother fuckers hang around to watch. They know I won't lay my hands on them because the cops are here.

I point to a house while looking at a smug man in his late fifties. "That's your house there. Isn't it?" I look at the house and back at him. My wicked grin and wide eyes have him uncrossing his arms and slinking home.

How Rayna hasn't noticed the commotion and come out to see if everything is all right baffles me. Truthfully, I'm pleased that she's oblivious. I know Alissa would scream at her or attack her if given the opportunity.

How Alissa hid her jealous streak also baffles me. Why would she want to be with me if she thinks I'm so fucked up? She once told me that I'm emotionally stunted with little chance of ever loving someone completely. She doesn't know me at all. Then again, I never let her see the real me.

A female officer drives into my driveway. After she's brought outside, I watch her frisk Alissa while she yells in protest. The officer finds a watch my grandfather gave me before he passed away, three of my rings, eight hundred and twenty dollars in cash, and all the photos I had ever taken of women in various positions and stages of undress. What was she planning on doing with them?

Those pictures are private and were secured in my safe, along with the money. I never showed her any of those photos, so how she even knew I had them has me curious. How she got into my safe without me telling her the code is also likely to haunt me.

I refuse to press charges but ask them how to put a restraining order on her to keep her at bay. After they give me the information, they send her on her way and follow her to make sure she doesn't go around the block and come right back to start trouble again. If she makes the mistake of coming back, I will absolutely press charges.

When I go inside, I put my stuff back where she took it from, and then check to make sure she didn't take anything that the cops didn't recover. After I'm certain everything is accounted for, I order a new and more secure safe. They'll deliver it tomorrow afternoon.

CHAPTER 16

After frantically rushing around to get everybody ready, somehow, I dropped the kids off at school on time. I start on the fifteen-minute drive to the dentist's office where I work while doing what I always do; I take this time to relax in silence.

Listening to music when I'm driving doesn't excite me like it does most people, especially in the morning. I can take it or leave it any other time of the day. This is my time to blank my mind as best I can before the busyness of the office consumes me.

Being a dentist is something I've always wanted to do, but I couldn't afford to pay for the continued education I needed to earn that degree. Instead, I had to settle as a dental assistant. It's not so bad. We do a lot of the same procedures, I just get paid less than they do.

No matter how much I try to concentrate on the drive, last night keeps flooding my thoughts. We made love. When I went downstairs to Coach's bed, I didn't intend to be romantic, but that's exactly what happened. I wanted it. I could even say that I needed it.

He was receptive to my tenderness and seemed to lose himself in my affection. It happened, and it was divine. I want to remember it as being one of those rare and perfect moments in my life that I will forever treasure. It may never happen like that again. I had a genuine connection to Coach, and it was perfect for both of us.

I click the phone button on my steering wheel to call my sister. She picks up on the first ring. "Hello, sister."

"Good morning! Are you at work?" I ask.

"Yeah, I just got here. I haven't gone inside yet. So, what happened?"

I wonder how she already heard about the commotion yesterday with my ex. "Oh, with Rick? Well, he really took it to a whole new level of idiocy this time. He got a bit out of control and then Coach came to my rescue. He punched Coach in front of the police and the kids, so they arrested him. They're charging him with assault and maybe trespassing because he wouldn't leave my house when I asked him to. But that charge might not stick because Ken initially invited him in the house. It was a giant shit-show. I'll probably have to hire another lawyer and go to court again." The silence is deafening. "Renee, are you still there?"

"Yeah, um." She takes a breath. "What the fuck? You rarely ever call me this early, so I was wondering what happened that was so crucially important you couldn't wait until later this afternoon to tell me about it. But, fuck! Holy shit, woman! Are you okay? The kids? How are the kids? Wait a minute! He punched Coach? That man has a death wish. Please tell me Coach beat that sardonic expression off his face?"

"Oh, no." I chuckle. "That wasn't why I was calling you. I suppose I should have called last night to tell you all of that. You asked me so many questions just now. I'll try to answer all of them. Well, the kids were shaken up and scared, but they seem to be okay now. I'm fine, too. And no, Coach didn't hit him back because the cops were watching. But he did physically toss him out of my house. So fun to watch."

"I'm sorry I missed it."

"It was great!" I snicker. "And, before you ask, Coach heard the yelling and came to see what was happening. He wasn't already in my house. He was at his place when it first started. Once everything calmed down, he offered to spend the night because he wanted us to feel safe. The kids pleaded with me to let him. So I did, and he stayed on the sofa-bed downstairs. Which brings me to why I was calling."

"Wow! So much action. I can't believe you didn't call me. You bitch! Okay, so continue the story and tell me the real reason you're calling me so early this morning," she urges.

"I couldn't sleep last night knowing Coach was in my house. So, I went downstairs and climbed into bed with him. He was awake, too. I made love to him."

"No, you did not!"

"Yes. Yes, I did," I confirm.

"Was he receptive?"

"Shockingly, yes. Very. I fucking cried," I confess, embarrassed at my feminine fragility, no doubt blushing even though I'm alone in my car.

Renee laughs as she talks. "You didn't? Oh my God, Rayna! How was he when you cried? Did he freak out?"

"He rolled me onto my back, wiped my tears away, and made slow, passionate love to me. It was heart-stirring. He was impressively tender and loving. Needless to say, this morning I was very nervous about how things would be between us over breakfast."

"And, was it horribly uncomfortable?" she asks.

I sigh and groan. "No, it was wonderful. He told me that he wants me and asked the kids if it was okay to take me out on a date. They surprised me; they want him to, so he asked me out in front of them. When I said I would go, he asked Ken if he could kiss me. You know, because Ken is the man of the house—Coach's words, not mine. Ken gave his permission and Coach laid one on me as the kids stood there watching and giggling. Strangely enough, it wasn't remotely uncomfortable. He was very respectful of me and the kids."

"So, you two are an item now, like, officially a couple?" She teases me the same way she used to as a child, with a silly song. "You and Coach, sitting in a tree, K-I-S-S-I-N-G."

"You are so immature!" I say, and she laughs. "In all seriousness, he's going to get bored with me. How can he not? I bore myself. I'll fall head over heels for him and he'll break my heart, leaving me more bitter than I already am. The kids will be hurt and think we failed because of something they did, even if I tell them otherwise. What have I gotten myself into? I must be crazy."

"You are not crazy. A little off the wall and over dramatic sometimes, but definitely nowhere near clinically insane. He's hot, and he seems to be really into you. Give him a shot, Rayna. You deserve to be happy. If it doesn't last, use your time together to make wonderful memories that you can look back on fondly while you masturbate. I'm joking, sort of. Seriously though, take a chance on him. Life is too short to be lonely because you fear rejection."

"Okay. I'll let this cowboy ride me until he finds a more interesting horse to run off with."

We both laugh, but I wonder whether I'm right to think he won't stick around.

"Before I forget to tell you, a friend of Coach's called me last night. We're meeting for coffee later this afternoon."

"You must let me know how it goes and send me a picture of him. I'm curious to see what he looks like."

"I'll text it to you. He already sent me one, so I sent him one, too. We agreed that there's nothing worse than spending time with someone you're not physically attracted to. It's awkward," she says.

The photo comes through and I'm instantly excited for her.

This guy is as big as Coach, but his face seems to be much more placid than Coach's. He's extremely attractive, exactly how my sister prefers her partners.

"Very nice, sis! He's smoking hot. Enjoy your date and don't forget to tell me how it goes."

We say our goodbyes and hang up.

I pull into a parking space, shut the car off, and take a few deep breaths before getting out. Here's hoping it's a pleasant one and nobody tries to bite me today. I'm so tired that my reflexes probably won't be as quick as needed to avoid a child's chomp.

"Rayna!" A voice that is way too familiar pierces the surrounding air, stabbing at my ears like an ice pick. I don't have to turn around to realize that Rick is approaching me.

"Do not start trouble or I'll call the cops again," I tell him as I turn to look at him with rage in my eyes.

He's walking closer but stops about five feet away and doesn't take another step toward me. His eyes shout regret. Good, he should feel shitty about what he did to me and his kids yesterday. The stress he piled on Coach, who's innocent in all of this, was undeserved. Okay, maybe he's not innocent, but unworthy of Rick's spite.

"I'm not here to start trouble." He runs his hand through his hair the way he has for as far back as I can remember. He adds, "I'm sorry about yesterday. Are the kids okay?"

Did I hear him correctly? "Are you kidding me right now?"

He shakes his head. "I don't know what I was thinking. I'm so sorry. I can't believe I got so angry. I'll apologize the next time I see them."

"And when do you think that will be? You can't honestly believe that they want to see you. Do you? There's no way you can think yesterday wasn't terrifying for them." I take a few steps closer to him, finding a wave of newfound anger like a momma bear protecting her cubs from a predator. "You fucking terrified them."

He begins, "I shouldn't have—"

"They don't want to see you. Coach is their friend, and they witnessed their father punch him in the face. Do you have any idea how devastated they are about that? I sure hope for your sake that he doesn't decide to sue you." I take a breath to calm myself. "You will not see the kids until they say it's all right. If you want to fight me on this, I'll see you in court. I have video proof that you are a cursing, angry man who was violent with the kids present. If you don't think I will fight you on this, try me. I am so fucking sick of your shit. I've taken it again and again for far too long, and it stops now."

I'm so furious that I'm shaking, but I am determined not to cry.

"Are you sure he's only the neighbour and not your boyfriend? He seemed to be a little too protective of you to just be the guy who lives next door."

The man is pushing his luck with me. If he doesn't stop, I'm going to kick him in the groin to hurt his brain. He thinks with his cock.

"First, who I date or don't date is none of your damn business. You lost the right to know what I do with my body when you had your fifth affair, and I finally wised up and divorced you. Second, if I were dating him, don't you think the kids would have told you by now? Oh wait, you don't listen to them when they talk, so how would you know?"

He raises his voice loud enough that my co-worker, Kelly, stops to watch to make sure I'll be all right.

"Don't fucking start that shit, Rayna! I asked a simple question, that's all. Are you fucking him or not?"

I take a few more steps toward him until I'm a mere foot away from him and then smirk. Hushed, so she can't hear me, I whisper, "He fucks me raw and I love it. I cum harder than I ever did with you. He enjoys thoroughly pleasuring me with his mouth, unlike you. When he touches me, it's all about me and my satisfaction, also unlike you. So, to answer your question; yes, that man fucks me hard with his thick cock, after I've kissed and licked every inch of his muscular body. And the best part is that you can't do anything to stop it. So, choke on that, asshole."

For a second, I wonder if I've pushed too far, but I will not back down or show weakness of any kind. I learned this intimidating expression from Coach. I don't even blink. I won't show him an ounce of weakness. He means nothing to me other than that he was the sperm donor that produced my children.

"Did you have to choose the biggest goddamn asshole in the city to fuck?" He runs his hand through his hair again. He looks defeated, and I revel in it. Rick adds, "I fucking nailed him, hard, and he barely budged. He's a tank. How do I compete with that?"

"Compete?" I question. He shrugs as if he thought he might get me back one day. "Did you honestly think I'd ever go back to you? I fucking divorced you! You're a shitty father, a lousy lover, a cheating asshole, and I never should have married you in the first place. The only nice thing you ever did for me was give me those amazing kids. And you're such a self-centered dick that you don't even appreciate them. One day, you'll wake up alone, accompanied by your mounting guilt. You'll tell the drunk guy on the barstool next to you that you're a father but haven't seen your kids in many years and don't even know what they look like anymore. How pathetic will that be? You need to get your shit together and start being their father and not just their biological sperm donor."

"How can I do that if you won't let me see them?" he snidely asks, revealing that massive chip on his shoulder.

"Prove that you're not an asshole, and I'll consider it."

"And how can I do that?"

I roll my eyes. "First, don't harass me at my job. Next, get rid of whatever bimbo you're dating and find a respectable woman, and treat her right. No more strippers or college-aged women. You're an adult. Grow the fuck up. That's all I'm asking. You aren't eighteen anymore, and you need to accept that. Now, I'm going inside and you're leaving. Call me when you get your shit together so we can discuss visitation, but you'd better give the kids some time to forgive you."

I walk inside to see all of my coworkers have been watching me through the giant plate glass window. They quickly pretend they were doing something other than listening in, but they aren't talented actors.

"Before anyone asks what's going on, I'll just say it now. He's being an asshole again and we'll leave it at that." I walk past them and head to the break room to put my purse in my locker.

Kelly slinks in behind me. "So, you're dating, huh?"

I look at her and shake my head. "Can we let this go, please?"

"All right, but if it morphs into something wonderful, will you let me stand in your wedding? Be sure to partner me with a hunky man. I'd prefer him to be single, please."

She walks as if she's a bride strutting down an aisle while humming the wedding march.

 *oach*

I'VE BEEN AT THE GYM, SITTING AT MY DESK FOR OVER AN HOUR, AND have gotten no work done. All I can think about is Rayna. Specifically, how she was with me last night. She made love to me, not just my body, but me: Simon. No woman has ever taken me down that rabbit hole. I wish I could go back.

Can we ever match that feeling again or will we forever try to get back there but never be able to? Was it simply a fluke? Why would she want to put herself in a position where she believes I'll only hurt her? I can't say that I blame her if she decides I'm not worth the risk and changes her mind.

I have to stop the what if's. Maybe I should get out from behind this desk and walk around, talk to some patrons. Few people are here this morning, but it's still early. Most people don't come to do their workouts until later in the day.

A beautiful redhead looks like she's about to stick her fingers where they might get pinched. What the fuck is she doing?

I jog over. "Don't put your fingers in there unless you'd like to get them broken."

She smiles shyly but doesn't say much other than a polite thank you. Her roaming eyes tell me all I need to know about her. She's a gym slut who works out for the sake of meeting men with muscles.

Best I leave her to her work out so she doesn't think I'm trying to hit on her. I'm definitely not interested. Normally, I would offer to stick around and help her, sort of feel her out. Then I'd bring her to my office to give her a more personal workout, but not on a morning like this after a night like that.

My cell phone vibrates in my pocket and I'm thrilled to have another distraction. I dig in and pull it out. My best friend, Tim, is calling.

"Hey, buddy. How's it going?"

He quickly replies in his typically smooth, deep voice, "Going good, Coach. You at the gym?"

"Of course I am, Tim. Where did you think I'd be?"

He chuckles. "I don't know, with your girlfriend maybe."

"Nah, she's at work and I'm here. So, did you call Renee?"

"Wow! She's fucking hot! Tell me why you aren't tapping that? Is there something wrong with her, like she has a tail or extra fingers? The picture she sent me only shows her face and shoulders, so I'm guessing the deformity is below the neckline. Seriously though, what's wrong with her?"

I'm amused by how excited he is. "You approve of her?"

"Yeah, but my question stands. Why don't you?"

As I make my way into the men's locker room to tidy up and make sure all is running smoothly, I answer. "Well, Tim, I've always liked her sister. A lot. I've been with sisters before, but this time it's different. I'm losing it, Tim! This woman has me all tied in knots and before you ask, I mean that metaphorically; I'd never let anyone bind me. I don't think I could ever submit to that degree." I chuckle. "Back to the subject at hand. I really like this woman."

Tim is silent. With the receiver next to my ear, I wait patiently for him to say something while I rearrange the dumbbells into their correct order, by weight. It irritates the shit out of me when people don't put things back in the proper spot.

He finally breaks the silence. "Sorry, I had to check the weather. I thought maybe Hell froze over and nobody told me. So, hard-ass Coach, who has ruined the hearts of many women—and their bodies, from time to time—is falling in love. How fucking romantic is that?" He laughs. "You know I'm only busting your balls. I'm happy that you've finally found a woman who'll put up with your shit and still want a somewhat healthy relationship with you."

"Thanks, but I've never ruined a woman's body, let's get that straight right now. I've used them until they're limp and bruised, but never ruined them beyond recovery." We both laugh. "So, when are you going out with her little sister?"

"This afternoon, actually. We're meeting for lunch, nothing special. Neither of us wanted to make it a big deal in case we don't click. We don't want to be stuck together for a whole evening of dinner and a promised stroll through the park or some bullshit like that, in case it doesn't feel right. We didn't want it to be too awkward if it's over before it starts. You know what I mean. Coffee and a sandwich are easy enough."

"She's really cute and kind of crazy, exactly how you like them. And she doesn't have extra fingers or a tail, that I know of, anyway. If I had met her before her sister, I'd probably have fucked her by now and tossed her aside, but I met Rayna first. I always thought of Renee as being off-limits to me. All this time I've lived next door, watching Renee strutting around, I couldn't understand why I never wanted to spin that little broad on my cock. Something kept telling me to leave her alone. Now I get it. Maybe she wasn't meant for me because Rayna was. Hey, can I ask you something and you'll keep it between us?"

"Yeah, unless it's really juicy, and then I'm putting it on a billboard." He laughs. "You know you can tell me anything and I wouldn't put it on a billboard. That's too expensive."

I scoff. "That's because you're a broke-ass mother fucker!" He protests. "Okay, last night, she made love to me and I absolutely loved it. Tell me the truth, am I turning into a pansy?" I ask, hoping he won't laugh hysterically at my soft-hearted query.

He takes a loud breath instead of teasing me about my insecurities in matters of the heart. "No, you're not a pansy. You're simply falling in love and that's outstanding, my friend. For the first time in your life, you found a woman who you consider being your equal."

"Nah, she's way better than I could ever hope to be. I don't know why she's so interested in a dick like me."

"It's got to be the sex. From what I keep hearing from the girls around the gym, and I quote, *'he's fucking amazing in the sack.'* Dude, the woman wants your pepperoni-sized pecker. Actually, I think she fell in love with your body before she got a glimpse of the wee fellow, but by then it was too late. I can't blame her for falling. It's a fine body you have, sir. Aside from the poor excuse for a cock, of course. I'm not into men but if I was..." He jokingly whistles a catcall. "Should I keep going with the tiny dick jokes, because I have plenty more where those came from."

"I'm so thankful you're not into men, but even if you were, a man's dick does nothing for me, even ones the size of elephant trunks, such as yours. I think I'll stick with Rayna for now, but I'll keep you in mind in case she smartens up and kicks me to the curb."

"Hey, I'll call you after the date to let you know how it went. I got to get going. My asshole fucking boss is glaring at me."

Tim's boss is his uncle and the two of them have a very close relationship. He raised Tim after his mother died when he was ten-years-old. His father was never in the picture because he died in a car wreck shortly after his mom became pregnant with him. His dad never even got to hold him. It's a sad story that Tim rarely talks about.

In a southern, teenage girl's voice, I reply, "Yeah, you'd better call me immediately after, girlfriend. I'll be waiting by the phone, crying into a tissue because you'll probably take too long to call me back and I can't wait to hear all the juicy details. Don't be surprised when I answer on the first ring."

He suggests, "Try the tissues with aloe, they are softer and won't scratch your pansy-like sensitive skin. Talk to you later, asshole!"

"Yeah, later."

After hanging up, I'm actually less confused about my feelings for Rayna. Tim's right. It's okay that I want her. Maybe I need her in my life.

As I'm exiting the men's locker room, I look over at the redhead who's bent at the waist with her legs together while she grabs her ankles. The chic is touching her forehead to her knees.

Damn!

Before Rayna, I would have been all over that tiny woman until I'd fucked her raw. I'd bet she's a pistol in the sack and a screamer. I like them loud.

She notices me walking up to her, watching her while she remains bent over. She waits until I'm within a few feet of her before quickly standing. She turns to look at me with a bullshit, disapproving expression.

I had better mind myself. I don't want to fall into her trap and play her game.

"Sorry, I didn't mean to stare. Can I give you a tip?" She nods cautiously while her eyes roam my chest, no doubt waiting for me to make a pass at her so that she can play the role of the innocent female being harassed by the big thug in a muscle shirt. "If you cross your feet, you'll get a better stretch. Try it."

She crosses her ankles and bends forward, not quite getting as close to her knee as she had been. When she stands, she's nodding.

"Thanks, I wouldn't have thought of that."

I'm sure she has and does it regularly.

"Yeah, no problem. We offer private coaching if you ever need any more tips. Whatever you're doing works well for you, but it's good to shake it up once in a while."

"Are you offering to coach me?" she asks in a high-pitched voice that would surely irritate me if she were screaming, even if she was coming on my dick at the time.

I'd bet it would be about as tolerable as nails on a chalkboard. I'm very turned off by her now. Something is seriously off with me.

"No, not by me. My schedule is already too full. Even if I could squeeze you in, I think you'll get a significant result if you talk to Carol or Lisa. They're very qualified." I glance around the room. "I think Lisa's already here, but Carol won't be in until this afternoon. I can go find Lisa and ask her to come and talk to you if you're interested. Otherwise, you're welcome to stop at the front desk before you leave to set up an appointment with either woman."

She's obviously disappointed. "I'll ask about it later at the desk. Thank you for the tip, though. I'm Reah." She puts her hand out to greet me, and I shake it politely.

"Call me Coach. It was nice to meet you, Reah."

She smiles flirtatiously as I walk away.

Through the mirror, I notice her watching me walk. She tilts her head and does a little dance like she's about to chase me, but she stops after only two steps, glancing around to make sure nobody saw her acting foolish. If Rayna wasn't in my life, I'd be all over that sexy little woman, but I'd have to put a piece of tape over her mouth just to get through it.

As soon as I set my cell phone on the desk, it vibrates. It's Rayna. The hairs stand up on the back of my neck. Something is very wrong. I can sense it.

I answer quickly. "Rayna? What's wrong?"

"Why do you assume something's wrong?" she asks.

"First off, you never call me. You text. Second, I got a terrible feeling when I saw your name. So, are you going to tell me what's wrong or will you make me guess?" I'm losing patience quickly.

"You are intuitive, I'll give you that," she says. Without meaning to, she nervously chuckles as though she's trying to lighten a tense situation. "Um, I don't want you to fly off the handle, but Rick was at my work when I got here this morning. I'm fairly sure I handled it, but it's Rick, so I can't be positive."

"That fucker has some balls!"

"Yeah, well, he's very jealous of you. I'm calling to give you a heads-up. He asked if I was fucking you. Initially, I refused to tell him, but he was getting out of control. The only way I could get him to shut up was to tell him that I was. It wasn't the right thing to do. I likely pissed him off even more. He's not acting right, and I don't know what's going on with him. I'm worried. If he confronts you, don't put your hands on him. He'll have you charged and then sue you. Try to have witnesses around you at all times."

"Don't worry about me. Do you think he'll confront the kids?" I ask, suddenly feeling like my chest is restricting as my rage builds. If he fucking hurts those kids, I swear I'll make that asshole suffer before I kill him. Nobody will ever find the body.

"I don't think so. Just to be safe, I called their school to let them know what's going on. They promised to keep them inside after school until I send someone to pick them up."

"Well, what good is that? He can send someone to get them, saying that you sent them," I say, getting a bit worried that she didn't think that through very well.

"Take a breath and calm down!" she hisses. "I'm not a fucking idiot! I have been raising these kids their entire lives and been dealing with their asshole father even longer. The school doesn't allow kids to leave with strangers who can't properly recite the secret sentence. Only she and I know it. If someone tries to pick the kids up, they will be sent to the office to talk to her before they even see the kids."

I crinkle my face and run my hand through my hair. "I'm sorry. I didn't mean to insinuate that you aren't capable of keeping them safe. That wasn't my intention. Those kids are very important to you. I want to protect them, and you. Try to give me a bit of a break, okay? I'm new to this."

"I get it." She takes a breath. "Rick gets jealous if he thinks there's someone in my life that isn't him. He's fine with having his tarts, but I can't have anyone." She sighs. "I just wanted to let you know that he might try to confront you. I don't think he knows where your gym is, or that you even own one, but I could be wrong. Just don't be alone. Promise me you won't put your hands on him."

"Rayna…" I hesitate because I don't want to promise that.

"Simon, promise me!"

She used my proper name. She must mean business.

"Fine, I promise I won't hit him. If he attacks me, I can't guarantee I won't break my promise to you. Rayna, don't worry about me. Keep yourself and those kids safe, okay? If you need me to pick them up at school, call me and I'll go. It's no problem. Besides, I like those little shits. They make me laugh."

"Thank you for the offer. If I get stuck at work and Renee won't be able to make it there on time, I'll call you. But I might call simply to hear your sexy voice in my ear."

"If you're alone, I can shut my office door and whisper in your ear while we touch ourselves."

She giggles. "Um, I'm not alone enough for that."

"Damn! Another time, then."

"Perhaps." I can tell she's smiling by her tone. "I have to get back to work. Maybe you can come over for dinner later, if you aren't busy."

"I'll have to get back to you on that, but it sounds good. Okay, call me if you need me for anything."

"I will. I'll talk to you after," she says before the line cuts out.

I'm furious at that bastard ex-husband of hers. That mother fucker confronted Rayna at her place of employment to ask her about me? Is he that much of a coward that he couldn't track me down to talk to me man to man? If I see that son-of-a-bitch, I hope I can keep my promise to Rayna. He'd better think twice before he hits me again. Before my phone hits the desk, it rings.

"Hello."

"Hey, asshole! How's it hanging?" It's Brett.

"Withered and to the left. I'm at work."

He laughs. "Yeah, I'm working, too."

Brett works as a programmer. I'm not sure what he does exactly, but he's a whiz on a computer. If mine fucks up, he's the guy I call.

After a lengthy silence, I ask, "So, what's up?"

"Um, not much. I was wondering how things are going with your neighbour. What's her name again?"

"Rayna. Good, I think."

"That's great. And the brats?"

I scoff. "They aren't brats. They're good kids."

"Have you given any thought to sharing her with your best friend?"

"No. Jeff didn't ask to share her, otherwise, maybe I would," I joke, using a fake name.

"And here I thought I was your best friend."

"Sorry, bud. And, ah…" I take a breath. "I think our days of sharing women are over."

"Fuck that! You'll come back to me. You always do. You'll play house for a while, get it out of your system. Then we'll fuck the hell out of her and be right back conquering bitches just like old times."

"No, we're done." I shake my head. "Even if I wanted to, Rayna would never go for it. She's not like that."

"You're fooling yourself. Give her the choice and she'll want to live out the dream of being with two hot guys at the same time, just like all the other broads."

"Not going to happen, bro." He groans. "I got to go. I'll call you next week and we'll have a beer. Okay?"

"If she gives you permission to go." He sucks air through his teeth. "All right, bye," he says and hangs up abruptly.

That fucking dude is weird, but I love him.

CHAPTER 18

 *ayna*

THE CHICKEN BREASTS HAVE COOKED AND SIMMER IN THE FETTUCINE sauce. The pot of boiling water meant for noodles sits on the stove, waiting for Coach to arrive. He texted earlier to let me know that he would for sure be dining with us.

I got out of work early so I would have time to pick up a loaf of Italian garlic bread and still be on time to pick up the kids at the sitter's. The bread has been cut and laid out on the baking tray, ready for toasting. The crispy salad rests in the refrigerator with homemade dressing in a cup beside it.

Everything is ready to go, and all we need is Coach. I thought he'd be here by now.

I pick up my phone to check if Coach sent a text and I didn't hear it vibrate. Nothing shows up on my alerts. My phone rings, startling me. It falls from my hand, but I try to grab it as it continues to drop. It flips through the air as I try to catch it, but each time I touch it, it changes direction. I finally decide to let it hit the floor. It has a protective case on it, anyway.

"Hello!" I answer quickly without checking to see who the caller is.

"Hey, it's me."

Coach's deep voice rings through the line. I hear several people talking in the background.

"Hi! What's with all the commotion?"

He clears his throat. "I was on my way home, but someone hit my truck. I'll tell you all about it later."

"Oh, shit! Are you okay?"

He must be if he's able to call me.

Coach chuckles. "Yeah, I'm fine. I didn't take the car to work today, thankfully, but the truck's a write-off. If you need to get dinner served, eat. I won't be there for maybe half an hour."

"I'm so glad that you're okay. We don't mind waiting for you. The kids had an after-school snack, so nobody will starve to death."

"I might be a bit off on the half-hour estimate. You should feed the kids. I'll come over after I get done here, but only if the offer still stands, of course." I can hear someone talking near him. His voice is faint as if he's moved the phone away from his mouth, but I can still hear what he says. "Yes, of course. I'd bet my house on that."

Unsure if he still has the phone to his ear, I say, "I should let you go. It sounds like someone needs to talk to you."

"Rayna, I have to let you go. I'll be there as soon as I can."

He hangs up abruptly. I'm left wondering why he wouldn't tell me the details of the accident over the phone. I do my best to let my worry roll off my shoulders. I turn up the burner on the stove to get the water to a roaring boil before slipping the pasta in, and then I turn up the oven temperature to prepare it for the toasting of the bread.

"Kim, come and set the table, please," I yell from the kitchen. Less than a minute later, she comes hopping into the room.

"It smells yummy, Mom," she tells me as she tries to look in the pot on the stove, but she's a bit too short.

I take her by her shoulders and pull her away from the stove. "Thank you. Get your nose out of there before you burn it."

"Is Coach still coming? I'm starving! Do we have to wait for him?" she asks, pouting while she drops her shoulders and slouches her spine to appear that much more pathetic.

"He just called. He'll be here in about half an hour. He got into a car accident on his way here." Her eyes immediately light up with concern. "Don't worry, he's not injured. By the time the noodles cook, he might even be here. If not, we'll start eating and he can catch up when he arrives."

"I'm happy he's okay. I like him. He can probably eat a lot of spaghetti. Will this be enough?" she asks, revealing her serious concern that he'll go hungry.

I am so proud of her for being such a caring young lady. After kissing the top of her head, I assure her. "Yes, baby. I'm sure we'll all have plenty to eat. There's salad as well, so don't forget to put out bowls."

"Do I have to eat salad? I hate salad!" she whines, her posture drooping once again. There was a fleeting proud moment.

"Yes, you do, and what's with the sourpuss attitude tonight?" I ask while stirring the water as I drop the stiff noodles into the pot.

"I'm not a sourpuss! I'm starving!" She bends her body in the same pathetic posture while plucking forks from the silverware drawer.

I take a cookie from the jar and hand it to her. "Here, eat this. It'll hold you until dinner is ready."

Kim pops up straight with a gleaming smile. She eats the cookie as she hums and sets the table. At least while she's humming, she isn't whining.

It doesn't take long for the noodles and bread to be ready. After draining the water from the pasta, I scoop the sauce into the pot of strained noodles. When I look at the clock, it's been forty-five minutes since he called. I head to the bathroom to pee and make sure my mascara hasn't smeared under my eyes from the blast of steaming water that enveloped my face when draining the noodles.

"Kids, come and eat."

As I walk into the kitchen, I see Coach standing with his head leaning over the pot, with a noodle looped over his finger as its being lifted to his open mouth. He sees me and freezes. His guilty grin has me cracking up.

He quickly slurps the noodle between his lips, making the evidence disappear, leaving a glob of sauce on his chin. Instead of wiping it off, he grabs me, and presses his lips to mine while he chuckles from behind closed lips. We both cackle like school children with sauce smeared all around our mouths.

Ken walks into the kitchen, followed by Kim. They look at us like we're the weirdest people in the world. We use our hands to wipe away the sauce as nonchalantly as possible. They need not know we were kissing again. We try to stop laughing, but neither of us can for a full minute.

"What's so funny?" Ken asks.

"I caught him sniping a noodle," I say, omitting the kissing part.

They aren't laughing, which makes us crack up again.

The kids and Coach sit down at the table while Kim asks him about the accident. I listen as I serve each plate with Fettuccine piled high with the chicken placed on top. The bread and salad also go onto the table, but I fill the kids' bowls before sitting down to the right of Coach. He doesn't tell us much information, just that he's okay, but his truck is irreparable. He jokes with Ken that he will not replace it and therefore, he'll be driving the muscle car all the time, wearing her out before he's old enough to take her for a spin.

"Rayna, this smells delicious. Thank you for inviting me," Coach says while looking at me as if he's about to lean in and plant another kiss.

I nod, then glance at the kids, hinting that he needs to keep his lips to himself. He picks up his fork and swirls it in the pile of noodles.

Coach goes back to his house shortly after we finish dinner, mentioning nothing else about the accident. I think there's more to the story. I figure he didn't want the kids to overhear anything gory in case he fibbed to Kim and someone really was injured.

The kids understand that accidents happen and sometimes people get hurt or killed, but he might not know how much he should tell them. I'm curious about the details. Thankfully, he's not injured.

The dreaded battle with my offspring to get them either in or out of the shower ensues. I cringe at the thought of what Ken might do in there. Why did Coach tell me that my son's likely jerking off? Eww!

The moment they're in bed and the house is quiet, I slip on my nightie and open the book I've been trying to get to for over a week, but never seem to have the time to read. These past few days, Coach has been a bit of a distraction; a fortunate one, but a distraction, nonetheless.

$\sim$

COACH

The second I walk into my house, I lift my pant-leg to see why my shin is so damn sore. I discover a bruise starting at the middle of my shin that runs along the bone almost to my knee. I rarely bruise, so the sight shocks me.

When the truck's door crushed in on me, I didn't feel any pain in my leg, or anywhere for that fact. My first concern was if I was bleeding anywhere. My second was how to get out of my truck so I could check on the people in the vehicle that struck me.

There was no way I could open the driver's door because it was smashed inward. I slid my ass onto the passenger seat but had to fight to get my legs to follow. There was no pain, just adrenaline. I was angry at how difficult it was getting my legs free.

When I finally got out, one woman and two men were telling me to sit on the grass and not to move, that I may have an injury and didn't know it because of shock. I was more concerned for the other driver, a woman, who was still sitting in her vehicle.

The second that I walked up to the driver's door, I knew this was no accident. Alissa was sitting behind the wheel, not saying a word. Her face was bleeding from her nose and mouth, but she could still sneer at me with pure hatred as she followed me with her eyes.

She hit me on purpose!

The cunt really is a crazy bitch. The fire department was quick to arrive and cut her out of the car while a paramedic gave me a quick once over and the cops took my initial statement. Thankfully, the police that showed up were the same ones who dragged her out of my house. They immediately assumed that she hit me on purpose but said that they couldn't put it in their official report until the investigators finished with their assessment.

I will do everything I can to ensure she's locked up for as long as possible and given a thorough mental evaluation. That bitch needs to wake up and realize that I am not a man to fuck with. I would have thought she already knew that from the intensity of our sadist/masochist type relationship.

She liked it when I was extremely rough with her. I could let my inner demon take charge, satiating his desire to hear her scream in pain and pleasure before satisfying his own physical needs. Most days, she left here with bruises about her body. She enjoyed pain, and I got off on finding novel ways to torture her.

The accident enraged me, but keeping my temper in check while I was at Rayna's was the true test. It wasn't easy, but I think I pulled it off. Maybe I should have been an actor. I would have made an excellent one.

Since I've been home, however, I still haven't been able to calm my anxiety, even after pounding on my heavy bag for nearly an hour. Even though I had gloves on, my knuckles ache. I'm exhausted but still furious. I need to see Rayna. It baffles me how that woman can calm the beast within me when no one ever could.

It's quarter to eleven. Maybe I shouldn't call her. She's probably in bed asleep. Dammit, why did I wait until it was so late to realize that I need her? If I text her and she's asleep, maybe she won't wake up to it, but if she is up, she'll text me back.

I want to hold her in my arms, that's all. Angry sex would be great, but as pissed off as I am, I might get carried away and scare the hell out of her. I vowed to myself a long time ago that I would never get aggressive with a woman when I wasn't completely in control of my emotions. I never want to take it too far.

The debate about whether to text or call her gives me even more anxiety. I don't want to seem overly needy. Maybe I should deal with my rage on my own and leave her out of it. I've been doing it my whole life, so why do I feel such an urgency to see her? And why can't I calm down on my own? How can she have such a powerful hold on me when we only recently started an intimate relationship?

RAYNA

I don't remember falling asleep, but I startle from chirping sounds, alerting me to a text message. The interruption of my sensual dream involving Coach is infuriating.

Coach was wearing black pants, unzipped, revealing the skin directly above the base of his beefy manhood. His hairless chest was bare, and his parted lips were lasciviously taunting me to taste them. My legs wrapped around his waist, and he carried me somewhere so he could ravish my body. My fingers weaved into his thick, inky hair. He was about to lay me down when my damn phone sang and woke me up.

I squint to help my bloodshot eyes focus on the small print. It's ten-thirty and my sister has texted me. She never texts this late. Something must be wrong.

Before reading the message, I dial her number and sit up with my heart pounding violently in my chest. It rings twice, each ring making my fear grow more and more dire.

"Hi, Rayna. Did I wake you when I sent that text?" she says with a spunkiness to her voice.

"What's wrong? You never text this late."

At least she isn't dead or in critical condition because it's not the cops or doctors calling.

She giggles. "Nothing, I'm fine! All is good, I promise." She snickers. "My date was this afternoon, remember? You asked me to call you to let you know how it went. So, I'm calling you now because he just left. I probably need not tell you that it went very, very well."

"He just left?" I roll over and read the time on the alarm clock, dropping the book onto the floor. It's barely past ten-thirty. "Did you take him to your apartment? Please tell me you didn't have sex with him on the first date."

"I did, indeed. And, let me tell you," she moans, "*dayum!*"

"How do you expect to have a long-lasting, loving relationship with someone when you have sex with them the very first time you meet? Come on, Renee. Why do you always do this?"

"Hey, you of all people have no right to give me shit about sex, dear sister. You were fucking your neighbour when you weren't dating. And you weren't having romantic sex either, so you can't criticize me."

"You aren't wrong. But, I've known Coach for three years, we've had many conversations, and gotten to know each other before we ever became intimate." I pause and then apologize. "Okay, I'm sorry for slut-shaming you."

I slide out of bed to pick up my book. I listen to her as I flip through the pages, trying to remember where I left off before I passed out, but quickly give up and toss it onto my nightstand.

She moans. "Oh, girl, he was so fucking good. It's not as if I've never had a man take complete control of a sexual situation before. I mean, I've been with dominant men, but not to the intensity of this guy. Tim was considerate but aggressive, if that makes any sense."

I have a wide, toothy grin because I completely understand what she means. Coach is rough and forceful while being caring and considerate. It's easy for me to lose myself in the sex we have. Being submissive has its advantages, but the harsher, more painful spankings are a bit too much sometimes. I'll happily take a burning ass if it gets him so excited that he pleasures me better than anyone ever has. It's a fair trade-off.

"It makes total sense. So, are you two going to keep seeing each other?"

"Oh, yeah! He's coming to pick me up tomorrow and take me to dinner. Who knows what will happen after that," she says with a seductive undertone.

"I'm happy to hear it. Maybe Coach is a good matchmaker."

She giggles. "Absolutely! I will have to give him a hug when I see him."

I scoff, wondering if she'll try to hump his leg when she hugs him. After shedding the image, I yawn.

"I'm happy for you, but I want to go back to sleep. Now that I know you aren't dead or dying, I can rest comfortably."

"Oh, shit, sorry! I didn't think you'd be asleep already," she says, apologetically.

"Normally, I'm not, but I started reading and then woke up to your text message. I didn't even know I was sleeping."

"Those are the best sleeps ever. That book must be boring; don't pass it on to me. Maybe the four of us can have dinner or something," she suggests.

I yawn again as I stretch, dropping my free arm to my lap as if someone paralyzed it. "That would be great. I'd like to meet him. Okay, I'm hanging up."

"Goodnight, sis. I love you!" she tells me.

"I love you, too," I say, hanging up and flopping over until my face is pressing into the duvet. I slowly turn my head and groan.

My bladder urges me to relieve it. With another groan, I drag myself to my feet and go to the bathroom. While I'm peeing, my mind drifts to how good it felt to have Coach's hot skin against mine. He brushed tears from my cheeks. I fell in love with him last night. How the hell can I already love him when we've only just recently become a couple?

CHAPTER 19

 *ayna*

As soon as I'm snuggled under my cool sheets, my phone sings its tune once again. The brightness of the screen burns my tired eyes, even through my closed lids.

Dammit, Renee!

I spin the knob on my lamp, and the room comes to life. The message is from Coach. It says that he's standing at my patio doors. Why is he in my backyard? I text back to inform him that I don't want to have sex tonight.

His reply begs me to come to the door. I groan but decide to go to the kitchen to see what is so important that it can't wait until tomorrow.

I'm rewarded with a cool breeze in my face when I slide the glass door open. Coach is standing shirtless in the shadows cast from a cloud-covered moon. He looks mountainous and intimidating.

"Come in but be quiet; the kids are asleep." He looks distraught. "What's wrong?"

He says nothing. Instead, he wraps his enormous arms around me, pulling me against his hard body. The chill of the night wears heavy on his skin. He lifts me off my feet and holds me as I dangle in his arms. My slipper falls, landing to the floor with a soft thud. Coach sets me down while looking toward the hallway where one of my kids would stand had the noise come from that direction.

"My slipper fell off." I step back into it. "Are you okay?"

"It was no accident," he confesses, adding confusion to my sleep-deprived mind.

"The accident with your truck?" I ask, and he nods. "Why do you say that?"

"Alissa purposely drove into my truck. I would have told you earlier, but the kids were here, and I didn't want them to hear. This is a complicated adult problem."

"Holy shit!" I say louder than I should have. Coach shushes me while I cover my mouth with my hand after the fact. I whisper, "Come with me."

I take his hand and lead him down the hallway, sneaking him into my room. After closing my door and locking it, I walk to my bed and lift the covers, sliding under them. Coach stands at the end, silently looking at it.

"What's the matter?" I ask. "Get in, it's chilly."

He looks at me strangely. "This is your bed. You lay your body down and sleep here."

"So?" I thought he'd be excited to get into my bed and lay with me, maybe even make love to me again.

"Sorry, I never thought I'd be getting into your bed. This is your sanctuary and you're inviting me into it."

"You brought me to *your* bed, so why is my bed any different?" I ask, not understanding his train of thought. Has he been drinking? That would explain a lot.

"No, it's different. I wasn't taking you to my bed for any other purpose than to give you pleasure while getting my rocks off in the process. I wouldn't be getting into your bed for that purpose."

He shakes his head while aggressively running his hand through his hair. "Never mind, I'm being stupid. Forget I said anything."

I pull the covers back on the other side of the bed and coax him in. "It's just a bed and it'll keep us warm while you tell me what's on your mind."

Coach slides in and lies on his back while looking around the room. He turns his face to me. His sunken eyes reveal how heavily his thoughts have been plaguing him. Something is going on, and I want to help him.

"Okay, talk to me," I whisper in the darkness.

He rolls his body to face me and his eyes scan my face. "You are so beautiful. Why do you want to be with me? Most women think I'm a fucking nightmare."

I smile. "You are not a nightmare. Yes, you have an aggressive side, but that's only one piece of your puzzle. There's more to you than that. I can see your marshmallow interior you fight so hard to suppress. You are caring, protective, gentle and you make me laugh."

"Last night, when you came downstairs, what we did..." He clears his throat; his eyes leave mine. "...that was new."

I hear the confusion behind his confession.

"We made love to each other," I whisper while brushing his cheek with my fingertips. "Have you never made love before?"

He presses my palm to his lips and then rests it on his cheek, covering it with his hand. "No, I don't do that. I can't stop thinking about it."

"Me either. It's been a very long time since I've felt close to anyone. For me, it was like we were joined and moving as one person. I could feel you; all of you. It terrified me and fulfilled me at the same time. That, I had never experienced before yesterday."

"Not even with that asshole when times were good?" he asks, referring to my ex-husband.

"Not even with him," I reply.

Coach closes his eyes for several seconds. "I think I love you, really love you."

I gasp and then swallow hard. "I think I love you, too. It isn't possible, is it? Can people fall in love this quickly?"

"We've known each other for three years. It's not like we were strangers before all of this." He looks confused, as if he's suffering with a moral dilemma. "I don't know what to do now. Tell me what I'm supposed to do. I never wanted to love anyone, but I did. I want you to be mine, and I want you to want me, too." His eyes squeeze shut as if he's riddled with anguish. "What happens if I let you in and you change your mind after I've given you everything that I am?" He rushes his words. "I might literally die."

"Feel it for what it is, I guess. I don't know if this will last or not because our worlds are so different. I can't have any more children so if that's what you need in your life," I shake my head, "I can't give that to you. Do you want to know my fears?"

He nods. "Of course."

"You're ten years younger than me and in a different stage of your life, so why would you even want to be with me? I fear that I'll give you my damaged heart and you'll soon tire of my boring life and then crush my heart into a million pieces. I won't survive it breaking again. So I'm just as terrified as you are."

Silence fills the room while we stare into one another's eyes, losing ourselves to the dimness of the room as it seems to darken around us. I see only his scared eyes as they reflect what little light exists around us.

I lean toward him and press my lips to his. I want him inside of me, not only physically but in my mind as well. I want his soul to dance with mine in the silence that surrounds us.

Coach rolls onto his back, pulling me with him. I straddle his waist. Our kiss is tender. Our bodies press together, parting for only a second so he can slide my nightie over my head, rendering me naked.

He sits up and his lips press to my nipple, suckling gently and rolling it between his thin lips. Every nerve in my breast awakens as the small nub stiffens just for him. My hands cradle his head to my bosom. A quiet moan slips away from him as he shifts to my other breast. His hands cup my butt, lowering me onto his erection.

He slips into me easily and completely, filling more than just my body. My heart feels as though it is swelling to twice its size. We gaze into one another's eyes and drown in each other's love.

His chest is warm against my breasts. With our lips pressed together, his tongue dances with mine. His firm grip pulls at my hips, directing me how to rock with patience. As he lies back, he takes me with him.

I'll revel in this moment forever.

Coach coddles my head in his palm as we kiss. Our bodies and souls have melted into one being. Oh, yes, he suits me like nobody ever has. Was he built for me and me for him? I'm losing control and I'm not afraid. I want him with me like this, always.

His body, my body, our body.

Our lips separate slowly, parting as we move together in a sensual, slow dance. His hips rock to meet my sway. My sensitive clit brushes along his smooth, heated skin. His grip urges me to ride him faster. His steamy mouth sucks at my nipple, shooting pulses of electricity straight to my clitoris, and pushing my mind and body toward orgasm.

I am consumed in the delirium of ecstasy.

My hips buck against him. I hold his face to my breast as his lips tug at my sensitive nipple with superb skill. I can't hold a thought as my mind clouds over.

The room disappears around us as I float into the glorious nothingness of ecstasy.

Euphoria.

He covers my mouth, preventing me from crying out as my body stiffens in his arms. My vagina pulses, pushes, and squeezes his swollen manhood as his hips hump with increasing intensity.

I jolt forward as a heavy breath bursts forth. My muscles ease, and I release his head to rest back on the pillow.

His eyes remain closed but they're weighted with genuine

pain; not physical pain but emotional. I have to save him from this inner turmoil. This is too intimate for him. He's falling too deep, and the fear of letting his heart go is excruciating. I have to pull him back.

"Take me as hard as you need to," I whisper.

His eyes widen and look into mine as if to thank me for seeing his struggle.

Coach immediately flips me off and onto my back beside him. He pops up onto his knees, quickly lifting and flipping me over so I'm on my hands and knees. He weaves his fingers in my hair, pulling my head back as he rams his throbbing prick deep inside my drenched pussy.

COACH

I fuck her hard, the way I like to, and don't let up. With all the strength I can muster, I hump into her, hoping to take myself away from the unfamiliar and overwhelming feeling in my chest. It's too much.

If she hadn't told me at that moment to take her how I need to, I might have died, or worse, I might have cried. What is this powerful feeling I'm having? Is this what love feels like? Why the fuck does it hurt so magnificently?

Her hair is silky in my hand, and I want to pull so hard that some will come out, like I usually do when I want to bury my emotions. But I can't do that to her, not to my Rayna. If she were anyone else, she'd be writhing in pain, and I'd be listening for the inevitable safe word to fill the room.

With my free hand, I hold her hip, pulling her back against me as I thrust forward, forcing my throbbing cock much deeper into her. I hammer her so ferociously that my legs spasm. Good, I welcome the pain. The severe bruise on my calf presses into the bed, and I revel in it. Physical strain makes my orgasms so much more sensational.

Rayna moans with each thrust and increasingly grows louder. Normally, I would enjoy her screams, but I have to think of the kids. I release her hair and reach around her face to cover her mouth. I pull her back until her head presses against my chest. I need to keep her cries muffled.

She grabs my thick forearm with a firm grip; her nails press against my skin. I continue to hold her face while she sucks in what little air she can through her nostrils. I know she's not getting all the air she desires, but I also know she'll cum harder this way. I have to keep her quiet, at all costs.

Her body stiffens, and her cunt squeezes my cock so forcefully I can't push into her. I muffle her scream under my hand, but it's still too loud. I pinch her nose with my thumb and forefinger, blocking any airflow and any sound from spilling into the silence of her bedroom.

She doesn't seem to care as her body rides the high of her climax, but quickly enough, she's frantically pulling at my hand. I hold for a few more seconds and then lift, but not completely. I can't let her face go in case she cries out and I need to shut her up quickly.

Rayna begins moaning so quietly it amazes me how well she's able to contain herself. She must have realized that I was only trying to keep her quiet, and she doesn't want me to muzzle her again.

I flip her onto her back and finally yank my pajama bottoms from around my ankles. I hurry to push my prick into her as quickly as I can; I don't want to be apart from her if I can at all help it.

My knees spread for better leverage. I lift Rayna's legs, folding her until her knees nearly touch her shoulders. I rest my fists into the mattress beside her. Her shins rest on either side of my neck.

There's nothing sexier than Rayna's orgasmic expressions, and I want to watch her lose herself.

I slam hard only once and hold steady, leaving my cock buried inside of her. Our eyes meet, and she smiles ever so slightly. I wink and then reveal my scary, aggressive expression. She bites her bottom lip and winks.

Excellent! She wants to feel my rage.

She's fucking *mine!*

I shift my weight forward, positioning her so my cock will hit her g-spot every time I pound into her. I pull back and ram, hard.

Her mouth opens, and her eyes close momentarily and then meet mine once again. She smiles.

I'm going to own her pleasure.

With my hand on her throat, I apply light pressure, not enough to hurt her, but it won't be comfortable. It's more of an intimidation than anything.

Without mercy, I fuck into her, straining every single muscle in my body.

Rayna's face is tense, but her bottom jaw is loosely ajar. I force each breath from her body with every merciless impact against her g-spot.

Holy fuck!

She's so goddamn beautiful.

Her legs force against me as her body stiffens and her delicious pussy pulsates around my prick, urging me closer to my own climax.

Her face shifts from a pained sexual expression to one of utter elation. But the calmness lasts for only a quick moment before the pained expression gradually returns and she's brought into another climax.

She cries out too loudly this time, before I can move my hand onto her mouth. She sucks her lips inward, between her teeth, biting down to force her lips closed, thus holding back the sounds of her ecstasy.

I'm relentless, not easing up for even one second. Not until I bury the pain in my heart. It doesn't ache anymore, other than from its rapid pounding.

If I can get her to cum one more time, I'll let myself go.

Fuck, I want to cum!

This is too fucking perfect and I can't take much more. My muscles burn from the incredible spasms. My back aches worse than from some of my toughest workouts. It won't stop me, and I refuse to ease up.

Rayna has to cum again.

Just one more, baby!

My inner demon wants me to set him free, but he'll be too rough with her. Tonight isn't about pain for pleasure, it's about both of us taking what we need to get us through the night. One day, she'll discover the demonic sadist inside me, but not tonight.

She slips her hand between her thighs. Her fingertips bump my cock as she masturbates her clitoris.

The touch has me clenching my teeth. I fucking want to cum, but not yet.

Her nails dig into my triceps, breaking the skin. I fucking love it!

"Hurt me, baby, I can take it. Cum for me."

Her eyes meet mine before rolling back as she loses herself in another powerful, cock-strangling orgasm.

That's it, I can't take any more. I let myself fall into the terrific absence of all mental focus. I give into the intensity of orgasm pleasure. I am lost in the darkness of my mind.

With a muffled grunt, my body jerks as hot seed shoots deep inside of her twitching body. My mind is in the distant abyss for what seems like an eternity. Oh, how glorious it all is. But it's only fleeting. I gasp and open my eyes to see Rayna admiring my face.

No longer able to contain my weight, I fall onto the bed beside her. My chest heaves and my lungs burn along with the rest of my body. With my arms at rest atop my forehead, I continually roll my ankles, hoping to relieve the spasms in my calves that are so painfully irritating.

Rayna rolls over and rests her head on my heaving chest. Her arm drapes over my abdomen, fingertips brushing along my ribs. I hold each breath as I struggle to slow my heart rate so her head stops bouncing on top of my chest. I place my hand on her upper back and caress her soft skin, but my arm feels like it weighs a thousand pounds, so I rest it against her with my hand spanning her back.

We lay like this, in the darkness that only midnight carries. Neither one of us speaks.

Time passes, I'm not sure how much, but I should leave before we fall asleep. Waking up with the faces of two confused kids looking at my naked body as I lay next to their nude mother would be a nightmare to explain.

"Babe," I whisper, "I should go." I kiss the top of her head as I brush a few strands of hair from her sweat-stained face.

Rayna groans. "I know. Will I see you tomorrow?"

"Of course! I live right next door and you're welcome over any time."

I sit up and search for my pants, finding them jammed against the footboard. After slipping them back on, I find her nightie and hand it to her. She pulls it over her head, covering the most beautiful body I've ever had the pleasure of laying my hands on. I kneel on the bed, leaning over to kiss her lips so lightly that we barely touch. Even still, I feel the electricity between us. Our eyes meet and hold each other's gaze.

"Thank you for this. I needed to know it wasn't a fluke." My words cut through the silence.

"What did you think was a fluke?" she asks, her voice sounding angelic.

"How I felt the last time we were together. I wasn't sure if it was real or something I imagined."

"And?" she asks while tickling my beard hairs with her delicate fingertips.

I turn my face to kiss her palm. "It was no fluke. How I feel about you is real. I know that now."

Rayna smiles at me and then leans up to press her lips to mine. Our breath mixes as we taste each other one last time. I breathe her in.

Goddamn, I love this woman!

"I have to go before I don't," I whisper and then pull away from her with incredible regret. I cannot submit to it.

Be a considerate man and leave.

I can't stay the night in her arms no matter how much I want to.

Walk away, now.

I peek out the bedroom door before walking out, in case a child is roaming the hall. I hear the slapping of her barefooted steps on the hardwood floor as we quietly make our way down the hall. I turn around and take her in my arms, scooping her up as if I had just married her and I'm preparing to carry her over the threshold. I cannot resist kissing her passionately one more time before I leave.

I set her onto her pretty little feet and then walk out the front door, closing it behind me. I wait until I hear the lock click before my feet chill in the cool, damp grass in the dead of night.

I welcome my bed by flopping chest-down, pulling a pillow under my head and sliding my hands beneath it to plump it up. My wet feet hang off the side of the mattress. I'm simply too tired to bother with covers. It isn't long before I drift off into a pleasant dream that doesn't seem to last long enough, as it's interrupted by the screech of my alarm.

It's morning, already? Damn!

CHAPTER 20

MY ALARM SCREAMS, PIERCING INTO ONE OF THE HAPPIEST DREAMS I've had in a very long time.

In it, I was much older than I am now. That part of the dream wasn't the best part, obviously. I was holding a beautiful newborn. What made it so fantastic was looking up from that perfect, sleeping baby to see Coach looking down at it with a wide, proud smile and a tear in his eye.

He referred to me as Grandma. The title shocked me and I looked toward the hospital bed. On it sat a beautiful woman, and she was smiling at me. I knew the woman was the grown-up version of Kim. She was a new mom.

I woke before I could find out the name of the baby or ask Kim how old she was. Was my dream a prediction for the future? I don't even know if it was a boy or girl. The blanket didn't give it away since it was the colour of burnt sienna. Most babies come wrapped in either pink or blue, but not in this dream.

Will Coach still be with me that far into the future? Is that what the point of the dream was, and not that Kim had a baby?

My thoughts drift to last night and how loving his eyes were in the beginning. They were all I could see. We had the best of both worlds last night; we made love, and then he took control of me, as he does so astonishingly well.

I could do that every day for the rest of my life. If he had spent the night with me, my body pressed against his, it would have been that much better.

All the kids know is that he just asked me to go on a first date. I can't suddenly spring it on them that he's spending the night. That wouldn't leave a very good impression. Throwing them straight into him sleeping in my bed might be a bit too hard to explain to their young, impressionable minds. I don't want them thinking their mom is easy, even if I am.

I jolt, realizing that I drifted off to sleep. Oh shit! Damn! After shooting out of bed, I knock on the kids' doors and yell that they have to get up and hurry because we overslept. I grab some quick sugar-filled breakfast treats and add them to the sandwich and fruit cup in their lunches, along with a juice box.

As I quickly make my way down the hall to my room, I remind them to hurry. Neither kid has opened their door and I doubt they're even out of bed, so I bang on their doors before flinging them open.

"Get up! Get up! Get *up!*"

I dress, put my hair in a ponytail and brush my teeth. They're whining that they hate it when I sleep in because they don't like rushing. Do they not realize how much harder it is for me to get everyone ready while they mope? I have to keep reminding them to do the things they would normally do in their unrushed routines.

Kim keeps asking if we can call in late so we don't have to rush, or better yet tell them we're all sick and aren't going in today. She wants to have a fun day. I remind her that I need to go to work so that we can eat, have electricity, and not spend the coming winter living in a cardboard box in an alley somewhere. She shuts up but sports an angry, pouty face.

Ken isn't voicing his frustration, but the angry stomping of every step is a constant reminder that I fucked up. I'm going to have to let Coach know that he shouldn't keep me up late anymore. It's obvious that I can't handle sleep deprivation.

We scoot out the door in record time, despite my slow-moving children. Verbally, I announce that I love them dearly. I considered driving off and leaving them to fend for themselves. Somehow, I get them to school before the bell rings and make it to work on time. Perhaps leaving later allows time for the congested traffic to clear.

I'm pleased with how well I pulled it all together and got us where we needed to be and on time. Now to get through the day without falling asleep or accidentally cracking someone's tooth because I'm too drowsy to pay attention.

When I get a break between patients, I text Coach to ask him if he slept in today like we did. He informs me that he woke at the right time, and so far, it's life as usual at the gym. How can he be so wide awake when I feel like I'm dragging a hundred pounds of sand in my ass cheeks? Seriously, I can't get myself in gear. I feel like I'm moving at a sloth's speed.

I also inform him that I forgot my lunch in the fridge because I was too worried about making sure the kids had something to eat in the car on the way to school. If I'd had something to eat in the car as well, I probably wouldn't be so nauseous now. He thinks it's funny and asks how long it will be before I get to sit down and eat. I tell him that I still have more than an hour to suffer through and that I've been munching on the sugar-free suckers we set out for the kids for after they've had their teeth looked at by the doctor.

This last half-hour before lunch seemed like it was four hours long, but I made it. I finish an older woman's cleaning and then make my notes. I inform the doctor about my concerns before heading to the break room to get some money from my locker. I'm going to hit up the sub shop across the street.

As I walk into the main lobby, I see Coach standing at the counter talking to Lara. I watch to see if they're flirting, but quickly realize that he isn't. However, the receptionist is biting her top lip and tucking her hair behind her ears. She's smitten. He keeps looking away from her, only meeting eyes with her now and then.

She stops talking. He glances at her, noticing that she's looking past him. He follows her line of sight and spots me walking toward them.

"What are you doing here?" I ask as he leans in to kiss my cheek.

"You said you forgot your lunch, so I'm here to feed you. Is it okay that I'm here?"

"Yes! How did you know it was time for my lunch break?"

"You told me in your text," he replies with a grin.

"Oh, that's right! So, you want to feed me? I was thinking about grabbing a sub. It's quick and somewhat healthy. Do you want to go there?" I ask, but he doesn't reply. He takes my hand in his and leads me through the glass doorway while my coworkers watch, some women sighing heavily.

"I had a better idea," he tells me as we walk through the parking lot, hand in hand. He takes me to a truck I don't recognize. "Welcome to my loaner truck. The insurance company is letting me use it until they can find a replacement for mine."

"Hmm, I like it. It looks bigger than yours was."

"Yeah, it's a full box. Mine was a short box."

Instead of bringing me to the passenger's side, he continues leading me toward the bed of the truck. He drops the tailgate. I see a few bags and two bottles of iced tea. He spreads out a red and black plaid blanket over the truck bed and part of the tailgate before lifting me up by my waist and sitting me on it.

"Scoot back a bit, babe."

I do as he suggests and watch him climb up and sit across

from me as our backs rest against the wheel wells. He hands me one bag and nods, signalling for me to open it. Inside is a plastic container with slabs of baked chicken placed on top of a Cobb salad. I smile and thank him. He's so focused on opening his salad that he only winks at me and gets back to wrestling with his container.

We eat in the warmth of the early afternoon sun, enjoying the heat of the summer before the day wears on and it gets too steamy to sit outside. I tilt my face up toward the sun and close my eyes, loving how its rays feel on my skin. The coolness of fall will soon be upon us. The air is already crisp during the night, and the grass is cold and dewy in the early morning hours.

"You take my breath away," he whispers, interrupting the silence of my mind.

I tilt my face back down and then open my eyes to look at him. He's watching me while uncapping his bottle. I shake my head and snicker, lightly kicking his shin.

"Cut it out!"

His wince is strangely wimpier than it should be for such a big, tough guy. It's not like I booted him, it was only a tap with the toe of my shoe.

After clearing his throat, he asks, "Cut what out?"

"Flirting with me. You'll get me in trouble because I might decide to make out with you right here in the parking lot, in the back of this loaner pickup. I'm sure there's a country song about that." I take a breath. "Has anyone ever told you that you're a terrible influence?"

"Once or twice," he replies while rubbing his shin. He flashes me a sexy grin that makes my tummy flutter. "So, you want to make out with me in the back of the pickup truck? I'll have to take you to a deserted road so we can do that." He grins wickedly. "Sound like fun?"

I laugh and shake my head. "What am I going to do with you?"

"You can do anything you want with me."

"Anything?"

"Yes, anything. Tell me, Miss Baxter, what twisted fantasies roll around inside that exquisite head of yours?"

I think for a moment, but I'm not able to come up with a witty response. "I'll have to get back to you on that."

"Take your time, there's no rush. I plan to be around for a while," he assures me, and strangely enough, I believe him.

His phone rings. He looks at me while he answers it, putting it on speaker. "Hi, Brett. You're on speaker. What's up?"

"Speaker, huh? Who's listening in?"

"Rayna's with me."

I cut in to introduce myself. "Hi, Brett."

"So, you're the special one?" He groans.

"Um…" I mutter, not sure what to say in response.

Coach changes the subject. "Why did you call?"

Brett, sounding upset, says, "To ask if you want to go for lunch."

"Sorry, I'm having lunch with Rayna as we speak."

He grunts again. What is it with this guy?

Coach adds, "I thought we said we'd have a beer next week."

"Yeah, all right." He takes a breath, then sharply says, "Rayna, I'm sure I'll meet you one day. Can't wait to wrap my arms around you." He snickers. "Okay, I got to go."

He abruptly hangs up and Coach looks like he has something on his mind, but I can't read him.

"He's a strange guy."

He chuckles. "You don't know the half of it, and you don't want to. So, fantasies…" He takes a breath. "Where were we with that?"

My cheeks burn hot. "Okay, for instance, if I said I always dreamed of doing a man with a strap-on, would you let me do that to you?"

The expression he wears tells me that he isn't thrilled with that idea. "If it's one of your fantasies, I'll do it simply to please you."

"But, do you think it might be something you'd like to experiment with?"

"I don't follow," he replies, taking a gulp of his iced tea.

I blush. "Well, have you ever thought about how it would feel to have something in your butt? It feels better than you might think. Is it a fantasy you might have but are too dominant to admit?"

He shakes his head. "No, I've never wanted to do it. I don't think I'd care to be fucked in the ass, but if it's something you want to do, Rayna," he takes a breath, "I'll do it for you. You only have to ask."

"Hmm, I'll let you know," I tell him after taking a long drink from my bottle and emptying it.

Coach grimaces when he gazes off in the distance at the people walking across the far end of the parking lot. "Rayna, I want to take you out on our first date tonight, if you'd be so kind as to accept the invitation. Not only you, though. I want the kids to come, too. I'm not only going to be in your life, I'll be in theirs as well. I think it would be a fun way to assure them that they mean a lot to me, too. Does that sound weird? Am I stepping into territory that you'd like me to avoid?"

I lean forward and touch his cheek, meeting eyes with him. "I think it's wonderful, and they'll appreciate you including them." I scoot myself closer to him so I can tenderly kiss his slim lips.

His hand slides up my bare arm, heating my skin instantly. To keep things innocent, I sit back in my place before I lose myself and behave like a lovesick teenager, making out in my boyfriend's truck. I giggle at the thought, but he doesn't seem to notice.

"When do you have to go back to work?" he asks while putting our empty containers back in the bags.

After glancing at my watch, I pout. "Soon, like now."

He nods, shuffling himself out of the truck with no difficulty. I struggle to slide my butt along the blanket to reach the edge. He takes my hand as I slip off the tailgate onto my feet, and then he slams it closed.

I walk toward the front of the truck; him following closely behind. He grabs my hand and spins me around, planting his lips onto mine, his other hand weaves through my hair. I place my hands on his firm waist, remembering how solid he felt as his body slammed into mine last night, granting me so much pleasure. I never wanted it to end.

Oh, shit!

I pull my face away from his and look around quickly to see if anyone is watching us. I have to do my best to be professional. Kissing him is definitely not going to help me maintain my coworkers' perceptions of me as being prim and proper. If patients are watching, they could complain.

I put my finger up and purse my lips, silently telling him to keep his distance. He cracks up laughing. I smile at him before making my way back inside the office.

Lara looks at me and waves a come-hither finger, urging me to her. Reluctantly, I see what she wants, even though I know it's to discuss my relationship with Coach. I like Lara because she's hilarious and always seems happy with life.

"Who was that beautiful beast, and why is he with you and not me?" She rocks back and forth with her hands overlapping her heart. "I want one, too. Wherever did you find him, and can I place my order?" She rattles off questions while jokingly pouting.

I chuckle at her silliness. "He's actually my neighbour. I've known him for quite a while, but we only recently started seeing each other. Sorry, but I don't have any other available neighbours that look like him. If I did though…" I walk away with my hands raised and my shoulders shrugging.

During my thirty-minute lunch break, Lara told each person in the office that I left with a hulking gentleman caller. Everyone had questions about him and a few spat idle threats of physical injury should he break my heart. This is out of character for me; dating. Maybe they thought I'd go through life single.

 *oach*

THE GYM IS LIVENING UP WITH THE REGULAR AFTERNOON CROWD AS well as a few newbies I don't recognize. As I walk through the free-weight section, I hear a tiny voice behind me call my name. I stop and turn, seeing that same flexible redhead that can put her forehead on her knees without much difficulty.

What's her name again? Shit! Rita, Reah, Renna… Dammit!

"Hi, how are you?" I ask, only to be polite. I have other things I need to get busy with, so I'm hoping she'll make this quick.

She stands with her arms clasped behind her back so that her overly enhanced breasts jut out, drawing my eyes. It's instinctual to look. I glance away, hoping she didn't notice, but I'm sure she did. It was her intention. She hasn't taken her eyes off me.

"I'm good, but I could use some help on that machine over there. Maybe you can show me how to work my Gluteus Maximus." She turns so I can see her perfectly round ass as she caresses it with her hands. "I think it's getting flabby. What do you think?"

"I think you look fine. How about I get Carol to help you?" I reply while purposely being passive with her.

"No!" she blurts out, spinning around while moving closer to me. With a flirty attitude, she adds, "I want you."

My body wants me to fuck this bitch like there's no tomorrow, but the constant interrupting thoughts of Rayna would likely make my cock go soft, anyway. Besides, risking losing Rayna for a slutty little tart would be the dumbest thing I ever did, and that would be quite an accomplishment. I've done a lot of stupid things in my life, but losing Rayna for a piece of ass would top it all.

"Look, lady, I'm in a relationship with someone so I'm not interested in your ass in the way you're hoping I am. A few months ago, I would have fucked you raw, but this is today, so I'll get Carol to help you if you need advise on your workout."

She crosses her arms over her chest and purses her lips. "Are you sure? I wouldn't tell anyone."

"Oh, I'm sure. Unless there's anything else, I really have to get back to work," I say as I stare at her with angry eyes.

I take advantage of her humiliation, making her squirm nervously under my gaze. This kind of shit makes my dick hard. Intimidating people like her and knocking them off their pedestal excites me every time. I should walk away before the swelling of my cock alerts people. She'll never leave me alone if she thinks she's the reason for my arousal. It's not her working me up; it's the control of the situation that's doing it for me.

After she huffs away, I turn and rush back to my office, shutting the door behind me. I reach in my pants and grab my swelling prick while still leaning against the door, preventing anybody from easily walking in. I squeeze firmly and stroke, slowly at first but working up to a more rapid pace. I pound my rock-hard meat while my pants slide down my legs. This isn't the first time I've jacked off in my office.

People walk past. The thought that they are mere inches away is a hell of a turn-on. With my free hand, I pull my balls down and away from my body until it hurts. I fist my cock as fast as my arm will jerk. Rayna's face pops into my mind. I see her lips slightly part, eyes squeezed shut, exactly how she looks as her orgasm sweeps through her body.

That's all I need to finish me. I cum quickly, cupping my hand to catch my jizz as my cock spits. After a few seconds, I bend to collect my pants and slide them up my legs. I use tissues to clean the mess off of my palm, and they stick to me and shred as I wipe. After a few calming breaths, I open my door and make my way to the men's room. I need to wash my hands before anyone greets me with a handshake.

Tim is drying his hands with a paper towel when I walk in. I quickly rush to the urinal and whip out my cock, not giving him enough time to put his hand up to shake mine. It's difficult to relax enough to pee right after I've spilled my seed. I want him to think that I had to empty my bladder so urgently that I couldn't take the time to greet him properly.

"Did you wait a little too long?" he asks while laughing. "I thought only children do that."

I chuckle. "So it would seem. Now I can't piss."

"Do you want me to run the water?" he teases.

"Would you mind?" I reply, looking at him over my shoulder.

The anticipation of the hypersensitivity from the initial urine flow might be why my body holds back. I groan when my urine flows and the tingles at the head of my prick tickle from the inside. Shit! I love and hate that sensation, but the soothing flow to follow is worth the initial discomfort. My sigh of relief has Tim laughing again.

He says, "Carol said you brought lunch to Rayna today. It sounds like you two are getting along very well."

Carol is one of our trainers.

"We are. Everything seems so much easier when I'm with her. She has this way of calming my inner demon like nobody ever has." I put my dick away and head to the sink to wash my hands. "I told her that I love her."

"Fuck, man! Wow!" He's shocked at my confession. "I never thought you'd say that to a woman. A man, sure; but not a woman. No way." He snickers, and I frown. "I'm proud of you, Coach. So, what did she say to that?"

I pull a paper towel from the dispenser. "She reciprocated." My smile is wide. "I'm happy, really fucking happy."

Tim launches at me, pulling me into a hearty hug and lifting me off the ground, which is quite the feat. Just then, a tall, thin man in his early forties struts through the door, stopping dead in his tracks. His eyes lock on the two muscular men hugging in the men's room. I know what's going through his mind.

We separate instantly. I quickly explain, "It's not what you think. I have a girlfriend."

Simultaneously, Tim says, "No, not what you think. He has a girlfriend, and he loves her. It was a congratulations hug."

I add, "Yeah, we're not gay. I mean, it's okay to be gay. We're just… We're not gay. Definitely not into men."

Tim adds, "Yeah, ah, no dicks for us. I mean, we have dicks, nice dicks, but we don't want other dicks. Gay is good, but, uh, not for us."

The guy snickers at our awkward overcompensation, which has us looking guilty. The thin man walks over to the urinal in a full-blown laugh. Not to seem like we're waiting to see his penis, we hurry out of the bathroom. That was an awkward situation.

"I'm happy for you, Coach," Tim says, patting me on the back as we walk toward my office.

I sit behind my desk and Tim parks his ass in the chair tucked in the corner opposite me. There's a pile of letters in front of me, so I sort through them.

"How did it go with Renee?" I ask.

His smile and waving eyebrow tell the complete story. I'll bet they had sex. If I know her as well as I think I do, she gave it up on their first meeting. Tim isn't a guy who would pass up a good fuck from a hot piece of ass like Renee.

"She is sexy, smart, funny and damn that woman is a flexible little thing."

"You fucked her?" I ask, my expression and shoulder shrug letting him know that I'm not surprised.

"No, it wasn't like that. I mean, we had sex, but she's not like the typical one-night stands I've had. I want to see her again. I like Renee. Okay, yeah, she's extremely sexual, but I like that in a woman." He pauses while I pop an eyebrow. "Dude, I took my clothes off, too, so you could say that I'm just as slutty. I have always wondered why it's okay for a man but not a woman. Shit, if I had a pussy and could cum as often as women do, I'd be naked and fucking everything that walked. And so would you. Don't deny it."

"I completely agree. I'd be fucking anything I could stuff inside myself. I don't think we men can handle coming that often, though. We'd probably drop from a heart attack after three in a row."

He smiles and jokes, "But what a way to go. Am I right?"

I agree wholeheartedly.

"I'm glad you two hit it off. If Renee makes you happy, go for it. She is definitely fine, and she is smart, I suppose. Even though we haven't had an in-depth conversation, I know that she doesn't drool on herself and her shoes are tied, so I assume she has some level of intelligence."

"You don't seem to like her very much," he concludes.

I shrug, wondering if I should tell him that she hit on me and then tried to cover it up with a lie. "I don't hate her. She's not for me, that's all."

"All right, enough about Renee and me." He leans on the desk. "Earlier, you said that Rayna calms your inner demon. Are you talking about your untameable, controlling, sexually sadistic inner demon?"

I chuckle. "Yes, that inner demon."

He furrows his brow. "But, you enjoy setting him free. If you're suppressing that desire, eventually it's going to show its ugly face. What are you going to do then?"

I look at him, knowing he's right. "Rayna is fine with what I've introduced her to so far. I haven't exposed her to the worst of my demon. I don't know how she'll respond. She's not as experienced as the women I'm usually with. I may have to keep that side of me secluded. I can't think about that right now."

"You need to talk to her. If you think you can go through life not expressing yourself sexually in the way you need to, it'll backfire on you one day. Find a way to let her know, Coach. You don't have to take my advice, but I highly recommend that you at least think about it."

Tim is right. No matter how much I try to tell myself I can keep my demon at bay, I know I'm only fooling myself. If she isn't accepting or willing to play, will she leave me? I would not expect her to stay if she's not into BDSM. I can be downright terrifying sometimes.

What if I end up cheating on her with a woman who accepts my freakiness? Fuck, I don't want to think about how much that would hurt Rayna.

"All right, you've said your piece, now get the fuck out of here. I have work to do, and you need to get your flabby ass working out. Hey, avoid that redheaded gym slut in the pink shorts."

Tim is definitely not flabby and knows I'm only joking. He's probably in better shape than I am. If he gets anywhere near the redhead, she'll likely pounce on him and start humping his leg. If I didn't have so much work to do, I'd lean out the door to watch her reaction to Tim as he struts past her. Rayna has a powerful hold on my heart, otherwise, I'd get freaky with that redheaded slut.

He leans out the door to see who I'm talking about. His whistle tells me that he sees her. "You walked away from that? I'm proud of you, man. You must really want to make it work with Rayna. All right, I'm out," he says, walking out and pulling the door shut behind him.

CHAPTER 22

THE WORKDAY IS OVER, THANKFULLY. I THOUGHT IT WOULD BE A horrible day because of how rushed it started. Since my lunch break, things have been looking up. It was sweet of Coach to bring me food and eat with me. I wonder where he wants to take us on our first date?

All day, I haven't been able to get him out of my forethought. It doesn't help that my coworkers have seen the surveillance video from the lobby. Thanks to Lara, who was more than happy to show the video, they won't stop commenting on him. I've had several requests for Coach to set them up on dates with his gym buddies.

My workday is finally over. As I'm about to walk out, Dr. Jessik calls out to me. "Rayna, can I have a word?"

"Sure," I say, and spin around as he approaches. I was so close to being out the door.

"I heard that you're dating now."

I nod. "Yes, I suppose I am."

He shuffles his feet nervously. "I didn't think you wanted to date anyone. It's been so long since you've had a man in your life. I thought you weren't interested in dating. If I had known, I would have asked you out a few years ago."

His words shock me. I had no idea he was interested. To be honest, I thought he was gay. I've never seen him with a woman. Nobody has.

"Oh," I reply, not knowing what to say to the man. This is awkward. And why do I suddenly feel guilty? I shouldn't. "I wasn't looking. He's my neighbour and I've known him for several years. It just happened."

"Well, I thought you'd come around one day and let me know that you were ready."

What? "I didn't know you were interested in me."

He smiles while his cheeks flush. "I have been ever since you started working here. You didn't know?"

"Um, no. You never told me, so how would I know?" I shrug. "Please, tell me you haven't been waiting for me to come around. You have dated other women, right?"

He shakes his head. "I've been waiting for the right time to ask you out. When you started here, you were married, and then you were going through your divorce. After that, you seemed shut down and uninterested. I asked you to go to the theatre with me about a year ago. But you said that you couldn't because you wouldn't be able to find a sitter with such short notice. You mentioned that you never go out anymore and didn't really care to, anyway. I figured you weren't ready to date anyone."

I'm taken back by what he's saying. He hardly ever converses with me. He seems terribly shy.

"Um, oh, okay," I say while looking at him with wide eyes and a gaping mouth. I quickly close my jaw and look away. "I'm sorry, Dr. Jessik. I had no idea."

"That's okay. I want you to know that if it doesn't work out with this man, I'm here. I'm a nice guy, Rayna, and I love kids. I have money, a house, and a secure job, so I'm no shlump."

I smile, wishing this conversation would end. I have no interest in him. He's too old for me and way too shy.

"You are a gracious man, but—"

"Okay, enjoy the rest of your day."

He quickly scurries away with his head down, hands tucked into his lab coat pockets.

"You, too!" I say, probably louder than I should have.

As I open the second glass door, the heat of the day engulfs me. I instantly feel the heaviness of the humidity. Yuck!

The heat rising from the asphalt is scorching. I can feel it on the soles of my feet as it bleeds through my running shoes. The days are unbearably hot, but the nights are cooling down considerably, so I know summer is nearing its end.

The interior of the car is sweltering after baking in the sun all day. Even the cloth seats are hot, heating my skin through my pants. I turn the key and the car comes to life. Super-heated air blasts from the vents, slapping me in the face, and taking my breath away. I immediately turn it down and push the buttons to lower all four windows. It's so damn hot in here. I feel nauseous.

It wasn't nearly this steamy earlier when I ate lunch outside with Coach. If it had been, we wouldn't have sat in the sun very long. I put my hand in front of the vent and feel cool air seeping from behind the slats. I spin the knob to turn it on high. I'm hoping to relieve some of this nausea. Now I push all four buttons to raise the windows, shrouding myself behind the tinted glass, setting me apart from the noisy world around me.

Before I can slip the shifter into reverse, the backdoor whips open and someone hops in. I spin around but don't recognize the man, a pudgy, white man about fifty years old, with a clean-shaven face. He's wearing sunglasses, a baseball hat, a long-sleeved shirt and blue jeans. All I can think about in my panicked state is that it's way too hot for that shirt. It's strange how I'm wondering why he didn't pass out in this heat today, but I'm not fearing for my life.

I'm immediately stunned when he points a gun in my face and

calmly says, "If you scream, I will shoot you. If you try to jump out or crash the car, I will shoot you. If you alert the cops, I will shoot you. Please don't doubt that I will. I don't know you, so I have no problem killing you. Drive, now."

My head is spinning, and I can't breathe. My face feels odd, like my nose and mouth have lost all feeling. Stars twinkle in my eyes and my hands and feet are numb.

Shit, I'm passing out! I try to take deep breaths but it's useless.

The world around me fades to black.

~

Coach

My phone rings and the caller ID tells me it's an unknown number. I answer with an angry tone, thinking it's likely a telemarketer. "Yeah?"

"Um, Coach?" The female voice sounds familiar. "It's me, Renee. Have you heard from Rayna today?"

Oh, I suppose I forgot to put her number in my phone when Rayna gave it to me. I never thought she'd call me. I passed it on to Tim and deleted that message from Rayna. Maybe I should add it to my contacts in case Rayna ever needs me to call her.

"Yeah, I had lunch with her. Why?"

She hesitates, spiking my curiosity. Finally, she replies, "The school called, asking me to pick up the kids because Rayna didn't show. When did you see her last and did she say she had to go shopping or something?"

The hairs all over my body stand on end. Something is very wrong. Rayna would never forget to pick the kids up from school. My heart pounds. I'm out of my chair with my keys in hand, ready to run out the door.

I have to find her.

"We ate lunch together, then I watched her walk back into the office at around one o'clock. I left and came back to the gym. She mentioned nothing about going anywhere after work, but I didn't ask if she had plans. I know she wouldn't be late for the kids because she's worried about the fucking asshole picking them up." I take a calming breath. "This isn't like her. Something's wrong. Did you get the kids?"

"I'm on my way to the school now. I don't know what to do," she says, sounding like she's about to go into full-on panic mode. Her sobs and snotty-nosed snorts begin.

As I'm rushing through the gym, alerting people who were minding their own business, I speak louder than I should. "First, calm the fuck down! Those kids need not know anything's wrong. You can't worry them about this. She probably went somewhere, lost track of the time, or her car broke down and her phone died. Who knows? I'm going to go look for her. Keep me posted."

I hang up and I'm out the door without a word to anyone. After pushing the auto dial number to Rayna's cell, I hear her voice asking me to leave a message. I'm instantly extremely worried and ready to kill someone if they hurt her. If that mother fucker ex-husband of hers has taken her, I swear on my life I'll kill that cocksucker slowly and painfully.

My truck is hot inside, but I don't care at the moment. I rev it up and drop the windows before taking off like a bat out of hell. I'll head to her place of work; it's the last place I saw her.

When I arrive, her car isn't in the lot and nothing looks out of place. I try the door, but it's locked. I bang on the glass, but nobody comes.

I get back in the truck and drive the most likely route she would have taken to the school, but her car is nowhere. Where the fuck is she? I call her phone again, getting the same voice message. Fuck! I search for Renee's number. She answers on the first ring, her voice soft like she's whispering.

"Did you find her?"

"No. I take it you didn't either."

"No, I'm at the grocery store she usually shops at, but I don't see her car in the lot. I was hoping she was here and stuck in a cash-out line."

I can hear the kids in the backseat of Renee's car. They're laughing and talking. It's a jovial sound. They have no idea that their mother could be going through hell right now. I'm thankful that Renee is keeping her concerns to herself.

"I'm going to call the cops. Something's wrong. I can feel it. I'd rather be overzealous than let this go on any longer."

She whispers, "Coach, I'm scared."

"Yeah, me, too." I swallow the lump in my throat. "Don't worry, we'll find her. You keep the kids oblivious for as long as possible. Hopefully, we find her before they know any different."

"I'm doing the best I can. We will find her." Her tone isn't convincing.

"Where does her stupid fucking ex live? I'm going to go talk to that asshole."

"No, don't! He'll only push you to hit him. You're too worked up. Call the cops and tell them about Rick and what he's been doing to cause trouble lately. Let them know that she has a recent restraining order against him. They'll question him. You stay away. Promise me," she hisses, sounding very much like her sister.

"Fine! I'm going to keep driving around. Did you ask the kids if she had something to do after work?"

"I already asked them. They said no," she reveals.

"Maybe you should go back to her place. I'll send the cops there to talk to you and the kids."

I can hear the tears welling up in her voice again. "I've driven the whole parking lot. She's not at the store. I'll take the kids home. Call me and let me know what the cops tell you."

"Renee, you need to tell the kids something. If the cops will show up, they might get freaked out. If you explain as calmly as possible, they'll be better off finding out from you."

"Good idea. I'll talk to them as soon as we get home," she whispers.

"Yeah, okay. If the cops tell me that they won't look into

Rayna's disappearance, I'll call you. Otherwise, expect them soon. If I find her, I'll call you right away," I promise.

My rental truck zooms down side streets. If there was a lot of traffic or an accident, she would try to avoid it, but her car is nowhere. Where the fuck is she?

The lump in my throat finally bursts and a flood of tears spill. I wipe them away, but the dam has broken.

I scream as loud as I can, "RAYNA!"

CHAPTER 23

THE LIGHT IS BLINDINGLY BRIGHT, EVEN THROUGH MY EYELIDS. I struggle to open them, blinking several times to clear away the fog my brain is waking from.

What happened? Why can't I move?

Fear yanks me awake. I'm hogtied, lying on my belly in the backseat of my car. A wad of cloth is in my mouth with something tied around my head to keep me from spitting it out. I want to scream, yet worry that the person who did this to me might try to hurt me.

What the hell does he want with me? He can't ransom me. I'm living paycheck to paycheck and don't have rich relatives.

Tears stream down my cheeks and drip onto the seat where my daughter usually sits. They expected me to pick them up at school. What time is it? Did my sister pick them up? If the principal calls Renee, she'll know something's wrong. She'll call the police, I'm sure of it. I'm never unaccounted for.

Oh, please, let them find me before this man hurts or kills me.

The car comes to a complete stop inside a structure. The man shuts off the engine and gets out, slamming the driver's door harder than required to ensure it closes. I'm expecting him to open the door I'm facing so that he can pull me out and do whatever it is he's going to do with me.

Please don't rape me!

But he doesn't open the door. The anticipation tortures my mind.

I remain facedown inside the car for what seems like ten minutes or more. It is sweltering in here, making it difficult to breathe. My lungs don't want to inhale the scorching air, and my throat is so dry that I keep coughing.

He must not be coming back. I fight against my restraints, trying to figure out how to untie myself, but the knot isn't anywhere my fingers can reach. I'm so frustrated that I scream, not making much sound through the cloth. If he doesn't take me out of this car soon, I will die from the heat. But, do I really want him to take me out? What will happen if he does?

The door whips open. A welcoming blast of cooler air rushes over me, giving me an instant sense of relief, even though fear runs rampant through me. The man grabs my arms and pulls me toward him. I didn't get a clear view of him when he got in my car, but enough to know that I didn't recognize him.

Now he's wearing a mask. That's a good thing, right? If I can't see his facial features, I won't be able to identify him in court. That means he's likely to set me free after he's done doing whatever it is he has in mind.

Please don't rape me!

He pulls me out of the car, dropping me onto my face and chest. Pain explodes from my cheekbone outward, radiating through my entire face. It feels like my eye has popped out of its socket. I scream louder than I think I ever have in my life, but it's muffled.

White stars fill my vision. Am I going to pass out again? No, not now!

A sudden force to my chest knocks the wind out of me, bringing clarity front and center. I can't breathe. The overwhelming pain is nothing like I've ever felt before.

Oh, fuck! Someone, please, help me!

Stars circle my mind again. No! I don't want to pass out. I struggle with all of my strength to gasp for what little air my lungs can manage without moving my ribs. The stars are clearing. I continue to force myself to breathe even though it's excruciatingly painful.

He lifts me by the rope's knot that binds my hands and feet together. The strain on my wrists, ankles, shoulders, and back is unbearable. I hope he puts me down before my skin tears or my joints dislocate.

I'm screaming as loud as I can manage, begging for him to put me down.

He drops me again, but this time, I'm prepared and hold my head up as best I can and tightened my stomach muscle so the blow won't knock the air out of me or further injure my ribs. Pain stabs at my ribs, instantly burning the moment my chest touches the cement floor. The swelling in my cheek impedes my vision. The pressure on that side of my face is intense. That nostril will not stop leaking.

It fucking hurts so bad!

The man is talking on the phone, but I can't make out everything he's saying; only a few words here and there. I hear him say: he has me, nobody saw, and he'll wait; but nothing else.

The pavement is cooler than the sweltering air, so I rest my throbbing cheek against it. It's going to swell my eye completely shut if I don't get some ice on it. I highly doubt he'd be kind enough to get that for me. I'm almost positive my cheekbone is broken.

"Don't worry, pretty girl, it'll all be over soon enough."

The man speaks as he cuts the rope between my feet and hands. My legs flop down to the cement with a thud, and my hands remain tied but now rest against my lower back. It's not great, but better than being hogtied.

I try to talk but obviously can't with the gag in my mouth. He can hear me trying, though. Maybe he'll remove the cloth. I would like that very much. It's getting harder to breathe because the one nostril is swelling. Panic sets in, so I scream, fearing that I'll suffocate, and the man won't even be aware of it.

The kidnapper flips me onto my back, pinning my arms underneath of me. He groans as he unties the mouth gag, removing the wad of cloth. I gasp but don't scream. The last thing I want is for him to put it back in. Besides, screaming would only make my throat and ribs hurt worse, as if that were even possible.

"Not a fucking word, bitch," he states while pressing on my swollen cheek with one of his sausage-like fingers. He's trying to get me to scream from the agony, but I fight hard not to give him that satisfaction. When he takes his finger off my face, he laughs. "Strong-willed, are you?"

The man tosses the mouth gag over my eyes and then walks away, leaving me lying on the cool cement. He's blocked me from looking around to see where I am, not that I recognized what little I've seen. I can hear him on the phone again but he's further away from me than before, so all I can hear are mumbles. I shake my head, hoping the makeshift blindfold will fall off, but I'm not that lucky.

Fortune seems to have left me today.

I silently plead to Renee and Coach to find me. I listen intently, hoping my subconscious hears one of them whispering to me, but I hear nothing except the kidnapper's mumbles. It's silly of me to think I could telepathically hear their responses. I'm desperate and holding onto whatever I think might get me through this ordeal.

I close my eyes and talk to my children, hoping somehow they will feel my love.

Kim, if this man kills me, please don't fear people. Not everyone is bad. Most people are honourable. Don't be angry.

Ken, don't seek revenge. Live your life to the fullest and be as happy as you can. Remember the pleasant times and don't focus on the last horrific moments of my life.

Kids, know that I love you with all of my being and I will be there to watch you pass through all the stages in your life.

Renee, raise my kids well, as I would have. I know you can do this; I have faith in you. That's why I put you as guardian in my will. I love you so much, little sister. I forgive you for hurting me. Find love and hang onto it.

Coach, find peace in your life. Don't be sad that you couldn't help me. This is beyond your abilities and it's okay not to be in control of everything. If I know you at all, you're driving around looking for me. I hope you'll be successful in your quest, but I don't think you'll find me here, wherever here is. If you can hear me, I'm inside some enclosure, like a garage or barn. I can't hear anything outside, like cars or people. Please find me before he kills me! In case you don't, you need to let this go. Don't hold the pain inside of you, it'll only weigh you down. I want you to find someone to love.

I pray that all of them can hear my thoughts or feel the warmth and love I'm sending them. If they can sense me thinking about them, it might bring them some comfort. I know they'll be searching for me and that gives me hope. It's unlikely they'll find me, but I can't think like that.

I shake my head back and forth, determined to knock the material from my eyes, but it only shifts, exposing my aching eye. It's not enough for me to see anything since it has swollen almost completely shut. The pain on that side of my face is outrageous, and the shaking only made it worse.

"Hey, bitch, I'm going to sit you in a chair. Can you behave?"

"I won't fight you." I speak with the softest, sweetest voice I can manage with my throat being so painfully dry. If he thinks I'm no threat, he might not further injure me.

He's much bigger than me; definitely not a bodybuilder, just big. He lifts me by my armpits and sits me on a solid steel chair. It squeaks on the floor when it slides against the concrete as my butt plops on it. He immediately unties my wrists but refastens them to the chair legs so my arms hang straight down by my sides. I'm relieved to have the blood flowing.

The mask is off, so I take this opportunity to look at the surroundings as he finishes tying me to the chair. It's an old wood barn. The mass amount of cobwebs on the ceiling and the level of rot on the unfinished walls give away its age. From what I can tell, the building is about large enough to fit three cars deep and three wide. It's a good-sized barn.

I take notice of all the huge toolboxes and how the tools are displayed neatly on the pegboard above the workbench. The floor is stained from the spills of oil and other automotive liquids. Some stains are fresh, but most have faded over time with newer stains overlapping them. A car is at the back of the garage directly in front of mine. It's covered with a light blue tarp, only revealing an extra-wide rear tire, like one that would be on a quarter-mile car.

The man says, "Don't say a fucking word and I won't have to shut you up. I'm sure you don't want a broken jaw to match that cheek. Do you understand?"

I nod and watch him as he shuffles his heavy boots to a workbench. His stride isn't as smooth as it should be. He has a limp from a possible wound on his left leg. He favours it. His ragged hair is black and hanging from the bottom of the baseball hat. I could use this information to help find him if he lets me go free after he's done doing whatever it is he has planned.

When he's close to me, I can smell his body odour, and it isn't pleasant. It's obvious he doesn't use deodorant, and if he does, he needs to change brands. I smell the oils and other chemicals in the barn as well. There's no doubt in my mind that this is a mechanic's garage.

I try to focus on what I can hear, but there's only silence. I must be in the county where the traffic rarely comes. If I hadn't been unconscious, I might know how long we were in the car.

~

COACH

Where the fuck is she? I'm so goddamn enraged. My heart feels like it's breaking over and over. Every time I imagine someone hurting my beautiful Rayna, an overwhelming, eerie sense of dread rips me apart.

Why would someone take her? Why?

I pull into my driveway and park, quickly sprinting across the lawn to Rayna's house. Three cops are standing inside the doorway. All of them have their hands on their guns with their free hands held up, telling me to stop.

I plant my feet outside of the door. I'm shaking from the rage that's been flooding through my veins since I got Renee's first call. I hear her instruct them to let me in, so they step aside and nod apologetically as I pass. They're only doing their job, so I won't give them grief.

She's sitting at the kitchen table with Ken in a chair next to her. Kim is on her lap, curled up against her chest with tears streaming down her pretty little face. She's trying to comfort the girl, but that's hard to do while she's just as upset.

"Renee, any word?" I ask, trying to keep my voice calm.

I don't want to frighten the kids any more than they already are. If they sense the violent rage that's eating me alive inside, it won't help to ease their worry. I know Rayna would want me to make the situation seem as light as possible for their benefit.

"Nothing," she replies. "The cops talked to Rick, and he has a solid alibi. I still think he has something to do with this, but they claim he doesn't."

I move closer to Ken and then rub his head like I always do. He gazes up at me with a sombre expression. Seeing the concern on his boyish face hurts me more than my own dread. I despise how desperate he looks right now.

The policeman looks up from his notepad, finally taking notice of me standing beside him. He immediately takes a step back while crinkling his brow and giving me the hairy-eye.

"Can you tell me where you were today?" he asks accusingly.

"Officer, I was working at my gym. I met Rayna at her workplace to bring her lunch because she mentioned that she had forgotten to bring one. I thought it'd be a pleasant surprise, and it was. We ate in the back of my rental truck in the parking lot of her workplace. I went straight back to the gym after she went back in the office. I was at the gym until Renee called to inform me that something was wrong."

"And where have you been for the past hour?" he asks while writing notes in his little pad.

"Driving all the routes she might have taken if she were going to the school to pick up the kids. I drove all over the place. Her car has vanished."

I stop talking because I have to fight off the urge to scream or burst into tears. That would not be helpful for the kids or Renee. Besides, if I throw a fit, that might get me arrested.

Renee and the kids look at me. They had faith I would find her. I tried but failed them.

Ken is still looking at me with desperation in his eyes. A child should never wear that expression. I have to turn away. I calmly walk to the bathroom and shut the door, barely making it inside before the tears burst forth. If those kids see me crying, they might fear that their mother is gone forever.

They have to believe that I'm staying positive. They see me as strong and dependable, so that's what I'm going to be for them. Rayna would expect that from me.

I pee while I'm in here and then wash my hands, and splash icy water on my pink cheeks and puffy, reddened eyes. After taking several deep breaths to gain strength, I slowly open the door with my shoulders back and my sorrow on the back burner.

Ken is standing in the hallway across from the bathroom, taking me off my guard completely.

"Is Mom going to be okay?" he whispers. His eyes plead for me to promise that she will.

I try to look stoic, not letting him see even a shred of fear. "The cops will find her. She'll be okay. Keep the faith, little man. We have to stay positive."

"How do you know? People kill other people all the time. The kidnapper could be killing her right now."

He erupts in tears. I see him as an inconsolable little boy, no longer like the pubescent teenager who seems older than his age. I take him in my arms and hug him tightly to my chest, running my fingers through his hair like I've seen Rayna do a hundred times before.

"Take a deep breath and keep telling yourself she's going to be okay. Your mom is smarter than anyone I've ever met, so if she can safely get away, she will. You know she'll do everything she can to get back to you and your sister."

"I know," he whispers, but sobbing gasps follow his gently spoken words.

I guide him into the bathroom and close the door. After looking in two different cabinets, I finally find a washcloth. I wet it with cool water and wring it out. I drop to one knee and wipe the tears from his cheeks. He takes the rag from me and finishes the job, holding the cool cloth to his eyes, hoping to reduce their heat.

"Can I ask you to do something that's going to be really hard?" I ask. He nods. "Your sister will look up to you for strength because you're her older brother. Little sisters do that. I need you to show her that you believe Mom's coming home, even if you have doubts. When Kim isn't around, you can cry like crazy to let it out." I lower my voice. "Don't tell anyone, but I cried, too; not because I think she's not coming home, but because I couldn't find her. I feel helpless, probably the same way you do. Just because I'm a grownup doesn't mean I have all the solutions. Can you be strong for your aunt and your little sister?"

He takes the washcloth from his eyes and swallows hard. "I

think so." His little chest gasps again from his heavy sobs. He takes deep breaths, hoping to stop his tears. It helps.

"I know you're hurting. We are all in pain right now. Can I tell you something else?" Ken nods again. "I love your mom. I want to marry her one day. I told her that, too, and she said that she loves me back. I probably wasn't supposed to tell you that, come to think of it. Anyway, you know she has to come home so she can marry me. If you approve, of course."

He smiles through his sadness. "I'd like that. I won't tell her you told me."

"You should never keep secrets from your mom. They seem to know everything, anyway." We both nod. "Okay, take another deep breath and let it out slowly. Are you ready to go back into the kitchen?"

"Yes, I can do this. I'll try to be strong for them," he replies.

"I don't expect you to be a superhero, just do the best you can, okay?" I suggest, ruffling his hair until he swats my hand away with a quick chuckle. "Bud, nobody will fault you for crying, okay?"

We no sooner get to the kitchen when the detective is called out of the room by another officer. Whatever she's whispering to him looks important. The officer shows the detective something on her phone. I hear him ask her to send it to him but can't make out the next thing he says.

He enters the kitchen with his phone in his hand. After it vibrates, he holds it up in front of Renee's face and asks her if she recognizes the person on the screen. She looks closer, sliding her fingers along the screen to enlarge the image. She shakes her head. Kim and Ken also look, but neither knows who it is.

"Coach, is it?" the detective asks. I nod. "Do you recognize this man?"

He shows me the picture on the phone. It's not a clear picture so the guy could be anyone. I have no idea who he is. He's a big-framed man, built like someone who's been doing physical labour his whole life, but not a bodybuilder.

"Wait a minute; I saw him when Rayna and I were eating lunch. He was walking across the parking lot. It was strange that he didn't seem to be in any hurry to get anywhere and he was dressed too warmly to be taking a leisurely stroll. He kept looking back at us, but I thought nothing of it. I mean, how often do you see two people eating lunch in the bed of a pickup in a commercial parking lot? I thought he was curious." I whisper, "Is that him?"

If it is, I'll never forgive myself for not watching him more closely to see what he was up to.

The officer nudges me toward the cupboards so we can whisper without risking the kids listening in.

"It looks that way. The video shows him getting into the backseat of her car. He's there for about a minute, then gets out, opens the driver's door, pushes her over, and he gets behind the wheel. He drives away. Officers reviewed the traffic camera recordings to see if they could track where the car went. We could follow the car for three blocks, but that's where the city cameras end. We believe he was taking her out of the city. We have cars doing an area search for them, but..." His words break off.

"I'm going looking. Where was the last place her car was seen?"

"You can sit yourself down right here and let us do our job. We're looking for her, don't think we're not. You're too upset to be out driving around. Stay here and take care of her family."

I nod, but I'm angry as fuck. I don't want to be here, helplessly waiting, accomplishing nothing while something horrible could happen to Rayna. But, when I look around the table, the kids and Renee are all looking at me with so much fear on their faces that I know I have to stay for a little while and be strong for them.

Dammit! Fuck. Rayna, where are you?

CHAPTER 24

 *ayna*

IT FEELS LIKE I'VE BEEN SITTING HERE FOR HOURS. MY STOMACH rumbles from hunger, and my throat is so dry it feels like I'm breathing shards of glass. That's not the worst of it. I really have to pee.

"Sir," I call out, trying not to be too loud, which might anger him. I definitely don't want that.

He looks at me. "What do you want?"

"I have to use the bathroom," I reply, dreading that he will either let me go, watch me the entire time, and possibly rape me while my pants are down. Or, he won't let me go and I'll have to relieve myself in my pants. I'd much rather option two if option one will lead to rape.

"What do you want me to do about it?" he hisses.

"Do you have a toilet I can use? Please, it's becoming urgent."

"No, piss your pants if you have to go that badly."

I do not want to piss myself. It would be even more

humiliating than I care to experience, especially if these will be my last moments alive. I'd rather not die wearing soiled pants.

"Please, sir?"

"I told you no. You aren't moving from that chair."

"I beg of you," I whisper, barely loud enough for him to hear me. Maybe he'll have a strand of compassion for me. I don't know how I can expect that of my abusive kidnapper. But he's a human being, so there has to be some shred of decency in him.

He stands and rushes toward me. Oh shit! I think I pissed him off. As he approaches, my fear is warranted when his foot lifts, slamming into my upper chest. The pain from my ribs is ghastly. Me and the chair flip backward, my head cracking on the pavement.

I can't breathe in, and my brain is spinning. Oh shit, I'm blacking out again!

Darkness takes over.

~

COACH

It's been about seven hours since someone took Rayna. Nobody can tell us anything new. My hope of finding her is fading and my faith in the detective's ability to come through has me itching to go find her myself. If I have to, I will bang on every door until she's found.

Why the fuck is this happening? Who took her? What for?

I stand up from the sofa, lifting a sleeping Kim off my lap and laying her down on the indented, warm spot my ass created. I toss the purple blanket from the back of the sofa over her tiny body and leave her to rest. She looks peaceful, as if she's dreaming of her mother being home and tucking her into bed like she should be doing tonight.

In the dining room, the police huddle around the table discussing information and potential leads. As I approach, the first officer sees me and stands between me and the table. I try to look around him to see what's so important that he doesn't want to share with me.

"What's going on?" I ask in a demanding voice.

"We haven't found any fresh leads. We tracked her cell phone and found it on the road two blocks from her work. We fingerprinted it, but he must have wiped it clean or wore gloves. We've talked to her coworkers and patients." He hesitates and scratches his head as if debating whether to tell me something. "Ah, there is one lead, but it's small. A witness saw the man get out of the backseat after she slumped onto the passenger's seat, as if she had passed out or," he takes a breath, "or if he drugged her. The witness can't be sure of what they saw. I haven't told Renee yet."

My rage has reignited, brewing deep inside me like lava. If I catch this guy, I will punish him until he begs me to kill him. I will bind that fucker and sadistically torture him and thoroughly enjoy doing it. My inner demon will rise and take over my body and mind, and I will welcome him.

The detective puts his hands up to calm me down. "Listen, you need to keep it together. If you go off, those kids will think she's dead. Why don't we go outside so you can get some fresh air?"

I turn with my fists clenched, nostrils flared, and my body stiff with rage. Once outside, I take a deep breath and purposely stretch my hands as I tilt my head side to side. This officer needs reassurance that I'm calm and not going to fly off the handle. As soon as he turns his attention elsewhere, I'll be in my truck and gone.

I will find her! These incompetent assholes couldn't find their dicks with a magnifying glass and a map. She needs me.

Rayna, please let me know where you are.

Before the detective goes back into the house, he tells another officer to monitor me. He must sense I'm about to run. I bide my time, waiting patiently for the cop to turn her back, forgetting that she's been appointed to babysit me. It isn't long before she chats with another officer. It's plainly obvious the two of them are having a sexual affair by how she's flipping her hair and he's puffing out his chest. I have to wait a few more minutes until they are deep in their conversation, and then I'm out of here.

I slowly pace back and forth across Rayna's driveway while the officer watches me. It isn't long before she turns her back to me. No doubt he's telling her what he wants to do to her when their shift is over. This is my opportunity.

As quickly as possible, I scurry across my lawn and hop into the truck, start it up, and pull out of the driveway before the officers realize I'm leaving. I watch in the rear-view mirror as the two of them run onto the road and throw their hands up, defeated.

I'd better get moving before they call in my plate and track me down. I have to find Rayna.

$\approx$

RAYNA

The man's phone rings, startling me from a pleasant dream. I was sitting at the dinner table with the kids and Coach. We were laughing and holding hands. It was lovely.

My one functioning eye opens. I'm sitting upright in the chair again. He must have righted me while I was still unconscious. My head aches, and my mind spins when I turn my head too quickly. I hope the vertigo passes soon. I likely have a concussion.

My bladder is even more full now and I won't be able to hold it much longer. I strain to hear what he's saying into his phone, hoping I might hear him say a person's name. If I survive this, I will track the bastard down myself if I have to.

"You were supposed to be here already." He shakes his head. "Where the fuck are you?" he whispers, pausing between sentences, I assume so the caller can reply. "So, what you're saying is that I have to stay here and babysit this broad until you decide to come?" He paces back and forth. "When might that be?"

He turns to look at me and shakes his head. "That wasn't the deal. No! You've got two hours and then I'm letting her go. Then I guess you'd better get your ass here! Yeah, fuck you, too!"

He hangs up the phone and tosses it onto the workbench. His beady eyes glare at me from behind the mask. "Looks like we're stuck together for a few more hours."

"Who are you waiting for?" I ask softly, fearing he'll hit me because once again I broke his command of not talking.

"Shut up."

"What are they going to do to me?" I ask in the sweetest, most innocent way that I can manage without sounding pathetic.

He looks at me and tilts his head. "I don't care. My job will be done. When that car pulls up, I'm out. What happens after that, I don't want any part of."

"I see," I whisper, looking pathetic and vulnerable. I wish tears would spill, but I'm so angry that I can't bring them on. "I have to pee. Please, may I have some dignity?"

"Fuck! You can't wait?" he asks with obvious irritation.

I shake my head. "No, I'm desperate. It's been hours. Please?"

"Fine!" he yells as he rushes toward me. I cringe, half expecting him to kick me in the chest again. He unties my hands from the chair. "If you try to get away, I'll beat you within an inch of your life. Do you understand?"

"I understand completely," I assure him, but if an opportunity shows itself, I will jump on it and fight like my life depends on it because I think it does.

He grabs my hair and stands me up, then brings the ropes in front of me, binding my hands together. The ropes are tight and hurt my wrists. I complain in a whisper, "They're too tight."

"Good, then you won't escape. Go that way," he tells me, pointing in toward the hallway.

First, the smell hits me, but when he turns on the light, I nearly vomit. The toilet is filthy. The bowl is coated with orange and black mould, and on the floor surrounding it is stained with urine. I'll have to hover. I ponder letting it go in my pants instead of risking contracting an incurable disease from using his toilet.

"Are you fucking going or not?" he yells, pushing me into the disgusting room.

The stench is gut-wrenching. I wretch, but there isn't anything in my stomach, thankfully. I can imagine the beating that would ensue after that.

"Can you shut the door, please?" I ask, fearing how intense the smell will be once it closes.

"Fuck no! If you have to go, go." He's leaning on the wood-panelled wall across the hall with his arms crossed over his chest, watching me.

I unbutton my pants and let them slip halfway down my thighs while bending forward slightly to pull down my panties in a way that prevents him from seeing my vagina. I hover over the filthy seat and immediately pee. I don't think I could have held it for another minute had I tried. Shit, this feels good!

I look for a tissue, but I see none. What the hell does he use to wipe his ass after he shits? A shiver runs straight up my spine when I picture his shit-streaked underwear. Yuck! He smells horrid, so I know his hygiene isn't up to par.

"Do you have any tissue?" I ask while not looking at him.

"Nope. Drip dry," he mutters. "Just do it quickly."

I can feel his eyes on me, seducing me while I perform a basic human necessity. He's disgusting, and I pray that he's decent enough not to rape me. Even though he kicked my chest twice, making it painful to breathe, he hasn't touched me sexually. At least not while I was conscious.

I pull up my panties, trying to avoid letting him have a view of my bits, but it's a struggle because my hands are bound so tightly. They've gone numb so trying to refasten the button on my pants is impossible. I wrestle with the zipper until I have it pulled up, and then try the button again, but my numb fingers can't manage the simple task.

My captor suddenly grabs the top of my pants. I didn't even see him approach me.

Panic ensues! He's going to rape me!

I swing my arms frantically, screaming for him not to touch me. He's unaffected with the hits to his chest and face.

I don't see his fist come at my face until it's too late to duck. It lands, shooting the worst pain I have ever experienced in my life through my entire face. It felt like my skull broke in half. Did my nose flatten under his knuckles and every one of my teeth break, too?

Blackness is taking the pain away. I'm falling but have no motor function to stop myself from hitting the disgusting floor.

This time, I welcome the blackness.

Coach

I'm stopped at the streetlight where the last traffic camera saw Rayna's car. I turn the corner where the video showed it turn. I drive slowly, looking at all the driveways and garages that have their doors open or lights on inside. Maybe I'll see her or her car if I get lucky enough. The captor won't concern himself with random people in pickups driving slowly.

I cruise up and down each street in this insignificant town, searching for a clue, any clue, but I find nothing out of the ordinary. I should drive faster before someone calls the cops to report a strange man scoping out houses.

She's not in this town. If she were around here, she would have screamed by now and someone would have surely heard her. It's so quiet around here that the slightest odd noise would alert people to find the source. Besides, small-town people know everything that everyone is doing. This kidnapper would have to be very sly for them not to have noticed his misdeeds.

The county is where I would take a victim, like Rayna's ex-husband, for instance. I agree with Renee; Rick has something to do with this.

It's all my fault. If I would not have gotten involved and tossed him out of her house, none of this would be happening. That situation escalated his temper. I should have stayed out of it. He wasn't hitting her, only yelling cruel things. Maybe I jumped the gun. I wanted to protect her, keep her safe. I fear I've made a bad situation so much worse.

"RAYNA! I WILL FIND YOU, MY LOVE!"

People in the surrounding homes can surely hear my screamed promise, and I don't care.

Call the cops! I haven't seen one yet. How can they be looking for her if I haven't seen them and I've been all over this town, twice?

*R*AYNA

The brightness of the overhead light burns harshly into my brain through my pupil. I can't even see a sliver of light through my other eye. It was swollen before he punched me.

Did he hit me so hard that he blinded me? Please don't let that be the case.

The world is spinning, and my face is in tremendous pain.

I look around as best I can. My guard has left me alone. My head spins with vertigo as I scan around the room. He really is gone. This is my chance.

I struggle with the ropes, pulling so hard that I feel my skin tear. My bones will soon break from the force. I don't care if I crush them, as long as I can get myself freed.

I'm unable to loosen them no matter how much I pull. Fresh blood flows down my fingers in streams; I can feel the warmth. Hopelessness consumes me, and that's when the tears fall. I'm devastated, not for my impending death, but for the sorrow the kids will surely feel. That is what's tearing at my heart. How will they grow up without a mother? Renee will raise them, but kids need their mom.

Someone will find me. I know they will, as long as I don't give up. I will survive this. For some unknown reason, I know this to be true.

I whisper it so the universe can hear, "I will not die today."

A warmth flows around me, easing my anguish like a loving hug, ensuring that I will survive. I smile softly and allow myself a moment to absorb the pleasantness of the air's loving caress. Snap out of it! Think Rayna, think!

I yell, "Hello?"

The smelly man comes out of the other little room by the bathroom, eating a sandwich. "You woke up. At least it was quiet when you were unconscious." I hear him smack his food around his mouth. "What the fuck do you want now?"

"I'm hungry," I tell him, unsure if I can chew anything with my face this badly beaten. He may have broken every bone on the left side of my face.

"You don't have time to eat. Sit tight, our company will be here soon enough," he says with a mouthful of food. A chunk of bread drops from his bottom lip after he mangled it in his mouth. "Why the fuck did you freak out? I was trying to button your pants since you obviously couldn't do it."

Dammit! "I thought you were going to rape me. Wouldn't you panic if you were in my position?"

"I suppose I should have told you what I was trying to do. Just sit there and shut up. It won't be much longer."

The man disappears back into that room again. I continue to struggle with my bindings, even though I know it's hopeless. Maybe the ropes will break free from the chair.

Our company will be here soon. Does that mean that I'll die shortly? I'm hoping they'll tell me why I'm about to die. Hopefully, the visitor cares to explain it to me. My present captor doesn't seem to want to answer that question. He might not even know.

Who is this mysterious person he's expecting? What will they do to me when they get here? Will the person torture me before they kill me or simply do it outright?

They don't have to kill me. They might keep me locked up somewhere. Neither option sounds very inviting.

Shit, Rayna, you have to get the hell out of here!

~

Coach

"Please, please let her be safe," I pray aloud.

I've been looking but can't find her car and the frustration has built to a breaking point. Where the fuck is she?

"Help me find her," I beg the universe to hear my pleas.

My emotions burst forth and I have to pull to the side of the road. I can't see through the waves of endless tears that flood my vision. I yell and pound on the steering wheel so viciously I fear the airbag might deploy, rewarding me with one hell of a punch to the face. I don't care. I need to let the rage out.

"RAYNA! Where the fuck are you? Dammit!" I scream at the tops of my lungs, collapsing against the steering wheel only after my rage turns into the pain of a broken soul and lost dreams.

Unable to yell anymore, I whisper, "Please. Rayna. I love you. Help me find you."

With my chin resting on the steering wheel, I breathe deeply and swallow hard, burying my emotions back inside where they belong. Outbursts like this will not help me find her.

What can I do now? Should I drive around more? I don't even know where to look; what town and how many towns? I could knock on the doors of every garage with its lights on. Is she being held hostage in a barn or a house? There are so many to search. Where would I even begin?

The evening sun hovers barely above the horizon and shines through the windshields of two cars as they pass by. It lights up the faces of the people as they go about their lives. They don't know that my Rayna is lost and hurt, or worse, she may be dead.

I squint because the sun's reflection off the second car's windshield stings my bloodshot eyes. As it nears, I'm shocked that I recognize him. A cold heaviness floods my veins, making me feel weak with dread.

What the fuck is he doing in this town? My hands shake, making it nearly impossible to turn the key to start the truck. I have to follow that car!

As soon as he turns onto the next road and can no longer see me in his rearview mirror, I whip the truck around to follow him. He won't lead the way to Rayna if he thinks he's being followed, so I tail him from quite a distance. He must know a vehicle is behind him. It's not like I can hide in the county where the roads are long and straight.

"Take me to Rayna, you mother fucker!" I say between clenched teeth. "You wait until I get my hands on you."

My fists grip the wheel. I want to pound the accelerator and catch up to him, but I know if I do, he won't lead me to her.

Time drags, each second feels like a full minute. My inner demon is seething in anger, causing me to shake uncontrollably. The car turns into a long driveway that leads up to a small blue house that could benefit from some maintenance. Two large barns sit behind it, both have lights on inside. There's a spotlight illuminating the one car that sits beneath it. It isn't Rayna's but now I know where that fucker is holding her.

Why would he take her? What does he want with her?

I never thought he was psychotic, but he is a dangerous man who could cause her great suffering. I have to help her.

My heart beats like a powerful drum. I want so badly to follow his car into the driveway and beat that fucker to death, but I'm not positive he's alone and can't risk another person, or persons, hurting her while I exact my revenge on the fucking weasel by ripping his head off.

So as not to lead him to think I'm tailing him, I continue to drive past where he turned while keeping an eye to make sure he isn't retreating out of the driveway and heading back in the opposite direction. I hope like hell he didn't recognize me in this truck. He can't know that I'm coming for him.

As soon as I'm far enough away that he won't see the truck pulling off the road, I shut off my lights and park so close to the ditch that I'm surprised I didn't slide into it. I shut my door quietly and run down the street as fast as I can.

I'm coming, Rayna! Just hold on!

CHAPTER 25

A DOOR SQUEALS AS IT'S JARRED OPEN. SOMEONE ELSE IS HERE. I HOLD my breath, hoping to hear their voice. It's a man. I'm not familiar with his voice. I wait, staring at the doorway that leads to the hallway where the men are conversing just out of my line of sight.

I wish the room would stop spinning.

My captor is leading the way for the other man. When I finally see him, I'm confused because I don't know who he is.

He is very tall, extremely handsome, and stacked with muscles. His hair is black and styled perfectly, using a lot of products, I assume. His facial features are sharp and masculine, his skin shaved clean.

As he nears, he looks me up and down, as if assessing me.

Oh, no! Is he going to rape me? Is that why I'm captive; for sex? Why wouldn't this stranger opt for a younger woman whose body is better than mine? He's obviously younger than me. Does he have a MILF fetish?

He grabs my chin, lifting my face up so he can get a better look at me. His eyes are ice blue and gorgeous. Right now, they scare the hell out of me, but in better circumstances, I would be attracted to him.

"Tell me your name," he asks in a deep voice while wearing an impassioned expression.

"Rayna," I reply, my voice shaking. "What's yours?"

He looks at my eye. "This is bad. I'm going to get my ass beat for this."

What is he talking about? Who will beat his ass? Is someone else involved?

I show no fear. "Who are you, what are you going to do to me, and why am I here?"

"You ask a lot of questions for a woman in your position." He turns to look at my greasy captor. "Is that why she looks like this?"

"She fell out of the car on her face and then she tried to fight me, so I had to shut her down. I had no choice," he replies, obviously nervous enough that he takes a step away from the handsome stranger.

I yell, "You had a choice, asshole. I'm not a brawny woman, you could have easily restrained me without breaking my face!"

I'm more pissed off than scared. What do I have to lose from ratting him out? If they plan to kill me, at least my kidnapper will catch shit from the man who hired him to do his bidding. He's not pleased that I'm all bruised up.

"Tie her to the rafters so I can get a better look at her," he exclaims to the pungent man. His eyes still burn into mine. "I want to play with you. Trust me, gorgeous, you will love this."

My captor immediately begins freeing me from the chair but doesn't remove the ropes from my wrists. I try to fight him, so he carries me to where he wants me. He unties me.

This might be my only chance to either get away or go down swinging. If they're going to kill me, I won't make it easy for them.

The instant I am free, I spin around, twisting Smelly's wrist when he grips my arm. The second he lets go, I punt his balls and then turn to run toward the door faster than if a bomb is about to explode in my wake.

I only get a dozen steps away when I'm grabbed by my hair and yanked back, falling to my knees. My blood-curdling screams should be heard a mile away. Perhaps someone will call for help.

He pulls me by my hair. My hands grab at the wrist of the sizable man. The man I kicked still crouches on the floor, gasping his breaths as he holds his aching genitals. He looks really pissed off.

My hair is set free, but only when his other hand grips my throat. He pulls my face close to his. His dangerous eyes blaze into mine. They're a beautiful blue but seem dark somehow. Perhaps his anger is changing his eye colour or my fear is clouding my vision.

His grip is getting tighter. He's choking me. I can't breathe.

My arms flail and punch at his wrist. My nails claw at his skin, hoping he'll let go, but he doesn't even wince. He seems to like that I'm fighting him. I kick at his shins, so he holds me at arm's length. I cannot reach his body with my arms or legs.

His words hiss at me through a clenched jaw. "Where do you think you're going? If I were you, I wouldn't try that again, you fucking little whore! Why don't you want to play with me? I'm not horrible to look at; at least, that's what I'm told."

He spins me around, loosening his grip on my throat but still rendering me captive. After pulling me back to his firm belly, he grabs my hair again and yanks my head back. I can't turn my head away from his full lips as they press onto mine.

His tongue burrows into my mouth. I try to bite down but the pain in my face is agonizing, especially in this position. Tiny bright stars fill my sight, so many that they're going black. I'm passing out again.

The bright lights once again bleed into my groggy mind, ruining a perfectly wonderful dream. It takes a few seconds for the fogginess to clear enough where I can think straight. He's tied my arms over my head with a hanging rope from the ceiling. My previously bruised and bloodied wrists ache. My toes barely touch the ground. I can't relieve my wrists from bearing most of my weight.

The blue-eyed man stands in front of me with his arms crossed over his chest. He's watching me, expressionless. Maybe he's been waiting for me to wake. I think he prefers me aware when he tortures me.

"What do you want with me?" I question with a weak voice.

"You likely don't recognize me because we've never officially met," he tells me. "I'm friends with Coach, best friends to be exact. We have been close for a long time." He smirks, then slowly circles me. "Did you know that we are both aggressive with women? It's true. He told me all about you and how vanilla you were before he got his hands on you.

"He also told me that he cares for you and because of that, he won't share you with me. That really hurt my feelings. We've been sharing women since we met. All the women we get with, that are worthy," he leans in to whisper behind my ear, "we fuck them together. He's usually in her ass while I fuck her cunt. My cock is too big for most women's asses, but not all. There are the rare ones whose asses you can drive a fist into, and I have." He shows me his massive fist.

"Are you one of those capable women? I would imagine you are not. We'll see, won't we?"

"Are you going to rape me?" I ask, already knowing his intention.

"Don't be like that. You will like my cock, I promise," he replies arrogantly.

Fuck! My worst fears are coming true.

"And, what if I don't?"

"It doesn't matter, because I'm sure I'll have a marvellous time. The more you fight me, the more pleased I'll be." His matter-of-fact tone ends with a sadistic chuckle.

"You're into submissive and master play like Coach, right?" I ask.

He looks at me while standing so close that we're almost touching. I can feel his body heat. This man is enormous, bigger than Coach in height and girth.

"Isn't it obvious?" he teases with a shifty sneer.

I reply, hoping to strike a chord. "From what I've recently learned about sadism and masochism is that the submissive is the one with all the power. Isn't that right?"

"It is unless they willingly agree to a power exchange."

"You believe me to be the submissive in this situation, correct?"

He snickers, looking at the rope that binds my hands. "Another obvious point. What are you getting at?"

"Since you agree that I am submissive, let me say that I have not agreed to submit to you, therefore, if you touch me sexually, it's rape which is not acceptable with the BDSM community, unless I say it's okay. Am I right? Are you a rapist?"

I'm hoping to get through to him but doubt I'll be successful. Maybe my words will get him to respect me and he'll feel some compassion. I wonder if he has it in him.

"I am whatever I want to be. You don't seem to understand why you're here," he says as he yanks my pants down to my ankles.

No! Tears stream down my face. I've never been very successful at keeping my emotions intact when standing up to people who intimidate me. This massive man is about to rape me and there's nobody here to stop him. I can't get away on my own, I know this to be true. My initial kidnapper has vanished, just like he said he would.

Oh, please, someone help me!

"Please, enlighten me," I ask, hoping to prolong the inevitable. The longer I keep him talking, the more likely someone is to find me.

He pushes his groin against my pantie-covered womanhood

and I wretch. His hands pull at my ass, humping me against his denim-covered bulge. He lets me go and I swing. I try to still myself using my tiptoes.

He circles me slowly as he explains. "I must say, I can see why Coach didn't want to share you. Your body is beautiful, exactly like he said it was. For a woman who's had kids, you look damn good."

"Why am I here?" I interrupt his speech with an angry attitude. "Get to the fucking point!"

"You want me to get to the point? Okay, here's why you're here. I want Coach. He's mine, not yours. If he has you, I have you; that's the agreement. We share our women, always. But not you." He lifts my chin so he can look in my eyes.

"He's keeping you for himself. If we stop sharing women, I won't get to have Coach anymore." He grimaces. "He's not gay, I get that, but I'll take him any way I can get him. If that means putting a whore between us, I can accept that. When he's in her ass and I'm in her sloppy cunt, I can feel his cock stroking mine. Do you have any idea how much that turns me on?" He steps back and takes a deep breath. His eyes stare off in the distance.

"It almost feels like he's fucking me. I can watch the expressions on his face change to reveal the agonizing glory of his impending orgasm. I know that if I push into the bitch all the way, putting pressure on his cock while he slams into her asshole, he can feel my cum wads pass through my twitching cock."

"So, you're gay? Is that what you're trying to say?" I keep my voice soft and understanding. "You love Coach and want him for yourself? I can understand that."

"No, bitch. I already had him, but you're trying to take him away. I had to see what was so fucking great about you that made it so easy for him to cast me aside. Tell me, bitch, what the fuck makes you so goddamn special?" he inquires with his face so near to mine that I can feel his fiery breath on my lips.

I'm thankful his breath smells much better than the other guy's.

The hate in his eyes is sinister and burning terror into me like daggers. I cast my eyes down, trying to think of how to answer his question to calm him. He's breathing heavily, and his hands form into tight fists. He's going to hurt me now.

"I don't know why he likes me. I'm nothing special. I mean, I have kids and an ex-husband who's an asshole. I'm older than him and our fitness levels are inharmonious at best. He's a workout fanatic and I'm definitely not. If I can avoid exercise, I will. I get enough of a workout cleaning up after my two children; it's a full cardio workout some days. I don't know what you want me to say that will make you not want to hurt me. Do you want me to break up with him?" I exclaim while tears stream down my face.

He kisses my lips softly and then whispers, "Break up with him if you want to, but there isn't anything you can say that will stop me from taking what's rightfully mine. He promised to share his ladies, *all* his ladies, and I know he won't let you go. Our sharing days are over unless I take you now."

"How will that make a difference?"

"Well, if I've already had you, he won't have any reason not to share you with me."

"Was it a binding agreement that you and he share every woman that either of you has sex with? Was it a verbal agreement or simply assumed on your part?"

He doesn't answer. He's circling me again.

"He said the two of you have tag-teamed a few ladies, but never once did he say that you have an agreement to share every woman. If he had, I wouldn't be with him. I don't want to be shared by anyone. Please, let me go."

I'm no longer crying because I don't think I have any tears left in me to spill. I'm completely drained, mentally and physically.

I whisper, "Just get this over with."

"Not yet," he replies as he grabs my t-shirt by the collar and with a quick jerk, tears the material, exposing my bra.

"Do what you will, but please don't kill me. I have children and I'm a single mom. Their father isn't responsible enough to care for them properly. Please?" I beg. I have no other option at this point other than to plead with him.

"Kill you? Fuck, I won't kill you. I'm going to fuck you raw before giving you back to Coach. He needs to know that I'm still here and we share our bitches. He'll understand."

He stands a few feet from me, looking my body up and down but not yet touching me. So far, he hasn't assaulted me, other than rubbing his groin on mine, but there was no skin to skin contact.

"He won't be happy if you put your hands on me. Coach will not share me because he knows that I'm not some whore that lets anyone between her legs. I would never agree to it. If you touch me, he will hate you forever, if he doesn't kill you. You know that, right?" I calmly state, in a last-ditch effort to get him to back off. "He told you not to touch me, didn't he? If you really love him, you'll respect him enough not to do this because it will anger him."

"Bitch, I don't care if you're the sweetest, most innocent chick in the world. If you're fucking Coach, you're fucking me, too. He'll come around."

A loud crash coming from the direction of the hallway grabs our attention. The man quickly yells, "Hey, what's going on out there?"

There's no reply from the greasy man who must be in the other room. He walks toward the hallway, leaving me hanging by my wrists, defenceless and nearly naked. At least he isn't raping me.

I struggle to free myself, but my body weight pulls the ropes so tight that my hands have turned purple. At least they don't hurt anymore. Nonetheless, I keep struggling.

The man gets near the hall entrance and stops. "Hey, buddy, glad you could join us. I was hoping you'd show up. She's ready for us."

"Where's Rayna?" The familiar voice brings me newfound hope.

I yell, "Coach! I'm in here! Help me!"

Coach comes charging into the room, heading straight toward me.

Oh, thank God! He'll make this stop and set me free. When he's near enough to see how badly beaten my face is, he spins around, slamming his fist against the jaw of the bigger man, but the guy doesn't fall.

COACH

Brett stumbles but doesn't go down. I hit him so hard that I'm amazed he's still standing. My rage is at a level where I might rip his fucking head off his neck. If I charge him again, I will probably kill him. He isn't worth going to prison. All it will take is for him to swing at me and I will take him out.

"What the fuck, Coach? We share every girl," Brett says while gripping his jaw in his massive hand and moving it back and forth to check if it's broken.

"Not this one! I told you to back off! Rayna is not for sharing. What the fuck did you do to her face?"

I reach out and grab him by the throat with my fist pulled back, ready to blast him again. I want to kill him. He isn't a skillful fighter, and he's fully aware I could seriously injure him. He's seen me fight, so he knows I can be dangerous. He might be bigger than me, but I'm stronger and faster.

He struggles to reply. "I didn't do that to her face. I'd never ruin that pretty face of hers. She's gorgeous. Well, one side of her face is still pretty."

He chuckles, and my temper roars. My demon is begging for freedom to let loose. If he gets out, he'll kill Brett.

I punch him again, slamming my fist into his eye. He swings low, catching my abdomen, but he's slow and I was ready for it. An inch higher and he might have knocked the wind out of me. I pull my fist back again and let it fly. This time, he blocks it with his arm.

His fist cracks me hard on my cheek directly in front of my ear. It stuns me for a second. Just as my mind clears, I see his giant mitt coming toward my face again. I release his throat and block his swing, grasping his forearm in a vice-like grip.

Unexpectedly, he laughs. So, I hit him again, this time splitting the soft skin under his eyebrow. Blood spills into his eye.

"Okay, enough, enough! I get it, you won't share her. We'll get another girl to share. You can have this one for yourself since you're suddenly so fucking possessive!"

I want to hit him again and again, but I release him instead, fearing that if I don't, I won't be able to stop myself until he's dead. Both of us are out of breath but my rage still burns through my veins and my inner demon is pacing in his cage, begging me to set him free. I take a few steps back, but my eyes remain focused on him, hoping to burn a hole through him.

"We're done! No more! Do you hear me? You are fucking done! I'm taking her out of here and you will not stop me. Do you understand?"

"Are you going to fuck me up if I say you can't have her?" Brett's tears spill, mixing with the blood that's still flowing from the gash over his swelling eye.

"What the fuck is wrong with you?"

He stands but doesn't come at me. He rants, spewing his thoughts in a rage. "Don't you get it? I want *you*, not her. You're mine. She doesn't deserve you, but I do. I've been here for you the whole time. We can be happy together. We'll even put a woman between us if you think it's too gay without one. It's time for you and me. Rayna can go back to her kids and her boring mom-life. She's no good for you. For years, I've been patiently waiting for you to come around, for you to realize that you love me and that we are perfect together." He looks pathetic and desperate as he spills his soul.

"What the fuck, man? We're done! You and me? Finished!" I hiss as I turn my back to him and rush toward Rayna.

He will not hit me anymore. Even if I hit him again, it won't hurt him as much as it will if I walk out of here and never talk to him again. When did he develop feelings for me? Was I oblivious to his advances? Could we have avoided this had I recognized his love for me?

CHAPTER 26

 *ayna*

DEFEATED, THE LARGER MAN DROPS TO HIS KNEES AND HIS TEARS stream down his cheeks. To make Coach understand, he professes his love through the desolate sobs of a broken man. "I fucking love you!"

"This isn't love, Brett," Coach says as he attempts to untie my hands, but the knot is proving difficult. "If you loved me, you would never do this. So shut the fuck up before I come over there and rip your fucking head off!"

Coach wraps his forearm under my butt and lifts me, enabling him to untie with the ropes that hold my wrists. As soon as the knot releases, my arms drop lifelessly between us. Pain erupts as my blood flows through my arms. I can't move them under my power, the agony is far too great.

Coach sets me onto my feet and gently touches the bruised side of my face. The pain in his eye hurts me worse than anything I've ever felt. He bends down, sliding my pants up my legs to grant me some dignity. He buttons them and then scoops me up, carrying my weak body past a shattered man weeping on his knees, watching the love of his life walk out with not another glance in his direction.

He holds me safely against his chest as he storms down the street. I'm not sure where he's taking me, but I don't care either. I'm with Coach and that means I'm safe. Coach doesn't put me down until he sits me in the driver's seat of his truck.

He kisses my forehead and asks, "Can you slide over?"

My hands aren't throbbing anymore, but my ribs stab at me when I shimmy from one seat to the other. I don't care. I'm just grateful he didn't rape me. It could have been so much worse.

The second he's in the truck, I push the button to lock the doors in case either of the men follows us. He looks at me with a remorseful expression that makes my heart ache. I lunge at him, pressing the sore side of my face against his chest. I clutch onto his shirt with all my remaining strength. He puts his one arm over my back, holding me securely as he starts the engine and puts it into gear.

Each bump in the road is agony, but I will not voice my physical pain. I welcome the pain in my face as it bounces off his tummy; it's a reminder that I'm out of harm's way. My ribs ache in this position, but I don't feel any grinding, so maybe they aren't broken. His heavy arm resting over my side isn't making them hurt any less, but I won't ask him to move.

We've been driving for a few minutes when I finally break the silence. "What happened to the smelly man?"

"Don't worry about it," he sharply replies, lifting his arm off my ribs to brush a few loose tresses of hair from my face.

"I need to know."

He sighs. "I hit him with a pipe and he went down like a rag doll."

"Is he dead?" I hope he is.

"I didn't stick around to find out." He clears his throat. "I needed to get to you."

"I hope he's in horrible pain. He's the one who hurt me." There's so much anger behind my words.

"If he isn't dead, he's close to it," he assures me. "How is your face?"

"It hurts. I can't see out of my left eye. I hope I'm not blind. He dropped me on my face, on the cement, when he took me out of the car. Later, I fought him, and he hit me so hard that I blacked out."

My throbbing cheek presses against Coach's firm, warm chest. It aches, but the pressure makes it feel better, or maybe it's that Coach is with me and that gives me so much comfort. I'm safe. I didn't think I'd ever get to say that again.

"I love you, baby. I'm so sorry," he apologizes.

"Sorry for rescuing me?"

"No, of course not. If it weren't for my lifestyle previous to you, this never would have happened. If I wasn't around, the bullshit with your ex wouldn't have happened either." He takes a breath. "I'm bad for you, Rayna. I've done nothing but burden your life. Everything that's happened lately is my fault, all of it."

He sounds like he's crying. I hug him harder.

"Simon, don't leave me. I love you. None of this is your fault. You saved me from my off-the-wall ex and from those assholes. I still can't believe you kept your cool and didn't kill him."

"It wasn't easy. I wanted to beat him to death. I didn't know he was so fucked up in the head. We had lunch together the other day, and he seemed fine. He was my trusted friend, and I loved him."

The truck turns left, then right, coming to a full stop.

He shuts off the ignition. "I don't know what happened to him. I am so sorry, baby. Can you sit up? We're here."

I clutch my ribs as I right myself. He brought me to the hospital. I need a doctor to look at my eye and tell me that my vision is still intact. X-rays would be nice to know if I have fractured ribs or if they're just bruised.

Coach opens my door and helps me out of the truck. "Can you walk? I can carry you."

"I think I'm okay," I tell him as I gingerly take my first few steps.

He holds my arm for insurance. My chest hurts from that asshole's boot kicking me twice. I hold my torn shirt closed. My depth perception is off because I only have one eye to see from. It doesn't help that my balance is horrible because the world keeps spinning around me. I keep swaying to the left.

The bright lights in the hospital are like sharp daggers stabbing into my one good eye. Tears quickly blur my vision, making it even more difficult to maneuver myself around without looking like I'm drunk. Coach immediately brings me to the receptionist, who's eyes open wide when he glances up from his computer screen.

"Come right in," the man says as he stands and presses a button to unlock the door. He raises his voice to alert the staff. "I'm sending one in right now."

I hear the scuffling of shoes as the door swings open and several people quickly approach me.

"We got her from here, sir," the one nurse tells Coach as she takes my arm.

A male nurse gently takes my other arm to assist. He tells Coach, "Follow us. We'll need to get some information from you."

A security guard approaches, immediately setting his accusing eyes on Coach. Maybe he thinks he is the one who did this to me. Idiot! Why would he bring me to get fixed up if he's the one that smacked me around?

"Coach, stay with me, please," I yell back to him.

"I'm not going anywhere, Rayna," he replies, interrupting a man asking him questions.

"Can you tell me who did this to you?" asks the female nurse who's holding my arm.

"There were two men. Coach knows the one guy." They help me up onto a stretcher in an empty room. "Coach saved me."

A person in a white coat rushes in, and the nurses clear a path for her. She informs me that she's a doctor, and she's here to help. She asks me question after question, which I answer as best I can.

They cut my clothes from my body and I'm now lying here wearing only my panties, but I don't feel self-conscious; they aren't looking at me as though I'm a woman with sexual parts. To them, I am a human body in need of repair. The doctor waves them off, letting them know to leave my panties on me for now.

The doctor rattles off a list of tests she wants them to perform as she tries to shine a light in my swollen eye. Her fingers gently pry at the bloated lid and it bloody hurts! I tell her that I can't see any light.

The nurses scatter, following up on the doctor's orders. Coach stands at my feet. He can see all of my injuries now that I am nearly nude. When I was hanging from the rope with my shirt torn open, he must not have noticed the bruising on my chest and ribs. He most likely saw everything with the crimson hue of his own rage.

He groans with so much regret in his tone. "Oh, my sweet Rayna! What the fuck did he do to you?"

Pain shoots through my face when she presses on my cheek. I fight not to scream, knowing that opening my mouth will only increase the pain. I can feel scraping, like bone rubbing against bone.

My stomach violently churns and before I can warn anyone, I turn my head and vomit all over the male nurse's uniform. I'm surprised at how much fluid I puke up because I thought my stomach was empty. I hadn't eaten or drank anything in quite a while.

They feed a butterfly needle into my vein, but I barely acknowledge the pain it causes. Almost immediately, I feel lighter.

Drugs! "Thank you," I say with a slur.

The pain from them poking at my wounds was making it so hard to hold back my screams. With the drugs flowing into my vein, I couldn't care less if they poke. The pain is still there, I simply don't give a shit.

After several X-rays and a CT scan, I'm told that I'll need surgery to fix my shattered cheekbone, and my ribs are badly bruised, but not broken.

I sign the paperwork to approve the surgery as they're wheeling my gurney into an operating room. I ask if they called my sister to let her know that I'm okay.

A different woman with kind eyes tells me, "Don't worry, everyone knows you're here. The police have been searching for you. Did you know that?" I shake my head. "You're going to sleep now. Can you count backward from ten?"

I begin, "Ten, nine, eight, sev…"

CHAPTER 27

oach

I TELL THE COPS AS MUCH INFORMATION AS I CAN, GIVING THEM
directions to the barn where I found Rayna. They want to know
all about Brett, our history, how I came to find her. Basically, they
wanted to know what role I played in this whole situation.

Their faces seem to soften once they understand I am the one
who rescued her and wasn't present when she received those
wounds.

After my interrogation, I'm walked to the X-ray room to get a
picture of my hand. It's swollen, and now that my adrenaline has
subsided, I can feel pain. I would turn down a painkiller if it's
offered.

The doc tells me it's fractured in two spots, but that I don't
require surgery; a splint will do nicely. She explains that Rayna
gave the hospital permission to tell me details of her injuries and
progress reports during the procedure. She is in surgery for a
shattered cheek and to relieve the pressure on her eye. I need to
hold her, make her feel safe, and prevent anyone from hurting her
again.

The doctor leaves to get a splint for my hand. Renee and the kids peek into the room across the hall.

"Hey, in here," I say loud enough that she'll hear me, but not startle the two people on the gurneys beside me.

Ken runs in first and throws his arms around me. "Thank you for saving my mom. I knew you would."

I hug him back with my good arm, and kiss the top of his head, "I'm happy, too, little man."

Kim hugs my arm because she isn't big enough to reach me on this bed. "Thank you, Coach."

"How is she?" Renee looks tired, almost defeated.

I'm impressed she was able to keep up a strong appearance when she needed to. Now that Rayna's safe, her emotions let go. I put my arm out and wave her toward me. She leans in, pressing her head against my chest. She weeps, soaking my shirt. I don't mind. I pat her back to calm her.

The kids stand at the other side of the gurney while I explain what I know. "She's going to be okay. They have her in surgery for a shattered cheekbone. Her eye is swollen shut so they have to work on that, too. They don't think her vision is affected, but they won't know for sure until the swelling subsides." I take a breath and smile at the kids who look scared.

"She has bruised ribs and a bruise on her chest. She also has a concussion, which they will monitor. Don't worry, she'll be okay."

"Holy shit!" Renee pulls out of the hug, wearing the same expression of rage I must have had when I first saw Rayna suspended by the rope. "Who did this and did they catch him?"

The kids listen to every word we say. Now that they know what to expect when they see her, it won't be such a shock when they do. I don't want them to hear the awful details of how she got those injuries. That's something Rayna can explain to them, should she decide to, but it's not my place.

"They know where to find them; if they stuck around, that is. I don't know that I should say anything more," I say, tipping my head toward the kids.

She nods and digs through her purse, pulling out a twenty-dollar bill. "Do you remember where the cafeteria is? I pointed it out when we walked by it. Go there and get something to eat. I'll meet you there in a few minutes. Can you get me a small coffee? Don't go anywhere else and don't talk to anyone other than your servers. Stay together, no matter what!"

Ken takes the money and leads the way as Kim follows closely behind.

"Okay, tell me everything. Did they…" Her words catch in her voice as dread washes over her face.

"No, as far as I know, they didn't rape her. I believe I got there before they could."

"Who did this to her and do you know why?" Her hand shakes as she tucks a tuft of hair behind her ear the same way Rayna does.

"It was two guys. One I don't know, and the other is… He *was* a friend of mine. He was a very close friend and I can't understand his reasoning."

She quickly replies, "What was he going to do to her? Why Rayna? I mean, if he's your friend, he knows how much she means to you. So why hurt her? This makes no sense to me."

"He told me that he's in love with me and wanted me for himself. I had no idea he had those types of feelings for me." I tell her, rubbing my beard as if that'll help me make sense of it all.

"I don't understand this. How the fuck could you two be friends and you not know he was gay and in love with you?"

I look at her and debate whether to tell her our history. If she's as stubborn as Rayna, she won't stop asking until I tell her. Besides, it'll all come out in his trial later, anyway. Everyone will know about my deviant sexual practices. I'm not ashamed of my life choices, but I'd rather Rayna and her family not know the disturbing details of my sexual practices.

I decide to tell her. "We used to double up on women. Apparently, he was in love with me and got his thrills from being that close to me. When I wouldn't share Rayna with him, he was jealous." I shake my head and cross one ankle over the other.

"In his warped way of thinking, he figured that if he could just have sex with Rayna, that I would change my mind, and we could share her. That way, I would still be his. None of this is logical. It's all my fault."

Renee takes my unbroken hand in hers. "Yeah, it kind of is." I look at her face, and she's grinning. "Seriously though, you can't blame yourself for having a friend who's fucked up, especially if you didn't know he had this messed up way of thinking. It's not your fault."

I look away from her and swallow down my regretful sorrow. I'm grateful this conversation ends when the doctor comes back in the room carrying three braces, each a different size.

"I wasn't sure which size to get. We'll try them on and make adjustments to see which will fit you best."

CHAPTER 28

OH MY GOD, MY FACE HURTS SO MUCH! WHAT THE HELL?

I whimper, it's all I can do. My throat is so dry, and my arms feel heavy. Where am I? Am I still in the barn?

"Help me!" I yell but it sounds about as loud as a whisper.

I try to sit up by pushing my body up with my arms, but my limbs feel like semi-cooked spaghetti noodles trying to hold up an elephant. I cannot muster enough energy for a second attempt. I lie here feeling defeated and confused.

It's so bright in here. This doesn't smell or sound like the barn.

Why is my brain in such a fog? What's wrong with me?

A kind voice comforts me. "Rayna, you're safe. You just had surgery to repair your face. You need to rest. Are you having any pain?"

I'm able to open one eye. It's barely a slit, but enough to see a pretty nurse hunched over me, looking at my bandaged eye.

I attempt to swallow the imaginary cotton in my throat, but I'm unsuccessful. I mouth the word, "Dry."

"I'll get you some water. How's your pain?" she asks.

I shake my head. "Bad."

"Okay, I'll up your Morphine. You'll feel relief soon."

She fiddles with the machine and then locks it with a key. I welcome the drugs.

"I'll be right back," she says.

I watch her seem to float out of the room as if her feet barely brush the floor. I feel light, as if I'm floating as well. I fall asleep before she returns, despite my determination not to.

Although I'm sure my dream was pleasant, I can't recall it. When I woke, I was instantly angry and wanted to retreat to the perfect dream. I hate everyone and everything right now. Time has no bearing on anything. Sometimes, I can't tell if I'm awake or asleep.

My face fucking hurts when I try to talk, and my stomach is viciously biting at my insides because I haven't eaten in...

What time is it? What day is it?

"Where am I?" I mutter with a hoarse voice.

I'm in an unfamiliar room. I like this one better than the recovery room; it's much darker. I'm a little less miserable. I roll my aching head to the side.

Coach is lounging in what looks like a very uncomfortable chair. His hand is in a splint. He's sound asleep and snoring, faintly. He looks so handsome with his head leaning on the wall, his face void of expression. I don't want to wake him, but I am so damn thirsty.

I reach for the jug of what I assume to be ice water, but my motor function is terrible and I can't grip it. If I try to lift it, it'll surely crash to the floor. Should I wake him?

When I swallow, my throat feels like it's sticking together and choking me. I try to cough but it's wimpy, like an exhale.

Coach startles and looks at me. He smiles as though he had assumed I was dead but came back to life.

"Hi, babe," he whispers as he stands up, taking my hand in his. "How do you feel?"

"My face fucking hurts," I tell him and then chuckle, but it causes horrific pain to my ribs so instead of laughing, I wince.

"Do you want me to get a nurse?"

Coach looks as if he's aged ten years, as if his guilt from feeling liable for his friend's actions is wearing on his soul. He looked so much younger when he was asleep.

"No, I only want you." My words sound frail but forced. He leans in to kiss my undamaged cheek and then my forehead. "What happened to me isn't your fault. I don't blame you. You didn't do this to me. Tell me you understand."

"I do. I know it's his fault, but I..." His words fail him. He swallows hard before lowering his head, burying it against my hip. He places my open hand on the top of his head and holds his over mine to keep it in place. I can hear the tears in his voice. "I should have protected you better."

"Oh, for crying out loud." Now my angry, drug-induced bitch is stepping in. "I told you it wasn't your fault. You could not have known he would go off his rock. How could you have protected me from him when you didn't know he was crazy? Do you think you should have been following me around everywhere I went, never leaving me alone? It's called stalking. Get that idea right out of that thick skull of yours," I say as I slap the top of his head, probably harder than I should, but my limbs are not yet fully functional.

He looks up at me with tears in his eyes. "I love you, Rayna. Get better and let me take you home. Marry me, my love."

"What?" I ask, unsure if he proposed to me or if I heard him wrong.

"I'm asking you to marry me," he repeats while smiling like a fool, eyes wide with anticipation.

I clear my throat and realize the imaginary cotton ball has wedged itself deeper into my esophagus. "Water," I say as clearly as I can manage.

He hands me the cup and helps hold it while I slurp its contents. I try to drink as much as possible, but my stomach protests. I'm only able to swallow two mouthfuls, but it feels wonderful as it slides down my parched throat.

"If you're serious about asking me to marry you, don't you think proposing while I'm lying in a hospital bed with my face broken is probably not the most romantic way to ask? Not like this, okay?" I smile with only half of my mouth. The opposite side of my face is horribly swollen.

"Okay, I'll go tell the nurse that you're awake. I'll be right back," he says and then sprints out of the room.

It doesn't seem like he's away very long, but I think I may have dozed off again. The nurse calls my name, and it irritates me. She says my name again and now I'm furious. I open my eye to seek her out and frown at her, maybe even cuss, I don't know. The drugs make everything seem like it isn't real; like I'm in a perpetual dream that keeps changing.

"There you are. How's your pain?" she asks with a voice I would normally see as pleasant, but I find it exceedingly annoying at the moment. I am so miserable, and she is simply way too peppy, but she has power over the drugs.

"It hurts, but I think I'm okay. My stomach is turning. I might vomit if I don't get some crackers and ginger ale," I say and then cough, grasping my ribs, hoping to make the pain halt. "Why does my throat hurt so much?"

"Sometimes when they sedate you, they insert a breathing tube, especially if they're working on your face. If your throat swells, they can still get oxygen into your lungs. It might hurt for a few days, but it will improve." She looks at Coach, who's been quietly listening. "If you go down to the cafeteria, you can ask them for some crackers and there's ginger ale in the machines by the elevators."

"Oh, I thought you might have some stashed in a room somewhere," he says with a shrug.

"Nope, we don't have stashes. You know, cut-backs." She shrugs.

"I'll go right now and be back in a flash." Coach disappears from the room again.

"I have to go pee," I whisper.

"Actually, you don't. You have a catheter. If you'd like, I can take it out, but you will have to page us every time you have to get up to go. We must assist you to walk to the bathroom, at least until you're off the Morphine drip. What do you want to do?"

"I'd better keep it in. I pee often, so I'll end up annoying you. When does the Morphine stop?"

"It's up to you and how you feel. If you don't want it, like it's making your stomach too nauseous, you can ask to stop the Morphine and take a different medicine in pill form or injection, something that might be more tolerable for you, but it won't work as well."

I shake my head and smile. "I'll keep the Morphine for now. I really hurt. Can you lift the head part of my bed? That might help."

"Sure! Tell me when to stop," she says as she raises the head of the bed.

My mind whirls for a quick second as my brain rights itself, making my stomach feel like it did a full somersault. Vomiting with sore ribs sounds like torture.

"Okay, that's perfect. Thank you. Do you know what they did in the surgery?"

She takes a tablet from her pocket and slides her finger across the screen. "Here you are." She pauses momentarily so she can read. "Basically, they had to put a plate in your cheekbone to hold it in place while it heals. Your eye socket has a minor fracture that will heal on its own, but your eyesight should be fine once the swelling subsides. You have some badly bruised ribs as well, which might also contribute to your nauseousness. In a matter of a few months, you'll look and feel as beautiful as you did before this happened."

I nod. "Thank you." I feel more at ease now that I know I'll heal up with no expected lingering issues.

She smiles and puts the tablet back in her pocket. "Ring the buzzer if you need me, okay?"

I nod as she rushes out of the room.

Coach walks in and gleams when he notices me sitting up. He teases, "Ah, look at you, sitting up like a big girl." He winks. "Is that better for you?"

"Yeah, I got dizzy during the ride, but I'm okay now. Thank you for going to get this stuff for me. Can you open the pop? I don't think my fingers are working all too well."

"Sure can, weakling," he teases with a smirk while cracking the bottle open. He hands it to me, never letting his hand get too far from it in case I drop it. I hand it back to him after only one small sip. The bubbles burn my sore throat. He sets it on the small table that hovers over my legs. He opens the bag of crackers and sets them down within my reach, besides the pop.

"Um, I need to thank you for saving me. I'm not sure if I did that yet. I don't know exactly what would have happened had you not shown up when you did. I'm sure it wouldn't have been good. He was about to rape me. He said he would send me back to you after he got his. Whether or not he would have let me go, I will never know."

Coach says nothing. He stares at my hand, which cradles perfectly in his sizable palm. I wait, but he remains silent. His jaw muscles flex now and then as he clenches his teeth. He's swallowing a lot. His face is flushed, and his eyes are glossed over. Is he going to cry again?

"Look at me," I demand with an assertive tone. He turns his face away from me, so I repeat myself. "I said, look at me, dammit!"

He slowly turns to face me, but when his teary eyes meet mine, I see an abundance of pain from a broken man. I lift my hand from his and cup his cheek, using my thumb to wipe a tear from his eye before it falls from his lashes. I smile at him, but the lump in my throat grows by the second. My tears erupt and spill down my cheeks.

Note to self: no crying until my swollen eye heals. This fucking hurts!

"Baby, I'm so sorry," he mutters between gasping breaths.

Coach stands and buries his face against my neck, pressing his forehead into my pillow. I try to hug him, but I can't get my arms around him, so I rub his thick arm instead, hoping it will suffice. I set my arm down when my IV needle wiggles in my vein, turning my stomach.

"I will only say this one more time and I need you to hear me. This isn't your fault. You saved me from a psychotic sadist who wanted to do horrible things to me. If you hadn't gotten there when you did…" I take a breath. "Tell me that you hear me."

"Okay, okay," he replies, his face remaining buried.

"I said, tell me you believe me."

He lifts his face until he can look into my one functioning eye. "It's so hard for me. A man should protect his woman, just as she should protect his heart. I didn't do my part."

I lift my hands and wipe the wetness from his rosy cheeks and then slap him hard enough that his head jolts. My smile is lame. His initial expression is surprise but soon, he grins and then nods, understanding that I'm trying to lighten the conversation.

"I love you." He kisses the healthy cheek with the gentleness of a butterfly's flutter. I'm grateful for his tenderness.

I whisper, "I love you, too."

"Do you want some crackers?" He stands and changes the subject.

"Maybe another sip of pop."

He opens the pop and helps me take a few gulps before putting the cap back on and setting it on the table. Dammit, that burns my throat, but my stomach is grateful.

"You look tired. Sleep," he whispers. "I'll be here when you wake."

"No. I will sleep if you promise you'll go home. Check on the kids and tell them that I am okay. They can come see me as soon as the doctor says it's all right. If they want you to spend the night, so they feel safer, it's okay with me. Just don't let my sister sneak down the stairs to make love to you, thinking she's me." I snicker when he tilts his head as if disappointed.

"If the kids want me to stay, I'll stay. No promises about your sister." He lifts his hand as is to slap an imaginary Renee. He grimaces. "That's not something you'll ever have to worry about with me. I'm not a cheater. Let me take a video of you so they can see that you're okay."

"Do I have any blood on me or anything yucky that might freak them out?"

Coach admires my face and then shakes his head. "You're beautiful." He aims his phone and says, "Okay, Mom, you're on!"

I look at the camera and try to smile, knowing I must look scary. "Hi, babies! I'm okay, but I may have to stay in the hospital for a while. Maybe tomorrow you two can visit me if the doctor approves. Aunt Renee and Coach will take care of you while I'm here. Be on your best behaviour. I love you both! I will see you soon."

He stops the recording and smiles. "All right, I'll go now. Promise me that you'll sleep. If you need anything, make a list and text it to me."

"I don't have my phone," I say, suddenly realizing that I don't know where my purse is. "My purse?"

"The cops found your phone near where you work; they pinged the signal off towers or something. They tracked it down, hoping you were with it. And I have your purse in the truck. The cops found it in your car and entrusted it to me. Your phone is probably in an evidence bag somewhere. I'm sure they'll give it back once it's processed if you ask them nicely. If not, I can get you another one."

"No, I'll talk to the investigators about it when I see them. They'll most likely be here soon to ask me a million questions. I'm suddenly very sleepy," I confess before a painful yawn erupts, bringing tears to my eyes.

He wipes away the tears from my uncovered eye and then kisses my forehead.

"Sleep, my love."

I plunge into the darkness of my mind. I don't even see him leave.

oach

Rayna has been home for a month now and she's healing nicely. Most of the swelling has subsided, but the yellow bruising seems to linger. Her face is still swollen. About a week after her rescue, the swelling to her eye eased and she could see again, which made her very happy.

She hasn't returned to work yet, nor has she left the house unless going to see a doctor and only if she has someone to drive her. I'm giving her plenty of time to regain her confidence and be independent again. She's nervous around men she doesn't know.

I expected her to have anxiety; I'd be worried if she didn't. The doctor that deals with the emotional aspect of her recovery said it will take time for the real Rayna to come back, if she ever does. He suggested we don't rush her or tease her about her fears, even if they seem irrational to us.

The kids have been amazing, helping her with everything from vacuuming to washing dishes. Renee has been picking the kids up at school most days and I do it on the days she can't.

Rayna is working on Rayna and I'm absolutely fine with taking the backseat while she does.

Today marks the five-week anniversary to the day that changed our lives, hers more so than mine. It drastically changed our sexual dynamic as well. I wish she'd come back and be the Rayna that is fun and ready to try new sexual experiences. She only wants to make love tenderly in bed. I don't mind that so much anymore, but my inner demon is itching to burst forth. I feel selfish when I think about my needs. I know she isn't ready.

I've been working out at the gym extra hard, usually until my muscles are on fire. It helps to keep me in check. I've also been beating the hell out of my punching bag. It temporarily satiates my demon's urge for aggression.

Renee has taken the kids to her place for the night, so it's just me and my lady. When we're alone, we typically watch a movie and occasionally make love in her bed. I don't even expect that from her but she says she wants me, so who am I to deny her? Everything is moving at the pace Rayna is setting and I'm cool with it.

"Can we do something different tonight?" she asks before putting a piece of garlic bread in her mouth.

I look up from my plate, very interested in this conversation. "We can. What do you have in mind?" I'm thinking that she wants to go watch a movie in a theatre, perhaps.

Rayna clears her throat. "Well, you remember how he had me tied, right? I want you to tie me up the same way but with my feet firmly on the floor. I remember how horribly my wrists hurt from hanging by those ropes, and I never want that pain repeated. My feet have to be flat on the floor. Then I want you to—"

I cut her off. "What? I don't think that's a good idea, Rayna. You want to repeat the most terrifying moments of your life and make it into a sexual game?"

"Well, kind of." She sets the bread on her plate. She looks at me with desperate eyes. "Try to understand. I want you to make it fun and pleasurable for me. You'll have to be very loving with me, of course."

"Why, Rayna?" I ask, not understanding her logic.

"Because every time I fall asleep, I'm back in that barn. My wrists are aching, my toes can't support my weight, and the fear..." She shakes her head. "Well, it overwhelms me." She swallows hard. "I had no control in that situation. I need to feel like I'm in control. He took that from me, and I want it back. Will you do this for me?"

I search her face for a flicker of doubt, but she doesn't blink. She seems stronger from having asked me. Maybe she needs this. It might end up being a great turnaround for her, helping her to regain her strength. If not, it'll be the most awful thing I'll ever do to her and it'll change our dynamic permanently.

How can I say no to her? I can never deny Rayna.

"Okay, I'll do it. If for one second, I think it's too much for you, it's over. I will cut the rope and that'll be it."

"Yes, sir!" she says, smiling playfully. "Will you fuck me while I'm hanging there?"

My cock twitches and my inner demon wakes from his long slumber. While trying not to seem too anxious, I ask, "Do you want me to?"

She grins the same way the old Rayna did when she wanted me. She assures me that this is the right thing to do.

"Yes, but don't let your sadistic side join in."

"My demon." This is the first time I've given her a title for it.

She ponders the name. "Your demon? Hmm."

"I promise that I'll be gentle."

I watch her face and swear I can see her ashen skin tone brighten as a flush of pink once again livens the paleness of the remaining yellow bruises, making her look almost exactly like the Rayna I know.

"Thank you," she sighs as if a weight has lifted.

I nod. "We can go to my house. I'll use the eye-bolt in my

ceiling. It'll hold the weight of two women. I made sure of it," I tell her with a wink.

She shakes her head and scoffs but knows I probably have tested it out exactly that way.

Instead of using rope, which I absolutely refuse to use on her wrists, because that's what he used, I secure soft leather cuffs on her. I string a rope through their cuff's loops, and pull her wrists together, knotting it in an easy release configuration. A clamp would take longer to free her from, so rope is best. While watching her face for any flicker of panic, I fish that rope through the large eyelet that's securely fastened to the eyebeam in the ceiling.

Before I pull the line and force her hands over my head, I ask, "Rayna, are you sure?" She nods. "What's your safe word?"

"It's red." She takes a deep breath while studying my face. Perhaps she sees the hesitation in my eyes. "Yes, I'm sure. I have to do this. I'll be stronger if I face it head-on. Just keep your *demon* on a leash or in his kennel."

I snicker because I adore the way she talks about my sadistic nature as if it were some type of devil dog. Somehow, she doesn't see my demon as being something bad, but something tameable. I like that very much, actually.

The beautiful woman standing before me is stronger than anyone I know. She's about to rewrite the most horrible event in her life, and I'm more hesitant than she is.

She mirrors me by taking a deep breath, then nods to signal that she's ready to begin.

I pull the slack from the rope, lifting her arms over her head until she stands straight with her feet firmly planted beneath her.

Fuck, she looks hot! My heart beats faster, and my cock swells in my jeans.

I assess her while silently reminding myself to keep my beast in check. This is about Rayna, not me. I watch her eyes until she looks up to meet mine. When I raise my eyebrows, she nods and smiles, proving to me that she wants to continue.

I move closer until I can feel the heat from her skin on mine. She smells so sweet, like a delicious dessert I want to taste and have melt in my mouth. My lips press to her neck and kiss gently. This is pure torture for me. I want to ravish her, spank her ass until it's hot pink, and then fuck her hard until she screams, and then fuck her more.

Her breathing has been calm and steady aside from the odd quiet moan escaping her lips. It's barely loud enough to hear. Slowly, I kiss down her body, ravishing her breasts, the tender skin on her tummy, and finally her sweetness. I'm careful to progress slowly, always touching her with a gentleness I'm not used to.

My tongue slithers between her labia, seeking the tiny button that fires her up.

She lifts one leg, resting it over my shoulder. I grasp her ass and push my tongue further back until I can slip inside her to taste her delicious nectar. My mouth sucks at her while she moans, her ass muscles tense and relax in my grip. Her whimpers shift to begging moans depending on where my tongue is.

I slip two fingers into her drenched canal. Rayna gasps, straining to push her wanting pussy toward me. My digits slide inside her with long, deep strokes. I think she wants me to pound her faster than I am. But she instructed me to tame my demon. So, for now, I'll be gentle, using sweet teasing torture. I have to remember to keep my demon in check.

She humps my face with increasing need. Her breathing is wild and loud. I want to make her cum, but not yet. She should enjoy this for a while. I'll get her to the edge, but ease off, only to bring her back to the edge of climax.

Before long, my fingers are filling her deeply and waving quickly while my tongue sucks and flicks at her swollen, stiff clit. She screams so loud that my ears ring. Her juices flow down my hand and chin.

Her body jerks feverishly, humping against my face, begging

her climax to continue and never stop. I don't let up until her body softens. She's shaking from the adrenaline rush.

I unzip my jeans and pull out my throbbing cock and stand quickly. Lifting both of her thighs with a firm grip, I take all of her weight while wrapping her legs around the small of my back. At no point does she feel any strain on her wrists.

Her face flushes pink and glistens with sweat; exactly how I like to see her. I press my lips to hers and kiss her with passion but not aggressively. I will keep my demon on a leash until she permits me to set him free. Even then, she won't experience his idea of sadistic pleasures; not now and maybe never.

"Fuck me!" she yells.

She need not tell me twice.

I push into her, holding as soon as I'm buried completely. We meet eyes and hold each other's gaze. My hips wave back and forth. I fuck her slowly and rhythmically, keeping her calm but torturing myself worse than if I had a hot poker buried in my brain.

Fuck! I don't know if I can keep him contained. She's bound and under my control for the first time in over a month. I know I missed this but had no idea how much.

I grunt through my frustration. She looks so fucking hot! I desperately want to pull her head back by her hair while I ram her like there's no tomorrow. She knows this is hard for me. It's still fucking, but not the way I like it, the way I need it. I'm so close, but so far from what I crave.

She whispers, "Harder. Fuck me harder. Let him out." I shake my head in protest, but she begs. "Please?"

I squeeze her ass cheeks and pull back, thrusting into her with the force I so enjoy. Her head tips as I pump into her hard and fast. I let my demon out to satiate his needs but keep him under control. I growl like a barbarian, but keep my eyes on her to make sure she's okay.

I grasp a wad of her hair and pull back on her head, exposing her throat to my teeth.

"Fuck! Yes!" she pants.

I bite hard enough to dent her skin but not shred into it. I span my hand beneath her ass and push my middle finger into her tight hole. I pull up, lifting her body and bury my finger. Now I can fuck her with the fierceness I've kept buried for far too long.

Rayna stiffens. Her wail launches me into a carnal fit. I pound into her with the ferociousness of a sadist. My demon's hedonistic growls echo about the room, piercing our ears.

It happens so quickly, my orgasm tears through me suddenly and violently. I cry out and pull her groin against me so tightly that I might crush her. Fire erupts from my balls, scorching the inner walls of my dick as hot cum blasts from me, filling Rayna's twitching body.

I stand as still as I can, involuntarily jerking. My body refuses to release my cock from her. My legs are quivering under the strain of our weight, which seems magnified at this stage.

If I can keep my eyes closed, maybe this will never end.

"Coach," Rayna whispers.

My eyes meet hers. Hers are half shut, her damaged eyelid drooping slightly more than the other. She smiles at me with beads of sweat on her forehead. I snicker, and her laugh follows. We laugh until my limp prick slips out of her along with my sticky seed.

"Please let me down now," she asks, suddenly not looking so light-hearted.

I immediately yank the rope's quick-release knot I used in case she freaked out and I needed to free her immediately. As soon as I release the rope, she pulls at the cuffs in a panicked state. She quickly tears at the buckles with her teeth.

Her eyes are wide and unfocused. I grab her shoulders and pull her against me, pinning her arms between us. She's shaking but doesn't fight the hold I have on her.

"Breathe, Rayna! Breathe deeply. You're safe. I love you. I'll get the cuffs off. Just breathe."

After the cuffs are off, she lunges at me and wraps her arms around my chest. I hold her for several minutes and then walk her over to the sofa chair. I scoop her up and sit, cradling her on my lap in case her emotions overwhelm her and she wants to cry it out. She needs to feel safe with me; to know I love her and that I'll never let anyone hurt her again.

A long time ago, I had a submissive that needed this kind of attention after every playdate. She would cry for about ten minutes, and then she'd get ice cream from my freezer. We'd eat while she'd talk about anything and everything, usually shit that bored the fuck out of me. I wasn't listening to her half the time, but I don't think she noticed or cared if I was.

Sometimes I wanted her to get the fuck out, but she was a fantastic lay and would let me do anything I wanted to her. Besides, as her master, it was my responsibility to ensure her mental state was solid before she left. I never let my submissives leave feeling emotionally weak. One day, she decided she didn't want to play anymore, and I had to respect that. I wished her well before sending her on her way.

Rayna has fallen quiet, and she's breathing slowly and deeply. I'm fairly sure she fell asleep. I remain still for what seems like an hour, watching her angelic face and hearing her breathing is so much better than the sex was, or the dinner we ate, or anything that's ever happened between us.

I thought she was gone and never coming back. I have her right here in my arms and this is where we'll stay until she wakes on her own. She is safe with me, and I would die for her.

Rayna

"Coach?" I whisper, gently rousing him from a deep sleep. He opens his heavy eyelids and blinks several times to clear the fogginess from his brain.

"I must have fallen asleep," he says after clearing his throat. He teases, "You fell asleep first."

"Why didn't you wake me? We could have gone to bed and been comfortable." My fingertips brush through his bearded cheek.

"You weren't comfortable?" he questions.

I smile. "That's the best sleep I've had since before," she takes a breath, "you know."

"Hence the reason I didn't wake you."

After slipping off his legs, I lean in and kiss him. I reach out to take his hand to help him stand, but he slides his butt to the edge of the cushion and hesitates. I wait, but he doesn't take my hand. He's rubbing his legs and rolling his ankles.

"Did your legs go numb? Oh shit! I'm sorry," I apologize.

"Nope, not your fault." He slowly stands up as a complaint groans in his throat. Once he's upright, he smiles, while looking down his nose at me. He's very intimidating.

"See, no big deal. I'm good."

"Come to bed, rest your gigantic body."

I take his hand to lead the way up the stairs and into his bedroom. We curl up under the silky blue covers and notice that the sun is already rising. We only have a few more hours to sleep before I need to get home for when Renee returns the kids. They need not see their mom doing the walk of shame. The thought makes me shiver.

"Are you cold, babe?" he asks and pulls me closer to him.

"No, not at all, but you can spoon me anyway," I reply.

He kisses the back of my head as his big arm drapes over my waist and I feel safe. It isn't long before we're both lost in dreamland.

CHAPTER 30

ayna

IT'S BEEN FIVE MONTHS SINCE THE KIDNAPPING AND MY PHYSICAL injuries have healed, but I'm still nervous around people I don't know. If they get too close to me, panic sets in, and I feel like I can't breathe.

I have returned to work and I'm not as worried to be out on my own, but I'm always aware of my surroundings. Maybe it's safer for me if I'm constantly on edge, ready to spring into combat if an assailant touches me. Although, I don't want to hurt an innocent man who's just walking past me and brushes my arm. It hasn't happened yet and I'm hoping it never does.

Coach's crazy ex, Alissa, made a deal with the court and ended up pleading guilty to reckless endangerment. It got her sentenced to six months in jail with a two-year probation. Coach was happy with that because he said that he hurt her emotionally and that's why she lost her shit and tried to hurt him.

He thinks it's fair, but I am furious that they didn't find her guilty of attempted murder. However, it didn't happen to me directly, so I'm working on letting go of my anger. Besides, I have my own problems.

The two men who attacked me face a whole slew of charges. The man who kidnapped me, who's name I learned to be Charley, spent a few weeks in the hospital and recovered completely. Except for the massive scar and the indent on his skull at the back of his head. He tried to have Coach charged for the assault, but the judge threw it out. They sentenced him to six years in custody. With good behaviour, he'll be out in three.

Coach and I don't think he got what he deserved. The thought of him seeking revenge keeps me awake at night. I dread the man's release and fear I will lose Coach if his temper gets the best of him and he hunts him down.

As for Coach's friend, Brett, he only got two years because he didn't assault me physically. He threatened sexual violence but didn't go through with it, other than removing some of my clothing. They convicted him for holding me against my will and physically assaulting Coach. They sentenced him to one year in jail. But because of good behaviour and overcrowding, he was paroled a few weeks ago and has to check in once a week with a councillor.

The court wouldn't charge him with hiring Charley to kidnap me because there was no evidence to back it up. There is a Peace Bond against him that's supposed to keep him civil toward me if we should be in the same location. If he tries to talk to me, Coach, or my kids, they will send him back to jail to serve out the rest of his sentence. So far, he's kept his distance.

Coach rarely lets me out of his sight. If he has to, like when I go to work, he made me promise to have someone walk me to my car and make sure I'm locked inside before they leave me.

I appreciate that he's doing his best to keep me safe, but it's impossible to have a companion with me all the time. I have a life to live and can't always have someone to accompany me.

When I put groceries in the car, I always look around before lifting each bag and turning my back to set it inside. There will be no sneak attacks on this girl!

When I'm in my car alone, I crank up the tunes on the radio and sing as loud and off-key as anyone can, and then laugh at how ridiculous I must seem to other drivers. I never used to enjoy the radio while driving, but it's my newest way of blowing off steam.

I can't yell or scream when I feel scared or overwhelmed. If I do, everyone will start walking on eggshells again, so to speak. I hated when everyone tiptoed around me, fearing I would break like a crystal goblet if they were to say or do the wrong thing. So, I take it to my car and yell through songs to maintain my sanity.

Coach's house has been on the market for two weeks, and the offers are pouring in. He said something about a bidding war, but I wasn't really paying attention to him. My mind was otherwise occupied, remembering when I was in the hospital and he asked me to marry him. I had told him it wasn't the right time to ask, and it wasn't. Well, it's been months, and he hasn't asked again. I wonder if he is nervous in case I shoot him down again.

I push open the front door and juggle the bags of groceries. I'm overloaded so I'll only have to make one trip, even though two trips would have been easier. It's almost as if it's a challenge to see if I can do it all at once.

After setting the bags on the floor, just inside in the entranceway, a sudden waft of deliciousness seems to slap my nose, awakening my senses and my hungry tummy.

"What is going on here?" I ask, as I walk up the stairs and watch them from the kitchen's archway.

Ken is stirring something in a pot on the stove. Kim is setting the silverware nicely on the table. Coach is nowhere to be seen.

"Did you two do all this?" They shrug. "Where's Coach?"

They say nothing, instead, smile at me. Kim gives it away by looking past me with a giggle. I spin around, expecting him to yell "boo!"

But he's down on one knee, wearing a perfectly fitted tuxedo.

Oh my God! This is it!

"Rayna, you have an incredible strength that amazes me every day. You are tough like a bull while having the gentleness of a ladybug's touch. You're wise when I am ignorant. You give me hope that even a schmuck like me can be loved by someone as perfect as you. I want to live out my days proving to you that I am forever yours, with every breath I take. I love you, Rayna. Please, marry me and make me the happiest idiot on Earth."

The kids stand beside Coach. Kim is giggling and jumping up and down while Ken video records the proposal on Coach's phone.

I stand here, not giving him any clues to what I'm going to say. I don't know why I'm making him wait. Each second ticks by, casting even more doubt on his face. How long should I make him sweat this out?

"Of course, I will marry you," I whisper.

A huge sigh of relief escapes him, as if he'd been holding his breath the entire time. He slips the most stunning, sparkling diamond ring on my finger. He pulls me onto his knee and kisses me lovingly, but PG-rated because of our young audience.

My tears fall as Kim leads me to my bedroom. She shows me a gorgeous red evening gown Coach spread out on the bed. She helps me put it on, and then brushes my hair and puts some lipstick on me. I slip on the heels that he bought to match the dress. I stand before the full-length mirror and admire how great I look. She smiles at me and tells me I'm pretty. I kiss her, then we head to the kitchen.

Coach admires my dress with a pleased grin before taking my hand and giving it a kiss as he guides me to the living room. Ken holds up Coach's phone as a beautiful melody fills the room. The kids watch as we dance closely to one another, except for the occasional spin requested by Kim. This is the most perfect proposal I could ever have imagined. It's so much better than the first one and more intimate than if he were to take a knee at a fancy restaurant.

The whole time we eat dinner, the kids are talking about the proposal with every single detail overly exaggerated to near fairy tale proportions, but we don't mind. We are in our own little world. Our eyes meet after each bite of food. This amazing man will be my husband.

We helped each other through some awful things, and we came out of them with a powerful bond. We are unbreakable now; stronger than the diamond I wear on my finger. He is mine, and I am his.

I have asked him if his inner demon ever urges him to choose another woman so it can play out its worst sadistic desires. He always smiles at me and tells me that no woman will ever stroke the horns of his demon the way I do.

OUR SEX LIFE BURNS AT BOTH ENDS OF THE CANDLE, SO TO SPEAK. Sometimes we enjoy the most tender and romantic lovemaking, where we seem to mould into one another and become one being.

Other times, he lets his demon loose, setting forth an evening of wild, vicious sex that takes its physical toll on us both. It eases his sexually aggressive nature while satiating my inner ravenous goddess. I am becoming a big fan of that side of me, thanks to Coach's demon. He says he's keeping his demon on a leash because I won't like him. If he's more intense than what I've seen so far, he might be right.

Soon we will marry, as we don't want to put it off any longer than necessary. It won't be a big, extravagant wedding; I've had one of those and it's not all it's cracked up to be. However, Renee will be my maid of honour. Her boyfriend, who happens to be Coach's long-standing best friend, will stand proudly beside him as his best man. So, it works out perfectly.

Renee has become someone I always hoped she'd be. She is no longer as scatterbrained, and she isn't hopping from one idea to the next, never finding something or someone to keep her entertained.

Tim holds her attention better than anyone ever has. She adores him, and he is head over heels in love with her. She's even been talking about having a baby or two. I never thought she'd love someone enough to commit to him and want to start a family.

As for my kids, they will grow up without their real dad in their lives. He moved across the country to live with some bimbo that he met online. He didn't even tell the kids he was leaving. When he was halfway across the country, he called me to ask if I'd do his dirty work for him. Like I had a choice. He's a coward and he'll never change. I'm glad he's gone, and I think they are, too.

The kids love Coach and he's so good to them. I wish he were their biological father, but he loves them so much that people assume he is.

They insist on calling him Dad, which seemed strange at first. It took a while before he could hear it and not smile like a proud fool.

I won't claim that our story is flawless from this point on because nobody's marriage ever is. We still have our trials, as does everyone, but I wouldn't change it for all the money in the world.

Who would have thought that two people, as different as we are, can come together and become an indestructible bonded force? I have calmed his bad boy ways, and he has saved me from my vanilla flavoured comfort zone.

I still sit on the patio with a chilled glass of wine and the book I've never read a single word of, and I watch the man who was once the mysterious, sexy, musclebound neighbour who turned me on by mowing his lawn every Saturday. Now, he mows *our* lawn while the twenty-something brunette, who's bought Coach's old house, sits on her patio with an open book of unread pages.

The End

ABOUT THE AUTHOR

It'll never cease to amaze me how people are so quick to jump at the opportunity to come into my basement, take off their clothes, let me bind them in rope, take photos of them, and then use those photos on book covers for all the world to see. I thank all the brave souls who've been so kind to pose for me.

Want to learn more about me?
Check out my naughty website!
http://www.pebbleslacasse.com
You can also sign up for my newsletter at
http://eepurl.com/dHMwqf
Don't forget to follow me on these social media platforms

ALSO BY PEBBLES LACASSE

Coaching Rayna: Bound Hearts, Book 2

Hello Officer

My Wife & Master Jake

Goldilocks & The Three Bear Brothers

Goldilocks & The Three Bear Brothers: Trifecta, Book 2

Little Miss Muffet

Still Waters Burn Deep *(preorder now!)*

A Run With Charley *(preorder now!)*

www.ingramcontent.com/pod-product-compliance
Lightning Source LLC
Chambersburg PA
CBHW050924030726
47503CB00007BB/2449